THE CAPE COD BICYCLE WAR

MODERN African Writing

from Ohio University Press

Laura T. Murphy and Ainehi Edoro, Series Editors

This series brings the best African writing to an international audience. These groundbreaking novels, memoirs, and other literary works showcase the most talented writers of the African continent. The series also features works of significant historical and literary value translated into English for the first time. Moderately priced, the books chosen for the series are well crafted, original, and ideally suited for African studies classes, world literature classes, or any reader looking for compelling voices of diverse African perspectives.

THE CAPE COD BICYCLE WAR

AND OTHER STORIES

BILLY KAHORA

OHIO UNIVERSITY PRESS • Athens

Ohio University Press, Athens, Ohio 45701
ohioswallow.com

Printed in the United States of America
Ohio University Press books are printed on acid-free paper ⊗ ™

ISBN (paperback) 978-0-8214-2416-2
ISBN (electronic) 978-0-8214-4096-4

Library of Congress Control Number: 2019954622

The Cape Cod Bicycle Wars and Other Stories was first published in 2019
by Huza Press, Kigali, Rwanda.

Cover design: Yves Honore Bisamage

To 'K' for being there.

Youth, *n.* The Period of Possibility, when Archimedes finds a fulcrum, Cassandra has a following and seven cities compete for the honor of endowing a living Homer.

Youth is the true Saturnian Reign, the Golden Age on earth again, when figs are grown on thistles, and pigs betailed with whistles and, wearing silken bristles, live ever in clover, and cows fly over, delivering milk at every door, and Justice never is heard to snore, and every assassin is made a ghost and, howling, is cast into Baltimost! – Polydore Smith.

Ambrose Bierce, *The Devil's Dictionary*

Contents

ZONING

O utside on Tom Mboya Street, Kandle realised that he was truly in the Zone. The Zone was the calm, breathless place in which he found himself after drinking for a minimum of three days straight. He had slept for less than fifteen hours in strategic naps, had eaten just enough to avoid going crazy, and had drunk enough water to make a cow go belly-up. The two-hour baths of Hell's Gate hot-spring heat had also helped.

Kandle had discovered the Zone when he was seventeen. He had swapped vices by taking up alcohol after the pleasures of casual sex had waned. In a city-village rumour-circuit full of outlandish tales of ministers' sons who drove Benzes with trunks full of cash; of a character called Jimmy X who was unbeaten in about 500 bar fights going back to the late 80s; in a place where sixty-year-old tycoons bedded teenagers and kept their panties as souvenirs; in a town where the daughter of one of Kenya's richest businessmen held parties that were so exclusive that Janet Jackson had flown in for her birthday – Kandle, self-styled master of the art of seventy-two-hour drinking, had achieved a footnote.

In many of the younger watering holes in Nairobi's CBD, he was now an icon. Respected in Buru Buru, in Westlands, in Kile, in Loresho and Ridgeways, one of the last men standing in alcohol-related accidents and suicides. He had different names in different postal codes. In Zanze he was the Small-Package Millionaire. His crew was credited with bringing back life to the City Centre. In Buru he was simply Kan. In the Hurlingham area he was known as The Candle. In a few years, the generation of his kid brother Giant Rat would usurp his legendary status, but now it was his time.

The threat of rain had turned Tom Mboya Street into a bedlam of blaring car horns, screaming hawkers, screeching matatus and shouting policemen. People argued over parking spaces and haggled over underwear. Thunder rumbled and drowned it all. A wet wind blew, announcing a surreptitious seven-minute drenching, but everybody ran as if a heavy downpour threatened. Even that was enough to create a five-hour traffic jam into the night. The calm and the wise walked into the bars, knowing it would take hours to get home anyway.

Zanze patrons walked into Kenya Cinema Plaza and a group of girls jeered at Kandle because he was going in the opposite direction, out into the weather. Few could tell he had been drinking since noon. Kandle was not only a master at achieving the Zone, he was excellent at hiding it. The copious amount of alcohol in his blood had turned his light-brown skin brighter, yellow and numb and characterless like a three-month-old baby's. The half-bottle of Insto eye drops he had used in the bathroom had started to take effect. He had learned over time that the sun was an absolute no-no when it came to achieving a smooth transition to the Zone. Thankfully, there was very little sunshine left outside, and he felt great.

'Step into the p.m. Live the art of seventy-two hours. I'm easy like Sunday morning,' he muttered towards the friendly insults. A philosopher of the Kenyan calendar, Kandle associated all months of the year with different colours and hues in his head. August he saw as bright yellow, a time when the year had turned a corner; responsibilities would be left behind or pushed to the next January, a white month. March was purple-blue. December was red. The yellow haze of August would be better if he were to be fired from his job at Eagle Bank that evening.

Kandle had tried to convert many of his friends to the pleasures of the Zone, with disastrous results. Kevo, his best friend, had once made a deep cut into his palm on the dawn of a green Easter morning in Naivasha after they had been drinking for almost a week. He had been trying to impress the crew and nearly bled to death. They had had to cut their holiday short and drive to Nairobi when his hand had swollen up with an infection days later. Kandle's cousin Alan had died two years ago trying to do the fifty-kilometre Thika-to-Nairobi highway in fifteen minutes. Susan, once the late Alan's girlfriend, then Kandle's, and now having something with Kevo, stopped trying to get into the Zone when she realised she couldn't resist stripping in public after the seventy-two-hour treatment. After almost being raped at a house party she had gone into a suicidal depression for weeks and emerged with razor cuts all over her body and twenty kilograms off her once-attractive frame.

Every month she did her Big Cry for Alan, then invariably slept with Kandle till he tired of her and she moved on to Kevo. The Zone was clearly not for those who lacked restraint.

Stripping in public, cutting one's palm, thinking you were Knight Rider — these were, to Kandle, examples of letting the Bad Zone overwhelm you. One had to keep the alcohol levels intact to stay in the Good Zone, where one was allowed all the wishful thinking in one's miserable life. The Bad Zone was the place of all fears, worries, hatreds and anxieties.

Starting off towards Harambee Avenue, Kandle wobbled suddenly, halting the crazy laughter in his chest. Looking around, he felt the standard paranoia of the Zone start to come on. Walking in downtown Nairobi at rush hour was an art even when sober. Drunk, it was like playing rugby in a moving bus on a murram country road. Kandle forced himself back into the Good Zone by going back to Lenana School in his mind. Best of all, he went back to rugby-memory land, to the Mother of All Rugby Fields, Stirlings, the field where he had played with an abandoned joy. He had been the fastest player on the pitch, a hundred metres in twelve seconds easy, ducking and weaving, avoiding the clueless masses, the thumbless hoi polloi, and going for the girl watching from the sidelines. In his mind's eye the girl was always the same: the Limara advert girl. Slender. Dark because he was light, slightly taller than him. The field was next to the school's dairy farm, so there were dung-beetle helicopters in the air to avoid and mines of cow-dung to evade.

He could almost smell the Limara girl and glory a few steps away when a Friesian cow appeared in the try box. It chewed cud with its eye firmly on him, unblinking, and as Kandle tried to get back into the Good Zone he saw the whole world reflected in that large eye. The girl faded away. Kandle put the ball down, walked over to the cow, patted her, and with his touch noticed that she was not Friesian but a white cow with some black spots, rather than the other way around. The black spot that came over her back was a map of Kenya. She was a goddamn Zebu. All this time she never stopped chewing. With the ball in the try box he took his five points.

Coming back to, he realised he was at the end of Tom Mboya Street. A fat woman came at him from the corner of Harambee Avenue, and just when she imagined that their shoulders would crash into each other Kandle twitched and the woman found empty space. Kandle grimaced as she smiled at him fleetingly, at his suit. At the corner, his heightened sense of smell (from the alcohol) detected a small, disgusting whiff of sweat, of day-old used tea bags. He stopped, carefully inched up against the wall, calculated where the nearest supermarket was, cupped his palm in front of his mouth, and breathed lightly. He was grateful to smell the toothpaste he had swallowed in the Zanze toilets. The whiff of sweat was not his. That was when Kevo came up to him.

'Fucking African,' Kandle said. 'What time is it?'

'Sorry we were late, man. Here's everything. Susan's upstairs. We just got in and Onyi told us you'd left.'

'I'm starting to lose that loving feeling for you guys,' Kandle said, taking the heavy brown envelope from Kevo, who began doing a little jig right there on the street, for no sane reason, jumping side to side with both feet held together. Passers—by watched with amusement.

'Everything else was sent to Personnel,' Kevo said, still breathless. 'So good luck.'

'Were you kids fucking? That's why you were late?' Kandle grinned, seeing that the envelope held everything he needed.

Kevo smiled back. 'See you in a bit.'

As they were parting ways, Kevo shouted to him.

'Hey, by the way, Jamo died last weekend. Crashed and burned. They were coming from a rave in some barn. Taking Dagoretti Corner at 8 a.m. at 160 – they met a mjengo truck coming from Kawangware. Don't even know why they were going in that direction. Motherfucker was from Karen.'

'Which Jamo?'

'Jamo Karen.'

Kandle rolled his eyes. 'There are about five Jamo Karens.'

'Jamo Breweries. Dad used to be GM.'

'Don't think I know him.'

'You do. We were at his place a month ago. Big bash. You disappeared with his sis. Susan was mad.'

'Ha,' Kandle said.

'Anyway, service in Karen. Burial in Muranga. Hear there are some wicked places out there. Change of scene. We could check out Danny and the Thika crew. You know Thika chicks, man.'

'I'll think about it.'

'You look good, baby,' Kevo said, and waved him off.

Kandle suddenly realised that he had forgotten his bag. It meant he was missing his deep-brown stylish cardigan, his collared white shirt, his grey checked pants, his tie. He should have asked Kevo to pick it up for him. Feeling tired, he almost went under again.

Since childhood, Kandle had always hated physical contact. This feeling became especially extreme when he'd been drinking. It had been worsened by an incident in high school – boarding school. One morning he'd woken up groggily, thinking it was time for pre-dawn rugby practice, and noticed that his pyjamas were down around his knees. He was hard. There were figures in the dark, already in half-states of readiness, preparing for the twelve-kilometre morning run. Nobody seemed to notice him. He yanked his smelly shorts on, and while his head cleared he remembered something.

Clutching hands, a dark face. He never found out who had woken him up that morning, and after that he couldn't help feeling a murderous rage when he looked at the faces in the scrum around him, thinking one of them had abused him.

Over the next few months, during practices, he looked for something in the smiling, straining boyish faces, for a look of recognition – he couldn't even say the word 'homosexual' at the time. With that incident he came to look at rugby askance, to look at Lenana's traditions with a deep, abiding hatred. Then one day he stopped liking the feeling of fitness, the great camaraderie of the field, and started feeling filled with hate when even the most innocent of tacklers brushed by him. He took to cruelty, taking his hand to those in junior classes. He focused on his schoolwork, became supercilious and, maybe because of that, ever cleverer, dismissive of everyone apart from two others who he felt had intellects superior to his. He became cold and unfeeling. His mouth folded into a snarl.

In spite of a natural quickness, he'd never succeeded in becoming a great rugby player. Rugby, he discovered, was not for those who abhorred contact. You could never really play well if you hated getting close. Same with life and the street, in the city – you needed to be natural with those close to you. As he went up Harambee Avenue, he realised he was well into the Bad Zone. Looking at his reflection in shop windows, he felt like smashing his own face in. And then, like a jack-in-the-box that never went away, his father's dark visage appeared in his mind's eye, as ugly as sin. He wondered whether the man was really his father.

After completing third form he had dropped rugby and effaced the memory of those clutching hands on his balls with a concentrated horniness. He became a regular visitor to Riruta, looking for peri-urban pussy. One day, during the school holidays when he was still in form three, he had walked into his room and found Atieno, the maid, trying on his jeans. They were only halfway up, her dress lifted and exposing her thighs. The rest of those holidays were spent on top of Atieno. He would never forget her cries of 'Maiyo! Maiyo! Maiyo!'

carrying throughout the house. God! God! God! After that he approached sex with a manic single-mindedness. It wasn't hard. Girls considered him cute. When he came back home again in December, Atieno wasn't there; instead there was an older, motherly Kikuyu woman. His father took him aside and informed him that he would be getting circumcised in a week's time. He also handed him some condoms.

'Let's have no more babies,' was all he said after that.

On Harambee Avenue, three girls wearing some kind of airline uniform came towards him in a swish of dresses, laughing easily. He ignored their faces and watched their hips. One of the girls looked boldly at him, and then, perhaps for the first time that day, a half-stagger made him realise how drunk he actually was, though it would have been hard for anyone apart from his father to tell.

And so the Bad Zone passed on. He quickly fished into his jacket pocket and came out with a small bottle of Smirnoff Red Label vodka, swigged, and returned fully to the Good Zone. Ahead of him was Eagle Bank. He smiled to himself. He forced himself to calm down and breathe in. The usually friendly night watchman, Ochieng, was frosty.

'You are being waited for,' he said in Kiswahili, shaking his head at the absurdity of youth.

Inside he was met by the manager's secretary, Mrs Maina, a dark, busty and jolly woman. She too was all business today.

'You are late, Kandle,' she said. 'We have to wait for the others to reconvene.'

This was the first time she had ever spoken to him in English. She had lost that loving Kikuyu feeling for him.

Kandle, who knew how to ingratiate himself with women of a certain age, had once brought Mrs Maina bananas and cow innards mixed with fried nundu, cow hump, for her birthday. She had told him later that they were the tastiest things she had ever eaten, better than all the cards she'd received for her birthday. Even the manager, Guka, coming out of his office and trying some, commented that he wished his wife could cook like that.

Mrs Maina blurted out another few words as Kandle waited outside the manager's office. She sounded overcome with exasperation.

'What? What do you want? Do you think you're too good for the bank?'

'No. I don't want much. I think I want to become a chef.'

She couldn't help it. They both laughed. Kandle excused himself and went to the bathroom.

When he was alone he removed a white envelope from his jacket pocket and counted the money inside again. Sixty thousand shillings, which he planned to hand over to the accountant to pay for the furniture loan he had taken out before he went on leave. Back in the bank, Mrs Maina told him that the committee was ready, and Kandle was ushered into Guka's office.

There was a huge bank balance sheet in the centre of the desk. Guka Wambugu, the branch manager, was scowling at the figures. The man was dressed like a gentleman farmer, in his perennial tweed jacket with patches at the elbows and a dull, metallic-grey sweater underneath, over a brown tie and a white shirt. All he needed were gumboots to complete the picture. Kandle noticed that the old fool wore scuffed Bata Prefect shoes. Bata Mshenzi. Shenzi type. Kandle held down the laughter that threatened to burst out of his chest.

Some room had been created on each side of the desk for the rest of the committee. Mr Ocuotho, the branch accountant, sat on Guka's right, looking dapper and subservient as usual, his face thin and defined, just shy of fifty and optional retirement. He was famous in the branch for suits that hung on his shoulders like they would on a coat hanger. He was a cost-cutter, the man who stalked the bank floors like a secretary bird, imagining the day he would have his own branch to run. He had once been the most senior accountant at the largest Eagle branch in Kenya, and had been demoted to the smaller Harambee branch only after a series of frauds occurred under his watch. As a result, though he was here representing the bank's management, he was partly sympathetic to the boy in front of him. He had been in the same position, albeit at a managerial level.

Next to Ocuotho, at the far-right corner of the desk, was a bald-headed man, Mr Malasi, from Head Office Personnel. He was wearing designer non-prescription spectacles. Kandle thought he recognised him from somewhere. At the far left, representing the union and, in theory, Kandle, was the shop steward, Mr Kimani, a young-looking, lanky, forty-year-old man with soft Somali hair and long, thin hands that he cracked and flexed continually. He also happened to be Kandle's immediate boss. He was the man behind the year-long deals in the department. On Kimani's right was a younger man, the deputy shop steward at the branch, Mr Koigi, a youth with a rotund belly and hips that belied his industry. He had had an accident as a child, and was given to tilting his head to the right like a small bird at the most unlikely moments. Like Kandle, he had worked at the bank for a year, and was considered a rising star. He was also Kandle's drinking buddy.

There was a seat right in front of the desk for Kandle. Just as he was lowering himself into it, sirens blared, and everyone in the room turned to watch the presidential motorcade sweep past, out on the street. The man, done for the day, heading home to the State House. Kandle grinned, and remembered shaking the President's hand once when he was in primary school, as part of the National Primary School Milk Project promotion. There was an old photo of Kandle drinking from a small packet of milk while the President beamed at him. The image had been circulated nationwide, and even now people stopped Kandle on the street, mistaking him for the Blueband Boy, another kid who had been a perpetual favorite in 1980s TV ads.

When the noise died down, Guka turned to him.

'Ah, Mr Karoki. Kandle Kabogo Karoki. After keeping us waiting you have finally allowed us the pleasure of your company. I am sure you know everybody here, apart from Mr Malasi, from Personnel.' Guka stretched his arm towards the bald-headed man in the non-prescription spectacles. His back was highly arched, as usual; his eyes were those of an old tribal elder who brooked no nonsense from errant boys.

Kandle suddenly remembered who the bald-headed man was. He was the recruiter who had endorsed him when he had first applied for his job.

Guka turned to the shop steward. 'Mr Kimani, this committee was convened to review Mr Karoki's conduct, and to make a decision – sorry, a recommendation – to Head Office Personnel.' He gave Kandle a long, meaningful look. 'This is not a complex matter. Mr Karoki decided he was no longer interested in working for Eagle, and stopped coming to work. Before me, I have his attendance record, which has of course deteriorated over the last two months. Prior to this, Mr Karoki was an exemplary employee. We have tried, since this trend began, to find out what was wrong, but Mr Karoki has not been forthcoming. What can anyone say? I am here to run this branch office, and eventually, as the Americans say, something has to give.' He paused, cleared his throat, and looked out the window with self-importance. Then he turned back to Kandle.

'The British, whom I worked for when I joined the bank, would have said Queen and Country come first. Eagle next. At that time, when I joined, I was a messenger. The only African employee at Eagle. I worked for a branch manager named Mr Purkiss, a former DC who made me proud and taught me the meaning of duty. I have been here for forty years. I turn sixty next year. It seems that young men no longer know what they are doing. When I was your age, Mr Karoki, no one my age would have called me Mister. I was Malasi's age, thirty-six, before anyone gave me a chance to work in Foreign Exchange. I was already a man, a father of three children. Now look at you. You could have been in my seat, God forbid, at forty. It is a pity that I did not notice you before this, to straighten you out.' He paused again. 'But before we hear from you, let us hear from the branch accountant, Mr Ocuotho.'

By now everyone from the branch was trying to hide a smile. Mr Malasi had a slight frown on his face.

'Thank you, Mr Guka,' Ocuotho said, clearing the chuckle from his throat. He spoke briskly.

'Mr Karoki is a good worker, or was a good worker. But after he received his June salary, which was heavily supplemented by the furniture loan he took, he never came back. We received a letter from a Dr Koinange, saying that Mr Karoki needed a week off for stress-related reasons. After that week, he did not appear at work again. This is the first time I am seeing him.'

Mr Malasi shifted in his seat at the mention of Dr Koinange. Kandle was looking at his boss, Kimani, who wore a grave expression. Feeling Kandle's eyes on him, he gave the most imperceptible of winks.

'What was the exact date of this doctor's letter?' Guka asked. Everyone waited as Ocuotho referred to his diary.

'Friday, 24 June.'

'Today is Thursday, 15 August. So not counting his sick and annual leave, Mr Karoki has been away for two weeks with no probable reason. And after eight weeks, he doesn't seem to have solved his problem.' Mr Malasi coughed, but Guka ignored him. The manager stretched and stroked his belly. 'Let us hear from the shop steward, Mr Kimani.'

Kimani straightened up. 'I have worked with Kandle for a year,' he said, 'and in all honesty have seen few such hardworking boys of his age. A few weeks ago he failed to appear at work, as Mr Ocuotho has mentioned. He called in later and said he wasn't feeling very well, and that something had happened to his mother. He said he would be sending a doctor's letter later in the day. I didn't think much of it. People fall sick. Kandle had never missed a day of work before that. I told him to get it to the accountant, give the department a copy, and keep one for himself. Then, of course, he went on leave. When he didn't come back as scheduled – I was to go on leave after him – I got worried and tried to get in touch. When we spoke, he told me his problems weren't done and that he claimed to have talked to Personnel. I told him to make sure that he kept copies of his letters.'

Mr Guka was getting agitated. It was obvious he was not aware of any contact with Personnel, with whom he'd already had problems. After he had accused the legendary Hendrix of insubordination, Personnel had decided otherwise and transferred the man to Merchant Services, which was a promotion. Hendrix was now Eagle's main broker. Guka had been branch manager for eight years; his old colleagues were now executive managers or had moved on to senior positions at other companies.

Guka loosened his tie. He remembered that he was due to retire at the end of the year. He wished he were on the golf course, or out on his tea farm, and reminded himself that he needed to talk to Kimani later, to find out whether there was any chance that the currency deals would start up again. It had been two months since he had received his customary Ksh 20,000 a week. He needed to complete the house he was building in Limuru. This was not going the way he had expected.

'I am not aware of any such documents or communication,' Mr Malasi offered.

'But as you all know, we are a large department. It's certainly possible we overlooked something. I will check up on that.'

Guka cleared his throat. 'I think the facts are clear —'

Malasi interrupted him. 'I think we should hear from Mr Karoki before we decide what the facts are.' Head Office Personnel had paid out millions of shillings to ex-employees for wrongful dismissal, and Malasi was starting to wish he had stayed away from this one and sent someone else. It was looking like one of those litigious affairs. For one, the boy seemed too calm, almost sleepy. And what was the large sheaf of documents he had in his lap? The reference to one of Nairobi's most prominent psychiatrists, Dr Koinange, had introduced a whole new element.

Dr Koinange happened to be on Eagle Bank's board of directors. The belligerent hubris of one old manager would be, in the face of such odds, ridiculous to indulge. Even if they managed to dismiss the boy, Malasi decided he would pass on word that Mr Guka should be quietly retired. As the oldest manager at Eagle, he was well past his sell-by date. Malasi decided he would recommend Ocuotho as a possible replacement.

Guka cleared his throat again. 'Young Mr Karoki, you have five minutes to explain your conduct.' His easy confidence had become a tight and wiry anger. 'Before you start, maybe we should address the small matter of the furniture loan you took out.'

Kandle quietly removed the white envelope from his pocket and placed the shillings, together with the contents of the large brown envelope, on Mr Guka's desk.

Malasi reached for the documents and handed copies to everyone. Kandle spoke in a quiet voice.

'Over the last year, my mother has lost her mind. Being the first-born, with my father's constant absences, it has been up to me to look after her. My sister is in the US, and my brother lives in a bottle. Two months ago my mother left my father's house in Buru Buru and moved to a nearby slum. At the same time, I started to get severe headaches. I could not eat or sleep, and even started hallucinating, as Dr Koinange, our family doctor, explains in one of these letters. He expressly told me that he would be in touch with the bank's personnel department. That is why I haven't been in touch. My doctor has.' There were tears in Kandle's eyes.

Guka sat back in his seat and glared at the ceiling. He tucked his top lip into the bottom, re-enacting the thinking Kikuyu man's pose. The Kikuyu Lip Curl.

Malasi looked up from the documents. It was time to end this, he thought.

'Yes, I can see that Personnel received letters from your doctor. I also see there are letters here sent to us from your lawyer. Why go to such lengths if you were truly sick?'

'I thought about resigning, because I did not see myself coming back to work unless my mother got better. But my lawyer advised that that wasn't necessary.'

One tear made it down his left cheek. Kandle wiped it away angrily.

'Do you still want to resign?' Malasi asked, somewhat hopefully.

'I'd like to know my options first.'

'Well, it won't be necessary to bring in your lawyer. No. It won't be necessary. We will review your case and get back to you. In the meantime, get some rest. And you can keep the money, the loan, for now. You are still an employee of this bank.'

He turned to everybody. 'Mr Guka?'

The manager glared at Kandle with a small smile on his face. He remained quiet.

'Mr Karoki, you are free to leave,' Mr Malasi said.

As they all trooped out, leaving Mr Guka and Mr Malasi in the office, Kandle realised that he had just completed one of the greatest performances of his young life.

He hummed Bob Marley's 'Crazy Baldhead' and saw himself back in Zanze till the early hours of the morning.

'Can I see you for a minute in my office?'

It was Ocuotho. Before Kandle followed him down the hall, he shook Kimani's and Koigi's hands and whispered, 'I'll be at Zanze later.' Then he walked after Ocuotho, into the glass-partitioned office right in the middle of the bank floor.

'Why didn't you tell me about your problems?' Ocuotho said, when they were inside. 'I thought we agreed you would come to me. I know people in Head Office. We could have come to an arrangement. You know Guka does not understand young people.'

'Thank you, Sir. But don't worry. It is taken care of.'

'You now have some time. Think carefully about your life.'

'That is exactly what I am doing, Sir.'

Ocuotho sighed, and looked at him. 'I have a small matter. A personal matter. My daughter is sick and I was wondering whether you could lend me something small. Maybe Ksh 10,000?'

'No problem. The usual interest applies. And I need a blank cheque.'

'Of course.' Ocuotho wrote a cheque and handed it over.

Kandle reached into his back pocket and counted out twenty 500-shilling notes from the furniture-loan money.

'Well, I suspect we won't be seeing you around here, one way or the other,' Ocuotho said, with some meaning. 'We'll miss …' But even before he finished the two started laughing. And it was from the liver and in it lay a national desperation. But it was a language that they each understood.

WE ARE HERE BECAUSE WE ARE HERE

Komora Kijana Wito sat outside his grandfather's hut watching Ozi village in its daily moments of morning wazimu, idleness, and petty quarrels. It was a week before the War between Tsana and Indian Ocean. His grandfather, Komora Mzee Wito, had come in with the first cockcrow after the meeting of the Gasa and was asleep in the main hut, so there was little for Komora Kijana to do before the old man awoke. It was early in planting season and outside the gate of their compound Komora Kijana now saw a few of the men going to the farms; some women singing while they cleaned their compounds; girls running off to the river to fetch water; young men beating the animals heading off towards the swamp and the forest.

Not for the first time Komora Kijana wondered what it felt like to have a baba, mama, sisters and brothers. The people of Ozi thought his grandfather, currently the most senior elder of the Gasa, was teaching him to become a mganga. The boys he had grown up with now spent most of their time watching Premier League DVDs in the small social hall, dreaming that they would one day play for Manchester United. After being cut they all now lived in their designated camp near the mangroves. His former headmaster, Mr Fito, had even stopped coming to look for Komora Kijana to convince him that he needed to go to university, so that option was also closed. All this was because of the Book that he was helping his grandfather write about his life. Komora Kijana could not do the things of other young men.

In another time he would already have started planning the trip upriver to steal a girl from beyond Shirikisho in a Malajuu village. Komora Kijana now remembered Mariam, the girl he had grown up closest to. She was the only one of his age who was not married because she was going to university. All the other girls of their age already had children. After he and his grandfather had started the Book, Komora Kijana and Mariam stopped seeing each other and when he saw her at the market recently there were no words, just an exchange with the eyes.

Now he wondered where his grandfather's breakfast was. It was getting late. Every week a different family was assigned to bring food for the elders of the Gasa. Komora Kijana remembered that this week it was the wife of Ukonto assigned to the Gasa's feeding. Looking into the sky he realised that she was already late. Komora Kijana was relieved, if only for her sake, that his grandfather was asleep. Not that the old man ate anything more than a few bananas and pounded pumpkin leaves every day. Ukonto's wife was nowhere to be seen and Komora Kijana stood up and decided to get on with the day before his grandfather woke up and demanded his attention.

He could hear the more active children already running around the homesteads – when he looked over the fence he saw the older ones release the chickens from their coops. The clucking birds complained about being cooped inside all night and immediately started scratching and pecking the ground. Cats of all shapes and sizes slunk from the newly open hut doors and stretched and lingered near the hearths. When the women of the houses emerged their cats circled them; some purred from beneath their mistress's kikois.

Older boy-children snatched the long cylindrical calabashes from the rafters of their mothers' huts and took to their heels to deliver their fathers' breakfasts to the shambas. The girls wandered out of huts that sat next to their mothers' and stood there scratching themselves with sleep till their mothers placed faded yellow plastic containers before them and barked a few commands. The girls reached for the ropes that held each yellow plastic container and slung it on their heads. They headed to the river chattering — more and more girls joining the line from all the homesteads. They all wore red gingham Ozi Primary School dresses. Some wore blue school sweaters, faded at the elbows. The girls all somehow managed to keep talking, some chewing leftovers from last night's dinner — a piece of cassava, yam, arrowroot, fried banana. Some even carried tin cups from which they sipped their tea uninterruptedly with skill and poise as they carried containers half their body-size on their heads.

Komora Kijana sighed, picked up a couple of water containers and followed the line of girls to the river, hoping to fetch water before his grandfather woke up. The girls giggled when they saw him and taunted and sang at him: *The young man who is the wife of his grandfather.*

It was cold by the river. The more reckless girls rushed to the water, cupped the cold water in their hands and splashed at their friends. Containers were flung aside as the smaller girls took to their heels. The ones who could not get away fast enough received an unwelcome gush of water down their backs and shrieked. Some pretended to cry and even produced tears. They were immediately mocked and threatened with 'death by crocodile'. Others did mini-impressions of their mothers and bickered and argued, with arms akimbo. Soon the disagreements turned into girlish laughter and containers were placed next to the pump and then the line of girls could be seen streaming back into the village.

When Komora Kijana noticed how swollen the river was he realised that the War between the Tsana and Indian Ocean was not too far off and he dropped the container he was carrying and hid it in the nearby bushes. Walking along the river he could see the farms, the men bent over digging up the burnt grass because they had to plant in a few weeks. Komora Kijana looked over across the river as the morning disappeared under the sun and he could see young boys carrying packets of food wrapped in banana leaves. The best farms had always been at the shores of the Tsana till the War started.

Komora Kijana found Mzee Jorabashora's son Hamisi working in the shamba. Hamisi had been his late father's best friend and was like an uncle to him. The man straightened and smiled at him and they both looked at the river.

'Has your grandfather told you when the War will happen?' the son of Jorabashora asked.

'He says a week at most.'

'Has he seen the river lately?'

'He sees its changes in his dreams ...'

Hamisi said: 'Look at the water. The War will come any day now.'

It was the third week of March and they discussed who had tilled the first bush and who had not. Thinking back to the past season Hamisi talked of men like Kase Morowa who waited till the last moment to put seed in the ground and did not take to the fields with the early sun. He then pointed at the shambas, which were all ready for the coming season. Komora Kijana nodded when Hamisi repeated what the old men of the village never tired of pointing out, that it was the footsteps of the woman who had become pregnant that required placing on the ground with care. Crops needed a brave hand. Even now there were still men who were asleep, who only took the path to the shambas when the dew had long evaporated.

A boy emerged from the trees on the other side of the shamba and came towards them. It was Jorabashora Kijana, the son of Hamisi. He waited to be greeted but his father ignored him. Komora Kijana could see boys on all the adjoining shambas bringing breakfast for their working fathers. Many of the men ignored the boys and continued working for long periods before they stopped what they were doing to eat.

Hamisi turned to his son. 'And now what is wrong with your mother?'

'Father, it is the government boat,' the boy said, rising on the balls of his feet with excitement. 'It passed this morning measuring the level of the Tsana. Everyone went to see it. The whole village is talking about it.'

'Is that what they teach you in school? To give answers to questions that you have not been asked? Did you pass by the mapera tree? Is that why my breakfast has to be late?'

The village mapera tree had not produced any fruit in the Nyuki and Moto generations, and the rebuke was meant for the boy's whole age-set – whose coming of age had dried the hundred-year-old tree.

'Baba, I told Mother to give me your food but she told me that water must be fetched from the river first. She said everyone is saying the river will be too muddy any day now from the rains.'

'Eh, she knows better than the Gasa when the War will come. Any day now there will be no food at all and my arm will drop from weakness because my food is always late,' Hamisi said.

Komora Kijana could see all the men in the adjoining fields unpeeling the banana leaves that held their breakfast to start eating.

'Father, may I go to school now?'

'Can't you see I am talking to Komora, who is old enough to be your uncle?'

The boy stood there waiting and when his father was not looking Komora smiled at the boy.

'When I was your age I would now be working next to my father,' Hamisi told his son. 'You children are very lucky nowadays.'

A few minutes later a few of the men in the adjoining shambas looked up as they finished eating and a few wiped their mouths with relish. Some of them waved in Komora Kijana's direction.

'What are you still doing here?' Hamisi said to the boy. 'If your teacher comes to my hut to complain that you are always late I will teach you what my father taught me at your age.'

The boy rushed off and his father looked at him with pride. 'He is a good strong boy.' Komora Kijana and Hamisi watched the river for a while and Komora said, 'I will tell my grandfather that the river is becoming a python.'

Remembering that he had started his morning drawing water from the river, Komora Kijana rushed there and filled up the container he had hidden away. He lifted the container with one arm with some ease and decided to take the long route back to his grandfather's hut to see how the village was preparing for the War between Tsana and Indian Ocean. Ozi village was 300 huts in total, big, medium and small as well as thirty small stone houses and two large ones with wide verandahs that belonged to Chief Mpango and the late son of Mzee Chilati Dhabasha who, a year ago, had been arrested after being mistakenly accused of being the famous terrorist Faisal. He had died in government custody and his father had left the house empty in anger. Ozi was the last inhabitable space on the Tsana before the mangroves by the river and the wilderness leading up to the sea. Komora Kijana now reached Ozi Primary School, which stood at the northern edge of Ozi, a clear mark of colour and design that stood out from everything that surrounded it in age and appearance. He looked out to the far end of the village along the river to the small bay where the farms, rice and bananas ended. Beyond the bay, kilometres of mangroves stretched along the river where the men went to fish or to hunt. The small bay also held the new fish-smoking facility from where the fishing boats left early every morning. Behind Komora Kijana, inland beyond Ozi Primary, was the indigenous forest called Kilu after the great Mbakomo mganga. Half a day's walk along the river on the edge of Kilu Forest was the larger Ungwana Bay, which for Ozi was the end of the world where the wild animals prowled. But in the other direction along a dirt track that became murram road all the way to the Malindi Highway, an hour away by Nissan or tuk tuk were the other Pokomo villages, and then the lands of the Ormah dotted the land. There was also a mosque along the dirt track navigable by car; there had been talk of a dispensary for two years but the floods and the wild animals thankfully kept Kenya at bay.

Komora Kijana reached the most densely inhabited huts in Ozi that formed a collective mass in the middle of the village. From that spot he stood in the middle of the rough triangle that was Ozi, with the Tsana as the base line. The pier boat launch with the fish-smoking house next to it was one angle of the triangle, the swamp-farms and the gate that led to the long road on the opposite corner the other. The chief's camp near Ozi Primary formed the top of the triangle.

He made his way slowly back to his grandfather's hut further from the river, beyond its flood level. His grandfather had moved there after the great El Niño of '97. Only the ancient hut of Gasa next to the kizio was on higher ground and, because of its special magic, was said to be the only place in the village unaffected by the floods since the Malachini settled in these parts when they came from Shungwaya.

When Komora Kijana reached the homestead his grandfather was still asleep and so he started with the kayapa hedge, heaping twigs and small branches that he had collected from the forest the previous day. He fortified the fence all around the compound till he was sure that even a senge pursuing a she-goat in heat would be deterred from entering the enclosure. He started a small fire and found the two walking sticks that his grandfather had instructed him to make for their forthcoming journey to the Constitutional Conference. Both heavy and strong, the two sticks were just about the right weight and firmness. He laid them back to harden against the small flame that came up. From inside his hut he brought out a long, hollow calabash container. He popped it open, holding it away from his face and nostrils to let the fermented porridge release its tang. He held it against the wind for a few minutes and soon enough there were yells of dismay in the neighbouring yards. Mama Kutula, their neighbour, appeared and shouted, 'You, Komora! Is that how you treat the friends of your dead mother? You will make me bring a smelly child into the world with your nonsense.'

Mama Kutula was heavily pregnant and complained loudly every day to the world about all the things that plagued her, including the increasing activity of butterflies, sparrows and swifts that were harbingers of the flood.

Komora Kijana noticed two eyes watching him keenly through the hedge. An arm appeared slowly over the hedge and placed a large wrapping that steamed away in the morning air. It was Ukonto's wife, Kerekani. His grandfather's food was almost three hours late. Kerekani was not allowed in the compounds of most homes because of her husband's lung condition. Most of the villagers feared their children catching germs from her that she, in turn, had caught from her husband. Ukonto had been predisposed since birth to a heavy lung that shed sputum and mucus all day long, especially in the wet rainy seasons. It was said it would have even been better if he had been born a mkabira in a land where the air is dry and there is no land to be tilled or river to be ridden. Ukonto now worked as a watchman at the government offices near Shirikisho because he could not farm.

'There are no children here to be sick,' said Komora Kijana, picking up the food. 'You can come into the compound.'

'Wewe, what about you?' Kerekani said, with habitual irritation, appearing from behind the bush. 'You think you are now a man?' Komora Kijana thanked her for the food and she left muttering. He winced when he tasted the first mouthful. The millet maize was too soft. Ukonto, it was also said, had weak teeth from his condition. Komora Kijana sniffed at the stew and it had too much pepper. He also saw that the vegetables were too dry.

Komora Mzee woke up with a few deep coughs. Komora Kijana waited for a few minutes and then went inside and they ate in silence. After the meal, the old man pulled the Book from the eaves above him and dusted off wasps' eggs and handed it to Komora Kijana. Then the old man started talking in his quick breaths and Komora Kijana wrote it all down with the Youth pen he was so proud of, a prize that he had been given for being first in his fourth form class.

A month ago the government delegation from Constitution and Water, Katiba and Maji, had come to visit Ozi village and invited Chief Mpango to the Tana People's Constitutional Conference. The Chief then asked Komora Mzee Wito instead to represent Ozi and the Malachini. With the coming Constitutional Conference the finishing of the Book became even more important. His grandfather said there was no better way to show the people of Katiba and Maji why and how the

Malachini lived on the shores of the Tsana. At the conference he planned to give the Kenyan government the Book of his life to explain everything about the Tsana and the Mbakomo, the Malachini, and Ozi.

Over the last month they had worked till late in the night but when the Gasa started consulting every evening about the coming War between the Tsana and the Indian Ocean they started working till maghreb. Then, Komora's grandfather would take his hand and they would walk slowly to the hut of the Wazee wa Gasa, near the kizio, and he would send Komora Kijana away.

Komora Kijana had lived with his grandfather since his parents died ten years ago during the last War between Tsana and Indian Ocean, also known as the El Niño of '97. Even when his parents were still alive Komora Kijana had gone into his grandfather's hut every evening to hear stories about the River, his people the Mbakomo, the downriver villages, the Malachini, his own village of Ozi and his clan, the Komora. But that one morning changed everything. Komora Kijana's father set out up the river to fish at Kau where the sea's waves at high tide pushed the fresh water trout. The floods had been expected any day and his father wanted to do his last bit of trout fishing before El Niño '97. But it was as if the Tsana had been waiting just for him.

Days later his canoe came back empty as the sea tides retreated from the force of the river. Komora Kijana's mother refused to leave her home till her husband came back. She was bitten by a snake washed out of its hole by the floods days later. When his father's head was found upstream, the rest of him taken by crocodiles, Komora Kijana's mother succumbed to the snake-bite. Komora Mzee was unable to speak at the funeral which was held quickly as the water climbed. And his sight and hearing started failing as the thick river spread over Ozi. Later, when the Malachini learned that the Kenyan government had panicked over El Niño's rainfall and opened the Seven Forks Dam upriver, known as the Seven Stone Men by the Mbakomo, without warning, Komora Mzee blamed his brother, who was Assistant Minister for Water at the time, for the death of his son.

Komora Kijana went to live with his grandfather. A year later, when he turned eight, he was sent to Ozi Primary School. When he learned how to write his grandfather told him that one day he would help him put down the old man's life in a book as a way of the Mbakomo recording their lives by the Tsana and even what had happened during El Niño '97. So, every evening, the old man told his grandson of his long life.

When Komora Kijana finished primary school his grandfather called the boy to his hut to tell him all the things that young men are told when they leave home. Komora Kijana did not expect to continue his education after primary school after his father's death but his grandfather sent Komora Kijana to stay with his brother, Komora Mzee Sazi, so he could attend high school in Ngao. After El Niño '97 the two old men had stopped talking when Komora Mzee Wito accused Komora Mzee Sazi of choosing the government and Kenya over Ozi and his own people. But he also said that Kijana Komora was his brother's son too when he sent him there.

Once Komora Kijana arrived in Ngao, Komora Mzee Sazi, whom his grandfather had fallen out with over the Tsana, laughed at this small victory over his older brother and said at least the old fool knew the value of formal education. The four years of secondary school went by quickly and every holiday Komora Kijana went back to Ozi. By Form 2 his grandfather was asking him to write down the things he told him every evening. Just before he did his final exams, Komora Kijana went back to Ngao before that last term and found that Komora Mzee Sazi had had a stroke and was bed-ridden. His younger grandfather lay beneath thick blankets surrounded by several hovering women. The photos on the wall next to his bed were littered with Mzee Sazi's wordly greatnesses – in one photo he stood with the first two Presidents of Kenya. One of the photos, with Mzee Jomo Kenyatta, had been taken at the site of the largest Stone Man, Masinga Dam, with the rest of the other Seven Stone Men in smaller photos. There was also a photo of a white man with his arm around his second grandfather.

Another photo had Komora Mzee Sazi standing before a tall building that said: MINISTRY OF WATER HEADQUARTERS. With a shaky hand and the smell of illness and lilies from the river, Komora Mzee Sazi scrawled a letter and asked Komora Kijana to go to Kipini Secondary School with the document and give it to the headmaster, Mr Fito. His younger grandfather also looked at him and said an odd thing: 'Now you have been given the power to read and you must not stop.' When he saw Komora Kijana's incomprehension he laughed and then fell back to the bed coughing. He died a week later.

After Komora Kijana sat his O-level exams he went back to Ozi. Two elders from Komora Mzee Wito's Sinbad age-group had died within a week of each other and his grandfather was worried he too would be called soon. They started working on the Book every day.

Komora Mzee Wito handed over an old brown-and-black diary with golden lining that he had been given by his brother when they were still close. The diary was embossed with the crest of the government of Kenya. At the bottom it said 'Ministry of Water'. The dates inside were from 1990. This became the Book. That had been a year ago.

Over this period Komora Kijana found some of the things that his grandfather told him strange but he wrote them down without asking questions. Mostly, they told of Komora Mzee Wito's past journeys along the river. Journeys without the maps that Komora Kijana had learned in school. Places that the maps in school never mentioned. Words that did not exist in Kiswahili or Mbakomo. Stories of men who could summon crocodiles and send them to their enemies. Of spirits in the hills and in the forest.

Komora Kijana came to understand that these things that his grandfather told him would be lost forever if they were not written down. At times his grandfather called one or two of the old men of Gasa, Mzee Jorabashora and the oldest man in the village, whose name was never said aloud, and they added things from their own memories and so the book grew.

Komora Kijana remembered one of those first evenings when his grandfather put the Book aside and reached up into the rafters of his hut and some ancient-looking scrolls fell from it. The old man handed them over to Komora Kijana and asked him to rewrite the words in the Book. The parchments had a kind of writing that the boy had not seen before but after looking closely he made out the words:

Imperial Majesty of Britain.
The Territory Ozi will serve as agent of the Imperial Majesty of Britain against the German Territory of Witu.

'Do you know what this is? This document shows that this village was given Madaraka by the Queen of England a long time ago. That Ozi was the first agent of England in the place we now call Kenya.'

And that was when Komora Kijana realised the importance of the Book.

A few days after the river began rising Chief Mpango's aides started going around the village with loudspeakers warning everybody that the coming floods were just days away. The whole village laughed and abused the aides. Serikali was always late. A week ago a messenger from the Malajuu had come with a missive from the Gasa of Baomo to warn them of the heavy rains that had already started upriver. The Gasa had sent him back with a young man from Ozi but this emissary was yet to return with news of how strong the Tsana was. Nature had already given its signs the day before when a large snake had appeared, sunning itself on the path to the swamp. Those who rose early missed the snake. And so it was Ukonto who had almost trod on the snake. When he saw it the heavy something that had sat on his chest all his life lifted away – he felt his mouth open and take in the morning air with such ease that he felt as if he was floating on air. The snake slowly slid into the grass and Ukonto saw it make its way into the Tsana and head towards the sea. Later, when the elders of Gasa listened to Ukonto's tale, several observed that a snake of that size had not been spotted in Ozi since the '97 Great El Niño War of Tsana and Indian Ocean. By the next day news of the snake was all over Ozi.

When Kerekani brought food for Komora Mzee Wito the next day she squealed at Komora Kijana Wito, 'My husband is healed. He asks when he can come and see Mzee Wito for his blessing?'

'I will ask him.' Komora Kijana knew that his grandfather would only bless Ukonto when he had cleared his land of bush.

The next morning before the sun was up the Tsana started swelling. For the next few days the villagers of Ozi village walked with tight backs and drum chests, breaths held, as they watched Indian Ocean fight the Tsana. As if connected to a huge river in the sky the Tsana pushed the ocean tides, the sea foam and its ancient salt back. The wind blanketed Ozi village with warmth during the day and when this was flung away at night, as if by an invisible giant hand, the cold deflated the people of Ozi. As the Tsana grew the air thickened and the people of Ozi walked up and down as if asleep. The children ran around trees faster and faster like twirling tops, as if mad, before collapsing to the ground. Babies' cries were picked by the spiralling wind and flung across the village. They refused to sleep at night, unheeding of even the famous Pokomo lullaby that forty-four years ago had become the tune of the Kenyan anthem.

Two days later the rain reached Ozi. It started in the afternoon, becalmed the children. Babies slumped on their mothers' chafing shoulders and only woke up to eat banana pulp with fish, their evening meal. Then suddenly the rain stopped, and another blanket of warmth covered Ozi village.

The younger generations of Nyuki and Moto spread out on the river's banks till mji Kau to cheer the heavy wind-swept victory as the swollen Tsana slowly pushed the sea back, past their village. The tea-brown waters from Mbakomo soils lapped steadily over the foreign metallic-grey liquid sea and Nyuki and Moto raced along the banks waving their arms, flinging their thin bodies into the air. The more foolhardy jumped and washed in the meeting of Tsana and Indian Ocean. Some young men even followed the victorious river past the Island of Kiundani where absent rich men of Ozi who had moved to Malindi owned rice fields; they skipped over the channel of

Suez to Kilunguni where Mbakomo weddings were held. They saw how the river churned the prawns from the beds in Chala Chala and they waved at the tourists' white faces peering from the tops of Polikani Hills where the German Meinherztgen had said he was building a hotel for the community but then kept all the profits for himself. It was whispered that the German still came in the dead of the night to give the money he owed to the old woman, Mama Mamkaze Witu, who had now been dead for five years, long after she had approved the building of the hotel. The German, it was said, left the money where her hut still stood every fifth day of every month, when all were asleep, to pay for the profits that he had kept for himself to stop Mamkaze Witu from haunting the hotel. That was strong medicine no longer seen in these days.

More young men jumped into boats and were buoyed by the climbing river. They eased past Camp Ya Tiro, where Mbakomo fishing tents were moored but now destroyed, past Bashwani, where they kept their sisal nets – now lost after being pushed out to the sea. Their boats passed Pajero, named after the richest Giriama man who had drowned himself because of debt. In Kivunjeni, they stopped and sang above the fish-breeding grounds where millions of eggs were planted by the Mbakomo gods to become fish and where their forefathers had harvested turtle eggs. When they came to Mlangoni, the door of the sea, they fell silent.

Hundreds of Mswahilis stood there, facing the sea, waving long white cloths calling for their beloved Indian Ocean to return and conquer the 'Tana', as they called it in their language. Low in the sky where they could almost touch it, hung a pale-brown, desiccated moon above the young foolish Mbakomos – a fearful sight they all looked askance at. They realised that their joy was the sorrow of others and they rowed back home. But once they reached the home shores of Ozi they forgot all they had seen and started dancing when their feet touched the ground at the victory of the Tsana over the Indian Ocean.

As the War raged the Wazee wa Gasa sat in the ancient hut at the top of the village. Their night talk swept the decades aside:

they remembered even older Wars between Tsana and Indian Ocean, before El Niño '97. They remembered the Wars of '37, told to them by the grandfathers, and '67 – the other great El Niños. They talked of how God helped the Indian Ocean every nine years to climb upriver and then the Tsana fought back every tenth year to overcome the sea. They remembered how, in their lifetimes, the Indian Ocean had increasingly become stronger than the Tsana. How it had pushed the people of Ozi and the other villages back from its door, almost to the lands of the Ormah who lived behind the Mbakomo, away from the river grazing their cattle. Before this new swelling, the Wazee lamented the Tsana's nine-year cowardice, and how it had failed to protect them or to give them all the good things it should have brought: the soil from the mountains in Meru to grow bananas, rice, millet, mangos, watermelon and sim sim; the fish it allowed to breed and thrive with crocodile and hippo, whose meat they loved so much. They remembered how the Indian Ocean had won the small and big battles in those nine years to bring drought every three years. They now worried about the Tsana's rage – once it conquered the Indian Ocean and the moon and the land it would come for Ozi. They instructed the celebrating villagers to abandon their homes and move to higher land in the forest. Many, however, were too drunk with river joy to listen and laughed, drunk on maize beer at the elder's emissaries. So, the Wazee waited for the flood even as everybody celebrated.

Then, just like that, the Tsana stopped raging against the Indian Ocean; the moon shrunk to an even smaller and paler hole in the sky, unable to help the sea, and the tides came back up the Tsana to Ozi. Those in Ozi with shambas near the mangroves stopped dancing first because the Tsana had now come into their homes. They were the ones who had lived with the salt that burned their land and rejoiced when sea-water was swept from their banana plantations and rice fields. Over the last few days, they had harvested salty catfish suffocated by the Tsana's fresh water. And so they were the first to tell that the river was coming into their shambas.

Now the air stilled and the rain poured all day in a slow, steady drizzle, picking up at night in a furious torrent. And it came up the banks, further and further, till even those who were cursed by distance from the Tsana's providence beheld a sight unseen in all their lives. Something they only knew in the tales of their grandparents from the War of '67 – there was water on their doorsteps. And so the village paused in its drinking and dancing and watched the Tsana. When the water reached their feet they still laughed, stopped what they were doing and danced away nervously till it followed them. Then, they saw the crocodile snouts, their gaping jaws beyond the old banks and they fled and rushed into their homes to pack their belongings and drive their goats and cattle to the swamp, to high land beyond the river. And so, the Tsana, as if pleased, lazily at first, crawled into Ozi land through furrows and channels. It then overflowed the channels and overcame more land. It now licked the furthest houses from its banks and even there, it woke the people up in their beds the next morning. These people who had been cursed to live at a distance from the river but had rejoiced at their temporary fortune only a few days ago also started moving like others but, because there were already numbers at the edges of the forest, they were forced to crawl beneath poisonous vines and enter the undergrowth; and there their children and babies trembled when the elephants trumpeted and the buffaloes bellowed not too far away.

As always, since the Malachini settled in Ozi the water stopped rising when it reached the ancient hut, where the Gasa sat inside. The hut was protected by old knowledge of the river and its ways, built in between its natural channels and history's study of the land's contours.

Komora Kijana was seated outside the hut of Gasa waiting for his grandfather when the old man called him. He went to the doorway and stood there because no one but the elders was allowed to enter. His grandfather appeared and came out into the daylight and handed him the Book. 'Bring your stool here.' And this is what he wrote as his grandfather addressed the Gasa:

My First Journey

When I was born the river was not where we, the Malachini – or us the people of Ozi, live. The River was at Shisrikisho when I was born. It was the British who brought it here. I am sure that the river will be elsewhere when you die and your grandchildren grow up.

I have travelled up the river. And it is these things I want to tell you. The British brought the sea to us – the river never came this way. Ungwana Bay is where the river went to that time long ago. When I was a boy we would watch the big pelican boat of the white man pass by our village – it made a loud noise that we had never heard before. Louder than thunder or any waterfall. I remember the British made my father and my uncles and all the men of the village dig the channel that became the river today. If the river had been left where Mola had placed it, the sea would not be attacking our land. Even now the days are too hot. Or too cold.

We, the Pokomo, come from Comoros. Because Comoros is small, our forefathers had to leave and over many days and nights came in small boats to Shungwani. I hear people calling it Shingwaya. It is Shungwani. Like I said, it is because people get the message wrong that things are the way they are in the world today.

All this place that we call home was forest and animals and all the peoples of the Coast were one. We were all Wakomora. Wakomora of the grass houses. The Galla made us start building mud houses. They were always fighting and we agreed to do what they wanted so that we could keep our land. Here at least, it was warm. Others were chased to where the Gikuyu have their God on top of a mountain. The age groups that we still have in our heads are part of the legacy of our forefathers: Gigiwa, my grandfather; Loda, my father; Japanisi, which is me; and the Gasa; Sinbad, the younger members of Gasa; Shombe, our sons; Moto, their younger brothers; Nyuki, the sons of my son and the ones who now think they are strong and call themselves 'Generation Man U'. Wembe, the sons of my son's younger brothers.

But first the Wakamora forefathers spread in Shungwani — some of you call it Shungwaya. Then they spread to Siu where that real Faisal was said to be, Pate, Kizunguti, Majimwale, Makoe. Then, they started travelling up this river we now call Tsana on their Kinga. The river was called Gamba then. They passed Lango la Simba where there were hundreds of lions but had to stop to rest.

One woman fell pregnant and when she stopped to give birth that is where the Pokomo settled. It is in the place that is now called Panda Nguo. Here the people started separating. Their tongue got twisted and because of the state of being pregnant (mbakomo) we became the Pokomo. Then they started spreading into Ndera, Gwano, Gwale, Kinakomba, Ndura, Zubaki, Malalulu and Malakote.

We had also separated from the Digo whose common food was mihogo; the Rabai who stopped because they liked raha hii (easy living); the waDavidi, also called the Taita because they looked white. And that is how we came to be here and live next to the river.

Our government was the Kijo. And every so often we made sacrifices on the river after planting and harvesting. We danced the kitoko and mwarabe. And we spread from Kibokoni to Garsen where the Ormah and their enemies the Somali live. The Ormah ran away from Ethiopia and on the way they started fighting the Somali who had always lived on the other side of the river. The Ormah came to us and asked for help and we hid them in huge baskets from the Somali. Ever since we have been enemies with the wakabira.

There is nothing wrong between us and the Malajuu. I have been travelling to them for years. There is also nothing wrong with us and Kenya. What is wrong is always the message. There are too many people talking. About us and them. About us and the Orma. About us and the Wakabira. About us as different peoples. Wandera, Wagwaro, Wasumbaki, Milalulu, Kwakomba, Mwinamwina. This river was our shield. Our Ngao.

His grandfather finished talking and Komora Kijana could hear the old men of the Gasa inside sneezing snuff from their noses. He heard them talk about how the Mbakomo lived in the balance of Tsana and Indian Ocean. How many of the people of the Tsana would die from this ancient battle now renewed but it was a death that was better than most. It was better than the desperation that was brought on by failure of the crops. The Gasa gave thanks to the strength of the Indian Ocean for nine years that allowed their sons to go upriver to fish. They talked of the risks of death by hippo or crocodile in the small boats on these fishing trips. They talked of death by the strong curses of other villages when Ozi was forced to steal from their shambas – clans up the river where the sea never reached and where crops thrived. This was better than death by buffalo, when Ozi was forced to go deep into the forest to look for food.

Over a low fire the Elders of Gasa murmured and gestured over all these things and commiserated with the people of the Sea, the Mswahilis whose lives would be taken away till the sea came back. They prayed that the other clans, their other people, the Malajuu, had not already been swept aside from the outpouring of the river from the Mountain and the opening of the Seven Stone Men.

Komora Kijana sat outside the hut of Gasa and wondered whether Mariam was okay.

All the young men who had climbed into boats and danced their way to Mlangoni to cheer the Tsana had now wisely left the river. Not far from the hut of Gasa there was a half-built stone hall with a flat roof – this was the youth social hall that was yet to be completed. The money from the Constituency Development Fund had dried up before the windows and the floor could be put in. But the Tsana was yet to climb onto the roof and so, happy and distracted, the young men stood on this vantage point and cheered the river against Indian Ocean.

The young men had been drinking maize beer since the War started. Most of the Nyuki and Moto generation were too young to remember the '97 El Niño War so they celebrated the majesty of the river shouting: 'Man U, Man U.' There was no electricity since the rains had started and they could not watch their Premier League DVDs so they sang the song of their favourite team.

Semikaro the councillor was among them and he put his hands up and they all fell quiet. Now he told that the water came from the upriver dams, the Seven Stone Men built by a government that did not care for them. The young men listened and became animated again, drunkenly shouting that they would go upriver and destroy the dams.

Semikaro hailed their bravery and promised to find them money from Nairobi for transport to carry out this important task. He also told them not to heed the words of the old men of Gasa who led the village and were past their 'expiry date'. The young men shouted they needed to choose a leader (Semikaro cleverly declined the great honour when they shouted and cheered Siad Barre, Siad Barre, his nickname from the aviator shades he always wore, that made him look like a giant insect) who they could send before the old men for support of their plan to kill the Seven Stone Men.

One tall, wide-toothed young man with a big mouth, the best soccer player in the village, wearing a Manchester United T-shirt, nicknamed Ronaldo, offered himself as their new leader. When the young men gave him their drunken vote of confidence he jumped from the roof of the stone building and waded confidently to new ground, to the ancient hut of Gasa and asked to be heard. He removed the earring he wore in his right ear like his hero, Ronaldo, and stood and peered through the open doorway. He spoke to the shadows as he could hardly see inside the hut and the old men grew grave when they heard his proposal. Komora Mzee Wito said: 'Kijana wa Mimili, you wear an earring like our daughters and mothers. Do you know what you speak of when you tell us of the Seven Stone Men found up the Tsana?'

'Fathers, with the blessings of Gasa all is possible.'

'Have you ever seen the Seven Stone Men? You speak with a mouth that should still be suckling. The Seven Stone Men cannot be destroyed. The whole of Ozi from a hundred years knows this. Even if my grandfathers from the time of Gigiwa and Loda, fathers and uncles from the time of before

Sinbad, my brothers and cousins from that of Sinbad and my sons and nephews of Shombe were brought back together as young men – they cannot destroy the Seven Stone Men. So you children from Moto and Nyuki have become nothing because you worship a football club far away. The Mbakomo have to live with the Seven Stone Men. It is time for you to start using your young arms to add mud onto the dykes of the river. The floods are here. If I still had the strength I would have locked you in the kizio myself. Ati you now call yourselves generation Manchester United!' Komora Mzee Wito spat on the ground.

Ronaldo left the hut and thought about the trip up the Tsana to destroy the Seven Stone Men. The furthest he had ever been from Ozi was when he rode upstream on a canoe with two of his best friends to 'steal' his wife from Ngomeni, which was half an hour away by boat.

He did not go back to the roof of the social hall where he had left his friends but went to join his young wife and two babies near the forest. The young men he left sang with new energy till it was clear that their Manchester United hero was not coming back, so they clambered into their canoes and rowed to Shirikisho with the little money that the councillor had left them and bought more millet beer.

The Tsana had now risen higher and the young men could only get off the boats beyond the swamp, which had become a small lake. They bought the beer and came back to their high outpost and started drinking again, dancing on the high concrete till they fell to the ground one by one, drunk. They did not feel the water come up slowly in the night as they slept and crocodiles pulled two of them into the river.

Semikaro had travelled to Shirikisho and when he came to Ozi the next morning he heard what had happened and stayed in the safety of Kilu forest. There he shouted at the government in Nairobi and the district headquarters in Garsen and swore revenge for the two young men who had been eaten by crocodiles. The whole Ozi world had become water.

Agitated by the words of Semikaro and worn down by the hunger and cold, some women in Kilu Forest started whispering that the Katiba and Maji government visitors the village had received before the Tsana had overcome the Indian Ocean and Ozi were to blame. Questions about the visit of the Katiba and Maji people now spread in the forest, asking what they had come to do and where they were now that Ozi was suffering. The forest spread with the news of these harbingers of ill. Different accounts were given of the visit. Angry, the people of Ozi asked why the Land Rover the men had come in had not been fed with saltwater from the mangroves to kill it. Or why the hair of the white girl who had come with them had not been shaved off as she stood because, more than anyone, she had brought the river's wrath.

The people in the forest now remembered how the British had favoured the Malajuu and given them their land because they thought they, the Malachini, were lazy. Someone asked how the elders could let the granddaughter of the British come back to their village, after all that had happened years ago. They told a version of the story over and over again of how the British had also stolen the river and taken it away near to where their big man lived so that he could travel by boat to the Ameru people far away near the mountains. They agreed that the British girl had now brought more bad luck to them.

Semikaro listened to the poisonous voices and sensed new opportunities against the Gasa. He did not correct them on many things such that the girl who had come to the village was Dutch or that Katiba and Maji had come to propose solutions to the Tsana's flooding. He turned to them instead and said: 'You people. The rest of Kenya does not take care of us. They have now opened the dams for us to drown. They have built dams in our river to benefit themselves. Now we suffer because of the dams.' The people all fell silent. The dams were too far away from them. They were getting hungry and somebody suddenly asked the councillor about the CDF funds and how that would help them in this time of need. He promised to see what he could do the next day. Deep in the night he rowed away in one of the boats to Shirikisho and never came back. Without the poison tongue of Semikaro they settled and looking around the trees remembered that Kilu Forest was their friend. It was their refuge in times like this.

The rain stopped as suddenly as it had started and because the air was calm and quiet everyone knew that the War between Tsana and Indian Ocean was over. Komora Mzee came out of the hut of Gasa and Komora Kijana led him home. The water had never threatened their homestead. They slept for days and when Komora Mzee Wito had rested enough he called Komora Kijana to his hut. The old man reached into the hut's rafters and removed the Book. He dusted it and handed it to the boy who opened the pages to release a pile of dead wasps to the ground. The old man sunk onto a stool at the far wall and started talking. The words from his mouth fell on the pages and now and again he paused and sifted the dead wasps through his hands and crushed them and continued talking.

After he finished, he sang the Pokomo lullaby the way it was supposed to be sung. Then, he looked at Komora Kijana and said it would soon be time to travel to the Tana People's Constitutional Conference. The old man handed Komora Kijana the Book and told him to read through as much of it as possible and to prepare for the trip. Komora Kijana could see that his grandfather had aged with the swelling of the Tsana. Over the last two years the old man had stopped taking his annual trip to Malajuu, up the river, to see the other Wazee wa Gasa. He had been building strength for this last journey to the Tana People's Constitutional Conference.

Komora Kijana spent the next few days reading the Book. When he finished and took it back to his grandfather, Komora Mzee Wito was unable to leave his bed. He called the boy to him. 'I am told that the river is back to normal and is moving again in its natural direction.' Komora Kijana held out the Book to his grandfather but the old man did not take it. 'This is now your Book. This is what I leave you. I cannot come with you but I will be with you in spirit. There is no time to waste.'

Komora Kijana slipped out of the village five days later in the early morning and only the Gasa knew he had left. Along with the Book, Komora Mzee Wito had given him a pile of papers that included an old map. He also carried a small bag that contained a calabash of water, three pairs of trousers, two shukas, four T-shirts and two shirts. He wore a cloth inside his trousers and there was a knot to the side where he kept the money his grandfather had given him.

It was still dark when he left and he wanted to catch a boat at Shirikisho village that he hoped would carry him to Ngao. From Ngao he would take a Nissan matatu to Garsen where he would spend the night. He now kept on foot through swamp and open grasslands – the track was treacherous and he ignored the likely looking firm grounds and took the steps of his childhood. The sun would be up in a few hours and so he rushed. The shadows of the crops of his people by the river – familiar banana shapes, blade-like knives of the maize, the shaded looming thick figures that he knew held mango fruit guided him. The last sound he had heard from his village was the sound of young men cheering at the village TV – electricity had returned and they were back to watching the recorded Premiership games they had missed during the floods. He could also hear the voice of the man far away in England talking everyone through the game. A goal was scored and the shouts of 'Man U! Man U!' came to him.

Now he wondered where Mariam was and how she was doing, and he knew she would have gone to university when he returned.

Komora Kijana touched the bag on his shoulder again and felt the Book inside and walked on towards the Mountain they called Kenya where the Tana People's Constitutional Conference was to be held. He remembered his grandfather's last words: 'At the conference you will find people asking you to keep explaining yourself. All you have to say is this: We, the people of Ozi, Malachini, we are here because we are here because we are here.'

THE RED DOOR

I n the old Datsun 1200, Julius Rotiken Sayianka and Eddie Muchiri Kambo roared off the Narok Highway, just before Suswa, building speed to clear a small rise where it had all become patchwork from the '97 El Niño floods. Juli took the Datsun into free gear heading downhill to the little seasonal Rift Valley Lake, now called Mwisho ya WaKikuyu after the last Maasai-Kikuyu election clashes. When the laga came into view, on the endless Savanna plain, a long boy lay under one of the Zebus. Juli shouted, 'Fuck!' from the safety of the cabin and hooted sharply. The boy's mouth was stuck fast on a wrinkled udder, feeding like a long leech. The conjoined cow-boy sketch, canvassed against wide sky, broke into two, righting the world.

Juli glanced at Chiri, switched off Snoop Dogg on the radio. They passed the boy's long form, observing he was at the cusp of manhood in his nakedness. Usually Juli would have stopped to find out which clan he belonged to but passing without acknowledgement was the right insult for the boy's animal act. Before them was Leakey country, the laga once a prehistoric lake on the floor of the Great Rift. Juli saw the long boy in his side mirror recede, noting the long cloth over his mouth.

'What's with the facecloth?' Chiri asked.

Juli peered into the side mirror. 'Even me nashindwa. Maybe his people think they can keep him from cow tit by tying his mouth. Matiti.'

Chiri, still learning about the ways out here in the wheatlands, saw Juli was serious. A young donkey stepped away from the Datsun's quiet roar, its jaws a metronome in the wind of the plain. Raising its head, the donkey brayed far into the northeast where the flat ended and the blue hills took over. The Datsun rumbled towards the other edge of the laga, a soccer field away from the long boy. Juli tipped the Datsun into the edge of the water to cool the tyres and let the makeshift blower exhaust slowly calm down.

Out in the open, Juli was tall, square-shouldered, hard and wiry, his head small and proportional, his face dark and firm. Chiri was shorter, lighter and leaned towards roundness in the middle. The long boy had shrugged off his shuka and was wading into the far shore of the laga. 'Definitely hii ni kichwa mbaya,' Juli remarked. Badhead. 'This time of year, August, morans should be in the forest. He looks old enough.' Juli sat on the water's edge on the driver's side of the Datsun, stuck his long thin knees in the air, slipped a Sportsman in his mouth, reached into his jeans and took out a plastic sachet full of stems. 'Na amebeba,' he said, squinting against the sun glinting from the laga. 'Did you see the size of him?' His mouth was full of miraa.

Chiri squatted to his left, furrowed his palm in the brown water, scooping it into his pits. Worrying the two-day grime he had picked on the road, he looked towards the far shore in response. Through the wet dripping from his face, Chiri saw the long boy had been joined in the water by his animals. Zebu horns and humps stuck out of the laga mirror. The donkey and goat-headed sheep dipped in and out of the water as if controlled by some giant hand in the sky. Chiri spat out the taste of Zebu from the laga water.

They'd been on the road for three days. Up and down the wheatlands, looking at potential farms to lease for the crop. Juli had been doing this for the last three years after school, banished by his father, Petro Sayianka, from Nairobi after his O-levels. Then, the two childhood friends had met again at Juli's father's funeral last March. Afterwards they started drinking into their common Buru past and one thing had led to another. Chiri had just walked out of his copywriting job at Ogilvy and Mather when they met at the funeral, and had been in limbo for three months. This was just two years after leaving Nairobi Uni in his second year. Juli told him about it all, this thing out on the road and the wheat farms in the Rift Valley and it started looking as good as any other decision Chiri had to make in the near future. Possibly Daystar Uni, maybe mtumba business. He didn't quite know. Chiri now looked at the low, intimate sky and lay back, feeling the warm dust through the thin grass on his back. Juli's voice played in his head and Chiri, his childhood friend who liked to talk up much more than he knew with a penchant for the fantastical. And so he had taken the percentages Juli had rolled on the harvest as added with a pinch of Kensalt. This Juli – who now lived in five-month cycles – in tune with the Narok wheat, which had two crops every year, and who still seemed to need the old illusions of their childhood friendship. Especially with his cold, smoothly shaven and imposing father in the ground. That evening, after the funeral, Chiri had listened to Juli speak with a freedom he had only heard in his friend's voice when they were much younger. This made Chiri wonder about his own father, whose death had not freed any of his own dreams.

Juli now stood up and went to the Datsun's back checking all the tractor and combine parts they had bought in Nakuru. He slapped the bags of seed, fertiliser and insecticide, ready for planting season. He came back to the front, opened the bonnet, poured water from the laga into the radiator. He stepped back as water shot up in an arc, fountain-like, and then lessened as the engine cooled. He cleaned off the deposits around the battery terminals, wiped the windscreen. Chiri did not join Juli's ritual. Since Juli's father died, Chiri noticed and respected his friend's sudden silences, tense and abrupt. He wandered off, made sure there was no wildlife around, and peed in the open field. He watched his yellow, alcohol-heavy pee splotch in the dust, stain the earth and disappear. When Chiri saw Juli look over to him, he strolled back to the Datsun and opened the broken glove compartment. The Marie biscuits had gone soft but there was still some of the Chelsea Dry Gin. He handed over the miraa to Juli, the stems now black and curled like a small dead bird's claws. There was also some choma left – mbuzi ribs crusted with fat, crawling with ants, hours-old tasty. Chiri wished aloud for some ugali.

'Maasais don't eat ugali,' Juli repeated. 'Spoils meat.'

Chiri skinned the ribs with his teeth watching Juli carefully pore over the miraa, talking all the while. They shared the gin between them and Juli stood up ready to get back on the road. But first he lit up the weed and that they did standing up, got their heads going for Narok, ready for the barmaids, the fights, the ugliness, the *ujinga*. The plan was to start planting over the next two weeks. Over their heads the July clouds were overcast, the rains would have started further south and west.

Just as they were about to get into the Datsun the long boy whooped and shouted on the other side of the laga; some storks on the lone acacia took off in witness. Juli, newly alert from the weed, the gin and miraa, turned like a dog.

'Never seen anyone in these parts swimming,' Juli marvelled, his voice low. Chiri heard the violent thing in Juli's voice that he remembered from their Buru teenage years.

'...This bubu here in no man's land. Uncircumcised.'

'Maybe he just wants to play,' Chiri observed. 'A big kid.'

Juli looked at him with a hard glint in his eye and Chiri looked away. 'A lot of blood was spilt here. So now that side ni ya Wa-kikuyu and we are on this side,' Juli said. 'Here on the border, the old ways are lost. Too many Kikuyus. They marry Maasais and they no longer remember the ways of the Red Door.'

'The Red Door?' Chiri asked.

'And that jitu thing remains here bila any respect.'

'And us?'

'Ero,' he said. 'We are passing.'

'And this Red Door?'

Juli smiled. 'For us it is everything. Kila kitu. You'll see. Mlango nyekundu and mlango nyeusi – where all Maasais come from.' Red Door and Black Door. Chiri had also noticed that Juli no longer saw himself as half-Kikuyu from his mother's side, let alone a hundred per cent Buru Buru raised. He waited to hear more lessons on wheat. Lessons on Maasais. How shitty Nairobi, Buru Buru were.

But in the mirror of the laga, Chiri saw Juli's face magnify and contort, thinking maybe about the boy, what they had come upon earlier. Maybe even of his father's death. But most likely of his elder fuck-up of a brother, Solo, who they were meeting in Narok later. Solo, who had just come from the UK after seven years of doing fuck all.

A muster of storks resettled into the small acacia tree. Suddenly a big head emerged right in the middle of the laga. Then it sank into the water. After a few seconds, a few metres from their feet, the dog-like face with newborn-baby eyes split the water, the fish mouth puckering through the handkerchief.

The long boy broke out of the water, hanging out for all the plains to see – tall against the Datsun's front, seemingly even longer than the car itself. Even when Juli stood up to full height, in his Safari boots, the long boy towered over him, as if in primal challenge. Chiri stepped back, almost bolting. Quickly Juli flicked his Sportsman in the long boy's face, and then he reached out, tore the cloth from his mouth and slapped him hard with an open hand and raked hard in a downward motion over the long boy's face. Juli raised his hand again and the baby eyes went wider than a Friesian's. Without the cloth, the boy's face was empty and slack and he started gushing at the mouth and eyes. He cowered under Juli, who lowered his hand and let the handkerchief drop. The long boy started bawling, making star jumps into the sky. His penis, like a fifth limb, jerked in all directions and then he bolted, an antelope on the plain. Juli picked up the handkerchief, went round, opened the car door, dipped his head and then came out, his face dark and triumphant. Chiri remembered the childhood Buru Buru fights, the same Juli look, the pointless violence.

'Ero…' Juli shouted. He hurled the Marie biscuits at the retreating figure. The packet made a long arc in the sky and then fell in the shallow water close to shore.

'Now his people will know why their cows have no milk at the end of the day,' Juli said to Chiri, picking up the white handkerchief and throwing it in the back of the Datsun.

Chiri stood at the edge of the laga and watched the unfortunate figure dip its fish mouth in the mud of the shoreside looking for the biscuits. When Chiri entered the car he did not look at Juli when he said into the windscreen: 'But yaani out here the price of milk is a beating?'

'Narok awaits,' Juli said, now relaxed. 'Time to plant.'

They chased down the dying sun, drained of energy and speech, sweeping past mostly trucks, the weed wearing off. When a Land Cruiser or Land Rover flew past them swiftly, Juli talked of its relative strengths, weaknesses.

Outside Narok town, they came to the commercial wheat farms, perfect like miniature Lego models, out of place against the acacias, the open grasslands, the *National Geographic* mud huts, the scrawny Zebus, stray jackal dogs and the omnipresent goats. Inside the endless fence there were rows of bright-red tractors and harvesters, and ploughed land dotted with young green shoots in furrows that went on as far as the eye could see.

Juli switched back to a monotone not unlike the voice-overs of the Western movies of their childhood explaining to Chiri how wheat was even in Bibilia, Old Testament, God's crop. Wheat grew flat like Maa land – unlike maize, which did not allow herdsmen to survey the most important thing in their lives: the cows. Wheat allowed the herdsman to sense the approach of the charging bull buffalo. Wheat did not hide snakes like cane or sisal.

They drove into Narok, reviving slowly from the endless flatness of their last few days. Narok in the evening was small-town alive to the evening breeze, the promise of mbuzi, beer and sex. Juli did his Narok ritual whenever they were back in town, taking the perimeter, through the slum known as London, then around downtown Narok's narrow streets that curved into the natural bowl that the town was built in, past the old market, the cattle sale still going on, the Diplomat Hotel where they did not recognise any of the cars outside. They came back full circle and someone shouted Juli's clan name, Rotiken, and they stopped, waiting. Obergon, a first cousin and prosperous absentee agricultural officer, waddled up, sweating meat, full of afya. His broad face was all smiles till he peered into the cabin and saw Chiri. He spat on the ground and said something in Maasai. Juli grinned.

'Habari, Kikuyu,' Obergon now hailed Chiri who ignored him. 'Habari mudu wa house,' he repeated sneering at Chiri. All of them laughed now, and Obergon turned to Juli.

'Lakini, let me ask,' he said. 'Tell me, you have finished planting?' His stomach was still heaving from laughing at Chiri. Juli threw his head towards the back where all the wheat season preparations were stacked. Obergon nodded in disapproval. 'Your mzee was always done by late July. Ni nini?' Now he looked at the purchases. 'Be careful. Do not leave anything in the open. Si you know there are a lot of Kikuyus hapa after the clashes.'

Juli nodded and said something in Maasai. Obergon said, 'Ai what's the hurry? Have you talked to Solo?'

'Kwanini.'

Obergon looked at Juli for a long time and then said, 'He has been drinking at Agip tangu lunchtime.'

'Kawaida. We have been driving for three days. Nakuru tafuta-ing supplies.'

'Listen. The Senyos are there. At Agip. The whole clan. You know what that means. Twende?'

And Obergon jumped into the back with surprising ease for one so heavy, hit the side of the Datsun and they drove off.

The Senyo clan sat in a semi-circle flank in the open-air part of Agip restaurant, like a large lion pride, potent with violence. Chiri whispered to himself the count — twenty-seven clan members. They had taken five tables — two doddering elders, talking with their gums with an ancient air of instruction to several men in their early thirties with hard faces. Some younger man-boys hovered around them. The women sat to the side in supplication, their cheeks ornamented with vertical scars, their litters of shy kids cowed by the men's harsh voices. Goat bones lay littered around them, spread over tables. Obergon observed that only the peripheral side of the clan, troublemakers and idlers were present. At least none of them would be carrying guns. 'But Lemeyian Senyo is here,' Obergon muttered, leading Juli and Chiri clear to the other side of the bar. Solo was nowhere to be seen. They sat on stools and ordered from the barman who was imprisoned behind chicken mesh, haloed in the light of a small lamp spewing kerosene to keep away the flies from the booze. Obergon ordered a glass of milk.

'See if you can find Solo,' Juli told Chiri. 'Avoid those animals.'

'Scream if necessary,' Obergon added. 'Kama mwanamke Mkikuyu.' Like a Kikuyu woman.

They heard Solo's laugh, crazy confident, before they saw him. As he came into sight, his face was flushed – he was yet to lose all the paleness he had cultivated in England. Solo ignored Juli, acknowledged Obergon with a manly handshake. Then, showing that he had not lost any of his boxer's speed, he quickly grabbed Chiri around the neck in a headlock, grinding his knuckles into his scalp. Chiri smelled the three-day booze, realised he had missed Solo. Juli and Obergon relaxed at seeing him, and looking over at the Senyos, signalled Chiri to finish his beer so they could take it elsewhere. But then they decided to have a second beer, Obergon and Juli exchanged a look confirming that Solo seemed in control. Juli and Chiri soon forgot all their concerns and shouted at the barman: 'Tumefungua mfereji' – the taps of our throats are open – and that is when Obergon shook his head and left.

Once Juli and Chiri re-started the conversation of their childhood, Solo inevitably wandered off. Then Juli and Chiri heard shouts and when they went to see what was happening, Solo was on the ground. He was bleeding from the mouth, rolling on his back laughing. There was a tall, burly individual pointing at him, shouting in Maasai. 'Kaa hapo.' Let me not see you with my eyes again. There was a girl next to him looking down at Solo with a perplexed look, as if she did not know what to do. Two of the Senyos appeared and greeted the man. 'Soba. Ni nini.' The tall man looked at Solo who was smiling from where he was on his back. 'It's this dog. He can't stay away from people's women.' One of the Senyo men looked at Solo. 'Kijana, is there a problem?' He came closer and stood over him. 'You want me to step on you?' The barman in the small cage, looking at Juli and Chiri said, 'I am not selling to you.'

The other Senyo man turned to Juli. 'Ndio. You are together. You are the ones disturbing women here.' At this the tall man said, 'Ero. Let it end there.' The Senyo men ignored him, looking at Juli, then the tall man grabbed the woman by the arm and they went into the next room.

'Let me not see you Sayiankas here again,' one of the Senyo men said, and they left. Chiri remembered all the kids the Sayiankas had beaten up in their childhood – this was a sight they would have paid to see. Solo stood up and they left.

Outside, Juli found a red public phone booth and called Nairobi as the other two waited outside. Chiri heard him say, ndio Mum, all is well – tume plant. Ndio the tractor is now working. And the Harvester is out in Mau Narok. And yes Solomon is here. Yes, he is helping with the work. This was his weekly report to Mrs Sayianka. When Juli finished they took the drinking to Diplomat Hotel where it was more civilised.

At 5 a.m. they left Narok bullet for Nairage Ya Ngare and were home in less than two hours. Grandma Sayianka, their gogo, querulous as ever, opened the door slowly and when she saw them burst into song.

When they woke up the next day in the afternoon Juli discovered that the supplies they had purchased in Nakuru had been stolen from the Datsun.

II

The Sayianka family's stone house at Nairage Ya Ngare was the first of its kind in the area. The first version, a small wooden bungalow, had been built by Petro Sayianka in the 1980s after he had bought the house in Buru Buru. Over the years as he prospered and his family grew so did the house, if it could be called that. More of a structure, it now sprawled with stone extensions, new wings, nooks and crannies made of mabati. Gogo had lived alone in the Nairage Ya Ngare house for years until Juli had been exiled by his father to the wheatlands.

Inside the house was a maze of corridors, cul de sacs, weirdly placed bathrooms and toilets. Most of the house did not have a ceiling underneath the mabati roof and sound travelled from room to room above the walls. One wing was

Gogo's living quarters, another their father's former room and sitting room − the rest of the house was completely separate and could only be accessed through the tiny kitchen which also led to the front yard. Chiri and Juli took two rooms in the shaded southern side, Solo slept in their father's old room.

Outside the house was a small shed and underneath was half an old John Deere tractor. The rest of the shed was littered with metal parts. Juli did not say much over the next few days about what they would do about the stolen supplies and so they slept, played cards, listened to the radio and talked late into the night. On other nights Juli pored over his late father's papers and books − reading about agriculture, wheat farming. Solo remained unusually quiet and read some of his late father's western novels and kept to himself. Chiri borrowed some of these and slept longer than he ever had since childhood. On the third morning Solo had regained his bravado at the breakfast table and plotted revenge on the Senyos. Juli remained quiet during these sessions. He had told Chiri that there was nothing to be done about the Senyos in Narok, especially now that the Sayiankas had lost their patriarch. Even Gogo laughed at Solo's contorted face, his reckless talk.

The next day Juli woke Chiri up at 5 a.m. and they drove to Bomet and bought new supplies, even if they were almost twice the price of what they had bought in Nakuru. When they returned to Gogo's there was a man standing in the compound. As they got out of the Datsun Juli said: 'That's the driver, Moseti Edwin.'

'Machini is okay?' Juli asked.

'Ndio.'

'Kweli. We don't need to go to the garage?'

'Ndio.'

'Na Harvester.'

'Also, that is okay.'

Juli beckoned Moseti and they went over to the shed.

'Naona there are parts missing … I am told that you gave the plough to Kagunya…'

Moseti looked at Juli with feigned shock.

'Si, he told me that you had talked.'

'Skiza — go and bring it back today. Leo.'

When Moseti left Juli pored over the old tractor under the shed and said, 'This used to be a John Deere tractor ... this is money. Watu here took advantage of us when Mzee died ... even that jamaa who was here. After this harvest I will wake up this old John Deere for my father. I've already done the hesabu of how much it will cost. Moseti will go with the Massey Ferguson Harverster to Mau Narok where they are already harvesting and here we will plant with the tractor.'

They started planting the next day. Juli had already leased farms in Suswa, Ngareta and near Narok town. Each of the three farms had a supervisor, two tractor drivers to do the planting and two boys to watch the seed, do menial small tasks. When Juli and Chiri went to the farm near town the owner said because they had been late he had given it out two weeks ago. A few days later they found a farm in remote Melili. They made sure the tractor work started the next day. Juli explained to Chiri the real numbers and how the acreage worked and how many bags he expected to harvest. Now that they were working Chiri saw a new Juli, older and watchful in the fields as the work went on. When he spoke now it was only of the basics, the figures. A good farm produced ten to fifteen bags of wheat grain per acre. Each bag was Kshs 2,000. Leasing one acre was Kshs 7,500-15,000 depending on where it was. Hiring a harvester and a tractor came to Kshs 1000 an hour. A tractor took half a day to spread wheat seed over ten acres. A harvester could take half a day to harvest ten acres depending on the shamba. Bottom line, if all went well you could double your money.

The planting took two full weeks and Juli and Chiri drove to and fro to make sure that none of the seed was stolen or wasted. Solo came out with them on some days and before long he declared that he was going back to the UK; that the dirty wheat life was not for him. On the days he did not come to the farm he went to the Nairage Ya Ngare bars and he came home late and found them spent eating ugali and sukuma greens. 'Naona you are pushing the week,' he laughed.

One evening Juli, tired and dirty from another day in the fields, watched him in the tiny kitchen, the light from the small wick dipped in the kerosene tin throwing their shadows all over the wall. 'I talked to Mathe leo. This joini. There is someone who keeps calling her in Buru from the UK. Asking to talk to you. Ati she has your son.' For a second Solo's face went slack and then he regained the knowing smile at the edges of his lips and looked at Juli for a long time and left without a word.

III

The wheat crop was now three weeks old and susceptible to rust, which could destroy the crop in two days. During this period, Juli and Chiri no longer came home at sunset. They stayed out making sure that the insecticide spray had been done properly and, when it rained, re-done. Now all day the rain poured lightly over them and they came straight to bed. Solo retreated from them, harbingers of knowledge of his secret wife and child. When they made it back early Chiri now sought him out, feeling for him with the guilty face he now wore around the house. On some days he convinced Solo to come out with them to the fields.

After a month all the fields Juli had leased had been weeded and it would be another three weeks before they started re-spraying insecticide, this time for weevils. Now, Juli and Chiri took several trips out south, past Narok town, looking for tractor and harvester work which was scarce mid-season unless it was for maize and barley. It was now August and they were mostly on the road. They went from farm to farm, asking randomly around whether anyone needed a plough, a winch, even a tractor carrier for transport.

On the road Juli continued his tutorials, his moods starting to swing with the vagaries of the wheat crop and the weather as the season developed. In their new idleness Chiri understood Juli's need to talk his farming dream into being, his voice at this stage betraying no fear of failure. In their road conversations Juli had long moved on from childhood to the more recent failures of their teenage years. Now when Juli talked against the pious mothers of the neighbourhood who had laughed when he failed his O-levels his voice was strained. He spoke with bitterness at their presence at his father's funeral, their looks of pity at his mother and the burden of her crazy sons.

For days Juli went on about the funeral again and again and in his voice Chiri at times heard Juli's gratitude to him for being there. And he was surprised as it was not like he would have been doing anything with his life that was of real importance. So, in between the planting and the wait for the crop to take hold Chiri played witness to Juli's plans, his triumphant return to Nairobi and Buru with a new car for Mama Sayianka like in the old days when his father was alive. But by the end of August, six weeks after planting, it was clear that their little Agip misadventure that had delayed the planting would prove costly. Their crop in Suswa and Ngareta, having missed a week's worth of rain, was fifteen centimetres shorter than the crops in the surrounding fields they drove past. They had planted when the rains were about to end. Then, in remote Melili, they spent more by having to import labour for another round of weeding as the locals were too proud to do such work, which they had not anticipated. In Ngareta, their second farm, which bordered the Mau forest, wheat rust thrived and the crop had to be sprayed over several times. In Suswa, the intermittent rain, driven away by strong winds, left a third of the crop stunted. That week, Juli did not call his mother with the fortnightly progress report. Instead they went drinking in Nairage Ya Ngare.

Their drinking binge moved between Top Life, Mara and Maji Ya Ngombe bars. After the first day they started drinking on credit and the three of them rediscovered a common ground over those blurred hours. Juli and Solo stopped circling each other. Chiri re-discovered a boyhood when he'd looked up to the older Solo who regaled them with tales of Manchester. Maybe they would have stayed indefinitely in between the three bars and the makeshift lodgings they crept to every morning if it was not for the news. A neighbour's boy found them in Top Life and told them that the Massey Ferguson Harvester had been spotted in the hills of Mau Narok without its driver. The news had been brought by a herdsman who was waiting for them at Gogo's. Juli beckoned at Chiri and they left Solo with his arm around one of the numerous Kikuyu barmaids. They found the herdsman on the road walking back and they stopped the Datsun.

'Machini iko Mau Narok. Imekwama kwa mlima. Mko na ndovu ya kutoa.'

You will need an elephant to move it.

'Uliona driver. Anaitwa Moseti? Mkisii.'

'Ai. Sitaki shida.'

'Twende? You show us?'

The man regarded Juli.

'Ati.'

Then, Juli changed his tone taking out the drink from his voice. The man started walking away.

'Two thousand shillings,' Juli said, and grinned.

The man jumped into the back of the Datsun. 'My name is Atelek.'

They stopped at the Nairage Ya Ngare Trading Centre and Juli borrowed fuel money from Johnny the Kikuyu bar owner at 15 per cent interest. They headed south first and were caught in passing rain heading towards Tanzania. In a few minutes they were in an indeterminate land where the rain fell with such relentlessness, it was as if time had shortened or space shrunk in the grey world. Now, for two full days, they managed no more than a hundred kilometres, stopping in trading centres, stuck beneath small kiosk fronts, abandoned cattle dips and, at times, under trees in open meadows. They did not notice at first when Atelek slipped away, back to the dry north. Without him, they kept at it because there was really only one road and little risk of getting lost if they asked along the way in the small trading centres where the event of a stranded Harvester was news.

One night, feeling as if they'd travelled almost to Tanzania, they managed to find a place to park the Datsun under a small shed in the middle of nowhere. They had started climbing and sensed they were already in Mau Narok. The world was a grey, stormy sea around them. With the incessant drumming of water on the Datsun's roof, Chiri could no longer remember what the dry world felt like. They had carried a bottle of gin and a few sips woke up the alcohol of the last three days in Nairage Ya Ngare in their blood. Juli's eyes were glazed: he was drunker than Chiri had ever seen him. And as he came to, Chiri heard the words: 'Let me tell you about Naimenengiu Forest. Naimenengiu is a magic forest near the Tanzania border at the edge of God's Narok. Uski Baba did not even wait for my Form 4 results – he sent me there after Highway.'

Chiri had finished school a year earlier than Juli even though he was younger and was already well into varsity when his childhood friend finished at Highway School. It was only later that Chiri heard from someone in Buru that Juli had been sent to shagz, back to the village his father hailed from. This magic Naimengiu Forest, however, did not sound like shagz.

'Naimenengiu ni the remotest place in Kenya after Turkana. Haiko, even on the map. There I started a shop. Ilikuwa so remote that I did not need to be at the shop all the time. Because everybody knew each other people were so honest that they just took what they wanted and left the money on the counter. One day I left the shop to smoke a cigarette, those days I was on Rooster ile non-filter, not so mbali far from the village. There were these rocks I used to see every day that looked quiet. I went there. I also wanted to read a letter Baba had sent. Just before I reached the rocks, I looked up. Haiya, sitting hapo on top was a lioness.'

Juli went quiet, the sound of the rain against the windscreen and when Chiri turned he saw that his friend's head had fallen to his chest. But Juli then continued, his eyes now fixed straight ahead. In his eyes Chiri made out something else – old memories and a bit of doubt.

'There in Naimenengiu I saw things. Have you ever heard the roar of a lion near you? Or seen a snake the size of your leg? Nilikua in that place for two months alafu one day the oldest man in that small village sent for me. When I went to his manyatta and stood outside his voice from inside said: "Now you have become one of us. Do you want one of my daughters? Do you want land?" I did not want to refuse him. When I remained silent, he asked me whether I was wanted by the government. The police. He said he could send me to his brother in Tanzania. To Mlango Nyeusi. The Black Door. I told him I had been banished by Baba. The old man appeared on the doorway shaking his head. He gave me five goats. He told me that I would always belong to the village. He said that Nairobi is not for everyone.'

'Catholic Parochial. Highway. You are Nairobi tao born and raised, man. You should have told the mzee that,' Chiri said. 'Those years for nothing. Pole, but to send you out there … I had a lot of heshima for him, you know that. But what was your father thinking?'

'My father …' Juli stopped and looked at him and then turned away: 'Out there huko we saw a car once in two months when the Canter from Narok brought me supplies for that little shop. We ate nothing but mbuzi. Sukuma wiki once in two months. One day I bit into a tomato and almost came just from the pleasure of it. For the first time I almost returned to Buru.'

'Yeah. But our paros, you know they are not always right. Half of the things my Mum goes on about… ' Chiri said. 'Wah.'

'Hapana,' Juli said, and turned to him. 'Chiri, if you'd listened to her ungekuwa still in campus.'

'Chief, let me ask you,' Chiri said, his voice hesitant. 'I do not know about you but I really tamani some fries.'

They both laughed and the world in front of them clapped in thunder.

'When Solo and I finished school Baba called us one evening, you know how wazees are, and asked what we wanted from hii life. Solo said he wanted to go to the UK. I don't think he was even serious. But me I was sent into the wilderness, to that shop. Because ati I was wild.'

'Everyone kila mtu, all of us were.' Chiri was still trying to push away the intense darkness with his eyes. 'That's why tuko in this party. To grow wheat and party.'

Juli ignored this. 'Alafu Solo sent a letter to Mum from the UK saying that he wanted to marry this mzungu girl. The one who has now been calling. Huyu Katrina. Then he wrote to Baba separately and said he had a wonderful business idea. You know how much he asked for? Five milli.'

'Million.' Chiri realised that he had said this aloud.

'That he did not want to continue with school. Baba then wrote to him and gave him his blessing. But he said, "Kwanza come back home we discuss." You could never fool Baba. He did not ask Solo about the mzungu girl.'

'Solomon, man.' Chiri laughed shaking his head. 'Always sly.'

'We didn't hear from Solo for one year.'

'Wah. I take back sly. Crazy, like a fox.'

'So Baba went all the way to the UK to tafuta him. When Baba came back he said zero. Sufuri. That's when he sent for me in Namenengiu. Being away from City he said had been good for me ... then he said I had his permission to start real life ...'

Chiri was trying to remember when exactly Solo had come back.

'Baba said I could make a life with farming wheat ... he gave me the John Deere tractor, and the old Massey Ferguson harvester. Alafu he leased fifty acres for me in Melilli to anza my life.'

'But just like that Baba left us. One day there was a knock on the door and there he was. Solo. We had not seen him for seven years. You should have seen Mum. But there was no time for questions. We were busy with funeral things. Mazishi. Then we started taking stock, you know how it is — what we had and of course we turned to Solo.'

A white Zebu cow suddenly appeared out of the darkness, its long horns reaching out at them. It peered through the windscreen, chewing slowly, then eased back into nothingness.

'Seven years. But we found out that he was bila degree. Nothing. Even now we don't know what conversations he had with Baba in the UK. He came back with only a serious drinking qualification and too much English. For every year Solo was in the UK, we could have bought a Massey Ferguson. I know because Baba used to send me to the bank to buy bank drafts for Solo. Seven Massey Fergusons. Or three John Deere tractors.'

Juli continued. 'I left Naimenengiu and when I tried to give the shop to the old man he laughed and asked what he was supposed to do with it. Then he said, do not go back. "Usirudi stay here with us." But then he saw my eyes and he said: "*sisi, ni watu wa mlango nyekundu*, we are of the Red Door. If you ever need anything, please come back." I know the people of the Red Door will always be there for me.'

Chiri could no longer hold his bladder; he opened the door quietly and started peeing on the side of the Datsun. Even before he finished, he heard Juli weeping quietly. Chiri let his friend grieve for his father, for his years in the wilderness. But the tears were more than that and Chiri sensed they were also for their lost Buru Buru childhood and all those who had wished failure on Juli — his St George's teachers, the Buru Buru mothers who feared for their daughters.

Then Juli stopped and said, 'You know, that old man did not know me from the animals in the magic forest. But he took me in, wanted me to marry into his family, he would have given me land. If anyone wanting to harm me came looking for me, the village would have protected me, say they didn't know me. That is the way of mlango nyekundu, the Red Door...'

'It cannot continue. Solo's behaviour.' Chiri heard a new hardness in Juli's voice.

'Baba would not allow it. Solo. He has let down the clan. He has let down the Sayiankas. He has let down our late father.' Juli paused, his face thinking through the mist that was coming at them. They had run out of miraa and without the busy chewing movements his face seemed like the Juli of old. '...And now Solo has a *mzungu* wife. And maybe all I really had of any value was that small shop in Naimenengiu.' Lightning streaked the sky above them.

Juli said, 'Fuck Buru and Nairobi. I can't go back there. If anything, I'd go back to Naimenengiu.'

Chiri tried to picture the small shop out there in the middle of nowhere.

'I need some miraa,' Juli said, and impossibly the first of daylight now emerged. And then it started pelting with hailstones.

Driving the whole day, they found the Harvester on the side of a hill deep in Mau Narok that evening. Like a strange windmill the machine tilted to the side, a small tower in the middle of all the nothingness. Moseti was nowhere to be found. He had fled after the machine got held in this rocky field in the dark. It was clear that Moseti had taken up an extra job in the night for his own benefit.

Almost half the wheat fields in the area had been destroyed by hailstones. They went to look for help and they found an old man of about seventy several fields down the road sitting at the edge of his farm holding wheat stems and bawling like a baby. Juli stopped the Datsun and they let the old man grieve and then asked him where they could hire a tractor to help pull away the Harvester. He sat up immediately and said he had a tractor.

'These kalenjins,' Juli said. 'He's liaing here and he can get a loan tomorrow. And get back on his feet.'

They also hired two drivers with the tractor and dislodged the Harvester. They started to tow it back to Nairage Ya Ngare. The rain lightened as they headed back north. At every trading centre, they saw people who seemed chastened by the hailstorm, re-emerging into their lives, walking like they were in a funeral procession. Chiri and the drivers took turns steering the Harvester. Up in the Harvester like a newly crowned king Chiri surveyed all the broken magnificence, steering through trading centres whose wheat crop had been destroyed in the storm. They passed field upon field, flattened, as if by giant hands. The Harvester had two small round mirrors mounted on long metallic rods and Chiri saw how dark he had turned, how lean his face had become and how rough and pitted his forehead had grown.

Theirs was not the only Harvester the storm had rendered idle. They met other blue, green and red iron giants headed north, made redundant by the Hand of God and the prolonged rains. The faces underneath Trading Centre stoops looked up wordlessly and went back to small, meaningless tasks. They finally left this funeral land and arrived in Narok on the end of the fourth day after they had set out. Juli stopped by the police post and paid some cops to track down Moseti.

The next day they visited Kinuthia, a mechanic who told them that the Harvester repairs would cost Ksh 200,000 and the spare parts could only be found in Nakuru. They left the machine with him. Before they set out to look for the money Chiri and Juli slept for two days from exhaustion. When they woke up, Gogo told them she did not know where Solo had gone. It was late September and they had ten weeks before the first harvest in mid-December. They needed to fix the Harvester quickly.

Juli went to Obergon to ask for a loan but it turned out that he was planning to get married and had no liquid cash. Juli who was only learning of these plans discovered from Gogo that his father had given Obergon half the bride price months ago. Since Petro Sayianka had died Juli had slowly found out the absurd amounts of money that his father had handed over to their innumerable relatives.

However, Obergon had a suggestion. Narok businessman Nkaiseri Ntimama was known to give loans. Obergon went to see Nkaiseri and came back with a report. The conditions for any kind of loan were vicious. The money Juli needed would be lent at 30 per cent interest and, in case of default, Nkaiseri would auction the Harvester and they would only be left with the tractor. After handing over the logbook, Juli and Chiri received a cheque for Ksh 1 million, paid Kinuthia for long overdue repairs, and then half the wages for the Suswa and Ngareta farms. When they went to Melilli, however, the foreman and the drivers and their boys demanded all their money to stop them burning the wheat. When they went to see Kinuthia to get a list of the parts they needed he suggested that they could get the parts even cheaper in Eastleigh. Kinuthia also now told them that he could not fix the harvester in Narok because the garage was too small. He told them he had a place in Kutus sixty kilometres away and they got the machine towed there. It was near the end of October. Before the trip Juli and Chiri headed to Narok and partied like it was already Christmas. When they went back to Gogo's they found Solo had returned.

IV

They sat in the cabin of the Datsun 1200 parked in Kinuthia's small town open-air garage in Kutus. They sipped warm Cokes laced with cheap gin, squirming and groaning in the oven-like cabin waiting for Kinuthia to diagnose all that the Harvester needed. The sun reflected off the metallic innards of the other ailing Massey Ferguson harvesters, John Deere tractors, circular gears with teeth and crank-shafts lying scattered in the yard. The bodies of old Canters, mini-bus matatus fenced off the working area of the garage. The garage reception was the shell of an old Mahindra Kenya Police Jeep.

It was hard to tell Kinuthia's age with his thin ropy arms and pulsating blood vessels on his forehead covered with grease. He came up to Juli to report his findings on their Harvester. Solo and Chiri looked on. Kinuthia said something in Kikuyu but Juli refused to acknowledge the language. Kinuthia looked into the blazing sky for a long time as if remembering recent trials in the Rift, tribal evictions and ethnic hostilities. He tried again. 'I see the sun is out with his familia,' he said. 'It is not the rocks that went ndani ya the differential. Ni gear shaft imeoza.' Rotten gear shaft. Kinuthia chewed at this and spat green in the dust and hefted the large metallic gear innard he had extracted from the Massey Ferguson. To think how a few days ago it held magnificent promise eating up the wheaten gold in the fields to brighten their days with cash.

'Gear shaft,' Kinuthia said again reverting to Kikuyu as if there are no other words for what he held in his hand. Juli looked long at him and the man seemed apologetic enough.

It was quiet in the heat of the garage, right smack in the middle of the day. All life – other than the three boys and the thin ancient man – was hidden in the shade.

'You said cheapest parts we can get are in Eastleigh?'

'Kama you are lucky yes.'

'Then, we will try and find our luck there,' Juli said.

'Mkifika Eastleigh go to Ndungu Motors and tell him I sent you. 5th Avenue,' Kinuthia said.

'I'll see you when we bring back the part,' Juli said. 'Don't sell my Harvester.'

Kinuthia said nothing, walked over to the insides of the inert police Mahindra that was his reception area. His head soon lolled back, a puppet dead to the world.

The boys slumped into the Datsun pick-up, and soon they were a small speck cutting through endless sky and scrub valley hurtling towards Nairobi. They passed Narok town without pause, travelling against a light rain and the approaching night that came up suddenly on them. They streaked past Melili, Suswa, Nairage Ya Ngare, Kinungi, Uplands. When a trading centre appeared as another speck on the horizon, they made out figures in the distance, coming out into the road with the old expectation. But they passed without pause, and the figure shrugged and shouted an old language in the wind. These were the string-town people who knew the Datsun 1200 that Juli had met over the seasons, mostly at the tail end of the harvest, a small god with wheat money. Barmaids, no-hopers, transients caught between older traditional times and the economic present, adrift. They retreated to the ancient physicality of the flat land and its dust, its blood and its old ways. They knew the boys in the Datsun 1200 would be back.

The small Datsun was loud when they reached the City, its cranky muffler throbbed, its large tyres awkward and self-conscious, leaving dust tracks on Uhuru highway tarmac. The boys went wide-eyed at Nairobi, the Mercs and the Beemers in the slow traffic crawl. It had been a while. They'd taken just under two hours to catch the Kangemi jam into Westlands. They headed to Eastleigh. Moving slowly in the traffic they took two hours to cross Westlands, and then Parklands and going through Forest Road finally managed to get to Kariokor, then past Ziwa. In Pangani the streetlights came back on and soon they were in Eastleigh. They drove till Juli nodded, '12th Avenue. Solomon, you know anything about that?' His brother remained quiet; his face was relaxed, curious — something had changed about him since his return. He seemed more speculative, less petulant, as if he had come upon a new secret knowledge. Now the last few hours seemed to ease away his permanent sneer at the big endless skies of the wheatlands. They found a lodgo and trudged off to bed.

Three days later everybody on 12th Avenue knew Solo, his restlessness had returned calling to the world. Juli and Chiri had washed themselves clean of all the Rift Valley dust in the arms of two Ethiopian women, unclasping the embraces of rural women from their memories. They felt like Nairobians once more. For a few days they ate, slept, drank and partied to oblivion – wheat, Harvesters and gear shaft forgotten for now.

They ate most of their meals at Somali Ndogo. All the regulars came to know Solo. When they went there Solo playing the local kept on saying out aloud here tuko in the sitting room of Eastleigh. He was so taken with the place he picked up all he heard and made it his.

Over the next few days they noticed a light Coastal looking man with a grave face who kept to himself, even if everybody in Somali Ndogo greeted him with heshima. Solo noticed this and asked one of the waiters who the man was and he said: 'Ahmed Salim'.

The boys saw this man, Ahmed, each day while looking for the Massey Ferguson Harvester spare parts. Ahmed only came in when the place was emptiest at around 11 a.m. and left at around 3 p.m. These were also their hours. They slept in late, tried to find the gear shaft and then headed out to the bars in the evening. Ahmed always carried a large black diary and he wrote in it all hours as if making the most important appointments on the spot.

One day the boys went into Somali Ndogo and the only table available was Ahmed's. Chiri and Juli turned to leave but Solo looked around and gestured at Ahmed asking whether they could sit at his table. He made the slightest of nods and the boys ordered breakfast. The businessmen were making quite a spectacle and the boys watched. Ahmed ignored all this for a while. When he stopped writing in his diary he looked up for a long moment and said something in Arabic that the boys didn't understand. He then turned to them and said in Kiswahili, 'Kunguni.' This word was straight from their school Kiswahili school days and Chiri who had taken Kiswahili in secondary school said: 'Bedbugs.'

Solo started on about his time in the UK for Ahmed's benefit. Chiri and Juli had noticed that he kept on increasing the number of years he'd been there whenever he met someone new. He also reduced the months he'd been back in Kenya. Ahmed said that he had lived in Tottenham and Birmingham but he was originally born in Lamu.

'Have you heard of the Mbarawa?' he asked. 'My ancestors are African and Portuguese.'

Solo was beside himself with Ahmed's news of also having lived in the UK. Chiri and Juli let him to do the talking for a while, exhaust his Manchester stories. They accepted Ahmed's invitation to his house when he said he had to leave.

The boys expected Ahmed to live in an apartment but when they got to the address that he has given them, it was a whole fenced-off plot. They went beyond the large gate and inside the building was split into two wings. Ahmed's two wives and their children lived on each side. Ahmed occupied the main wing, straight though, opposite the large gate. The rest were all his offices. They were taken to a large open area with a TV and couches. Ahmed joined them and they were served fried coconut and a purple slushy drink the colour of iodine that they could not get enough of.

'Maybe this is some kind of Sangria? Without the pombe,' Solo said loudly and leaned back on the long sofa. 'Ah. This is the life. Eastleigh kweli.'

'I am a Forex dealer,' Ahmed said as they crunched away at the fried coconut. 'I represent my family's business interests in Nairobi. We are based in Dubai.'

'We are farmers,' Juli said. 'At least I am. These two are kati kati between things.'

Solo jumped in. 'Me, I plan to go into business,' he said, looking at Juli. 'I studied law. Mr Ahmed, you know Sussex University I am sure?'

'Please call me Ahmed,' he said. 'Even if I grew up in Lamu here Eastleigh is now my home. This place is in a bad way. I need partners from outside Eastleigh. We might be from different worlds but all of us are interested in money. Many young people in Eastleigh now … all they want is to get high or drunk,' Ahmed said. 'They say they are frustrated – I tell them that should give them all the more reason to work.'

'Tunatafuta gear shaft. Massey Ferguson combine harvester … '86 model,' Juli said. 'Can you help? We were told that we could find it in 5th Avenue but we found the place closed.'

Ahmed looked at him. 'I am sure I can find what you are looking for in twenty-four hours. I know someone who works at CMC who supplies Eastleigh on the side. For now my house is your house. I know that your hotel is only good for sleeping – you can spend your other time here. All I ask is that you do not bring alcohol here.'

He stood up. 'Feel nyumbani. Mtaniambia more about the farming. I now have a meeting with some people from Mogadishu. We talk later.'

They were shown into a room with couches and a large–screen TV. They vegetated for hours. Strange men walked in and out of the compound all day to see Ahmed. Chiri fell asleep. Solo and Juli had nothing to say to each other so they watched another DVD: *Pulp Fiction*. Solo got up halfway through the movie and went looking for Ahmed. The sun was about to go down.

They chilled till Ahmed joined them for supper. They all ate quietly for a while and then Ahmed turned to Juli.

'Let me ask. I hear that Maasailand has a lot of business opportunities with leopard skins, ivory, red mercury, and smuggled gold near the Tanzania border. I know a lot of government people doing that business. Solo told me you know Maasailand well.'

'Kweli, its true about that business. I've heard that too,' Juli said, his voice strained. 'Have you managed to find the shaft?' There was an abrupt silence and Solo said: 'We are all good friends now. I am sure we can do more business than a gear shaft.' Juli looked at him and remained quiet.

The next day Juli and Chiri spent the morning looking for wholesalers who dealt in cereals who might be interested in their harvest and then headed to Ahmed's in the afternoon. There were four cars outside and they looked at each other, thinking of heading off to relax elsewhere. But they knocked on the gate and one of Ahmed's men opened the door and rushed away immediately. There was no one in the small courtyard when they entered. Ahmed's wives usually sunned themselves in their buibuis during the day but now even the children were not out playing. In the courtyard, Juli and Chiri headed to the open area where the large-screen TV was and Solo emerged from the office at the end of the courtyard. He was out of breath as if he'd been sprinting. 'Where have you been? I've been waiting for you. Kuja you have to see this.' Juli ignored him and picked up the remote and flopped on his back. Solo looked at him, grabbed Chiri's hand and started dragging him towards the office. Juli stood up and they followed Solo.

Inside Ahmed's office were two women dressed in expensive buibuis and wrapped in a cloud of scent. Three very fat men sat on sofas. Ahmed welcomed the boys like long-lost relatives. Two other men dressed in lab coats stood to Ahmed's side.

'These young men are in business and I am trying to help them,' Ahmed said introducing them. 'They are large-scale farmers. I hope you don't mind if they join us.' The three fat men and two women nodded. They were all Somali. The younger woman smiled at them. The older woman seated in the middle of the group ignored them. Her fingers were covered in gold rings and she had bangles that went all the way up to her elbows.

Ahmed said: 'I have learned a lot about farming in the Rift Valley from these boys in the last few days. It might be something I want to invest in. So I thought as a matter of trust because we have not known each for a long time I would also ask them to my home. They might also be interested in this venture we are working on.' He nodded at the boys.

'We are all here in Nairobi to do business. We all know how tough things can be. When our fathers and families did business a long time ago things were very simple. Because of how things are in Somalia now we are lucky that there are new opportunities.'

His face turned grave. 'I will ask you for confidentiality in what I tell you. A lot of the money that has always been in the Somali economy is now here in Eastleigh. And this I tell you in the strictest confidence. A big opportunity has come our way from a friend of mine who was in the Somali government. When the war started a lot of money was looted and he was asked to be one of the caretakers of government funds. To transport these large amounts of money a special dye was used so that the money could look like normal black paper. My friend managed to bring some of the money over the border before all the looting started. Now the money is in secret locations in Kampala, Juba and Nairobi.'

Chiri looked to Juli but his face was empty.

Ahmed continued: 'A lot of the powerful people in Somalia have now disappeared after the War. They went to America, England and changed their names. I now tell you that that money in my friend's hands will not be claimed for a long time. My friend now needs some of the money to facilitate his own passage to Australia with his family. He came to ask how he can clean the money.'

Juli leaned back, relaxed, watching Solo completely caught in the moment.

'Cleaning the money is not the problem,' Ahmed said. 'Finding the chemicals that governments use is not even the problem. Money to buy these chemicals is the problem. I see all of us as partners. But before we enter any further discussions I want to show you all something.'

The two men in the lab coats headed off to one of the doors in the spacious office and opened it. They all streamed into a long room, a chemical lab with no windows. There was a long table on one end and a long series of cupboards on the other end. There were stools along the table. On the long table lay test tubes, beakers, calipers and glass containers that the boys remembered from their O-level chemistry classes. There was also a strange box-like machine on one end of the long table and next to it, a money-counting machine.

The two lab-coated men led everybody to the long stools. They all sat facing Ahmed on one side.

'I want to show you how this chemical I am talking about works.' The technicians arranged a flat tray and then put aside two beakers and turned to Ahmed.

'Excuse me,' Ahmed said. He went back into the main office and came back with two bottles, a paper bag full of white powder and a small stack of paper bills that was black in colour. Ahmed placed them on the table and nodded at one of the technicians.

The man greeted them in a strange accent. 'I know you are all wondering where I am from. I come from Liberia. Like Somalia our country went to war and I was lucky to settle in Kenya to do business. I used to be a banker in my other life in Monrovia. I have experience with the government ink that Mr Ahmed told you about.'

'In my country we call these notes, black money, negative notes. I have been helping peoples with negative notes for a long time. Here,' and he pointed to the two bottles, 'we have the original solutions. SSD solution powder it is called. It is made from international mercury. See it. We have it all here – we can use it to solve the problem of negative notes. We will solve all the problems. We will go through the process.'

Everybody was watching carefully. Chiri was distracted by the man's English and a small laugh threatened to start in his stomach and explode. Juli noticed and frowned at him. Chiri excused himself and headed off to the toilet. He had a good hysterical laugh behind closed doors. When he was sure it was all out he went back to the lab.

As the man from Liberia talked he removed five notes from the small wad and placed them on the trays. Then he put on plastic gloves and slit the packet of white powder with extreme care. He started rubbing the black notes with the white powder very carefully.

'Dollar yes,' he said. 'This is the black dollar. It needs to be cleaned. This is a dollar note. What is going on now – this is the anti-air powder. We can open it now and make it dollar.' Now his voice had picked up as if he was talking in a church or on a Christian programme on TV. He was really getting into it.

'Brothers, and sisters too. Madam, you can see we want to put it on top of the black dollars. Let's put it in the tray. The anti-air powder is put on the top of the black currency. It's going to be robbing on top of the currency body. On top of the currency body. Robbing back and front. Robbing back and front. This powder is very very important in the robbing of the black currency.' The man from Liberia rubbed the notes even more.

'You want to pour this powder on the body – rob it again. Robbing it on top of the black currency. Black Somali dollar. Now take this solution. This is what is shaking is called SSD solution. Then take solution and what is shaking is iodine, which is shaking so that you can mix up the two. Yes, yes, yes. It is now shaking. And then you are going to pour the solution first into the tray. Inside the tray. Pour the solution inside the tray. Inside. Pour inside the tray – you smell its power. This is a very powerful solution for cleaning. Cover your mouth and eyes and noses. Please. It is taking all the powder inside the tray in the solution. So he can peel out the code – the government code. This is just lab test.'

He poured from the first bottle into the tray and then the second. And then he rubbed again.

Ahmed stepped forward and took over again. He introduced the second man in a lab coat.

'This is also a professional technician who has fifteen years' experience in this field working with bank chemicals and can also vouch for this process.' The man from Liberia who performed the note cleaning picked this up. He was now sweating, excited.

'This man I tell you,' he said, 'he knows in and out about all world currencies. He has done this work in Dubai, Mogadishu, Saudi Arabia, Ethiopia and even Brazil. You can see the currencies are coming to life. Coming to life. Our technician is a professional on it. Performing. Your true note is coming to life.'

They all watched as the dyes on the black note fell off. The man from Liberia picked it up and held a US dollar bill. 'After this process you can eat your money anywhere.

We can guarantee it with our company licence. Hundred-dollar note. Performing it. Money is clean. Money is clean. We have done the cleaning fantastic. Performing it. Performing it. The cleaning has done. Fantastic.'

Then, he looked at Ahmed with the hundred-dollar bill in his hand. Ahmed nodded and the man handed over the bill to the woman with the bangles. 'This is our present to you, Madam. We want you to eat that money to see if it works.' The younger woman started clapping and the three fat Somali men smiled. The older woman nodded as if to say thank you. Ahmed led them all out of the lab back to his office.

When they were all seated Ahmed said, 'We need to buy the SSD solution and the anti-air powder. My associates promise that they will give us ten per cent of the money we clean.'

The older woman spoke for the first time. 'Mr Ahmed, we have known each other for a long time. Thank you for your time. But this is no small matter. We will have to think about this a bit more. We will be in touch in two days.' The three fat men and the two women then stood up and bowed. And then they left and a trail of perfume swirled in the office.

Ahmed smiled at the boys. 'You see how real business is done.'

The boys staggered out of the office. Their heads were spinning. They went and sat on the couch and remained silent for a long time.

Solo said, 'This is the kind of deal that everybody waits all their life for. We've been wasting time uko Maasaini, ati farming. This is the deal we need.' He stood up like somebody about to run a 100-metre race.

Juli was still seated on the couch staring into space. 'We need to leave this place immediately and never come back,' he said quietly. 'We need to go see Mathe, talk to her and explain everything about the loan we took and see what she says.'

With this mention of their mother, Chiri looked around and it suddenly felt strange – their being here, Ahmed's high walls, the smooth, cemented yard. His other life, dropping out of campus, taking time off to sort himself out, now felt like a very long time ago. He now wanted to go back to Buru to his mother.

'There is nowhere I am going,' Solo said, and paced about. Juli blinked and looked at Chiri, who had never seen him scared.

'Najua you still have money left from the loan. I want half of it,' Solo said. 'I am the one Baba sent to the K to do a business degree. There was a reason why.' He is panting. 'We are not children. Everyone has to make their own choices. I want my half now.'

Juli looked at him long and hard. Solo's lips were still purple from the slush drink. He looked like he'd been punched in the mouth and then treated with iodine. The sun had gone down. Juli reached into the shorts where he kept the money. He stopped. 'Tafadhali, let us go to CMC and just buy the parts and leave. There are no parts here.' He then said a few words in Maasai, in entreaty to Solo.

But Solo's face was now one of pure hatred. 'I want half of the money,' he said. 'I do not want to ever see wheat again.'

Juli laughed in frustration. 'Umesahau wheat money paid for your fees in the UK. Yaani you've forgotten that's what made our father.' He looked at Solo who just stood with his fists folded at his sides.

Juli said nothing, reached inside his jeans and removed a wad of money and started counting. 'One hundred and fifty,' he finally said, and handed the money over to Solo. His last words to his brother were in Maasai.

It was midnight when Juli and Chiri left Eastleigh and headed to Nakuru. Juli said they would also have to put up the tractor as collateral for the spare parts they needed because they now had to buy them from the showroom.

V

One week later they were back in the wheatfields when they received the news. Solo was in hospital. Pumwani General. Juli and Chiri had been working hard against Nkaisery Ntimama's deadline to pay the first loan. They'd managed to get some money from Kinuthia against the tractor to survive.

The message about Solo was sent by Juli's mother to Gogo who sent a herdsboy to tell them out in Melili. They still had at least five days to make sure that the wheat was sprayed against rust, weeded again to be ready for harvest in a month's time. There was no way they could leave immediately. When that was done they headed back to Gogo's and went straight to bed but just an hour later they were woken up by Gogo screaming at them. She asked Juli why he cared for Chiri more than his brother.

The next morning they sped to Nairobi in the Datsun 1200. Once again they passed the small towns, the wheat life. They were happy to be just two in the car. They remembered old childhood acquaintances and friends. They listed the failures of Buru. They spoke of the more successful ones of their childhood acquaintances with a bitter envy – of their stupid lives in suits and ties. They moved on to the departed. Ken, who died when his liver failed. Older than them, he'd taught them soccer when they were kids. They remembered a neighbourhood girl Njambi who, it was rumoured, became a prostitute at nightclub Florida 3000. They went back to the larger-than-life oboho pretend-criminals of their childhood. Jack Marley. Don Silver. Ochi Mastuko. Before they got to Eastleigh, Juli said: 'About Baba's death. I remember hearing the news. I was playing pool in Buru Shopping Centre Mateso when I heard the news …' Chiri looked at him but then he did not say more.

They were not able to see Solo immediately when they got to Pumwani General – he was in a procedure. They were relieved; they needed to rest but instead they ended up in the original Mateso Bila Chuki in Huruma – suffering without bitterness, they crawled to bed in the morning. They only got up at lunchtime. Juli said he had to do something and drove off alone. Chiri hoped he would not do something stupid like go to Ahmed's. He was relieved when Juli came back after an hour and picked him up. When they got to hospital they found Solo in a bed in a corner. Next to him were beds with women and their newborn babies.

Solo's face and arms were all swollen. There were also large blotches of purple all over his body. Solo tried to smile because he couldn't talk – his lips were torn and his front teeth were all broken. The purple blotches reminded Chiri of the gentian violet (G.V.) purple medicine of their childhood misadventures – the iodine that had salved their wounds.

All Solo could say from his torn mouth was: 'It was Ahmed.'

Juli and Chiri stayed close by to bring him the medicines he needed, and food – the hospital did not provide much more than a bed. They received a list from a nurse so they could go to a chemist to buy the medicines. After a week Solo was discharged and he went to Buru Buru. Juli and Chiri paid the hospital bills and, without any money to drink or even eat at the hotel, ended up in a kiosk on the edges of Eastleigh near Mathare. They ordered some tea, and the girl serving them asked whether they wanted a garatathi. They looked at her and shook their heads. When she brought them strungi they called her back. Wapi maziwa – where is the milk? The girl sucked her teeth and came back carrying two small clear plastic bags with very watery milk. Hii ndio garatathi.

Juli stood up and went outside to smoke. Chiri picked up his strungi tea and followed him. Juli turned to him and said, 'You know in Nairage Ya Ngare they are pouring out milk into the ground because its too much for them to drink. And now we are here drinking strungi. Kuna shida.' There is a problem.

They stood there and Juli smoked hard, his mouth straining at the cigarette. Not far from where they stood was a barren dusty patch where some kids were chasing around some round juala plastic that they used as a ball. Some of the kids seemed healthy but many were dressed in rags. Chiri could not tell whether they were street chokoras. Or why chokoras were playing with the neighbourhood children. Beyond the playground was some sort of administrative chief's camp. Close to where the children were playing there was a small heap of garbage. Black plastic bags were picked up by the wind, flew around the children and some were held by the strands of barbed-wire fence of the chief's camp.

Chiri held up the small paper cup of watery milk in his hand.

'You remember lorry ya maziwa?' Juli asked. The milk lorry.

'Yes,' Chiri laughed. 'Fresh bread in paper packets. And here we are drinking milk in jualas. To think you went to Catholic Parochial, and my Mum struggled to take me to St George's...'

'Yes, but look at those kids,' Juli said. 'At least we grew up with Tetra Pak milk.'

'Hey man, Buru together till we die. Maybe we should go back home for a few days.'

Juli shook his head. 'No, my friend. I can't. Not like this. What would I tell Mathe who thinks all is great with everything. But you should go see your Mum. Like me, you are now also the man of the house. Maybe not now but at some time you will have to go back to Nai things. To things the way we were raised in Buru.'

'What are you saying?'

Juli said, 'I have a plan. Solo is lucky to be alive. The jinga went back to confront Ahmed after he lost the money. And can you imagine refused to leave his house. But maybe he will be good for something for the family after all after this. I will head back and tell the Ntimamas that he was robbed and almost killed and he lost the harvest money. I hope out of respect for my father those dogs will let me work for them till I pay the debt. Then, maybe I can go back to Buru.'

'Juli ... I am not ready to go back ...'

Juli looked at him. 'Sisemi, I am not saying you go back now – just think about the rest of your life. This wheat thing is not your life.' He lit another cigarette. 'I have never thanked you for being there for us after Baba died. Asante. Nobody else was.'

Small dust devils swirled where the kids were playing. They whirled, gathered force and soon everything was covered in dust. The larger dust devil headed towards Chiri and Juli. Chiri remembered how when they were kids and dust devils appeared they always tried to throw a plastic basin over them – it was said that was the way to trap Satan. Juli and Chiri now did not move away from the larger devil. They just held their hands over their eyes and foreheads and stood against it as it came.

VI

Early November. It was three weeks to the harvest. Juli and Chiri spent the long days in sobriety, beaten and stony broke back in Nairage Ya Ngare. They drove to the fields passing fields that belonged to others that were turning golden like a TV Unga advertisement. Juli knew they would be lucky if they harvested half what they had expected. Things had gone badly while they were in Eastleigh. In the shamba in Ngareta, birds had eaten half of the crop. In Melilli, the workers Juli paid in full refused to return. In Suswa, there were huge gaps in their wheatfield from the scant rain. Out in Ololonga, where Juli had baulked at the leasing prices but where his father had always planted, a bumper harvest was expected.

They went back to the house one evening and Solo was back. Clean, dressed in new clothes. Other than his broken teeth Chiri and Juli could not believe that he had recovered so quickly from the Eastleigh beating. They sat outside in the evening sun and Chiri listened to Solo go on about how the English sun only retired at 11 p.m. in the summer. Chiri imagined himself elsewhere, far away from here, anywhere, back in school. He wondered whether his Mum would keep her promise made months ago that if he went back to university she would take a loan to pay for him.

On the night of Jamhuri Day Juli paid for Chiri's first barmaid from the sale of the parts of the old John Deere in the garage that he had so long wanted to revive. Chiri was up most of the night: after every round of sex, the barmaid drunkenly repeated, 'Kereti is my name, Kereti is my name.' Juli kept on banging the wall in protest at the noise, unable to sleep. Miraa had dimmed Juli's interest in sex; he no longer bothered with his barmaids. After a torrid night, Chiri came to understand Juli's and Solo's penchant for these rural women. They had no anxieties, they did not need to pleased – the physical exchange was an uncomplicated transaction.

When Chiri woke up the next morning, he felt an immediate discomfort in his shorts, a nagging feeling. He couldn't pee. When he squeezed the middle of his penis it leaked a yellow pus. The pain was strange, small and sharp, recurring and shifting into his groin, the bottom of his stomach. But the leaking didn't stop. His penis felt like a disassociated part of him. When he went to the kitchen, Juli looked up and could tell from the way Chiri walked. He pointed and Juli laughed long and loudly. Solo wandered in and Juli shared. Ame-burn. Chiri remembered the brothers' strange and sudden reunions in childhood when it came to the perverse, the tragic. They were grinning as if he'd just passed a singular rite of passage. Taken another step into their brotherhood. They all sipped strungi tea from chipped cups in the small kitchen. Chiri awaited to hear the day's plan – anything to distract from the throbbing down there. But Juli just watched him with a curious expression on his face.

Chiri felt the leak in his shorts come on again. He would not be going anywhere. He could already imagine being in the heat and dust in this state and all he now wanted was to be in his Buru bedroom. He had thought of heading to the Trading Centre to confront Kereti but with Juli that could end up very badly.

'What should I do?'

Solo chuckled at the fear in his voice. Juli continued to look at Chiri curiously, like he was trying to learn something new about him.

'Some pills will get you right.' Juli said. 'Antibiotics.'

The two brothers said they would check on the Melili shamba to see when they would harvest. Chiri wandered through the empty house all morning. He headed outside and covered every inch of the compound. By midday, the pus was now constant; the pain had spread to his lower stomach, his upper legs. There was a smell in his nostrils of rot. He headed back into the house and could barely walk in the wetness; he had run out of toilet paper. He lay down and all his ears strained for was the familiar roar of the Datsun. When he peed, the pain was at its worst. Juli and Chiri did not come back at sundown and Chiri managed to fall asleep from exhaustion.

In the middle of the night he was shaken awake and when he sat up Juli stood over him, wobbling. 'Sasa. Here. Take two now and two in the morning.' The eight large yellow pills were wrapped in a small, grotty piece of brown sugar paper. Chiri gobbled the pills gratefully. In the morning his pee was sulphur yellow. The pain had gone down. The pus had reduced. But the smell was even worse. But now he felt like he could run five kilometres. He took another dose.

When Juli and Solo headed out, they turned briefly to see whether Chiri wanted to come with them to the fields. Being in the house alone had grown on him so he smiled weakly and shook his head even if he thought he could do it and survive. Over the next two days the pills coloured the edges of his vision in a yellow haze. He read Petro Sayianka's westerns most of the day and into the night. He went to bed early and sometime in the night not sure whether he was dreaming heard the brothers stumbling around in the dark, drunk.

But on the morning of the third day, the pain was worse than before; the pus had come back and it had streaks of red. Chiri found Juli outside, sitting under a tree, looking terrible from the night before. The Datsun was nowhere to be seen. Juli looked up.

'Solomon took off with the car,' he said.

When Chiri told him about the increased burn, Juli winced.

'Ai that's bad – now you have to be dungwa'd. Don't worry this happens if you do not take the medicine immediately after infection. I'll get some money for you from Johnny when Solo gets back.' They waited for Solo till 2 p.m. and then Juli jumped on the tractor. Chiri watched him go off, his long body bumping along the road, heading to the farm in Ngareta. Chiri sank to his knees: the pain was unbearable. He couldn't even wear shorts any more. Juli had given him a shuka and he tied it around himself like a skirt.

Juli came back hours later. 'Pole, Johnny has gone to Narok for supplies,' he said.

'I left a message for him. We should be able to sort things out tomorrow.' Chiri smelled maize beer on his breath.

'Hangover,' Juli explained. 'You should have some for the pain,' he grinned. 'For your makende.' Chiri knew that it would also kill the effect of the antibiotics. But he took a swig from the gourd that Juli offered and winced at the sourness. He felt lightheaded.

When Solo eventually came back late in the night he was even more drunk than Juli. He found Juli and Chiri in the kitchen, eating kunde and brown ugali. Solo laughed. He pulled a toothpick from his jeans with some delicacy and started picking his teeth, flicking specks of goat meat on the ground.

'Where is the Datsun?' Juli asked. 'Lazima I finish the Suswa harvest tomorrow.'

'... Ei ran out of fuel,' Solo said. 'It's in Nairage Ya Ngare. Outside Top Life.' He dropped the keys near the small tar lamp. 'Empty like you, little brother.'

The tiny lamp flame threw Julis's head in a shadow dance against the wall like a genie. Juli's voice was quiet. 'Kumanina, you fuck-up.'

Solo grinned. 'Ah, Julius, the big wheat farmer speaks. Bwana ngano.'

Juli said, 'Fuckin. You should have stayed where you were. Dead to Baba and everybody.'

'Na wewe all you have done is harvest where Baba planted. Now let's wait and see what happens to your crop.'

They attacked each other like rabid dogs. They probably hadn't fought since they were kids. Back then, Solo used to come out on top. Now Juli, taller and hardened by the wheatlands, seemed to have the advantage over a Solo softened by England. They crashed around the kitchen, smashing everything. Juli rushed Solo trying to dictate the fight, make it a wrestling match. Solo wanted to keep it to a boxing contest so that he could use his speed. He caught Juli with a right to the head but the momentum was still with his brother. They rolled on the ground without either of them gaining an advantage. Juli wanted to pin Solo to the ground and did for a moment, smashed his head back into the concrete. But Solo unleashed some punches to his neck. They grunted, cursed each other.

Then an unearthly scream rent the house. Gogo. She yelled for her son, their father. Petro. The brothers fell apart. They looked at each other with pure hatred. Gogo appeared at the kitchen door. She cursed them on their mother's life and asked them to leave the house. No respect for your dead father. They sat shocked, but defiant still. Gogo relented when Solo looked up at her and said something in Maasai. She started wailing.

The next day, two very old men appeared at the crack of dawn. The brothers were summoned to the kitchen in council. The old men spoke:

'We raised your father when he was a boy. So, you will listen to what we have to say. Sisi wote ni Mlango nyekundu.' We all belong to the Red Door.

But before they continued, they summoned Chiri and asked him where he came from. 'Buru Buru,' he said, looking at the brothers who remained quiet. The old men told him he needed to go back there; these were sad and strange times for the Sayianka family to be borne alone by those inside the Red Door. When the old men finally left, Juli and Solo told Chiri he did not have to go anywhere but he needed to stay out of sight for a few days.

The pain had spread to the whole of his waist area and Chiri took to maize beer. Juli left in the morning and did not return in the evening. Solo stopped drinking after the fight and he seemed to finally become the older brother that Chiri remembered when they were in their teens. He talked about his time in the UK and how much he had missed the family, in many ways Juli most of all, who he knew would always be there for him when he came back. Chiri knew that Solo would never repeat this in front of Juli. In the end it was this sober Solo who managed to get some money from Gogo to take Chiri to the clinic. The injection was excruciating but in two days the leak had dried up.

When Solo and Chiri woke up, they found Juli's room empty, his clothes gone. The Datsun 1200 was found parked at the junction of the Narok road. Solo called their mother but Juli was not in Buru Buru. Christmas was a week away. They waited for Juli for another two days but he did not come back. Just less than a week before Christmas, Solo and Chiri went to all the three shambas with Obergon and harvested what they could. They paid off all the smaller debts. The Ntimamas came for the Harvester. After that was settled Solo put all the farming equipment up for sale. Not much remained after paying Kinuthia, at least not enough for the Sayianka clan bash that Mama Sayianka wanted to thank the clan for their help with the funeral. But it would be enough for the immediate family to live off for a few months. Mrs Sayianka, their baby sister Esther and Solo.

Three days before Christmas Chiri prepared to go back to Nairobi. He knew he would have to go back to uni. He was done with the wheatlands, the drinking, the women, the adventures. He hoped he had not caught HIV from Kereti. He decided that he would work hard to become adept at those things that are built by a Buru Buru childhood: go back to uni, get a degree, an office jobbo, buy a Toyota. The things Juli had rejected by going back into the wilderness. Chiri knew he would never see the Sayiankas again and that Juli was better off with the old man in Naimenengiu, the Magic Forest, where the ways of the Red Door remained alive. Before he left Chiri thought about Juli and could see him out there sitting by the small shop, where lionesses prowled and snakes crawled and the rules were different.

The last night in Nairage Ya Ngare he dreamt of the long boy by the laga. In the dream he found himself on a plain somewhere around the laga. The sky was pale white with a small yellow sun. He started running and feeling airless took to the empty sky, flying. But when he tried to climb higher something held him back. He gathered momentum covering great Rift Valley distances but was unable to shoot away into the sky. So he flew close to the ground over Narok, Nairage Ya Ngare, Suswa, Melili and Mai Mahiu, and where the land climbed into congested Kikuyu-land, Kinungi, Limuru and Nairobi teemed in the distance.

He turned back and saw some giant storks heading towards him. Feeling a strange communion with the birds he turned to join them but still at some distance away he noticed that the stork in the lead was larger and he slowed down, unsure. Coming closer he saw that the leading stork was a man-figure with wings – and then he recognised the face. It was the long boy from the laga. His face was completely fishlike, with very sharp teeth. Chiri turned quickly and flew off and he could hear wings behind him in pursuit. And then, the laga appeared below them. Chiri dived deep into the water and then there was a splash behind him, then a voice – a grown man's voice that was not quite right.

'Nataka to play. Play. Play. Play.'

That's when Chiri discovered he could no longer fly.

COMMISSION

Jameni, I lost the silver bracelet my nyanya had given me when I was a little girl when I heard the news that he would appear on the Goldenberg Commission. I ran around our small shamba and through the fence to his clan on the next shamba to tell everybody and the bracelet fell and I did not feel it leave my skin. Imagine. I told his Gogo in the small house we lived in and Uncle Rotiken, our closest neighbour about one kilometre away in his also-small house, about the Commission. It was only when I saw afterwards that I had torn my bui bui on the Ngombe barbed-wire fence, and that there was a scratch with blood on my shoulder, that I saw that the silver bracelet was not on my arm. Ai there I was with my shoulder open to the world to look at the blood because my head was full of the news of the Commission. I remembered nyanya's madrassa when I was a small girl and slipped the cloth over my shoulder and went to check it inside, away from the eyes of the world. That is how bad the last years had been in forgetting how I had grown up and that is how good this news was. The silver bracelet was always leaving my arm and I knew nyanya was trying to tell me something. That maybe I should not have stayed in Olokurto. But when I took my steps again I found the bracelet near the fence.

The first time the CID came to pick him up in the police Land Rover we wondered whether we would see him again, even if a new regime had now come into power. He came back after a week and said that he had been asked to be part of the preparations for a Commission looking into Goldenberg. He said this government would not let the sins of the past be forgotten. I knew that we had stopped hiding when he also said that we had to start preparing for a new life. He even said that we would travel to the Coast to see my parents who I had not seen since we came to Maasailand, and that was six years ago. The silver bracelet stayed on my wrist and did not slip off even when I was digging with Gogo, or washing the girls or the viombo dishes.

Alafu he was picked up again by the police Land Rover to go to Nairobi to testify and he went wearing the blue suit that had been bought for him by Transparency International. While he had been preparing with the Commission the news of what he had done had come out and Transparency International had come to us. Now he sent more news: they were going to give him an award and maybe even a job for the brave thing he had done. He said we would then even be able to go and live in Nairobi. Inshallah. At least they had bought him the blue suit while he was doing the work of the Commission so the government would take him seriously. When the newspapers announced the Commission and said that he would be one of the witnesses, some people here in Olokurto thought he had done a stupid thing not a brave one by not taking the money like many had all those years ago. Maasai jinga, they said.

The few days when he stayed with us before he went back to Nairobi we noticed that he did not go quiet maji ya mtungi for long periods like he used to. He started talking talking quickly again in English as if he were practising for our new life to come. He had always been good at talking talking like an offisi person and even when we had not been able to leave Olokurto he read the newspapers that wrapped the meat when we could afford it once a month. Before we had two daughters, Amina and Fatu, he had impressed my father with his knowledge of the Koran when he came to tell him that he wanted to marry me in Mombasa. Even if we had a wedding he still had to be given permission by my parents properly in the Muslim way for me. That is the way of the Bajuni who used to be my people. I knew Allah would plan for us when we would go for the final blessing. The Koran says that man just says. It is God who decides.

Then when he was away, the newspapers said that one of the very powerful ministers who had been in power during the last regime had gone to court to stop the Commission. We knew how the country was and I was scared. When he called us at the red jamii telephone at Olokurto trading centre he laughed and said that hii ni tsunami. No one can stop an idea whose time has come. His English over the phone was stronger than this powerful minister. But as I walked back to the farm I knew that a minister in Kenya is more powerful than English. That is why wanasiasa say the important things in our languages, then the other takataka in broken Swahili and in English.

The Commission, we were told, was meeting at Kenyatta International Conference Centre, the most important place in Nairobi. We all knew about KICC but I had never seen it. Gogo shook her head and laughed and said it looked like a big mboro, tall and long, that had been built in the middle of Nairobi so that wanaume leaders could feel strong and good about themselves even if wananchi were going through many problems. Gogo's feet were old and angry and made her say things like that. I could not stop thinking about a big mboro growing in the centre of Nairobi and I was ashamed. I missed him in our bed. I asked Allah for forgiveness.

We were told the Commission had started. I could not go to Nairobi to see him because we could not afford it even when everyone asked me in the trading centre unaenda unaenda? There was only one TV in Olokurto at the Good Hopes Bar. Gogo and I were called to go see him kwa Commission. We did not have any money for soda and we carried chai from the house. The barmaids from Molo, who had come with their people after the '92 clashes and served at Good Hopes Bar, looked at Gogo and me with fitina eyes and sengeyad sssss at us in Kikuyu. But they did not know Gogo was Kikuyu before she married Guka and had not forgotten the tongue of atiriri.

Everyone on the television at the Commission looked serious sura ya kazi and Gogo kept on falling asleep. When he appeared on TV after a few days of Commission I felt happy and remembered when we first met in Mombasa. He looked so beautiful on TV that Gogo and I looked at each other and said Ai Ai Ai. The barmaids from Molo ssssd ssssd and looked at us with macho za papa. 'Kweli, the eyes of the shark,' my nyanya used to say, 'are dead, but binadamu are not far.' These Molo women, whom Gogo said she did not know why they came here, knew my husband because of that time he had thought he was carrying the world on his shoulders. Men ndio hivyo they think the world is on them. He refused to come home and was always in Good Hopes Bar and slept in the lodgings next door. Gogo had said she would send him an engoki and then kill herself and come back to make his life a wilderness. The dawa medicine power of the gogos of UMaasaini is not to be played with.

In the TV he looked as if he worked in a bank in Nairobi in the deep blue suit, white shirt and red tie from Transparency International. I quickly sent for our baby, Fatu, and Amina who was already a little girl, to be brought to the bar to see their Baba. Ka-Joyce the youngest daughter of Uncle Rotiken who was in likizo from school was looking after them. I said she must dress them in the Bajuni way so that people would not think we had forgotten our religion by sitting in a bar. And I touched the silver bracelet and knew nyanya would be happy because this is what she had taught me.

I had never been to a bar before then. When I came to Olokurto I had tried to start a madrassa. I did not want to forget my mila. The ways of the Bajuni. When I was growing up in Lamu my father was always at the mosque or the town square. There were no bars of Good Hopes. My mother only left the house to go visit other women of her age in their homes or the market. The market here was for cows and men and I did not have any friends to visit. I wanted to teach the few Muslim children here who stayed in the trading centre the Koran, and to say their prayers five times a day. I was taught to wash five times after saying my prayers. Five times. When Fatu and Amina were born they were not held up so that the traditional call of prayer was said into their ear. That is why I had started the madrassa so that they would not forget the mila I had come from. And now they had to come to Good Hopes to see him.

I showed Amina and Fatu their Baba on TV and Fatu pointed and laughed. 'Bara, bara,' she said. Even the eyes of the Molo barmaids became woi and they gave her a Fanta for free. Good Hopes Bar was full of men smelling of wheat ngano farms. The men went very quiet during his testimony and said that we should be given anything we wanted because of what he had done for the country. For that day he was on TV saying what had happened we ate as much as we wanted at Good Hopes.

He told in English how he had joined the Central Bank of Kenya in 1990 and worked as a clerk for two years. There was this big man who had a very big head tumbo kubwa with many thoughts asking him questions but he was not scared. I could not understand everything and I explained to Gogo kijuujuu because they were talking in English.

'Then, what happened?' the lawyer asked.

'I reported to work every day at 8.30 a.m. and left at 5 p.m.'

'Can you explain to the Commission how you became involved in Goldenberg?'

I could not keep track of all the questions with my slow English. When the big-headed tumbo kubwa wakili-lawyer asked him how much money was involved he kept quiet for a few minutes and then he said: 'One million dollars was involved.'

The lawyer said: 'Did you say one million dollars?'

'Yes, Your Honour; one million dollars.'

It was like a DVD movie. There was noise in the court and everyone in Good Hopes Bar cheered. They said: There he is, your husband, the hero.

I remembered how we met in Mombasa all those years ago when he was running away from those bank people who had stolen the money and I wanted to cry right there in Good Hopes Bar. Shukran to Allah.

Before I met him all I knew was the Coast. I miss bahari, the sea how it smells. I miss eating fish. His people here say that samaki are insects and God did not create human beings to eat insects. Ngai. For six years since we came here I have only eaten kuku chicken five times because his people do not also eat birds. I had to hide and buy the kuku from the other Molo Kikuyus who own the food kiosk in Olokurto. When I went there I did not wear my bui bui so nobody recognised me. When I asked for the chicken in my Swahili that had stopped being sanifu the woman selling knew who I was. I knew she knew because she asked if I also wanted mbuzi ulaya. Pork. Ai. Salaam Aleikum. I touched the silver bracelet and remembered nyanya. The boiled kuku stayed in my mouth for a whole week and I could feel it scratching in my stomach. I prayed to Allah for forgiveness.

I was only sixteen when we met in Mombasa. When I finished my Koran studies in madrassa and primary school in Lamu I had gone to live with my sister, Hadija, in Majengo. She worked at the port and opened a small biashara for me to sell mboga, fruits and other takataka. I met him when he started coming to my stall to buy fruits.

'Habari-yagho! Fungia-mimi-hiyo,' he would say in his strange voice, pointing at mandizi. It was completely foreign to me. Even then he spoke mostly English. I also used to work in a salon and I used to see him with this Taita girl with big eyes who used to come in to do her hair. Then, I did not see her again. One day he just came to me at the stall and he said: salama lakini. He said he wanted to see my parents. By then his strange accent had disappeared. I had always thought he was a Mbarawa, a Bajuni from Somalia.

The ways of men are very strange. I told him to tell me what he wanted. My mother had told me when it comes to men and women there should not be too many stories. When he offered me a bitter lemon, I refused because he had not declared himself. I asked him about his Taita girlfriend who used to come to the salon. He said she liked money too much. Aieee, I looked at him because I had seen them holding hands. He said that he had become a Muslim and wanted to marry a Muslim girl. I laughed and then saw that he was sura ya kazi serious. He even showed me a letter from the Kadhi to say that he had become a Muslim. I pushed away the barua from the Kadhi – these were not the things for a girl of my age to read.

We met two times because that is the way it is with us. That was enough. With us Bajunis, you say what you want. No stories. Hadithi mingi. And if you want to marry me and I like you, you go see my parents. No wasting each other's time.

Then, he started to visit me at the home of Hadija my sister. At first I used to run away when I saw him to go and watch mapenzi Bollywood films with a Tanzanian boy, my friend Jomvu. My sister asked me why I was playing this game of panya na paka, cat and mouse. After my sister spoke to me I became close to him. The time he came and he saw me with Jomvu his neck started swelling and his ears turned red. Imagine. I pretended not to see. I wanted to see whether he was serious and he did not just want to tongoza me.

Jomvu was maskini and could not pay Ksh 30,000 and buy my parents a sofa set and a bed made of mvuli hardwood. So, I became engaged to him instead. Nobody in my family knew where he was from. They also thought he was a Mbarawa. At our wedding, only his brother and his brother's father-in-law came. The men from my family wore kikois and rubber-thonged sandals on their feet with the women in bui buis that only showed their eyes to the world. In those days there were still songs during our weddings. The sheikhs had not yet refused us to sing and make poem mashairi. We could not afford to bring the famous Juma Bhalo but the cousin of my poet who had been one of his musicians came to the wedding to sing. Then, my father said we must give our new family a chance to speak.

Hai. We wondered what Kiswahili these people were speaking. It turned out to be Kikuyu Kiswahili. What if it had been Maasai? I would never have married him. The words come out of the mouth like a waterfall. I've become used to it at Olokurto because this is what my ear listens to all the time.

He explained that he had been born out of ndoa and had no father. His only family was his brother and his brother's father-in-law. He said his mother had died and we felt pity for him. We did not question him when he said his relatives were far away. Like many other things, I only knew later that he was hiding from the government of Moi. But he was able to give mother and father a jumbo sofa set and bed made of hardwood podo.

When we arrived in Olokurto everything was so different from pwani. I had never seen a Maasai in a shuka, only those Kikuyus who used to jump for tourists on the beach who were warani bandia. I did not even know how food came from the ground. Gogo tried to teach me all these things. She laughed at me at first and then she grew angry when she saw me put back the potato waru stalk in the soil thinking that another potato waru would grow from it. When she asked me to go and bring ati firewood I went to Olokurto and bought charcoal. When I tried to cut wood with an axe I almost cut off my toes. He helped me with the firewood and shouted, how would I become the Maasai woman of the house. Gogo could carry huge bundles of firewood easily. I had never seen my own mother carry anything. She would have dropped dead fofofo on the spot.

In Lamu and Mombasa people don't walk anywhere because the sun will kemea you and ask you where you think you are going. I could not even walk to the Olokurto trading centre. In Mombasa, I just threw Ksh 5 at the manamba even to go to the shops. But in Olokurto everyone we knew stayed so far away, we had to walk.

Aii, the food. I could not understand how anyone could eat so much meat. I was used to coconut mnazi rice and samaki. There was no bread or sugar just a cup of strungi, sugarless black tea, for breakfast. I forgot everything for a while when Amina was born till she was one and a half.

My tongue refused to pick up Maa though my children could speak it. My Swahili changanisha mixed with Kikuyu. I found myself saying Ngai and calling the fence, iriga. Waru ati for viasi potato. We do not have such words in Tikuu.

One day I saw Gogo, who used to drink raw goat fat, give it to Amina mixed with cream. Amina cried at first but she became used to it. Gogo said that it would make her strong and she would never fall sick.

After this I told him that I wanted to visit my sister and pick up some things. He said that Gogo would take care of

Amina if I was going for a short time. So I went to my sister Hadija in Mombasa. Hadija did not ask me anything when I stayed and stayed without saying when I would go back. My nephews and nieces laughed at me when the words came out of my mouth. Hadija told me to stop speaking like a Mmbaara in front of neighbours and friends.

He sent messages begging me to go back and it was only when I started missing Amina that I went.

Gogo sat me on a low stool when I arrived and told me what had happened to him with the Central Bank, banki kuu. She said this to make me understand why he kept quiet with mawazo. After I came back I became used to everything slowly and slowly and I forgot the ustarabu that I had been raised with.

After the Commission ended we did not see him for a month. Gogo and I went back to the things we had always done. We only had four goats and three cows to take care of. Even if he was a hero and our lives were going to change, Gogo and I went back to the shamba to look after the maize, beans and potatoes we had planted. One of Uncle Rotiken's sons brought us the newspaper and he was on the front page with his name in the headlines. After that every few days we were brought a newspaper and sometimes there was a photo, sometimes just his name. Then we received a message that even if the Commission was over that he was now working with the government and he was helping them with the case against those who were involved. I was scared again because these were important men. Imagine. They were going to go back ten years and find all those who had taken money back then. Gogo and I did not even have five small shillings and we borrowed milk from the kiosk for Fatu.

We then got a letter from him that was delivered by the police Land Rover and inside was a postcard with a picture of KICC. There was another one of the sea and his words that said that we would be going back to see my parents soon. The postcard said many other things about his whistleblower business in Nairobi but I was thinking about how we would go back to Lamu to see my parents. Inshallah.

The policeman who delivered the letters asked whether I had a message for my husband and he said he would pick it up the next day. He also smiled kama papa ya baharini and said he wished he had someone like me to wait for him. He was carrying a big gun when he said this and spoke funny. Gogo said this was because he was from Kisii where there were many ogres. We had come to know the police from the Olokurto post because they are the ones who brought his letters and took our messages to him. We did not like them because they were not from here. But I did not fear the police as much as the warani. Every harvest the warani came to our house because I was not Maasai to ask for meat and milk. They liked to go to the houses of Kikuyus and those who were not Maasai and take things. We hid the cows and goats because they would take them if he was not here. The warani did not come when Gogo was there because they feared she would send them an engoki curse.

When I showed Gogo the letters and the postcards from him that the policeman brought she started crying. Then, Amina came running into the room and when she saw Gogo she started crying and then Fatu was crying and I found tears falling down my face. I had to be the one to remain strong but at night when I went to bed I cried.

When I asked Gogo in the morning whether she had any message for him so that I could take it to the police post she wiped her tears and put her hands on her head and looked at the sky. Uncle who came every evening to see us when he was not here brought us some githeri and uji and we all held hands and prayed together. All the years we had been here he would get angry and say that people in the reserve thought that God would do everything for them. Before the Commission and the change of regime when his Uncle had come to pray with us in our hour of need he refused to join us.

When I went to the police post to send the message the police told me he had said that we could go visit him in Nairobi for the award ceremony by Transparency International. Gogo said that her feet would not carry her to Nairobi and that it was just better if we were given the money because Fatu did not have milk. The people he was working with did not send us the money for the matatu fare. They said that they would give us the money when we reached Nairobi. I do not know which matatu these people travelled on that gave receipts. When we told Uncle Rotiken all this he said the Good Lord would provide. Uncle even if he was Christian was always praying every day like my Muslim baba.

Uncle called a meeting of the family elders to do a small collection for our trip. He said that I could not go alone with Fatu as Gogo was now too old to take care of her. Uncle offered to come with me to Nairobi. We were not able to raise the fare for many days and then Uncle got a donation the day before the awards from the Anglican Church in Narok.

We woke up very early on the morning of the awards. Uncle said that we would reach the city by 2 p.m. in time for the awards in the evening at 8 p.m. The people from Transparency International who had not sent us the fare said they would meet us at the big matatu stage in Nairobi near Tea Room. The driver and the manamba between Olokurto and Narok were very kind because the matatu was owned by somebody from our clan. When we told them we were going because of the Commission they told us that we did not have to pay because we were the people of a great hero.

When we got to Narok it was the day of the cattle market and there were many people. It was like I remembered Mombasa. There were old men in shukas standing on their long sticks with simba eyes looking at everybody like something had happened and they were wondering about it. They looked and spat and then looked again. They shouted in the air as if they had just thought something from their past in their heads. When a woman in a shuka passed in front of them they raised their sticks as if the woman was a cow and she would run and laugh. The old man pretended to be angry and shouted at her that if he was still a young man she would see. And I could see that the women's eyes were shining at this and their faces settled like cool water in a pot.

At times Land Cruisers came running very fast through town and they did not stop because they were carrying mzungus to the Mara. The mzungus inside were covered in kofias and they wore big glasses and looked like insects. Fatu pointed and laughed and tried to sing the song that Gogo had taught her about mzungus.

Palikuwa mtu moja
Jina lake ni Smithi
Alipenda mashamba
Tangu kuzaliwa
Smithi smithi
Smithi smithi

I told her shhhhh and put my hand over her mouth. I had worn my green bui bui and I had drawn henna on my hands and feet for the awards for him. Old men in shukas pointed at me. I could understand some of their words and I heard them say that I was a jinni. A spirit. In Olokurto, when I walked for my prayers in my bui bui, children jumped up and down. I did not understand what they were saying. Then Amina told me that they were saying 'paka paka' in Maasai. Black cat. I wondered whether the old men were calling me a green paka.

Because of Fatu I was allowed to sit in front of the Nissan where it was more comfortable. Uncle was also directed to the front seat next to me because he was old. The manamba said we should sit there because the back was too hot for old people and babies. But then the manamba said that we would have to pay double if we did not share the seat with a third person. Before we entered the matatu Uncle had said that the new Kibaki regime had come to power and taught the matatu men manners. But now the manamba started shouting that we are going express and that it was a hundred shillings extra. Uncle Rotiken pleaded with the manamba that the only extra money we had was for our lunch but the manamba said that he also needed lunch too. He said even the owner of the matatu needed lunch kitu kidogo too. And even the policeman at the checkpoint needed lunch kitu kidogo too. He said everybody needed lunch kitu kidogo in Kenya.

When Uncle said that God would take care of everything and that we were going to Transparency International Awards because of the Commission, the manamba became kali and said that there was a Commission every other year and the country had still not changed. He started singing Ouko Inquiry. Muge Inquiry. Ndungu Land Commission as he collected all the money from the passengers before we left the Narok stage. Uncle looked very old like Milka our cow before she died last year after he handed over the money. We were lucky we had not paid for the matatu we had taken from Olokurto and had extra. I wondered when the President Kibaki manners would reach Narok.

There was a sticker on the windscreen of the matatu that said: *Dear Passenger, this is the place of my business. Please respect me and I will respect you too. Thank you dear passenger.* There were many stickers and I tried to read them all on the journey but Fatu would not let me. When she slept another one said: *God made Man. Man made money. Money made man mad.*

On the way the matatu broke down just after Mai Mahiu and we were told to wait by the roadside. We could see a small church that was very old where we stopped. Uncle said that Italians had built it during the First big war of the mzungus. I took Fatu under a small tree outside the church. The building reminded me of Lamu. I played mkono tupu with Fatu and then we slept there on the grass and I dreamt that my parents had grown very old and were about to die. When we were woken up and told that the matatu had been repaired it was already late afternoon. I knew from the dream that I had to tell him that we had to go see my parents soon.

We knew we were near Nairobi when we saw KICC from a distance. It became bigger and bigger as we got closer and I laughed when I thought about what Gogo had said. Uncle Rotiken looked at me and thought I was just happy. I asked Allah to forgive me. When we reached Nyamakima in Nairobi it was saa kumi. Four o'clock. The police had told us that he had said there would be someone waiting for us. Everybody quickly ran off from the matatu and we were left there alone. Nairobi was like the big hill for ants that is outside Gogo's house that looks like it's breathing because of the movement inside. Amina had learned how to stay away from the anthill but Fatu was always getting bitten and crying when she forgot and stood too near. Now Fatu looked around at everything with big eyes. My father had always said that you had to be careful in Nairobi.

We sat in the matatu and we were not sure where to go. We did not know what the Transparency International people looked like. We had been given a simu to call. We knew that the ceremony was at eight o'clock at a big hotel on Thika Road. Uncle asked the manamba whether he knew Transparency International. The manamba had been eating miraa for the whole trip and his mouth was green and his eyes had become very big. He pointed in the direction of KICC, 'You see that big mboro – all the Commissions are held there.'

When we left the matatu Uncle started asking everybody where the Commission or Transparency International was but they were busy like the ants outside Gogo's house. There was a very thin man who was shouting that the hour of the Lord was at hand. Brothers and sisters look carefully. See the signs. Repent. He held a book in one hand and a handkerchief in the other. You see this cloth and you see this book. Which one should you trust? When he saw us looking at him he said, Yes, elder brother, sister and little sister. Choose one. Choose fire or eternal life.

Uncle said that we should go to Tea Room and have some chai and try and look for a telephone booth to call the Transparency International offices. We went to Tea Room, the famous restaurant that all people travelling from upcountry know well. Fatu was hungry but did not cry because all the people around us scared her. Tea Room was full of people of all shapes and sizes with bags travelling all over Kenya. I saw that they did not put their bags down when they ate and held them like children. I did the same and put Fatu down. Uncle used some of the coins left to buy Fatu soda and mandazi and some chai for me. We had carried some ngwaci and I gave Fatu some and she fell asleep. It started getting dark and the waiter who had brought the chai came and told us that we had to leave because we had finished eating. Time was money. There were other travellers that needed the table. The manners of these Kibaki times were also yet to reach Tea Room.

Uncle begged the waiter in Kikuyu and told him that we had come for the awards because of the Commission. He went to call from a phone booth and when he came back he said he had spoken to someone who had told him that we should take a taxi to a big hotel called Safari Park Hotel. They said that when we got there someone from Transparency International would pay.

When we found the taxi the driver asked us where we were going and Uncle said the Safari Hotel on Thika Road. He looked at us suspiciously as if he did not know why we were going there and then he said: 'Haya twende.' We left and went through the streets at such a slow speed that even the people who were walking were faster than us. Fatu kept sleeping and I could watch all the things of Nairobi that I had never seen. Everyone was rushing this way and that way leaving work and I wondered whether he would be like that when we lived here like he had said.

After a long time we left the crowds of people and the buildings everywhere and the roads became wider but the cars increased and we stayed in a long line of cars for a very long time. It looked to me like we were always going around KICC at a distance. My green bui bui had folded like a mzee's skin like I had been sleeping in it. I looked at my hands and the henna was not as bright as it had been when I left home because of all the dust I had picked up on this long journey. Then the sun went down very quickly. It was not like Olokurto where it gave a long warning and took a long time to go to sleep. We became like blind people and we did not know where were going. Uncle said we were now on Thika Highway when we found more cars and went as slowly as we had in town.

The driver kept looking at us and saying, 'Ati you are going to Safari Hotel eh? Nyinyi Safari Hotel eh?' Uncle looked at him and said, 'Ndio. Safari Park Hotel.' Gogo had once told me that Nairobi people are never sure of anything, that is why they ask something many times.

We reached a big gate and there were many watchmen. They refused the taxi to go inside and asked the driver to park on the side. Uncle said that is how all watchmen are with old cars. It was now almost 8 p.m. and we wondered whether we would be late. He would be very angry. After a long time the watchman came and said they have tried to call the people at the awards and nobody was picking. They said that they had sent their people to the awards to find someone to come. We would have to go and park on the side of the highway and wait. The driver reversed the car and we went and parked and waited. Then, the driver began asking for his money. Uncle said that the Transparency International people would pay him.

'Ati nini,' the driver said. 'Mzee, is it the international people that are transparent that I have brought here or you people from the reserve? Let us please respect each other. I need Ksh 2500 or I will take you to the police. Just here. Not far away.'

Gogo had also told me that people in Nairobi think taking you to the police can solve all problems.

Uncle said: 'Please please tafadhali. We were told to come here by Transparency International. Let me go and see whether they have been found.'

Uncle got out of the car and went back to the gate and he did not come back for a long time. Fatu woke up and started crying and the driver said he had been working since 5 a.m. and that if Fatu did not stop crying we should wait outside the car.

Then, he looked at me. 'Ngoja. And if you run away...'

I told him that I could not run very fast and he smiled like a papa ya baharini. 'You women are the worst. You do not like to pay for anything.'

I told him I could leave my bag but he looked at my green bui bui and then pointed at the silver bracelet that nyanya had given me and he said, 'Leave me that I will give it back to you when your Mzee comes back.'

Fatu started crying again and I could see she was tired of the taxi and the heat. I slipped off the bracelet, gave it to the man and got out of the car. Even before I put down Fatu to straighten my bui bui the taxi drove away.

I looked around and there was nobody on the side of the highway where many cars were passing. Fatu and I sat on the side of the highway and I thought of nyanya. The silver bracelet had been trying to run away for a long time and now it had left me.

Then I heard Uncle's voice in the dark, Maimouna Maimouna. I said 'Ndiyo,' and I saw him coming towards me with a woman and a man. The woman dressed in a suit like his came and picked up Fatu and asked her name. The man greeted me and asked where the taxi was and I said it had left me. He said he was very sorry. I did not say anything about the bracelet. We went into the hotel and they said the awards had started and we had to go in immediately because it was going to be on TV.

Ai, there were so many people and they all looked like those we saw on the television. I wanted to go and jump in the fountain outside and wash Fatu and myself. There were even mzungus who had come all the way from Ujeremani. All because of what he had done. They said many things about him. That he was brave and he was honest.

We were so tired that we did not listen to any speeches. Ai, I just looked at the people who were all shining. There were many tables with a lot of vino and everyone spoke na utaratibu. Kweli hii ni ustraabu. Fatu had seen him when we entered and said: 'Bara bara,' and then smiled and fell asleep immediately. Many people came to me and said what a brave man he was and that I was lucky. One woman came up to me and said I was also very brave like him even if nobody said. She said she worked for – ati, they were called African Woman and Child. She said she even wanted to interview me because I was an African woman and Fatu was an African child and we were also important. She touched Fatu the way some people touch their dogs and went away.

Even the wife of the President apologised because she could not come. Mama Lucy. The man who came instead came to the table where we were all sitting and greeted us. He said Mama Lucy thanked him for what he had done for the country. The man said he had integrity. And that was the name of the award he had won – Integrity Award.

Before everything finished he stood there before everyone and he said: 'Ladies and gentleman, I did what I thought was important for the country.' We all stood up and clapped vigelegele.

Soon after me, Uncle and Fatu were taken by the people of Transparency International to where we would sleep. He did not come because he had to talk to all the important people and all the people from the newspapers and the TV. I remembered Tea Room and how we had been chased. And I remembered the silver bracelet that was a blessing from nyanya and I did not feel sad about it anymore because everyone saw what he had done was important.

He came in the morning and we all went for breakfast. He looked like he was from Nairobi and we were just people who were here to shangilia him. And then he said to me again that everything would now change. He said that we would be in the newspapers with him and I was ashamed because I had brought the dust from Olokurto. And then, the Transparency International people came and said he had to go. They gave us money and said that was for the matatu and the taxi even if we did not have receipts. And they put us in a big car and we were driven all the way back to Olokurto without him.

He did not come home for almost a month after that. He was always in the papers and now they always called him the whistleblower. Mpiga firimbi. Yaani we wondered like a referee. We were the supporting mashabik on the sidelines of a football game we did not understand. He sent letters saying that he was almost getting a new job at OP, I did not know what this OP was. Uncle told us that it was the Office of the President. He wrote and said that he was helping people in the new regime to fight corruption. He also said that he was working with a filmmaker and a publishing firm so that his story could be written and his life could be made into a film. So that what he had done would not be forgotten. I did not want Amina and Fatu to forget him so I showed them his photo in the newspaper every day and Amina ran around singing in the compound about her Daddy and told all the other children about it. Gogo had given her a little calf and she asked whether her Daddy would only come back when it was big.

When we came back from Nairobi, Uncle became sick and we were told it was pneumonia. When we went to see him he said in a small voice that I could not hear very well that my husband had done a very important thing by going to the Commission. When Uncle got worse the clan took him to Narok Hospital. Even if he had raised the fare for us to go to Nairobi nobody did the same for him. A week later he died in hospital and we buried him and my husband did not come. He sent his condolences but everyone knew that he and Uncle had not been very close. I was ashamed because I knew that Uncle had died from being tired after taking me to Nairobi and because we had been kept waiting outside at night for so long. His family did not show any anger at me – they just looked very tired like the old cow Milka and said that they trusted in God. At the funeral the pastor from the AIC church said that all of us were going to a better place and that was where God had taken Uncle Rotiken. After Uncle died I started thinking about my parents and the dream I had had outside that small church by the roadside. I wondered when he would come so we would go see them for the final blessing of our marriage.

Then, one day he came back. It was a Saturday and Amina was on her school holidays. We were hoeing weeds from the beans and sukuma wiki in the garden with Gogo because it would soon be harvest. We heard the sound of a vehicle rushing up the hill to our homestead. At first we thought it was the police and we were happy we would get some news. Then, we saw the minibus from the shamba kwa bara bara before it disappeared in the trees. Then, we heard shouting and we knew it was him and went into the compound. The minibus had stopped outside the small gate and there he was with several men who we did not know.

I felt dirty and wished that I had instead gone to wash and prepare for him. He stood at the gate and held out his hands and hugged me even if I still had mud on my hands and my dress. He bit my lips with his teeth and I could feel a little blood on my tongue and I could also smell something like Fatu's cough syrup on his breath. I remembered when I was a child when my mother gave it to me and I missed the sea. I knew he was not sick but that he had started drinking again.

Gogo started wailing and ululating in the old way. The rest of the family had heard the minibus because very few cars came all the way here. They came and started stamping and celebrating their son who was now a national hero. He wore a brown suit and light blue shirt with black shoes that were shiny and I could tell he had put on weight. His skin had lost the dust of all those bad years we had been running away and I wondered whether he would now still stay with us. Gogo brought Amina and Fatu from the house where they had gone to hide because of all the men. Amina went to him but Fatu hid behind Gogo. He picked Amina up but she tried to stretch away and he laughed and said she would get used to him again. He then picked up Fatu but she cried and he told her that her future was bright because her father had testified before the Commission and the country would be a better place when she grew up. All the men who had come with him laughed. They were much younger than him. One had a camera and took many photos of all of us. I had always thought about how he had looked when he had worked in the Central Bank before I met him. *And now I could see*. He had cut his hair, he had shaved his beard and he looked like the old photos that I put away of him before we met. He no longer looked like us upcountry people but someone from the city. Becoming a hero had made him bigger and stronger. Even if he had been away just for two months he was now someone different. He was somebody in a newspaper like a politician. Someone to be listened to. Someone who had been to a Commission. The whistleblower. Mpiga firimbi.

The rest of our family brought milk and we cooked tea for all of the men but we could tell that he was restless, that he wanted to be left alone with them to discuss the big things that they had left in the city. He excused himself and he stepped out with one of the younger men who carried a notebook with him wherever he went. They went towards the fence and I could see them through the wooden planks of our kitchen hut. I saw the young man with a notebook give my husband an envelope. When they came back they drank the tea but did not touch the bread even if we had sent one of the nephews all the way to the trading centre to buy it. I kept it away for Amina and Fatu for the next day. My husband said that these were the men and one woman from the publishing house and the film company. He said that he would take them to Olokurto and make sure that they found a good place to sleep. He reached for my hand and squeezed in some money and when I looked I saw it was Ksh 10,000. Maybe our lives were really going to change.

I waited for him but I fell asleep and he did not come home that night and I remembered the Kikuyu barmaids with the papa eyes and the sss sss. Later the next day at midday the minibus came to the house and when we went outside we saw it was only the driver. He said that my husband had sent him with some things for us. We took all the kiondos he gave us and they were full of roast and raw meat, sodas, and milk and biscuits for the children. That night I cooked some of the meat with some waru potatoes for him but he did not come and I went to bed. We were lucky to have meat after so long but he wasn't there to eat it with us.

Then in the middle of the night there was banging at the door. Fatu started crying and when I opened there he was and he could not stand properly. I helped him come to the house and when he sat I removed his shoes and his coat. I had not seen him drunk like this since Gogo had said she would send him a engoki curse a few years ago. He kept on saying that he had gone to the Commission and the most famous lawyer in the country had said that without him there would have been no case. He said that he had met ministers of this country. That he would meet Mama Lucy soon. And as he was talking he fell asleep fofofo on the sofa without eating.

The watu wa film and the writing people stayed for five days and he only slept at home for that one night. Imagine. When they left he came back to us and when we lay together at night I wanted to ask him many things. But it was not like those years that we had suffered together. For the first time he asked how things had been while he had been away. And could I say. What. We had just been waiting for him. I did not want to ask him whether he would be going back to Nairobi.

A few days later one of the men who had come before in the minibus arrived at the house. My husband told me that he was a writer and he also wanted to talk to me. 'Anataka nini?' I asked. He was the one I had seen giving my husband that envelope. He also said he would be leaving with the writer because they needed to work together on the book of his life. Ai. This one did not look like a writer. He told Gogo and me that his name was Kahora. Gogo asked him what the name of his people was. He thought for a long time and said Wa Njama. Gogo asked the writer many questions about his people but we could see that he did not want to talk about them. Gogo says do not trust anyone who does not talk about his people. The writer's eyes were very watchful kama chui even if his face was like a baby. Round and brown. We had heard my husband calling the writer Billy.

When the writer asked me questions about when we met in Mombasa I did not remember many things because I had stayed in Olokurto for so long. This Kahora wrote everything down. He also carried a small cassette player and he put our voices in it. I could see my husband was happy to have somebody to listen to him after all these years. Gogo and I sat in the kitchen and we could hear their voices day and night talking politics and the future of the country. My husband said that the writer knew people that he would help him start an anti-corruption NGO, and that the book he would write would make my husband famous. He said that the writer was also helping him with getting government to recognise what he had done for the country. He said there was a lot of logistics. Gogo said that all this would also make this Kahora famous.

But we were also happy to talk to Kahora too. We told him things we had forgotten ourselves. When he asked me about our life in Mombasa, I was happy to have someone listen to me when I remembered my old home. He talked to Gogo about her daughter, my husband's mother and she told him everything. Kahora put our voices in his small radio. Then, he took our voices and left.

Now, it is months after the Commission and our lives are still the same. Sometimes I try to talk to him about things here and even about going to see my parents but he has become only interested in politics. He praises the new president all the time even if he was also in the old regime for very long. He listens to me the way he now listens to everybody with a wise strange face I do not know. Even those who are powerful now come all the way to see him because they see him as a leader. He seems to understand things even if I no longer know who he is. It is not like it was before he became a hero.

Our councillor even visited us for the first time. He said that he should join the ruling party and run for office because he is well known. He now walks with a confidence like the politicians. At the trading centre people greet him with respect, even those we still owe money from our time of difficulty.

We have not had a good harvest. I am now worried because Amina has to go to school next year and he has not said where the fees will come from. He says that the bank will pay him because of what they did to him and so we wait. In our room the glass award that he won with Transparency International just sits there with the dust of Olokurto. The blue suit he was given so that government could take him seriously also hangs on the wall being eaten by insects.

Kahora comes and goes every few weeks and they discuss corruption. They talk about it the whole day. I hear the word Goldenberg often but I am now tired of it. This Goldenberg. He has explained that we did not have anything at all, all those years, because the previous regime was corrupt. That if you do not fight corruption your life is worthless because you will be left with nothing. He says that is why he has to join the fight against corruption. Then he leaves again for Nairobi.

Gogo cannot walk because her legs ache too much. I kept the money he gave me from the envelope and I arrange for her to be taken to Narok Hospital. At times like this I feel that I am fighting for our family by taking care of Gogo and our two babies while my husband is fighting something else that is not with us and is far away. This corruption.

One day I discover that I am with child. He is happy. He says that this child will be born in a new country. A new country that he was part of making. He talks against the old regime. It has become like a song that plays for too long on the radio. I still have hope that the government will give him a job. He has stopped going to the Commission or writing the book with Kahora. He now travels many times to Nairobi to take his papers to different offices. He has an old friend at the Central Bank who was just a grade above him and is now the Deputy Governor. If he had not said anything about the stolen money he would now also be a very big man. Imagine. But we would never have met. That is the way of Allah. I want to explain all this to Amina our daughter. But how can you tell all this to a child of six years old?

After a few more months he has not heard anything from all the places he took his papers. Some days he becomes quiet like he used to be, before the Commission. We have come to have little again but at least now he is here with us. There is no more meat and little milk. Even with this regime, just like the old one, money is very important.

I have started going again to the small madrassa that I used to teach at every day. I walk up to the hills every chance I get. I also go to the stream and sit beside the water and think. I think about Gogo and the stories she tells our children about warani and the ogres they kill. I think about my nyanya and look at my arm where the bracelet used to be and left a mark. I think of Baba and Mama and picture them down at the Coast in Old Lamu town. I can see them heading together to the mosque and I know they will pray for me. He says we will go and see them soon. This government moves slowly like the last one and we wait. When he says this his face becomes like a shadow but then he looks up and I see he has not given up. Yet.

THE GORILLA'S APPRENTICE

That last Sunday of 2007, just a few days before Jimmy Gikonyo's eighteenth birthday on New Year's Day – when he would become ineligible to use his family's Nairobi Orphanage Lifetime Pass – he went to see his old friend, Sebastian the gorilla. Jimmy sat silently on the bench next to the primate's pit waiting for Sebastian to recognise him. After a few minutes, Sebastian turned his eyes towards him and walked towards the fence. Sebastian's eyes were rheumy, his movements slow and strained. Their relationship was now full of that strange sense of inevitable nostalgia that death always brings, even when the present has not yet slipped into the past. It was a feeling not without some pleasure.

Jimmy removed the tattered pass from his pocket and read the fine print on the back:

This Lifetime Family Pass Is Only For Couples And Children Under 18 Years Of Age.

The *Sunday Standard* beside him said: NAIROBI, KISUMU, KAKAMEGA AND COAST PROVINCE IN POST-ELECTION VIOLENCE AFTER PRESIDENTIAL RESULTS ANNOUNCED.

There was a sign on the side of Sebastian's cage: Oldest Gorilla in the World. Captured and Saved from the Near Extinction of His Species After the Genocide in Rwanda. Sebastian, Born 1951, Genus: Gorilla.

It was cold that Sunday morning, which was strange for late December. When Jimmy looked around, every one of the animals agreed, each with its unique brand of irritation. Eleven in the morning, when the animals were fed, was the best time to visit the orphanage. The church-going crowd that came in droves in the afternoon was still worshipping, so the place was empty. Until Sebastian had started to fall sick, Jimmy had helped the handlers in the feeding tasks: crashing and clanking meaty hunks against the carnivores' cages, and forking in bales of grass and leaves for the others.

He had come here first as a toddler. They acquired their Lifetime Family Pass in the days when his father was a trustee of the Friends of Nairobi National Park. His father soon found the trips boring, and for some years, Jimmy had come here alone with his mother.

When Jimmy was twelve his father left them, and Jimmy began to come on his own, except for the year he had been in and out of hospital. That year, he borrowed a book called *Gorilla Adventure* by Willard Price from a school friend. He had read it from cover to cover, in the night, using a torch under the blanket and eventually falling asleep. He woke up to find the book tangled and ruined in urine-stained sheets. He had received a beating from the owner that had increased his resolve and love for the Mountain Gorilla. For the rest of that primary school year there would be more playground violence on account of his beloved primates when he took the lonely side in arguments on whether a gorilla could rumble a tiger, or whether a polar bear could kill a mountain gorilla.

Feeding time was Jimmy's favourite moment of the day at the park – sacks of cauliflower plopping into the hippo pool, the dainty-toed river horses huffing. These times became the fulcrum of his weeks, defining his priorities and spirit more than his mother's war with the doors of the small Kileleshwa flat they now lived in; her diurnal conflicts with the cheap dishes which she had to wash as they could no longer afford a maid; their strange and sometimes psychotic neighbours; her boyfriends.

Week after week, year after year, he listened to the screeching conversations of vervets devouring tangerines, peel and all; the responding calls of parrot, ibis, egret: magenta, indigo and turquoise noises fluttering in their throats like angry telephones going off at the same time.

Real life was Evelyn's College for Air Stewards and Stewardesses, where he had attended for a year. Real life was the thin couch he slept on. Real life was his mother screaming that he needed to face Real Life. Waking up on Sunday morning and staring at the thin torn curtains of the sitting room, the stained ceiling that sagged and fell a few inches every week, and smelled of rat urine, Jimmy often felt he needed to leave the house before his mother asked him to join her and her latest boyfriend for breakfast. Real life was the honey in her voice, the gospel singing in the kitchen as she played Happy Families for her new man.

Jimmy was more sensitive to light than most. When he was sixteen a blood clot had blacked out his sight for months and he had spent most of that year in hospital. 'Picture an ink stain under his scalp,' the doctors had told his mum. 'That's what's happening in your son's head.' The stain had eventually been sucked out, and the doctors had triumphantly given him large black X-ray sheets for his seventeenth birthday.

After fifteen months of seeing the world in partial eclipse, light came alive for Jimmy in the orphanage, glinting off slithering green mambas and iridescent pythons, burning in the she-leopard's eyes high up in her tree.

Every July he had watched the two kudu shrug off the cold with dismissive, bristling acceptance, standing like sentinels blowing smoky breaths in a far corner of the enclosure. When the sun travelled back north from the Tropic of Capricorn over November, the two hyenas' hind legs unlocked and straightened, and they acquired a sort of grace. In August the thick-jawed zebras and black-bearded wildebeest heeding the old migratory call would tear from one side of their pen to the other and, finally exhausted, grind their bodies into the ground, raising dust and exciting even the old toothless lions. Over the last year as Sebastian became more subdued, Jimmy spent more of his Sunday keeping him company.

He could sit for hours like Sebastian, rendering the world irrelevant. In the orphanage, everything outside became the watched. And Jimmy knew all about being watched. What his mum called love.

That last Sunday of the year there were still visitors at the orphanage. They carried their apprehension like a badge a day after the election results were announced. All who passed the gorilla pit noticed the slightly built, light-skinned young man with brown hair, a zig-zag bolt of lightning on the left side of his scalp, above one ear. He would have been thought good looking but there was something wrong with his face, a tightness; a lack of mobility.

Soon the crowds would arrive, some from church, others rural primary school children in cheap, ugly browns and purples, wearing leather shoes with no socks, smelling of river-washed bodies, road dust, the corn-cob life, meals on a three-stoned hearth. Jimmy knew all about these children – had lived among them, and become one of them after his father had left and his mother had taken them to her parents' in Kerugoya for six months.

On holidays like today, foreign tourists would crawl out of minibuses and crowd the fence as they flipped through the pages of Lonely Planet *Kenya*, carrying water bottles, cameras, distended stomachs and buttocks, wiggling underarms, like astronauts on the moon. They watched with strained smiles as their children actualised Mufasa and other television dreams, as they chatted about cutting their trip short, with all that was going on. The children made everyone jump, clanging the metal bars of the cage, trying to get Sebastian's attention, throwing in paper cups, sticking out their tongues at the immovable hairy figure and having their photos taken. After taking tens of photos in a myriad of undignified poses, they would throw Sebastian several of these souvenirs when the warders were not looking.

When the sun crossed its highest point in the sky, faraway screams rent the air. The gazelles and impalas stopped grazing and looked up in their wary way, tensed to accelerate from zero to a hundred as they had always done. The old lions seemed to grin, yawning at a sound they understood only too well, and licked their chops. Smoke billowed in the air from a distance, and loud popping sounds could be heard. In half an hour, as if in response, the crowd completely thinned, and Jimmy was left practically alone beside Sebastian's cage. In the quiet, beautiful afternoon they started their dance, small mimicking movements they shared. Scratches and hand flutters, heads bowed forward and swaying from side to side.

'That must be Kibera. Maybe time I also left, old man.'

Over the last six months Sebastian had avoided making eye contact with Jimmy. At first Jimmy had taken offence, then he realised that Sebastian's eyesight was failing. He had cataracts, and his eyes and cheeks were stained with cakes and trails of mucus. Sometimes Sebastian would join their weekly ritual of movements for only a few sluggish moments, then turn away and slowly walk to the shade.

They could hear screams coming from Kibera and see a large mushroom-cloud as a petrol station was set ablaze in Kenya's largest slum. Sebastian raised his head ever so slightly to catch the breeze, and he began to pace, nostrils flaring and mucus streaming. He lifted his palm and beat it on the ground in time with the faraway popping of gunshots. Jimmy had read all the books there were on gorillas, and he knew all about their sense of community, their empathy, their embracing of death.

Jimmy had been born not far from State House where the president lived. The house he remembered smelled like the orphanage. It smelled of the giant pet tortoise that had disappeared when he was eight. When he had cried for a week his mother brought him Coxy, and the house came to smell of rotting cabbage and rabbit urine. Later, when he was older, Mum allowed him to keep pigeons, and they added to the damp animal smell of the house. It smelled of the bottom of the garden where he eventually strangled Coxy and the second rabbit, Baby, and drowned their children, overwhelmed by three squirming litters of rabbits; the piles of shit to clear. His mother found him crying at the foot of the garden and said, in consolation: 'What are rabbits anyway? Your father is a rabbit. Always up in some hole.'

He didn't keep pets after his father left. They moved into a small flat with skewed stairs and smirking girls in tight jeans who chewed minty gum all day and received visitors all night. Mum said it would still be all right because they were still in Kileleshwa and not far from State House.

'James,' she would call out, from the chemical haze of her dressing table, 'pass me the toe-holder, pass me the nail polish remover. Come on, James, don't be spastic. Your daddy liked that word. Wait till you become a steward; you'll fly all over the world. With your mum's looks you'll be the best,' she would laugh in the early afternoon, a glass of Johnnie Walker Black next to her. 'Then you can stop spending time with that old gorilla. You know, when your father left I thought that we would just die, but look at us now.' She would then put on her lipstick and flounce out of the apartment to meet a new man friend. (I've no time for boys. I need a man. James, will you be my man? Protect me.)

Sebastian rose, slowly coming to rest on knuckled palms. Jimmy watched the gorilla stand on his hind feet and move in the other direction, slowly, towards the other side of the cage. He was listening to something. Jimmy strained, and for a while he heard nothing – and then he felt against his skin rather than his ears, slow whirring sounds, followed by sharp, rapid clicks. A dark, tall man walked into view. He walked with his head tilted. And with his dark glasses and sure firm steps, he could have been mistaken for a blind man. He went right to the edge of the gorilla pit, squatted, and, looking down, spoke to Sebastian in a series of tongue clicks, deep throat warble and low humming. Sebastian bounded to the bottom of the wall standing fully upright, running in short bursts to the left and the right, beating his chest as if he were welcoming an old friend. Then Jimmy distinctly heard the man say something in what he recognised as French. He could not understand any of the words, except, *mon frère, mon vieux*. The gorilla-talking man walked away briskly, and Sebastian slumped to the ground and went back to his customary place. Jimmy saw the man walk to the orphanage noticeboard next to the warthog pen and pin something on it. He felt that he recognised him from somewhere; the way that one feels one knows public figures, beloved cartoon characters, celebrities, doctors or shopkeepers.

Jimmy scrambled up, picked up his bag and waved goodbye to Sebastian. Now that his pass had expired, the Sunday visits would be infrequent. But what he had experienced told him that those future visits, however rare, might be the most important in all these years he had been coming – an opportunity to talk to Sebastian. He walked over to the poster the man had pinned to the notice board. With a thick felt pen he quickly blacked out the theme and wrote:

Come And See
The Amazing Man
Who Can Talk To Gorillas

The man who now called himself Professor Charles Semambo knew that the Jamhuri Gorilla series of lectures would attract animal science experts from the ministries, and university students – but the rest was decided by the availability of rancid South African wine, grouty sandwiches and toothpick-impaled meatballs. He had learned that the renewal of future contracts was decided in a Nairobi shark pool – the consultancy circuit was no better than the River Road brothels he visited – and the lectures were where one met and impressed the major players in the game.

He could smell the mustiness and sweat coming down from the higher levels of the auditorium where members of the public sat. The bucket-like seats comically forced people's knees up into the air – and Semambo went through the two hours allocated for the lecture briskly, enjoying such minor distractions as a glimpse of red or white panties between fat feminine knees. It was his standard lecture: Gorillas 101. Habitat. Classification. Physical Characteristics. Behaviour. Group Life. Reproduction and Life Span. Endangerment.

After the lecture, he allowed the five mandatory questions from the audience. As usual, these were either of a post-doctoral nature from the front row of specialists or idiotic juvenile comments. One man stood up and pleaded for the museum and the new government to compensate him because a gorilla from a nearby forest where he lived in Kakamega had eaten his child. He said he had voted for the Opposition because the previous government had failed to do anything about it. Those around him laughed.

'Angalia huu mjinga. Hakuna gorilla Kenya. Ilikuwa baboon.' There are no gorillas in Kenya, fool. That was a baboon. The man started weeping and had to be led out.

Then the last question: 'It-is-said-that-far-in-the-mountains-of-Rwanda-men-have-learned-to-talk-to-gorillas. Do-you-think-there-is-any-truth-to-such-claims?'

Semambo felt the ground shift slightly beneath him, but as hard as he tried, he could not make out the face that had asked the question. The projector light was right in his face, hiccupping because it had reached the end and caused the words on the screen to blink. **Seeking New Habitat Grounds In The Face of Human Encroachment: The Mountain Gorilla in Rwanda.**

'Is that a trick question?' he responded smoothly. The audience responded with light laughter.

'If I say yes, I might sound unscientific, and you know what donors do with such unscientific conjecture, as the esteemed gentlemen sitting before me will attest.' In the front row, the museum politicos laughed from deep inside their stomachs.

'You might have heard of Koko, the famous gorilla who was taught sign language,' he went on. 'It is claimed that he is capable of inter-species communication. I think a lot of it is pretty inconclusive. So the answer would be no.'

The piercing voice floated again. Insistent. The face still invisible.

'I am asking whether you've heard of men who can talk to gorillas, not gorillas who can talk to men.'

The audience was bored. A couple walked out noisily. Then he saw his questioner. He was just a kid, slight and lithe, about sixteen. Then he remembered — he had seen him a couple of times at the Nairobi Orphanage. Was it possible? Then, unbelievably, the young man took a photo of him. The angry click felt as if it was right next to his ear, the flash lit up the whole audience and general enforcer of dictums such as: CAMERAS NOT ALLOWED IN THE AUDITORIUM.

'Excuse me. Excuse me, ladies and gentleman. I want to allow the young gentleman the courtesy of an answer. There might be something in what he says. I also want to remind you, young man, that cameras are not allowed in the auditorium.' There was an uneasy laughter. The herds needed their wine and pastries. Semambo hesitated.

'But since you all have to leave I will take the young man's question after the lecture.' There was light applause.

Baker, the museum co-ordinator in charge of the Jamhuri Gorilla Series of lectures, suddenly emerged from the shadows at the back. A naturalised citizen, he had lived in Kenya since the 1960s as a functionary of one sort or another through three regimes. He was useful because he provided a sort of international legitimacy to the thugs who ran the government. When things swung his way, he could be a power broker of sorts, a middleman between a defaulting government and paternal donors. He slid to the front of the podium.

'Let us give Professor Charles Semambo, our visiting expert on the African Gorilla, attached to the Museum for six months, a big hand. And please join us for wine in the lobby.'

After glad-handing all the museum officials, Baker came up to Semambo, his face red with embarrassment.

'Sorry about the camera.'

'Get it,' he said tightly. He struggled for a smile then said very deliberately. 'Please get me that fucking camera.'

'Charles, it's not that big a deal.'

Semambo wiped the sheen of sweat from his face. It was a bad move to bully Baker. Although he remained self-effacing, one could quickly find grants and fellowships drying up. He looked around to make sure no one was within earshot and with a nod of his head he led Baker to the side of the room away from milling bodies. He removed his dark glasses, reaching for a softer, more conciliatory note. 'Winslow, you have no idea how big a deal it is. I want that camera. Introduce me to the boy. I will do it myself.'

Even if it was fourteen years ago, Semambo clearly remembered the day he had erased his past and come to Kenya. He had met his contact in a seedy restaurant near Nairobi's City Hall. It seemed a confusing place at first. People sat gathered around tables, wielding folders and clipboards and pens, all having various meetings it seemed. Was it some sort of game? Bingo?

He met the man at the bar.

'This restaurant markets itself to wedding and funeral committees.'

'Ah,' said Semambo, laughing, 'Where the balance sheets of living and dying are produced. They are counting the cost of life. Very appropriate. Well, here is the cost of mine, exactly counted, in the denomination you asked for.'

The man looked at him and laughed back. 'I don't know why. I have to sleep at night you know? Our old man is friendly to your side. Me, I just think you are all butchers...'

A title deed, four different Ugandan passports with appropriate visas and work permits, a pin certificate, an identification document and his new name.

But hiding was not easy. There were always people looking. The papers would be drawn up in twenty-four hours, and he would end up in Arusha before the tribunal in front of more men in dark suits and unsmiling eyes. And the questions would start. The camera flashes would also be unceasing. A couple of million dollars could only buy you so much.

When he turned away from Baker, Semambo was surprised to see the kid standing not five metres away from them. He had been mistaken – the kid was probably closer to eighteen. He had good teeth Semambo saw – a rarity in Kenya.

'Have we met before?'

'No,' the boy said. 'But I've seen you at the Nairobi Orphanage. When you come and talk to Sebastian.' The boy's voice was a quiet whisper. 'Sebastian. The gorilla. He's dying, you know. I need to talk to him before he goes. Can you teach me?' The boy added breathlessly, 'He has maybe two months. He's old. Could even be sixty.'

'Yes. I know who you are talking about. And you are?'

'Jimmy. Jimmy Gikonyo.'

'Call me Charles. Can we talk in my office? Or even better, let's go somewhere quieter.'

'Sorry, but my mother expects me home early.'

'I understand. Where do you live? Maybe we can talk on the way as I drop you off. I don't generally allow people to take photos of me.'

'I'm sorry. It's just that I thought I recognised you from somewhere. Not that we've met.'

It was two days after the presidential election results had been announced, and it seemed as if half the drivers in Kenya were in a deep stupor and had forgotten how to drive. Semambo counted three accidents during the fifteen-minute drive from the National Museum to Kileleshwa through Waiyaki Way, then Riverside Drive. They turned off at the Kileleshwa Shell petrol station and the boy gave him directions to a large, busy high-rise off Laikipia Road. It was only 7 p.m., but there was a lot of movement in the parking lot where the boy lived.

Two girls stood insouciantly outside the grey building as if waiting for a bus. A green Mercedes Benz drove up and both jumped in, laughing gaily, waving and blowing kisses at Jimmy. The Benz almost collided with a Range Rover that was coming in. The Benz driver, an old African man, threw his hands in the air. The two young men in the other car, one white and the other Asian, ignored him, screeched into the parking lot and bounded out of the car. They also waved to Jimmy as they passed the car. Semambo noticed Jimmy's hands clench tightly.

There was a slight breeze gathering leaves in the now quiet front of the building. It could not, however, drown out the frantic hooting on the main road right outside the block of flats. Semambo suspected that this went on all day and night. Even from inside, one could see a long queue of walking silhouettes, probably going to Kawangware, through the hedge – a parallel exodus of the walking and mobile classes. Back in 1994 when Semambo had first come to Kenya, Kileleshwa was still keeping up appearances – now it seemed victim to all sorts of ugly aspirations and clutchings: tall ice-cream cake apartment buildings that crumbled like Dubai chrome furniture after a few years.

'Will this be fine with you? I'll wait here for the photos, then we can talk about gorilla-talking lessons,' Semambo said.

'You have to come in and meet my mother. She won't allow me to spend time with you if she doesn't know who you are.'

Semambo looked up through the windscreen. There was a female figure three storeys up, a slight woman. She stood there smoking, dressed in only a slip, one hip forward, shoulders and back slouched. Jimmy waved and after the most imperceptible of nods, the woman smiled.

Semambo never used lifts. He bounded up the stairs and was not even out of breath when he knocked on the boy's door. Jimmy's mother was beautiful. A beauty of contrast, of failure even. The frowns and lines of her forehead, the crumpling skin astonishingly frail. Semambo knew that many men had probably mistaken the same evident pride for intelligence. Her mouth and jaw, perfectly symmetrical, trembled with drunkenness and skewed lipstick: she seemed on the verge of tears.

'Please come in. James tells me that you are to be his teacher.'

Semambo could smell the whisky on her breath. The flat had an extremely low ceiling and he had to stoop once he was inside. She prattled on. He sat down and looked around. There was a bottle of Johnnie Walker Black on the cushions where she must have been sitting. There were two glasses – one was empty. The cushions on the floor were crumpled.

'I hope you like whisky.'

The flat was crowded with the triumphs of the past. There were photos of three strangers, a young man, woman and boy in different settings. The young man in the photo seemed the studious sort, uncomfortable and self-conscious, with his hand held possessively in every photo by a Claire fifteen hard years younger than the woman in front of him.

Jimmy carried both his parents' features. The world in the photo seemed to have little to do with the small flat Semambo found himself in. He could not stretch his legs and his knees were locked at right angles. Because Semambo was mildly claustrophobic, he noticed that everything in the flat was in miniature, as if Claire had had to crowd in a checklist to serve as a buffer between herself and a fallen life. The Cheng TV, the Fong music stereo, Sungsam microwave and the cracked glass table; all had been chosen to fit the flat's small specifications. Every appliance in the room was on; even the small washing machine in the corner.

The TV was muted. It showed a crowd of young men dancing with pangas, a shop in flames behind them. A washing machine gurgled as Dolly Parton sang an old song in the background. There were two doors to the right, probably the bedrooms, Semambo thought. He could, however, see blankets underneath the other wicker two-seater where Claire was now slumped, peering at him beneath suggestively lidded eyes. 'Thank God for whisky,' she purred. 'One of the last pleasures left to an old woman like me. What you do for fun?' Her voice sounded breathy and Semambo was uncomfortable. He was no prude, but these were uncertain times, and with her perfume and cigarette smell, her drunkenness and incoherence, she promised nothing less than forgetfulness and the loss of control.

She poured herself another shot. Semambo wondered where the boy was. He had started to acquire a grudging regard for him; most teenagers would have taken on a long-suffering sullenness with such a mother. Jimmy treated her like a slightly loopy older sister. He now appeared from behind one of the two doors. 'Mum. Professor Semambo and I need to talk.'

Her face went blank for a while, and the mouth trembled. 'I am going to bed. You men are no fun at all.'

She went through the door that the boy had come from and slammed it. The TV showed a soldier in fatigues creeping against a wall and then shooting down two young men.

'I need some air,' Semambo said. The boy beckoned and opened the other door. It led into a small room that opened onto a narrow balcony overlooking the parking lot. Semambo crossed over into the open and looked down at the behemoth of his Land Cruiser.

Some distance away, towards Kangemi, fires burned into the night, black smoke billowing towards the City Centre. The screams in the air were faint, the gunshot pops muted, as if coming from another country.

'While some fuss about whether to eat chicken or beef tonight, many won't see tomorrow morning. We are in the abyss and the abyss is in us.'

He turned and removed his dark glasses. His face was thick and flabby, layered with dark pudge and there were two large scars running down his neck. Jimmy felt that he needed to back away from the balcony.

'Do you think that it will get much worse?' he asked.

'Only when you see the fires in your parking lot.'

'I never thought that the end of our world could happen so slowly. This all started when Sebastian fell sick. Will you teach me how to talk to him?'

'That might not be possible. Maybe I can tell him how you feel. That might be enough. Let us go see him. His time might be nearer than we think. Just like ours.'

On the Langata side of the city, the screams and wails began. By the time they were near the Nairobi Animal Orphanage their faces were lit up in the cabin of the Land Cruiser by the fire on Kibera plain. They sped down Mbagathi Way, turned up Langata Road, past Carnivore restaurant as if driving around in hell. Figures danced in the road, yelling and waving pangas, grotesque in the firelight. They did not try to stop the Land Cruiser.

'Hide in the back and whatever you do, don't come out. Your kind can only excite them.'

Once they were clear, Jimmy jumped into the back seat.

'What do you talk about with Sebastian?'

'Can you imagine what Sebastian has seen of man since he was born?' They had reached the gate of the orphanage. 'Get back into the boot and hide.'

A guard came up to the Land Cruiser smiling brightly and peered into the car. 'Habari, Professor. What brings you here at this time of the night?'

'My old friend is dying, and I need to see him.'

'He hasn't eaten today.'

Jimmy sat back up as they drove in.

In the orphanage, the animals' nocturnal sounds drowned out the sounds of fighting from the neighbouring slum. Then, for a while, everything was quiet. 'I don't think Sebastian has long. Kibera over the last twenty-four hours has aged him impossibly. Nothing alive can take the past he has come from and then have to repeat it in old age.'

When they finally got to the gorilla pit, Sebastian lay on his side, heaving. Semambo rushed to where the wall was at its lowest and jumped into the enclosure, landing as silently as a cat. Jimmy passed him his bag through the front metal bars. Semambo went back to the gorilla, crooning all the while. Sebastian tried getting up, but with a giant sigh, lay back. A huge light climbed up in the sky, followed by a large explosion. Sebastian twitched without moving. Semambo removed a long syringe from his bag and filled it with fluid.

'Goodbye, old friend.'

Jimmy ran to the back wall and scrambled to where Semambo had jumped down. When he hit the ground inside the cage he felt something give in his left ankle. He hobbled to the middle – Sebastian had stopped moving. Semambo removed a small razor from his bag and shaved the left side of Sebastian's thick chest.

'His heart.'

Semambo plunged the long needle into the small, naked spot and pressed the syringe home, and in that single motion the gorilla sat up immediately. He started clawing at his chest where the injection had gone in, roaring madly and beating his chest until the rest of the animals joined in, drowning out the din of man, and fire and death.

Sebastian whirled his arms like windmills. Semambo stood without moving, and Sebastian wrapped his arms around him, roaring enough to drown out the rest of the world. Jimmy had scrambled away to the edge of the cage and Semambo's face turned apoplectic, red, crisscrossed with blood vessels. His glasses fell off, and his light eyes turned darker and darker as the two figures became one.

THE UNCONVERTED

That morning, in matatu No. 36 Dandora–City Stadium, I was thinking of the hardness of men's hearts, enyewe roho ya binadamu ni ngumu, as I had read in the Book of Jeremiah before I left for my daily work for God at St Stephen's on Jogoo Road. I remembered how the prophet Jeremiah had asked the men of Judah to circumcise the foreskins of their hearts and cease evil deeds. Next to me in the back seat of the mathree was a well-dressed mama on my right by the window and a kijana schoolboy in an Upper Hill School uniform. We were elbow-in-armpit squeezed. Those who were standing were being pushed back against us like beasts of burden. The words of Jeremiah made me think of the cruel and rude tongues of the street boys I taught at St Stephen's. The mama opened the *Nation* on her lap and it spread like a blanket across the schoolboy and me. She held one tip and the schoolboy the back page tip and he started reading Sports and she read Lifestyle and she started saying ai ai ai ai at the things of the world. 'Lakini dunia,' she said loudly, and the schoolboy sucked in air. Now, because of reading the *Nation*, she could not balance and at each corner the matatu took her flesh in its purple dress tent and poured over into my grey pastor's uniform. When I felt the joto of her body I thought of the Book and of Jeremiah to make the warmth of her flesh go away.

'Pole, Pastor,' she squeaked and smiled.

'Ni sawa, Sister,' I said. Tuko msalabani. We are under the cross, all of us. I had not seen her before on this mathree route that I used every day to go and do the work of God.

Then, I looked at the *Nation* for the first time. When I saw him I immediately felt a pain like that of being cut. That pain that goes into the marrow of manhood. And even the memory of the smell of GV medicine when I became a man filled my head.

There, on page three, was my brother Kariuki. I read that he had been arrested carrying three grenades in Eastleigh. Now the kijana and mama squeezed me as more people were coming into the matatu. I asked the mama whether I could read, just pointing my mouth unable to say more. And she smiled, 'Only if you pray for me, Pastor.'

Kariuki, the *Nation* said, was one Khalid Hussein Ibrahim, a twenty-eight-year-old suspect. Then, from somewhere in the traffic outside, I heard Les Wanyika's 'Sina Makosa'. The chorus 'chuki ni ya nini', maybe it was in my head. There was no music in the mathree. And the song became louder and I put my face in the newspaper. And I touched this Khalid Hussein Ibrahim. And I heard her squeak. 'Uko sawa, Pastor?' The schoolboy smirked at me.

I sat back but it was still my brother Kariuki in front of me. Even the sweat of my whole body and hands when I touched the photo could not rub off the black ink of this news. The image of the man who was my brother, Petro Kariuki, not, as the ink said, Khalid Hussein Ibrahim. The schoolboy glared at me and I felt in my heart for him growing up in these times. He would be in my prayers. The mama shut the window and the Yolanda perfume of her covered us and there was no comfort. And when I said, 'No, no, no, tafadhali, please,' she opened the window again. And I remembered Jeremiah again. I reached into my pocket for the piece of paper where I had written the verse:

Circumcise yourselves to the Lord; remove the foreskin of your hearts, O men of Judah and inhabitants of Jerusalem; lest my wrath go forth like fire, and burn with none to quench it, because of the evil of your deeds.

We were passing Hamza, Makadara, Jericho, and Landhies Road. Mbotela. Salem. It was six months after Westgate and there were grenades being found in the city

every other day. I turned back to page one without asking
and the lady looking at my face said, 'Sawa, Pastor.' Then,
she squeaked, 'Nani amekufa.' And now even those who were
standing understood. That is what death did. Someone said:
'Pole,' and others shook their heads. I read again about my
brother Kariuki-Khalid. I looked up and saw the Monday
morning faces in the mathree looking at me and so I looked
at those we were passing out along Jogoo Road instead. Tuko
msalabani. I read what he had done again. Even if he had died
it would not have been bad like this. I remembered the deaths
of those who had been accused of bombings in Mombasa and
everywhere and how the police made them disappear. In these
times I knew I might never see Kariuki again.

The mathree paused in traffic and the men walking past
to Industrial Area looked up at us. The manamba shouted
at them: 'Punch. Inda. Kusimama. Punch. Inda.' The men
trudged on, so the manamba laughed, jumped down and
mock-walked and sang on the spot: 'We Are a Walking
Nation. Punch. Inda. Punch. Inda. We Are a Walking Nation.'
Some of the men even laughed and then picked up a sudden
speed that left us stalled in Jogoo Rd traffic. I could hear 'Sina
Makosa' again.

A man, slightly older than the others in the Walking
Nation, face hooded in bright purple, legs in an extremely
flared pair of red jeans, appeared beneath our mathree perch.
He swept up a small dust-storm in his slow hunched approach
that swallowed the brownness of this part of Jogoo Road – the
railway quarters from the 20s, the torn plastic sheets of the
mitumba vibandas. His hooded face looked up at us with our
Nation – his nostrils open, his eyes red against the morning,
hostile in a measure I hardly saw any more nowadays. The
faces around him looked tired and dusty. His, I noticed, was
an old face, deprived and sly. I remembered it from all those
boys of the Kaloleni, Majengo, Huruma of my childhood and
Kariuki's, stuck in the ditches and grooves of that record of
want in huku Eastlands. 'Chuki ni ya nini', Les Wanyika sang.
The man now smirked at my pastor's collar, rubbed thumb and
forefinger and listened in silent glee to his finger music.

Now, we could see CBD buildings and the city in the distance and it smothered me in its choke, thrum and weight, its smoke blanket. And I remembered some TV news from somewhere that had warned that a grenade looked like a pineapple – the Swahili word 'mananasi' – and I thought of the grenadeness of grenades and the acid of pineapple, what it did to teeth, and how mananasi were God-made to fit a man's hand. And I had no doubt that Kariuki had done what the *Nation* said.

I got off the mathree while it was still moving. 'Wacha kungethia,' the manamba urged and I almost fell, still thinking of Kariuki. The manamba laughed, 'Tuombee leo Pastor,' and I smelled the brew on him. Yes, I would pray for him and us all. I had missed the mathree St Stephen's stage three stops mbali and I walked back from City Stadium to St Stephen's and the world had not changed with news of Kariuki. I reached the gates of St Stephen's that were never shut and stood before the dusty compound with tufts of yellow parse Kikuyu grass that would turn into wild bush if last week's rain kept up.

The cathedral loomed, a husk this Monday morning, empty of jana Sunday's song and worship. And Ochieng the caretaker, who I did not see till he was upon me, said: 'Habari, Pastor Kamau. Leo there are more boys.' And he stood there and then I suddenly realised I had not replied because he asked uko sawa. I sent him for the *Nation*.

I went across the yard to the Children's Home, to my homeless street boys who came and went with the four winds. I knew that some of them would no longer be with us today. We had been told by the police at Bahati to report when any of our boys disappeared. They said Al Shabaab was recruiting from the surrounding neighbourhoods for training in camps in Somalia.

Inside the boys' classroom, with the ancient desks and shelves and the smell of dry bare wood, I removed The Book from my desk. But I stood there looking into the large cupboard trying to remember all The Books it had once held and around the room where everything that had once been stored was now stolen and lost. Then, Ochi brought the *Nation* and looking at Kariuki-Khalid again, that first prick straight to the marrow of the bone of manhood came at me again: *Circumcise yourselves to the Lord; remove the foreskin of your hearts*; the smell of G.V.

Now I struggled to open the sacrament-thin pages of The Book with my sweaty dusty hands. The pages of the Book of Jeremiah breathed their age out at me stirring the floating dust. As I read the boys slunk in one by one, late, in sin to the day, muttering Mwalimu-Father Kamau in my direction. I read my last verse and shut The Book. I saw that three of the boys were new, and that two who we'd brought in from the street — Mambo and Kung'u — were no longer with us. That was the way of the stray-cat appearance and disappearance of the Home. I saw Kariuki's long form in a camp in Somalia.

The day wasted away, and I became even more frightened for Kariuki as my ears rang with the boys' voices chanting the multiplication tables. And I felt, still the injection in the marrow of things when I was cut and told I had become a man. *Three times twelve, forty*, the boys chanted. I made them start again for their error. There would still be time for the boys to repeat the Lord's Prayer. At the end of every line I would say his name: Kariuki.

When my mother took Kariuki in he had been like these boys, thin, his face like a panga till he smiled. We believed he could become like us, go to our Pentecostal church, eat githeri and do small business. The hurried way he spoke without ceremony when he first came to stay with us stilled under the hand of my mother. And in a year, his eyes lit up and you could see the brown grow in them, laughing and direct when he was asked why his hair was so kimira like mucus. These questions came from fitina neighbours who came in to Mum's 12th Avenue mini-market — renamed Mama Ngina Mini-Market after the First Lady's children's home near St Teresa's and known by everyone as Ngina's. Where Eastleigh, Majengo, Pumwani street children came in flocks for milk and bread till Mum convinced them to get off the street and join the real Mama Ngina home. Where the neighbours also asked for charity, and rarely paid at end-month till they started calling Mum 'Mama Ngina' because of her kindness. Kariuki would not answer their questions of his kimira-ness. Instead, he would just look at my Mum because she was his answer. Mum would shout and laugh at the questions and say, 'This is my new boy, Kariuki,' then turning to the boy in mock-anger, 'Tell me you don't know anyone in your family with kimira hair?' The neighbours would sign the Karatasi Exercise Book against the borrowed bread, milk and sugar, look at Kariuki, and shut the ledger that kept their silence, their mouths pursed in debt.

Even before I read the *Nation* that morning on Route 36, the whispers about Kariuki had come to me across Pumwani, Eastleigh and Majengo to St Stephen's a year before, through the transient flocks that came to us every Sunday to listen to our famous choir. This was still in the days when the former Minister and greatest choir-master Kenya had ever known, Darius Mbela, came to worship and lead the singing at St Stephen's. Mama Maina, a senior member of mama wa Kanisa, who had also known my mother, and who had one of the longest lists in that old faded Karatasi exercise debt-book when Mum died, tugged me aside after the first morning service. 'Kamau, nikii. What is wrong with you?' she peered at me. 'Aaauuui, what is wrong with you, Kamau? Are you with us?' she said loudly. 'You have not heard your brother Kariuki has converted? Why are you pretending? He has thrown away the name your kind mother gave him. He has turned Ngina's mini-market 12th Avenue into a madrassa.' I was still new at St Stephen's and I clutched The Book and smiled at the other watumishi women watching us. I smiled and she spat on the ground because she knew I already knew. But I feared for my place at St Stephen's and how I would feed my wife Gathoni and two-year-old son Solomon Kinyua.

'He even dresses like a mukorino woman, in a long white dress.'

These were the first harbingers of what Kariuki would become. The beginning of his becoming Khalid Hussein Ibrahim. I wondered if I had not gone to the US whether he would ever have become Khalid. We had both received our birthrights. Mum had paid for my departure to the US and she had given Ngina's mini-market to Kariuki. But what could I say to Mama Maina and not be guilty?

That afternoon in class, I now wondered about the missing Mambo and Kung'u in forsaken Kijee or Salem doing what boys do there. I did not believe what the police said about the camps but I would have to report to Bahati Police if they were not back in forty-eight hours. Maybe Kariuki had decided to become Khalid when he saw what the Mandrax, Roche and Ngwai of our childhood did to all those boys on 12th Avenue that we'd grown up with. Kariuki could not have been much older than boys like Mambo or Kung'u were now when he started wondering where he had come from. He might have become angry. I could see some of that chuki in some of the boys in front of me now. I could see the cold fire I had seen in the vijanas Kariuki and I had grown up with on 12th Avenue. It was like the burning ice that we put in our mouths when we could not afford Lyons Maid ice-cream, when the ice-cream man's bell rang every Saturday because Eastleigh and most of Eastlands was still safe. For ten cents we bought a small piece of burning ice and puffed out smoke with oboho coolness to be like the notorious Ochi Mastuko Thunder, the oboho thief. 'Chota. Deliver what you have if you do not want blood,' we screamed at each other pretending to be like our hero. We practised the Ochi Mastuko oboho look. Ochi had eventually been shot by Patrick Shaw, English Reservist, 70s and 80s Kenyan policeman number one.

These boys in front of me now grew up without even bothering to feign meanness, a deep chuki; they grew up with it in their bones. They grew up with two meannesses, the chuki of today's Eastleigh, Majengo, Calif, Mlango and Baha, and the second chuki of the papers, TV siasa, the *Nation*, the politician Sonkos of the world. This second chuki was a way out from the first chuki. It was grenade-throwing anger. It was the real *foreskin of their hearts.*

When the day ended, the St Stephen's church bells rang and I sat down heavily as the boys ran off and left me with an axe in my head. I peeled off my Pastor's sweater and shirt soaked with my exhaustion. I sat there for a long time and after a while heard the boys reciting the Eucharist out in the field with Pastor Muchemi. There was little joy in the recitation even in the childish voices straining for manhood. I could hear a mocking to their call to God, like the angry crows that swooped down on St Stephen's at lunchtime. Before I shut the wooden windows of the learning room, I looked outside in the dusty courtyard lit by a long pole with a single bulb at the top. The local gangs had smashed all the other security lights inside the compound and the streetlights outside. The boys' voices rose and fell in chorus under this solitary light, against the sound of matatus and going-home vehicles on Jogoo Road, the clamour of hawkers, and the dust of the day rose into night. I was about to swing the wooden windows shut when I made out in the eerie light the head of the tallest and skinniest boy, Abdul. I could see the teeth of all the other boys moving but not his. Instead, his face held a smirk. I suddenly realised that the smirk was aimed at me and not the ceremony to which he was indifferent and had never been part of. The shadows had played with his face and I had not seen him watching me till I shifted. I wondered why his father had not picked him up at this hour and where he'd been all day.

I knew Abdul's father, Mr Siad Abshir, from the old neighbourhood. He was an old Somali friend of Mum's from 12th Avenue, whose family and ours had known each other since the 80s. Mr Abshir was a courteous old man who had made generous contributions for the upkeep of the Eastleigh children that Mum took in and sent to Mama Ngina Children's Home. The Abshirs and my mother had even once appeared in the *Nation* newspaper with the former First Lady for saving boys and girls from becoming like the oboho thief Ochi Mastuko Thunder.

A few months before Mr Abshir had called me at home in the evening about Abdul; Gathoni frowned as I listened to his hushed tone. Abdul, he said, had been arrested as a terrorist suspect and taken to Pangani. Mr Abshir had been made to pay Ksh 150,000 for his release. I heard weeping in the background, Mrs Abshir and her daughters, probably. 'Father Kamau, can my son please spend his days under your care at St Stephen's,' Mr Abshir had asked, 'even if he is not a Christian? Till this evil goes away. I do not want him hanging out here in Eastleigh. It is not safe. If he spends a month under your care at St Stephen's, Abdul will be okay, like you, Kama and your brother Kariz.'

I thought about Kariuki's old neighbourhood name, Kariz, and how he had spent his childhood with us, and how he'd not turned out okay.

Now, I went outside. The boys had finished singing something about travelling with the Lord in the old ship and were walking towards their quarters for the night. I waved at the two watchmen, Mwami and Okoth, and they returned the greeting. 'Asante Mwalimu-Father Gerald.' I did not correct them. I had asked them to use Kamau. I noticed Abdul standing in the shadows down the corridor. For a second, it seemed as if my brother, as I remembered him, was standing in the shadows. I almost said his name. Abdul smiled at me and I saw two other shadows move when I emerged into the corridor from the doorway. There stood Mambo and Kung'u, the other boys who'd been missing all day. I remembered seeing them with Abdul now and then. They all wore the same smirk, the same loose cast to their shoulders and necks, the lounging attitude I'd seen from all the smoking and snorting when we were boys in Eastleigh. Abdul said something and the other two boys attempted a deep manly laughter. Abdul then looked up at me and said it louder: 'Father Kama, uliskia we threw another grenade in Eastleigh.' I realised he was very high on something. Then he said, 'Father Kama, siwezi make home tonight. I will kesha here till morning with Mambo and Kung'u?' The two other boys stirred behind us. I could see their lopsided crazy-high grins even in the dark. I beckoned Mwami one of the watchmen over and asked Abdul not to move. Mambo and Kung'u were marched to the quarters by Okoth. The giant searchlight of the night Eastlands security helicopter fell on us and swept past the St Stephen's compound. 'I need to call your father and ask him whether you can stay here tonight,' I said. Abdul looked into the sky waving his arms. 'Ama tuchukue one of those to Eastleigh. Chopper.'

Mwami laughed.

Then, Abdul said: 'Kweli si uwongo Baba is in Mogadishu. Bizness. What do you want me to do, Father Kama? The Eastleigh curfew. You don't know I am a terrorist. If I try and go home now I will sleep at Pangani Police.' He said this as if it was the funniest thing in the world and I wondered what he had taken.

When Okoth came back I asked him and Mwami to go back to the gate.

'I'll call your mother from the office,' I told Abdul.

He just looked at me and said, 'I saw your brother, Kariz kwa *Nation* newspaper.' His voice had changed. I looked at him and now he was still a kijana. The helicopter light came over us again and then we were left in the dark.

'You know your brother Kariz came to the 12th Avenue mosque last year and in front of everybody he burned his ID. Then he choma'd muguka and said it was because it had taken over his life. That's when he became Khalid Ibrahim Hussein. At first we laughed. But he started talking out in public on 12th Avenue kila siku saying he had returned to us from the Unconverted. Baba went to see him and told him to remember your malaika Mother who had taken him from the street. After one month Kariz started being respected and everyone listened to what he was saying.'

I remembered some of the other families from the old neighbourhood who knew Kariuki. 'Only your father talked to Kariuki?'

'Kwanini?'

'And the Adans?'

Abdul laughed. 'Only Baba is rich and stupid enough to remain in Eastleigh. Hao akina the Adans went to Canada.'

Now Abdul had sweat on his forehead, his eyes straining, his face loosening as if there were worms under his skin. His mouth tried to smile but something inside refused and his face listened to Jogoo Road noises.

'I even heard Baba telling Mama about you one night. He said, "You remember Kamau Mama Ngina's kijana?

He is now a pastor and a good man who will help us." Baba said that your mother was an angel on earth. A Kikuyu malaika on earth.'

'Why do you joke about grenades?' I asked him.

'Si, serikali says I am a terrorist.'

The helicopter light came over us again.

'When I was taken to Pangani they asked me whether I thought I was Al Shabaab. I told them if I was Al Shabaab they would never have caught me ... then look what they did.' He pulled his T-shirt down and along his neck there was a fresh, long, dark worm of a scar that came alive under the lights. Abdul continued, his voice trembling: 'Si-believe you were born in Eastleigh. Kweli? You, a Kikuyu from Eastleigh called Kama with a Kikuyu Somali Brother called Kariz. And now they are saying he's a terrorist.'

He laughed at the word terrorist in some kind of pain, the kind that always wants to share. And I was suddenly tired. It was getting late. Gathoni would be worried. I told Abdul that it was okay for him to stay the night. I called Mwami who walked him to the boy's quarters.

I walked to Jogoo Road and this time took a No. 58 matatu. Soon we were on Mumias Road past Buru Phase 5 and then Buru Phase 4 and the air was changing. Tipsy teenagers lounged against walls and stood by shops, weary mothers walked hurriedly to cook for their families, men in cars drove past us. Far from St Stephen's and my childhood I felt relief. Abdul's voice in my ear now sounded foreign in the bright Buru streetlight.

At Buru Shopping Centre, I watched all the Buru people get off matatus coming from work, shopping at the new Tusky's, getting haircuts and new hairdos at New Florida Salon, leaving Kagena Gym. We swung past Mateso Bila Chuki Bar, Suffering Without Bitterness, and looked at the men sitting in the outside area with puzzled faces, lifting the bottled burden of their lives up and down to their mouths. Here, the paper on my lap with the photo of Kariuki now seemed crumpled and unreal. I thought of Gathoni, and how she would now be washing our son Kinyua.

I got off the matatu at Phase 2 and just there on Rabai Road was my small servant's quarter. I could see the naked bulb through the thin curtain. Gathoni's slightly pregnant figure, bulb-shaped, gladdened my heart. And when I saw the newspaper in my hand, I looked at the photo and realised I could no longer really remember Kariuki as he had run in my head all day. In Buru Buru he had disappeared from my head and I knew I would not tell Gathoni because she would make me go and see him. We had already been through enough with Kariuki when we first met. I could not be his keeper again. The lights inside calling, I dropped the newspaper at my feet. And I was not sure I would ever see him again wherever the government would take him.

A tall man passed behind me and I saw him go to the back gate of the main house next door to ours. I did not recognise him. My neighbours were a family. The tall man turned. He was very brown with an oblong face.

'Hello Pastor, I am your new neighbour.' He had a voice like a mzungu. 'I am Maxwell. Maxwell Kamande.' I shook his hand and he went in.

There was some familiar music playing in the distance. Kenny Rogers, I think, and there was the smell of roast choma not too far away. I did not go inside immediately. I remembered 'Sina Makosa' again from the morning and it picked me up. Buru Buru picked me up. And then I realised I could hear 'Sina Makosa' because I was whistling it.

II

Almost three years later I was in a Route South B matatu on Mombasa Road when I read it in the *Nation*. There was Kariuki again, a worn and older 'Khalid Ibrahim Hussein', as the newspaper called him. He was to be released after being in remand prison. The police spokesman said that they had ascertained after investigations that the activities in the 12th Avenue madrassa that he had first been arrested for had gone on without his knowledge. Khalid, the police spokesman added, was a 'confused but innocent' individual who had been used. Further investigations into Mr Khalid's previous life as Petro

Kariuki from Eastleigh had convinced the police he was not guilty. For his own safety Khalid would, however, remain in police custody to help with investigations.

Three months after I read about Kariuki first being arrested in the *Nation*, I had left St Stephen's. I joined Methodists for World Youth, a Scottish NGO, as Programme Officer, Street Youth Rehabilitation. After six months my new boss, Angus MacDonald, an energetic twenty-four year-old Scotsman from Aberdeen, moved us to a one-bedroom Methodist bungalow in Upper Hill. He swore that he would make me a Youth Expert in two years. When I left St Stephen's I pushed Kariuki chini ya maji, into the background noise of our lives. I forgot about the St Stephen's boys. I forgot about how Abdul had disappeared – it was said to Somalia – to train as Al Shabaab. He left me a Koran written in Arabic in my desk drawer next to my Bible. In the Koran I found a small piece of paper. *You will learn. Abdul.*

I never learned Arabic and Gathoni and I did not turn around our lives in this row-row-row-your-boat-gently-down-the-stream manner that I describe. Over those three years Kariuki was away we went through what Gathoni said were pingu za maisha. Life's ropes. The Lord's fire. Gathoni lost 'St Njeru', as we came to think of him, after a miscarriage in that first year. After a year we tried again and we were blessed with Celestine Wangari, now nine months old.

That evening, after I read about Kariuki's pending release in the South B matatu, perhaps remembering the loss of St Njeru from those days I'd seen Kariuki in the paper, perhaps feeling more charitable from moving to the other side of Uhuru Highway, I wrote to Kariuki and told him about our lives over the time he had been away. I even told him about our losing St Njeru. A few weeks later, I found a letter from him on my side of the bed placed there by Gathoni. I read it and knelt on the side of the bed and asked the Lord to help me shed the foreskin of my heart. When I opened my eyes, Gathoni stood there with five year-old Kinyua holding her leg tightly and asked me what I was doing. I showed her the letter.

Dear Kamau, my brother,

How much I needed to hear from you. I wanted to write to you some of the times but time goes so fast in here and I was afraid. I am afraid because of all the things I did and how angry you were. How did I get here? Things happened from my anger. Niliona I had been found kwa mtaro. But now I come from Allah. Converted. I'm happy Mum did not see what became to me, her SON. I made 12th Avenue MINI-MARKET into a madrassa that brought bad people. I am sorry. How is Mr Abshir? I am so sorry. How is 12th Avenue?

In truth I am Somali. Kikuyu. Kenyan. In life I am your brother even if I was taken in by Mum. Now I am at peace. The police will release me soon. I have to work with them to find the people who used the madrassa for hiding grenades. Our Mama Ngina's. I have been angered but please trust me. I have been in muguka but now Allah has shown me the rightful path. Can I and you meet? How is Gathoni and Kinyua? I'm so sad about Njeru. Mum said always God is mystery. Allah is there for me.

Your Converted Brother, Khalid Ibrahim Hussein.

Gathoni told me that I must write to him and we started exchanging letters every two weeks. His release took another nine months. The letters came with stamps from different parts of the country and I wondered what he was doing with the Kenya Police. I thought about him constantly now.

For the first time in a long time I went back to 12th Avenue and the old neighbourhood. Slowly I was told how Kariuki had turned our mother's Ngina's Mini Market into an off-licence – Wine and Spirits – and then a muguka and bhangi den after I had gone to the US and Mum had passed on. Then, how he'd gone half crazy from the substances and was taken to Mathare Mental Hospital and how he went into rehab when he came out. Then, as Abdul had recounted, how he had burned his ID and all the muguka and started going to the 12th Avenue mosque. He had brought in new strange people who had turned Ngina's into a madrassa. 'How could he have lived all these lives?' I asked Gathoni one evening.

She looked at me and laughed. 'You talk as if you've been a pastor all your life. Your brother was converted just as you were saved in the Lord. He has a plan for Kariuki just like everybody else. Mungu asifiwe.'

I met Kariuki at City Centre Bus Station after he was released from police custody. I saw all the things in him I'd been wondering about – the muguka years in his brown teeth, the cut, dry lips and wraith-like form from the formaldehyde-lined alcohol, the brown eyes from the bhangi. He still held the stillness he'd always had, that aloofness that had made the girls in the old neighbourhood mad for him. But that quietness was now older, thinner, he was like a jinni, a ghost. He was dressed in an old threadbare coat, worn Bata Mshenzi canvas shoes, shiny polythene trousers, a polythene shirt without the top buttons. A stranger, ten years more worn than the *Nation* photos. A terrorist only in the imaginations of some stupid government serikali person. He carried a small carton with a green book tucked into his coat pocket. He smiled and his eyes gave off that brownness and directness that I remembered as my brother and I felt like crying. His movements were uncertain like somebody coming out of a long illness, coming into the light, like a new calf.

'Sasa, uko salaama?' he asked.

'I'm well …' I said, and out of habit almost added 'in the Lord' but left that bit off. Instead I said, 'And everybody else is fine.' I'd worn a T-shirt that said 'St Stephen's Methodist Choir' instead of my Pastor's uniform to meet him. He smiled, his face held against the sun. 'I'm fine. Just fine. I'm happy you are here with us,' I said. Even in my T-shirt, my pastor's collar in the wardrobe, Saturday, I felt the usual rift slowly opening between us. He was now impossibly tall and this made him seem more vulnerable, a banana tree in the middle of nowhere, swaying in the wind.

'How is Gathoni?' he said.

'Always tired. Tired but happy with the new baby Wangari.'

'And Kinyua?'

'He is impossible. But we've told him he has an uncle.'

'Wacha. He wants to meet me?'

'What do you think?' I said this without thinking but he just grinned, possibly too glad to be out of custody to take it any other way. There seemed to be too much to say now to get into the usual things immediately. At the Bus Station, we wound our way through the maze of hawkers' wares on the ground, bodies crowding out of the small stalls. There were some hard stares at Kariuki, his small carton, his colour, height, and thinness. I heard a hateful whisper behind us. Mushumari. Kariuki remained oblivious, his eyes were firmly lifted to the dust-choked buildings above. We came to the small Sikh temple, colourful and dusty, older than its surroundings, filled with small business stalls. I wondered about his time away, the madrassa and his links in old Mombasa town. We walked to the former Tusker bus stop on Ronald Ngala Avenue where the taxi was waiting. I said, 'I now live in Upper Hill.'

He looked at me, at the taxi driver. 'Do you mind if we just drive around the city? It's been so long.'

I knew he meant he wanted to see Eastleigh, the old 12th Avenue neighbourhood. We took a loop through Luthuli Avenue, past New Eden where we had lost our virginity to Tanzanian malayas, down River Road biasharas and butcheries where Kikuyu businessmen chewed at toothpicks, rubbing their stomachs in satisfaction after their lunch. We drove into Ronald Ngala Avenue again to Racecourse where that Rwathia building had collapsed and killed twenty people, then back to Kirinyaga Road where men stood haggling over stolen spare auto parts and the muindi shop owners looked on chewing pan. From either side of the back of the taxi we both surveyed the present but were caught up in the yesteryears. We went round Globe Cinema roundabout, where street kids drifted to the windows of the taxi and stared at us when we slowed down in traffic. Their lips were distended into glue cans, their eyes hanging mask-blank, and I remembered St Stephen's. Kariuki opened his window without fear and spoke softly to them and the smallest of charcoal bits seemed to come alive in their dead eyes, just a small flicker that immediately died though I could not hear what he had said. And I knew that Kariuki was a better man of God than I would ever be. I knew he was a good Muslim. We left the City, went past Kariokor where we would hang around as kids waiting for nyama choma scraps and we could still smell the burnt meat from those years and my stomach made angry noises.

We entered Eastleigh through 11th Avenue and headed towards our old street. I'd been nine when Mum had taken him in and this is where he had followed me around like a puppy. Here I taught him his first words of Kiswahili, Kikuyu, Sheng and English. Then, I felt a hand on my arm and turned. Kariuki looked stricken. 'Siwezi. I just can't. Not yet.' I asked the taxi driver to turn around and we drove away from the dangers Kariuki had left, to my family, to my new life in Upper Hill.

Gathoni and I pretend now that we live in the real Upper Hill that we are finally on the Lord's straight path of prosperity but the truth is that we are really living in Railways quarters and this could be anywhere. Muthurwa. Dagoretti. Pipeline. The large bungalow we live in is old and damp and Wangari is now getting wet lungs. That's what Doctor Nkendi said when we took her for a checkup. Yes, we still go all the way to Eastlands, to Buru Buru because we can't afford medical care in our new neighbourhood. *Wet rungs.* Doctor Nkendi went to school with Gathoni and she always gives us a discount. Here in Upper Hill we wake up to the 6 a.m. train's rumble and schedule our days to the Mombasa-Nairobi-Kisumu express timetable. There is nowhere for Kinyua to play so every Sunday after Church at Methodist, Valley Arcade we take the long route, drive through tree-lined Lavington, Riverside Drive and marvel at the life of others. When Pastor Muchemi left St Stephen's before me he graduated to an old Toyota Crown, and I bought his tea-green Daihatsu Charade. We are saving to buy a Subaru Legacy in eight years. That is our small vision twenty-something.

When we got home Kariuki retreated into his old quietness. I was not sure why I thought we would have a lot to talk about, catch up over what had happened to him, to us, to things over at 12th Avenue. We had a great dinner though. I was surprised at how Gathoni reached out to him, kept the conversation going and made him laugh. We all listened to her at the head of the table and I could not remember the last time I'd seen the lines smooth out from her face, and glimpses of the Nanyuki girl I'd been lucky to meet come through. I realised that motherhood had hidden her need to entertain, to be entertained, to cook for guests. Wherever we had stayed she'd tried to start a church prayer and bible group, a cell, but it had never taken off. That night, Kariuki stuffed himself with the yoghurt kienyeji chicken and coconut rice even if it was a bit watery. Gathoni had grown up boiling things and too much water had always been the default side to her cooking. I did not feel that we avoided any subject and that first night Kariuki came home I felt like Gathoni and I would really succeed in eventually making a happy home. There were moments I saw glimpses of the Kariuki of the *Nation* photo, Khalid the accused, the quiet man, the still maji ya mtungi. I really hoped he had put all that anger aside. I was not sure of his arrangement with the Kenya police. But I did know that Kariuki would never lose his natural *chuki* for authority. I remembered his roho for teenage pranks against the two-man police patrols in Eastleigh of our youth, a rocket cracker hurled during Diwali that almost got us shot. And I became afraid again. Before Gathoni put the kids to bed, I helped her clear the dishes, and she came up to me, squeezed my hand and whispered that everything would be sawa. She went off to bed with Kinyua and Wangari and from the kitchen I watched Kariuki sitting alone with bowed head, somewhere faraway. I wondered at his conversion and my being saved in the blood.

III

'Converted to what?' Saved from what?' This is what the man who had been my real father said when Mum left the changaa business on the banks of Mathare River, took to the Bible and opened what would eventually become Ngina's Mini-Market. My father chose the changaa den on the banks of Mathare River instead of us. Then the '97 El Niño came. Passed out on the banks of Mathare River he was washed away, a dry husk, too drunk to fight the tide, to fight for life with us.

Before he died he would come to visit us now and then, stop drinking and even stay for a week or two. Then, he would leave. It got worse after Kariuki came to us. The last time my father was with us the changaa really took hold of him and he called Mum a shumari lover for taking in Kariuki and giving him a home and a name. Then Mum kicked him out for good but his Airforce Uniform, the smart navy-blue sweater with wings, light-blue shirt and dark-blue trousers continued to hang in her room. I was twelve and Kariuki was seven and had already lived with us for three years. When the body of the man who had been my father washed up during El Niño we went to retrieve it at the City Mortuary a few weeks later. I remember him on that slab, a Borana-looking Kikuyu who looked shumari more than anything else, even more than Kariuki. Embalmed, drained of changaa, he looked more like Kariuki's real father than mine. We buried him at Langata Cemetery and I saw Mum cry for the first time in my life. A few of his changaa den friends joked and poured him his last drink in the coffin.

Mum never mentioned him again till I finished my KCSE O-levels. Then she said, 'Your father always spoke of America when you were younger. That is where he would have wanted you to go.' And so I started the Going to America visa dance of the time.

Over two years after seven attempts at different visas, with three different names and passports, I finally got my student visa. I remember that evening when Mum called me from my room. In those days I was drinking and smoking and chasing girls up and down Eastleigh like everybody else of my age. It was also a time of the first real changes in Eastleigh from a real mtaa to what it has become now.

'You are never to come back,' Mum said to me that evening. It was July and it was cold and she was wrapped up in blankets. The bank statements I'd used to prove to the Embassy that she could afford my upkeep in America, my bright new blue passport open on the precious US Visa page lay on a stool in front of her. When she said this I thought of Iman Adan who I had grown up with and was now seeing. Back then it was not so strange for a Kikuyu boy to be with a Somali girl. But I would never have wanted Mum to know. When I remember that night I always wonder whether Mum and Gathoni would have gotten along.

Mum had picked up the bank statement and shaken it. 'This money here I have to return to Mr Abshir. He lent us money for the US bank statements for the Embassy.' She sat back and wrapped herself tighter against July. We sat there and looked outside the window. You could still see clear across the Mathare Valley to Muthaiga where VP Kibaki lived. There were still city council streetlights in Eastleigh in those days. This was before the exhaust and the light industries, before the war in Somalia that changed Eastleigh because of all the money that poured in. There were still some farms – the houses, even the mud ones, looked province rural not slum undeveloped. We had not even learned to envy the things across the Valley, the presence of that wealth was meaningless as the clear moon of that night I sat with Mum.

'Go to Mr Abshir tomorrow and thank him for your visa,' she said. 'He will give you back the title for the mini-market. He is holding it as security for this money for the statement. She looked again outside the window. 'When you get to America you will do everything to make sure that your brother is with you after two years.'

Facing us was a photo on the wall cabinet that Mum had taken recently because I was leaving. There we were in front of Mama Ngina's Mini-Market just after church where we had gone to pray for journeying mercies. Mum wore the long, light-blue dress she always wore on Sundays. She seemed crumpled, stooped with Kariuki and I on each side of her. Kariuki had lengthened, his hair curled up, his face sharpened, a stranger who had wandered into the frame.

'Things are always changing here,' she said, looking at the photo. 'When your father was younger, just a few years older than you are now, he was in the Air Force and everything was good. The Air Force took him to America to train.' I already knew bits of his story, dropped like seeds throughout my childhood. He had flown secret missions in Northern

Kenya and bombed Somalis. And that's why he had started drinking. He had become a Ngoroko, part of a special force of killers who fought in the Shifta War. When he came back he bought this house for us and left the Airforce.

But now Mum said: 'Kariuki is your real brother. After your Baba left a woman came to our door. A Somali woman. She asked me for your father. I told her she could find him at kwa Mama Pima. Then, I looked at her and she was not the kind of woman to send into Mathare. I asked her to come in. That woman was Kariuki's mother.'

And so I learned that week before I left for North Carolina where Kariuki had come from. We were of the same father but different mothers. Our father and his mother had met in Garissa. The Airforce man and the teacher. After the Shifta War, Kariuki was no longer the son of a Somali woman but the son of a ngoroko. He would be killed if he stayed there. And that's how he came to us.

Mum said, 'He's your brother. You need to take care of him.'

I went off to Winston-Salem, North Carolina with this information and a promise to Mum to take care of Kariuki I soon forgot. I did not even come to her funeral because my student visa had expired. I could not leave America unless I never wanted to return. I'd left the Community College she had sent me to without a diploma. I continued where I'd left off in Kenya with the drinking and after years in the wilderness, in transient jobs, I washed up at a small Methodist church in Granite Quarry, still in North Carolina, and got saved. I remembered the promise to Mum about Kariuki. I went back to school, to a Methodist Community College to train to become a pastor. I returned to Kenya two years after the training. I had been away for a total of eight years.

When I returned to Eastleigh, Ngina's Mini-Market was no longer there. The quiet streets, even the tarmac from the roads and the open spaces were gone, even though there was much more money about the place. I went to see Mr Abshir and he told me that the last he had heard was that Kariuki was in Mombasa and was working with the people of a politician called Sheikh Balala. The small Methodist church in Granite Quarry, North Carolina had referred me to the Methodist Pastor Training school in Eldoret. During a holiday break I tracked Kariuki down and went down to Mombasa, to Old Town and eventually found him. When I'd left for the US he'd been sixteen years old and he was now twenty-four.

'What do you want to be?' I asked. We walked to Fort Jesus and ordered tea at a kiosk. He looked at me. 'I don't want to be anything. I'm now converted. I'm doing the work of Allah,' he said. I was sweating profusely, even in the shade, dressed in my Pastor's uniform. Kariuki was dressed in some sort of white robe and looked as if he had emerged from a cool-box. 'Why don't you come back to Nairobi with me, stay with me for a few months and we can see how to go about things? There is also social work there with the Methodist youth of Majengo and Bahati if that's what you want to do.' Then, he said something I found strange back then. 'I respect you and think that the work you do with street boys is important but I think my place is here in Old Town.' The waiter brought us our drinks, hot tea for him and cold sugar cane juice for me. And I sweated even more and he seemed even cooler.

'Dawa ya moto ni moto,' he said.

This was before all the US State Department Travel Advisories and there were all these middle-aged German and British women wearing almost nothing walking around heaving in the sun, dripping in oil and sweat. I noticed Kariuki's agitation when they passed by and smiled at him in invitation. He had become a very good-looking man, tall, slim, light, with Bajuni looks; his time at the Coast lightening his skin. He looked out into the street and his tone changed. 'Why don't you stay in Mombasa for a bit here with me? I want to get married to a girl in Mwembe Tayari.'

When he said this I saw glimpses of the old Kariuki. I became his brother again. And then I mentioned Mum and my promise that I would take care of him. When I said this something in his voice changed. 'Kama, but where were you when our mother fell sick? We could not find you in America. Would you even have known about Mum if it wasn't for

Mr Abshir?' He remained silent. 'But everything happens for a reason. Now, I want to serve Allah.'

I had never heard the word Allah said to me directly and coming from him I became angry. I heard something in his voice I could not change. We had grown up with many Muslims in Eastleigh but it was something at the edge of our lives, different days of the calendar: the Fridays of their worship and the Sundays of ours; Christmas not Ramadhan. I could now imagine him on the narrow streets of Old Mombasa talking in his new Swahili accent and I was afraid of it all. It was not real to me. I realised I had never seen him so serious about anything.

'Then, what are you doing with this man, Sheikh Balala?'

He looked into my face as if trying to see how I knew about Sheikh Balala. Then, he said, 'Look. Look. What do you see?'

The fat white women winking with their eyes of tamaa at everything. The men in their white kanzus. The women in their black bui buis.

'Foreigners own everything here at the Coast,' Kariuki said. 'The Unconverted. This is what Sheikh Balala is fighting against.'

'If you get in problems with the government ...' I started to say, and then I remembered Mum but I looked in his eyes and in them I was no longer his brother. I was another unconverted on the street.

We parted ways and I travelled back upcountry. I received a phone call from him a few months later. There had been political riots at the Coast and I'd been scared when I saw how the riot police had beaten up youths in old Mombasa town. When I spoke to him I was grateful to hear the fear in his voice, the old Kariuki I knew. He had nowhere to go. Sheikh Balala had been arrested and deported to Oman. Even though Kariuki hadn't told me, I knew he had been married very briefly but that had not seemed to work out.

I had been seeing Gathoni for a year and I was at Baraton, in the final year of my Bachelor's degree in theology and so I asked her whether Kariuki could stay with her family in Nanyuki till I finished my remaining year of study. I hoped the practical and religious nature of her parents would help him rethink things. But immediately Kariuki went to the Nanyuki farm owned by Gathoni's parents he found the local mosque. Gathoni said that when she was a child she always thought it looked like a small vanilla ice-cream cone – a white minaret with green markings.

It was already bad enough with Gathoni's parents not wanting her to marry me, a boy from Eastleigh. It was only when they found out that I was a man of the cloth that they blessed our future union. I'm not quite sure what happened and Gathoni has never given me the full details. And I have never become close enough with my in-laws for them to tell me. One day the family woke up and Kariuki had disappeared.

I finished my course at Baraton and set up house with Gathoni blessed by the Lord and we had our son, Solomon Kinyua. A few months before I read of Kariuki's arrest in the newspaper on Jogoo Road, I had my last major fight with him. I had heard he was living in a mosque in South C and I went to see him. It was worse than our earlier meeting in Old Mombasa Town. This time, I shouted at him for almost ruining my relationship with Gathoni and her parents. I was still dressed in my pastor's cloth and he was in his white robe. And there we forgot these contexts, our Eastleigh 12th Avenue street upbringing bringing back the brawling vijanas we'd once been. That was the last time I saw him. Later, I heard that he had gone back to Mwembe Tayari and was living with the family of the woman he had briefly married. Then, I read about him in the *Nation* in that Route 36 mathree. Petro Kariuki, who had become Khalid Hussein.

IV

It was a Saturday morning. Kariuki had been living with us for nearly two weeks. With all the memories I found myself wandering aimlessly about the sitting room, poring over materials for a Youth, Cultures and Leadership conference I was going to attend in the coming week. It was one of those terribly moist mornings before a hailstorm and I was restless. There was something on Al Jazeera about 9/11 and all these families were being interviewed about whether they knew their neighbours had been terrorists.

Gathoni, Kinyua and Wangari were out and I didn't know what to do with myself. I was distracted and was trying to convince myself that it was the best thing for my family that I search Kariuki's room. I somehow summoned up the courage and finally went in. His bed was neatly made with the green Koran lying on top and then I saw a small carton on the other side of the floor against the wall. I tugged at the sisal knots that held the small carton. Inside was a threadbare T-shirt, a pair of loose, cotton Swahili-type trousers, some clean but old underwear and some akala tyre sandals. Underneath were some papers: an ID application in the name of Khalid Ibrahim Hussein and a police form reporting the loss of another ID in the name of Petro Kariuki. I went outside and heard the chanting and the *shake shake* of a calabash, and the rhythms of a small drum. I opened the gate slightly, and there were about twenty figures, indistinguishably female or male, apart from the bearded leader. The strange team did a little jog, bop, bump of shoulders, in slow rhythmic piston-like movements with knees and shoulders under their different-coloured dresses.

They were Lejo Maria. We'd called them Orchestra Twende Mbio when we were vijana. They floated above the Upper Hill dust, the latest push for glass and steel infrastructure in our Upper Hill. A strange band from another time in this day and age of the Coca-Cola complex, the World Bank Building and Crowne Plaza Hotel. The band seemed even more incongruous than the dusty little Railway quarters that we were part of, that could not surely last any longer with all the development. The tall, bearded individual who led the band shook his head, making a chugging noise from somewhere in the depths of him, a strange atavistic sound.

The sun poured out sweat from the Lejo Maria leader and his Jik-White robe was soaked through. Then the man stopped suddenly; his band dropped their instruments and Upper Hill seemed to fall silent. The man called out to the skies and held a black Bible above his head with long arms that seemed to touch the sky. And the band members all chanted across the new steel and glass landscape. A few construction workers trudging past looked up in weariness and then wandered off. One or two hawkers eased up, held their wares – padlocks in all sizes, torches, electric and car battery cables – in tentative half-gestures but gave up when they saw how intent the band was on something that they could not readily observe. I heard one of a pair of hawkers mutter 'Jaruo ici' and it irritated me. I had seen Lejo Maria hundreds of times chugging up Jogoo Road and never thought about them. But suddenly their appearance in that neo-Nairobi landscape of new steel and glass, finally accepting Kariuki as a Muslim, made me curious as to the different forms of faith that men picked up.

Looking at these men and women in front of me, and their routines that had once seemed outlandish, I could now see a calm and peacefulness in their faces. It almost seemed that their leader was chanting away their worries as they whispered back in response. I wished that my own worries too could be cleansed away. There was something frightening about the leader's devotion. Then, I noticed one of the Lejo worshippers at the back of the small orchestra. Tall and stooped, his face was filled with the ridges of his forehead and his nose and his lips were bright pink. I could see the ravages of changaa. He removed a small bottle from his pocket and sipped at it even as he jogged on the spot and his head bobbled. He passed this onto the man next to him and they continued dancing. A small crowd of onlookers now gathered behind the band and that is when I saw Kariuki. He was looking on intently. I retreated quickly behind the gate and looked through the small peephole at him on the edges of the crowd watching like everybody else. There he was with that old stillness. After a while, he came towards the house. I stepped back, pretending to be looking at the conference programme as he pushed the gate open and came into the compound. I could hear the worshippers pick up their pace and move off in the distance. We both watched them through the light hedge as they headed west towards Kenyatta Hospital. I was suddenly aware that I was smiling and he watched me with a curious face. Then, he said suddenly: 'Would you have been so against me if I'd joined Lejo Maria?' I remained quiet and he looked around. 'Where are Gathoni and the kids?'

'Enjoying Nairobi. You've eaten lunch?'

'No, I'm not hungry,' He leaned against the fence and looked up at the sky and then turned to me. 'I want to invite you somewhere next week.'

I looked at him and he smiled. 'Where? You mean a mosque?' I asked.

'No, brother. No. Something else. We are doing something else. In Eastleigh. 12th Avenue.' He looked at me closely. 'Would that be okay?' The sounds of Orchestra Twende Mbio were disappearing in the distance and Kariuki seemed to be listening. I could not refuse. We both looked out into the now empty street waiting for the rain.

'Lejo comes here every Saturday?'

'I don't know.' We remained quiet for a while.

Then Kariuki started in a different voice. 'You know when I looked at the Lejo Maria preacher and his face, it's as if his whole body had disappeared into something bigger than the present. He was so at peace.' Kariuki went quiet and then started again. 'It reminded me of my first days going to the mosque. That Lejo man seemed out of control, but also *in* control. In a strange way it also feels like that on muguka ...' He looked away. 'Do you know what I mean? Did you ever feel like that when you became saved? This thing called the Holy Spirit.'

I was sitting on an old bench we had acquired from the church and placed in our compound and now stood up at his question. 'Is that what you felt when you became a Muslim? Like you are on muguka?' I tried to keep my voice level.

'No, it's not quite like that.' His eyes had become troubled and I recognised the old Kariuki I had known before I went to America.

'With muguka one feels the sense of control come on but after a while that goes away. With Allah one feels like they are finally in control. And it cannot be switched on and off. Like at peace.' He said this slowly, as if thinking it through as he spoke. I tried to talk but my mouth was completely dry.

Kariuki then said: 'I have been to hell and back, if such a thing exists. When you left you cannot believe how Mum became old suddenly. She stopped going to the mini-market in the morning. And from then on, I think I started looking for that peace that Allah now gives me in muguka ... I went through a lot in those years you were away.'

The clouds had now gathered and the heat had become unmanageable and there was the smell of a coming rain.

Kariuki looked at me. 'Brother, I am also at peace because you came back.'

I now wanted to tell him about my drunken years in Winston-Salem. How I'd wandered up and down America till I ended up in the small church in Granite Quarry. I wanted to tell him it all and how I had also suffered but all I could say was just, 'All that matters to me is that you don't suffer anymore. Stay with us.' My face was itching. 'Come back to Christ.'

His face became defiant. 'Why are you so scared of suffering, Kamau? Why are you so scared of suffering that you cannot do anything apart from the life you grew up in?'

I tried to say more. I tried to say that I had felt a great peace when I came back and saw him. He looked at me and saw I was trying and the anger in his face went away. He reached into the pocket of his kanzu. He now removed a piece of paper.

'Is this yours? I found it in the room. On the floor.'

I took it from his hand and looked to see whether he knew I had been in his room looking at his things but his face was back to the new calmness he had returned with after being away. I opened the piece of paper, read it and put it down between us on the old bench.

Circumcise yourselves to the Lord; remove the foreskin of your hearts, O men of Judah and inhabitants of Jerusalem; lest my wrath go forth like fire, and burn with none to quench it, because of the evil of your deeds.

He nodded, looking at the piece of paper, and the rain started and we went into the house and sat in the sitting room. The materials for the conference lay on the table and he picked up the programme. 'Youth-Alliance-of-Churches. Ati Youth,

Cultures and Leadership,' he laughed. 'What do these people know?'

I reached into the pile of papers and held the list of participants idly.

'Maybe, you should come – I could ask my boss to put you on the programme. Then, you could really tell them.'

But he had wandered off again in his head and then he said: 'All the places I've lived in – Mwembe Tayari, Old Mombasa town and 12th Avenue. When you see the hopelessness and energy, despair and hustle, anger and tolerance, all mixed up, something happens to you …'

He did not need to finish. The Lejo Maria music trailed at a distance like our thoughts of the years behind us. We sat there quiet for a long while. And sunk below the tall steel and glass of the new Nairobi, we waited for Gathoni, Kinyua and Wangari.

WORLD PAWA

J emimah Kariuki is becoming Chinese.

'Charity begins at work,' she says at every desk she stops at in her workplace, Domestic Revenue, ExtelComms Inspectorate. She licks her lips — a nervous habit from childhood — trying to recruit members. A few have promised to join the Chinese venture, Kianshi Multi-marketing, that she has just signed up as an agent for: Mama Kitu, the Domestic Revenue manager's soon-to-retire secretary, who has a sausage and 'Buru Buru free-range' eggs business; Bob 'just call me Bobby' Onyango, who offers green card opportunities for a price, and who starts asking Jemimah whether she can hook him up with red cards to go to China — Bobby says he needs a new product and he sees potential in their working together; Assumpta from Engineering. Then there is Silas, the intern from Domestic Revenue, and Dennis Wafula from Wires and Cables, who needs something on the side to help him pay school fees for his twelve children.

'The new Kenya is Dholuo and Gikuyu. Working together. Kenyatta na O.O. Oginga Odinga. Kenyatta Mboya — Okuyu meets Kisum City,' Bobby says.

Many at the office who have bought green card promises from Bobby are yet to go to the States and are disappointed. Soon, the office's informal marketplace can't stop whispering about Jemimah's new Chinese thing. Wires and Cables, who have shiba'd from the bribes they have gotten from stolen copper cables, start deriding it. Accounts starts looking for small ways to deduct her salary and clip her wings because of this latest sign of Jemimah's irritating ambition. All the messengers want in but are unable to cough up the Ksh 500 they need to join the Chinese scheme.

This is how it works: Kianshi offers the best consumer products from China at very affordable prices based on flexible payment instalment plans; agents receive Chinese goods upfront based on how many members they can sign up. Jemimah is determined to be the number one Kianshi agent of all the twenty-five based in the city. She met the head of Kianshi Multi-Marketing in Kenya, Han So, five months ago and has since gained his confidence. Recently, Han So asked her to come up with a more identifiable Kenyan name for Kianshi. She was his choice for that select assignment among many other Kianshi hopefuls.

Later, at lunch, Jemimah stands in the queue with other junior clerks from her department, at Mama Jacinta's. The kiosk has a smoky stillness and midday sunbeams bullet through the recycled wood walls. Once in a while, there is a large crack as the iron-sheet roof suddenly expands and contracts from the lunchtime sun and a cloud of hot githeri washes the interior. Bessie, Jemimah's work best friend, is closest to her in the line for food. Bessie's back is to the counter, so she does not notice she's holding up the queue. Assumpta, tall and beautiful as always, stands in front of her. As she listens to Jemimah, three cheap suits from Accounts breeze past her, get their lunch, hungry eyes on Assumpta.

One says, 'Sasa Beejing?'

Accounts is all male, a hundred per cent juvenile. Beejing – their latest idiotic joke making fun of the International Women's Conference in the Chinese Capital – is now doing the rounds in Accounts, spreading to Wires and Cables, and will finally be legitimised in Field Division.

Jemimah is speaking to Assumpta, who nods, her eyes roaming in their perpetual panic. Jemimah's eyes are caught by Assumpta's mouth – large, large and soft and painted carefully, and never grimacing or stretching. Bessie laughs and says, 'It's a private-sector mouth. The girl will never last here.'

Jemimah says at Assumpta's mouth: 'Not America, Chaina is the next world pawa – everyone knows. You need to buy new Made in Chaina. Thas why I'm selling Made in Chaina. Na-Sell World Pawa.'

'Yeah, yeah,' says Assumpta in her serious way, 'I went shopping in Cheng Du last year. Their kitchen tiles are very good.'

'Korea, Iddian, Firipino watever,' Bessie says. 'I forgot my purse in the office. Can you pay for me?' Bessie has been forgetting her purses and having her handbags stolen ever since she lost her Nigerian boyfriend two years ago and stopped living what she used to call *la vida loca*. During friendlier moments, like month-ends, Bessie commiserates on their present vertical immobility in life with a standard sigh.

'My sista mon, Jemmie,' She says this in her slow, stalking and deliberate way, in a passably bad Nigerian accent that, with time, has acquired old Jamaican reggae lyrics. Bessie is long rather than tall – like a gawky giraffe calf. 'Pay for me beans and chapati, please.'

'Jemmie' suggests to just about everyone that Bessie is unlikeable because she is high maintenance. She hates it when Bessie calls her 'Jemmie', though her short quirkiness has learned to shrug this off – like many things about Bessie – because of her marketing training at Kianshi. Part of her understands that her plump, round-shouldered lightness is complemented by Bessie's dark, long features.

'Kwisha,' says the young man behind the counter, with a smile, and a flourish of the sufuria lid. He bangs two lids together, 'Chakula. Food finito.'

Accounts are already seated, enjoying what was supposed to be Domestic Revenue's Chapati Madondo.

'Aieee ... Kijana, not again!' Bessie says with her elbows.

Kijana laughs, 'Last month's money. Mama Jacinta anakutafuta.' He bangs his lids again, and a cheer rises from where Accounts are seated. Domestic Revenue has to do chapatis and Stoney Tangawizi. They all leave the queue. Bessie glares at Jemimah who stands, oblivious of their food disaster, still talking Chinese products to Mama Jacinta. Mama Jacinta owns the kiosk and is making her way to the till when she sees Jemimah. It's too late for Mama Jacinta to hide. She is tired of listening to this Kianshi biashara every day.

'Kianshi is Chinese. They do multi-level marketing. Selling Chinese products. Wait a minute … here it is,' she says to Mama Jacinta, as she riffles in her bag. 'As it says here … I will photocopy this for you. No, you don't have to pay for photocopies. I'll do them at the office.'

Mama Jacinta holds up her hand. 'Ngoja,' she says. She quickly scribbles on her receipt book: Photocopy − *Jemimah to pay*.

'Kianshi is a large-scale global enterprise group. Advanced biotechnologies. Advanced… you understand. Kianshi boasts a rapid average annual growth rate − 270 per cent…' Jemimah suddenly remembers the video presentation on presentation, and juts out her chest to project her voice.

The kiosk has quietened down with all occupants masticating away their lunchtime. Light beams shooting through the holes in the mabati walls slant as the sun moves across the sky.

'Three years minimum,' Jemimah continues, still standing and explaining to an entranced but sceptical Mama Jacinta. 'I plan to be Kianshi head marketer. You have the Ksh 500 to join for me? There will be benefits later.'

'Chapo Dengu,' shouts a late customer, pushing Jemimah aside from the counter. Jemimah remembers where she is, makes her way and sits down, ignoring Bessie's angry glower.

Now Jemimah sips at her soda, too excited to eat because Mama Jacinta might finally sign up. Counting in her head everyone in the building they work in, she does not notice Bessie appropriate her chapati. Mlima House. She thinks of all those Ministries: Labour, National Planning and the defunct Heritage. Five askaris at the gate, the women selling felt-tip pens near the chain fence around the compound, the two police and four receptionists. Eighteen storeys in the building, fifty people per storey.

She turns to Bessie. 'Like the wheel of a bike, every ka-spoke is number one. With 10 per cent of kila mwananchi in our building − thas ninety people,' she says, removes a pen from her bag, and starts making notes. 'I need to invest in a scientific calculator,' she says. Everyone sitting at the Domestic Revenue table removes their toothpicks from their mouths and laughs.

'Shock on you,' Bessie says to Jemimah. 'Aloe Vera products are better,' she leans in to whisper, 'the cream tightens it *down there*.' Jemimah knows that Bessie is angry with her for making them miss out on madondo and chapati, talking up China. She will make it up to her when she becomes a senior marketer at Kianshi and take her to the Oriental restaurants she likes so much. Jemimah has not asked Bessie to join Kianshi. She fears that her sista will be highly successful. After Obi left, she thought of introducing Bessie to Han So's brother-in-law, Jin Shu, but decided he was too short for her.

Obi, the Nigerian boyfriend, was thrown out of the country leaving Bessie rich with a Yaya apartment, two hair salons in South B and West and a cyber café in Westlands, at least for a few months, till Obi started sending his associates back to Kenya for it all. The properties, as well as the dark platinum 5-series Beemer, the Hutchings Biemer furniture. Bessie was left with some Dubai 24-carat gold trinkets, a pair of Dubai Donna Karan outfits, a queen-size gold bed with a smaller mattress (concentric squares), her stocky puppy, Boss, who looked a bit too much like Obi, and an almost life-size poster of a Dubai Tiger, all yellow and gleaming and photoshopped and crouching in a mass of cartoon-like jungle-ness.

Bessie lived with Jemimah for a while and they became friends. Jemimah knows she is Bessie's only company at the office. But the days of doing Chinese, Japanese or seafood for lunch are long gone with Obi and his money.

That Friday afternoon there is no one in the Domestic Revenue's cardboard and mkojo-smell office on the fourth floor at Mlima House. Everyone is running around, collecting money for the coming weekend from their various office enterprises. *Saa nane na forty*. It is quiet. Jemimah is relieved and exhausted after two hours of detailed calculations in Mama Jacinta's small, hot office kiosk and is now thinking about the potential in the Mlima House offices. Mama Jacinta, it turns out, is a member of GLD, Amway, Aloe Vera, Herbatronics, and five merry-go-round schemes. When Jemimah hears this, she tries to convince her: 'Kianshi is special. All members are a FAMILY. Chaina is the next World Pawa. Everyone knows this.'

Friday traffic, shouts and smells rise from the street, the burning blue saucer of sky outside the curtain-less windows, grit in her eyes and the perpetual smell of urine and chemical lemon toilet cleaner: the things she is trying to get out of her life.

Jemimah remembers the last Kianshi video she received in her P.O. Box. VISUALISE, the video says: she daydreams, driving up Community, on her way to the office. But wait a minute – passing by, drifting towards the leafier Nairobi suburbs, further west into Karen, Adams or Hurlingham – a non-working and free woman unencumbered at 3 p.m. on a weekday afternoon. Following the setting sun in the opposite direction to her 5 p.m. reality, downtown Eastlands. She has calculated. With hard work it could take up to two years.

So, immediately she gets to work, she starts drawing up the generational multi-level mind map structure for Mama Jacinta and writing up her recent lunchtime projections for her sponsor, Mr Han So. She looks around the tired ExtelComms office she knows she will be leaving soon. Jemimah underlines beneath the projections she has placed on paper – IDENTIFY GOALS NOT NEEDS – then starts working again on the new name Han So has asked for.

'Chenya, Kinya,' she mutters rolling her tongue. Enunciate the vowels. She does not see the slouching figure before her for a moment. When she opens her eyes the intern she is assigned to train that afternoon is standing at her desk. Both his hands are placed on her desk.

'... Er Sammy.' Her head is still on the Kianshi figures and names, but she switches haraka. 'In-this-department-we-deal-with-telecommunication-revenue. We-get-photos-from-all-over-the-country-that-show-pipeline-meter-reading. Edit-and-forward-to-IT,' she says in staccato.

'Eh,' the boy says, and stares at the front of her blouse.

She ignores his stare and, after they go through the meter counter photos for half an hour, looks around and, making sure there is no one within earshot, pulls back her shoulders and says in a new tone that she has learned from the Kianshi video: 'Ever heard of multi-level marketing? While everyone is doing silly tu-small businesses in this office there is money to be made.'

The intern jerks back, 'Is this part of my internship?'

Jemimah ignores the Friday lunch beers on his breath, notes with surprise the expensive patterned yellow shirt he is wearing. Han So has taught her to look for potential signs of new agents and members for Kianshi.

'Nice shirt. You are a dyed-in-the-wool multi-level marketer,' she says and bares her teeth trying to smile.

'What you doing after work?' he asks. They are alone in the office – 3.30 p.m. 'By the way… my name is Walter.'

'Si Silas?'

He grins.

Even better, she thinks. A thick skin. Not easily offended.

'Skiza,' she says smoothly, 'I can't join you. Marketing training seminar. 4.30 Westlands.'

Walter walks away and picks up the phone at the next desk, dials and stares at her.

Jemimah fishes a small mirror from her bag and carefully moves it over the new red suit with padded shoulders that she is wearing. It is one of a batch she bought in Ngara after joining Kianshi. She has thrown out the chiffon dresses with erratic hemlines and balloon shoulders that she wore when she had moved to Nairobi from Karatina. Out too, the softer skirts with shorter hemlines and white blouses bought from Wangari at Posta. Bessie had always made fun of her, saying the clothes made her blend into ExtelComms like a good Made in China weave. She purses her lips, and applies lip gloss over a cold sore.

Some men from Wires and Cables have joined the intern in looking at her from over the far corner of the partitioned office. One imitates her with a clipboard. She ignores them: decides that, after all, Walter the Intern is not going places with Kianshi and heads out to meet Han So.

They meet near Parliament at the C & A coffee house. Whenever they meet, Han So likes to watch how the establishment works and even asks her questions that make her feel good about herself.

'You think they make money here?' Han So asks. 'Where do they buy coffee? Who are their main customers?' Silly questions, she thinks.

She pretends to study the C & A coffee shop. After the mandatory month's training, she has been judging everyone around her as either a multi-level marketer or a non-marketer. Or, even worse, the bottom of the marketing heap – the traditional marketer. Han So has trained her to be wary of these. Traditional marketers like the father of her eight-year-old son, Kim. Traditional marketers like her parents back in Karatina. At first, even with Han So's training, the criteria she used to tell who were marketers, non-marketers and traditional marketers was vague and instinctive. But now she has watched Han So at work and she has caught on to some of his mantras.

'I think this coffee shop is in the shifting stage from non-marketer to marketer,' she offers.

Han So looks at her blankly, like she is mad. When she tries to tell him about Mlima House he does not seem too excited. He instead asks her about ExtelComms products, and listens carefully. She asks Han So about the results of her latest test and he says the results are yet to arrive.

When Jemimah had gone to the Kianshi opening seminar at KICC, she had been impressed by Han So's opening presentation, which she had paid Ksh 500 to attend.

'You must avoid the number one problem of Africa: thinking luck, not hard work, will solve your problems.' Now, this is something she never tires of telling her focus group during the seminars Kianshi arranges. The twenty-five Kianshi Nairobi agents are split into five focus groups that meet every Saturday to discuss marketing strategies. After the strategy sessions anyone is allowed to volunteer to give a testimony. Han So has said that she has improved in her testimony telling.

She never tires of playing what they call 'the testimony game' with the five other multi-level marketers in her Kianshi focus group every Saturday. Each session is Ksh 1,000. All have undergone the one-month training period together. Jemimah can't always remember their names. They are a sight – an exercise in Han So's faith. An old, recovering alcoholic who lost his senior marketing position at one of Kenya's largest HMOs, some bright kid just out of International School of Kenya, Han So's ever-grinning brother-in-law, Jin Shu. The rest hover on the edges of Jemimah's memory. The nervous oddity of the group doesn't matter in the face of Han So's motivational speeches, 'Magnifying glass catch sun, bring power, focus energy. Then fire! Catch potential!' They all cheer and become one but whenever they try to use the same words it doesn't sound right. They've all tried this public voice in the mirror. 'Magnifying glass catch sun, bring power, focus energy. Then fire! Catch potential!'

At first, she used her experience from her time at the New Redeemer Church of Christ in Karatina where she had trained to become a pastor before she came to Nairobi. She had to leave while she was still training after she started an affair with Pastor Muremi who refused to leave his wife for her, even after they had been seeing each other for at least one year. She thinks that the Karatina church testimonies did not work at Kianshi because of these unhappy memories. Han So encourages the use of personal experiences to sell products. They also practise this in the focus group. 'When I first arrived in Nairobi two years ago, I lived with my relatives ... Mbari ya Mundia', she says. 'They hated me, but I loved them. I know I will meet many people like the Mundias when I am out there selling.' In reality, the Mundias she uses as a teaching guide were vaguely hostile and pleasantly indifferent to Jemimah. She finished the testimony by saying: 'In the end, Mundia wa Steven got me my first job because I had sold myself and marketed my skills. I moved to a high-rise bed-sitter in Kayole. In Nairobi, you start small small, so I started saving for better things. And I am here now.'

Presently, they finish their coffee at C & A and because Han So is still observing what is going on in the shop, Jemimah removes her notebook. Han So watches: how fast the waiters go to new clients? How fast the orders are? What everybody is ordering? Jemimah thinks of how far she has come since she joined Kianshi. With her new expertise she now categorises everything aloud to practise her marketing voice: national politicians, newscasters and people starring in TV ads as either traditional marketers or multi-level marketers. During such sessions at home, her current come-we-stay husband, Miano wa Miano, curses and mutes the TV.

'Sawa, let's listen to YOU, nye nye nye … nye nye nye,' he says. 'All the time. Nye nye nye … Go on and on. Endelea …' Miano wa Miano urges with a hardcore relish that he has developed from being a spare parts dealer on Kirinyaga Road. Miano wa Miano knows how to sell spare parts and makes a lot of money so she cannot understand his contempt for her new venture. 'Where is the demand?' he asks, in anger. Miano wa Miano took care of her while she was still finding her way in Nairobi. But, a few months ago, there was a huge crackdown on spare parts as part of a racket of stolen cars in Nairobi and the cash has dried up.

Once, during these regular TV battles, Jemimah switched off the TV in a huff during one of Miano Wa Miano's favourites – *Nderemo ya Mabingwa. Win-A-House Contest.* She then watched him calculating whether her action warranted some form of physical action. He gave her a speculative look and all he said was: 'Niki-win the house; you won't be coming.' She ignored him as he walked out of the door and made him sleep on the floor after he came back after three days, drunk, meek and dishevelled. He becomes quiet when he drinks because of the lean days on Kirinyaga Road.

'Being multi-marketer, very challenge,' Han So has told her when she tells him about the lack of support at home.

Jemimah recognises the uneasy détente that becoming Chinese has created between her and Miano wa Miano. She finds him useless now that she has more money but likes the new sense of power over a man. She wonders what he'll say when she tells him about her son. For now, she is too busy to engage in a retaliatory aggressive short-term competition with him.

And so her son, Kim, remains undiscovered by him.

The after-work crowd starts thinning in the coffee shop, heading to the bars. Han So is satisfied with his observations and they leave.

On Monday, happy and high after three weekend meetings with Han So, Jemimah comes to work wearing a dress from China that Han So has given her from the Kianshi products. He always says that the best way to market Chinese goods is also to use them.

'It is a Qipao,' Han has told her, and she repeats that to all at work. It is a long flowing deep-blue garment with aquamarine herons on the breast flowing over the shoulder to the small of her back. Jemimah ignores the snickers from Wires and Cables.

Han So explained: 'Also called Cheongsam. Not only for Chinese woman but beautiful all woman. Come in many style. You can sell here in Kinya?'

Her boss, PK Maina, calls her into his office. 'Kama unataka kuvaa hiyo stupid national dress you do it in your home.'

'This is Chinese silk! It is called Kipao.' She storms out of his office. People stare and laugh through the glass partition of PK Maina's office.

'Mambo ya wanawake,' he mutters, shaking his head.

Even Bessie is not as supportive. 'Imagine me coming to work in a Nigerian agbada when I was with Obi. If and when I could. And Jemmie, you know what I mean – I had the money and the man.' When Bessie says this, she places her fingers on the sides of Jemimah's eyes and tugs upwards: 'Chinese.' Sideways: 'Japanese.' And downwards: 'Portuguese.'

Bessie then puts her hand flutteringly to her chest, leans back and says: 'Nigerian.'

Both women start laughing hard.

Over the next month, Jemimah notices that Han So now asks her more and more about ExtelComms products – and one day he asks her whether she can get copies of shipment invoices, credit notes and local purchase orders from the office. When she manages to sneak away the documents he wants she is surprised at how happy he seems. He even promises her more Kianshi products over the next month.

Then one day he asks: 'Your boss is good man... can talk?'

She pretends to think and says: 'He's a traditional marketer.' Two years ago, she had an affair with her boss, PK Maina, when he was not the present brusque top-heavy man given to picking his teeth to distraction in the afternoons at the office. She was still in the white blouse, tight skirt phase. Jemimah stopped sleeping with him when he started telling everyone he was 'eating Beejing.'

Soon after, Jemimah met Miano wa Miano and moved in with him, and she hasn't thought of PK Maina in a while. She asks Han So about the differential margins between Kianshi cosmetics and golf equipment. His eyes glaze over from behind his thick glasses and he curses in Chinese. 'No time for joke. Time for serious. You introduce me to your boss?' he says with a smile, tapping his chest, and almost pushing his hand into her face.

When he calms down, he asks: 'You know... er how you say it... where government company you work for buys...' He pretends to be picking up a telephone receiver. Bessie always tells her that men will change after a certain period of knowing them and she wonders whether this is what is happening with Han So. She tells Han So about PK Maina's recent scorn at the Chinese dress he gave her and this time he laughs and says, 'Time for serious. You introduce me to boss?' She decides to forgive Han So for his strange behaviour.

Jemimah invites Han So to her office and introduces him to PK Maina. She leaves the two of them alone and they talk for three hours. Now and then she turns, everyone does, and watches the two through the transparent government glass. Finally, they laugh and shake hands. When Han So comes out of PK's office she walks him out. She can hear Accounts making their loud stadium whispers, 'Beejing, Beejing na Ka-Chinese boyfriend.' She also hears Bessie's loud laugh.

When she comes back, Bessie says: 'Now you know how I used to feel when you'd call Emenkua, 'Obi''.

'Your boss he good man,' Han So says to her later when they meet after work at the open-air restaurant near KICC. She realises, for the first time, that he's much shorter than her. She has always thought of him as big. She can put her hands all around his upper frame. Until now, she has never contemplated physical contact with him. Now she notices his small tight thrusting hips, and a charcoal-coloured mouth – smoke and beer and a certain knowledge. She wonders what their children would look like. Pink to medium-brown depending on the time of day, she decides. She thinks about her son and Miano Wa Miano.

Last night, she kept waking Miano wa Miano up with screams from a recurring bad dream. Her son Kim appeared in a field of maize in the dream. He wore his grey, black and white boarding academy uniform. Starting at the foot of the field he wandered into the long stalks and she watched as the lilting green leaves started to whirr like blades as he walked in harsh sunlight.

Miano wa Miano woke up to her thrashing and, still semi-drunk from the previous night, found this arousing. She pushed aside his gropings. These dreams have been going on for weeks. Miano wa Miano has decided that Jemimah has kifafa. He has also found a payslip lying around, full of scribbles and evidence that there is another budgetary presence in her life, but he has said nothing.

Han So is saying, 'Your boss is good man. He agree to buy Chinese phone. We soon talk about computer. You do not listen. This is important.' She wonders whether she should leave Miano wa Miano because her life with him is now affecting her concentration during these Kianshi meetings with Han So.

'I am sorry,' she says in her best Kianshi voice. 'I have come up with a name that sounds Kenyan for Kianshi. Kenshi,' she tells him. He nods.

'When are our products arriving?'' she asks.

'Factory in Shanghai burn down. Six months.'

Later that afternoon, PK Maina passes by her desk and whispers: 'I like your kajamaa. Anaelewa Kenya. He taught me some Chinese words.' He leers: 'You know what tongoza in Chinese is?'

The moment Jemimah has been dreading comes. Han So is to visit her two-room high-rise bed-sitter in Kayole to see whether it is safe to store Kianshi products there in the future. She cannot remember what the pamphlets says about home storage and she is worried that her home will not be good enough as a Kianshi marketing outlet. She is scared that when Han So sees where she lives he will think she cannot make a good Kianshi agent because she is not ambitious enough and lives in a hole. She has postponed visiting her son Kim at his Academy in Athi so she can receive some goods Han So has said he wants stored as testing for a bigger Kianshi venture. The school no-visit she can tell will be another trigger on the escalating hostility from her mother, whom she has not spoken to for three weeks.

Jemimah makes sure the maid removes all the wet clothes hanging in the small corridor leading to her room. She removes the vitambaas from the red velvet jumbo sofa set, looks at them and puts them back. She opens all the windows trying to make the room larger and removes a cracked mirror that hangs on top of the TV. She stares at the small pile of books from her days as a Sociology student at Maseno. Looking at a household list on the wall, an account from one of the local shops in which she has scribbled the little Chinese she has learned, Jemimah feels small and hopeless. She crosses out the Chinese words. They are from a book Han So lent her when she joined Kianshi. He has said that, as the most promising agent, when the time comes, she will go for training at Kianshi headquarters in Beijing. She takes her monthly shopping list down from the kitchen wall.

Mwangi Shop List – July

Mafuta Boy 1kg
Milk (30 pkt) niúnǎi
Bread (8) miànbǎo
Ugari

Ketepa
Tomatoes
Waru
Boga
Degu
Beans
Bebe
Hey-Ho
Mchere

With nothing to do but wait till Han So calls her, she walks out of the door and, looking down from the dangerous balcony with the low railing, her phone rings. She can see the city in the distance, and when she turns she can see the huge white emptiness of the quarry behind the block of flats.

'Haai,' she says into the phone.

'Mathee,' she hears. It's her son, Kim.

As she looks down from the balcony she is surprised to see Han So emerge from a small Canter parked outside the block of bed-sitters. She had hoped he would call first.

'Mathee …'

'Kimani.'

'I couldn't make it… this weekend.' she says. 'Sorry.' She feels like crying and is not sure why.

'Mathee. Una homa? You sound funny.'

'Kimani. English. English. Argh… leave that Sheng, Daddy… How are you?'

She can see below how the neighbourhood kids have gathered around Han So. 'Jackie Chan, Jackie Chan,' they shout, chopping their hands and kicking in the air. Han So laughs and shouts and, with a flourish, takes a Kung Fu stance and kicks out in the air:

'Ha!' The kids cheer.

Han So looks up, sees her and waves her down. Relieved, thinking he might not come up after all, she clacks down the five flights of stairs in heels, still on the phone. Looking at the huge white quarry at a distance she feels a sudden heat on her face, the white dust it brings caking her face.

'Mathee. Mi si mlami.' her son says. 'Sitaki English.'

'Kimani!'

'Okay. When are you coming? Will you bring Kenchic?"

People are lighting jikos everywhere on the corridors of each floor. Saturday maize and beans, githeri gas everywhere, the smells of her mother's life. There is a burst water pipe. Water overflows from the third floor to the second in a stink.

'Soon. Soon,' she says to her son. 'Your school is so nice. Green, big. Like where I grew up.'

'Mum imejaa wa Cambodia.'

'Kambas cannot be trusted but they are not bad people … Are there any Chinese children?' she asks.

'Hakuna ma Jackie Chan.'

Jemimah paces herself, tiptoeing through the last flight of stairs – she wants to finish with her son before she meets Han So. On the ground floor. She sees that some of the bigger kids are playing with him. He can't see her. The kids stare at her phone. If they were alone and at night she would lose it.

'Bye Dadee… I will call tomorrow.' She straightens her dress. Her face feels tight with white dust from the quarry.

'They like leettle monkeys,' Han So smiles, looking at the crowd of kids gathered around.

Jemimah is thankful that Miano wa Miano is not at home. He has not come in since last night, Friday. Han So's men start stacking boxes everywhere in the small house.

Jemimah is happy when Han So doesn't ask to go up to her house.

They watch the men carry the boxes upstairs. When one box falls down the stairs Han So curses furiously: 'Carefle. Carefle.' Small containers and packets of seasoning fall and flutter to the ground. Han So hands out an armful to Jemimah.

'For you. Good friend of Han So. Chinese seasoning. Like Loyco.'

She laughs. How long did it take for her to stop saying 'Loyco'?

As the men go up and down she notices an oil stain on one of the boxes. 'For cooking. Chinese fat for cooking. Some for you. Good friend of Han So,' he says.

He turns to the small kiosk metres away from where they stand. 'Come, let us dleenk soda dleenk,' he says, his hands fishing into his pockets. He waves the kids over and ends up buying over fifty sodas and thirty mandazis.

'Ha ha ha. For good fliend of Han So.'

Han So leaves her and goes to talk to Mwangi, the owner of the kiosk, for about twenty minutes. Han So then comes outside and waves at the men. They bring over five cartons from the Canter. Jemimah sees Mwangi shaking his head.

'Angalia hii label. These Omo packets are torn and they are in Chinese.'

'Half-plice. For good friend of Han So,' Han So says. Mwangi stops when he hears this.

'Half-plice?' he asks. Then he laughs and shakes Han So's hand.

'Money half yours,' Han So whispers to Jemimah as they walk out. She likes his lips near her ear, his hair tickles and his breath is strange and exciting. 'If you can supply this area with these goods. Boxes have electrical goods from China... silk from China... Some to sell. Toothpick, clockradio. Big and small. Yes? Till Kianshi product come from Shanghai.' Jemimah does not mind working with strange goods till the proper Kianshi merchandise arrives.

Han So never comes back to Kayole after his one and only visit. The Canter comes every Monday at 11 a.m. to Jemimah's house to pick up the boxes she is storing for him. Miano wa Miano says nothing when he notices the full shelves in their kitchen, their small bathroom laden with Vim and Jemimah's dressing table full of Lady Gay and Limara all written in Chinese. Things are bad on Kirinyaga Road after the police crackdown.

Han So still comes frequently to the office to see PK Maina. He does not bother telling her of these visits – now he just waves from a distance. The days when he does come over to her desk are only when she has some money for him from the Chinese Royco seasoning, Chinese Vim toilet detergent, Chinese Kiwi shoe polish and Chinese Eveready batteries that she has distributed and sold for him in Kayole, Komarock, Umoja and Dandora.

After six months, Jemimah and her focus group are still waiting for Kianshi products. This does not seem to bother Han So, who has given her money to rent out the flat next to hers so that she can store all the Chinese goods that he is now bringing in. She distributes these Chinese goods to Jogoo Road, Bahati, Kaloleni and Burma.

One Friday, PK Maina comes in wearing a deep-blue silk shirt and a glossy tie with herons that shimmer in the office dust.

'Have you heard that your Beejing boyfriend bought Maina a car?' Bessie says.

Jemimah first learned about Kianshi when a street vendor handed her a small promotional leaflet in a matatu. 'Make Money. Sell Chinese products. Call No. 0740444888 and attend seminar at K.I.C.C. February 5th ' the leaflet said. That's when she met Han So. A small man wearing a flashy tracksuit and dark glasses with an even smaller identical half standing by his side. JinShu, his brother-in-law wearing exactly the same clothes. There were about two hundred people at the seminar. Han So's helpers sent away all those without employment IDs – leaving about twenty-five people in the small hall.

Once, during these first meetings she asked him what China was like and for the first time since she had met him he grinned. 'There is story of famous Chinese government official with heart of general. Name is Lin Tse-hsi. My father name me after him but I don't use that name here. In 1830... 1840; I not remember exact. He refuse British product but greedy Chinese government official agree. British then bring opium and people become weak. British first say they sell to China, world power. British say British products are world power. And that Chinese will become strong. But come opium. And then opium war or Anglo–China war. Me not like that. Want to make China strong and Kenya strong. Bring products that make Kenya and China strong. Bring Kianshi. Bring World Power.'

Now almost a year since starting her Kianshi adventure Jemimah is the biggest supplier of local consumer products from China in the whole of Eastlands all the way to Gikomba. Though it is not through Kianshi Marketing as she planned, she has come far since the '97 El Niño floods when she moved there. The days of getting home at midnight after wading through half of Nairobi and squeezing into matatus are over. Now Kayole is no longer nights spent staring and listening to the rushed pounding of rain on her ceiling at three in the morning waiting to start the next day. She thinks that in another year she will be able to buy a small Daihatsu Charade. And maybe even move from Kayole and get a bed-sitter in Buru Buru or move to Umoja. She is now the one looking after Miano wa Miano.

One Tuesday morning, she climbs into her usual 5 a.m. matatu. As the matatu pulls into the city centre, a dirty brownish light fills the sky. It is August again and the cold months are behind Nairobi. By the time the matatu gets to Lower Hill, Mlima House, she is warm from FM 101.8's Breakfast Show offering cash prizes, and a climbing sun.

Before she settles down, three men in brown and grey suits and grim, bland, smiling faces show up at ExtelComms. They walk directly into PK Maina's office. Everyone can see something is wrong. Two of the men sit in PK's visitors' chairs and the third, a fattish individual with folds of skin for hair, sits behind PK Maina's desk. PK Maina remains standing, alert like a schoolboy with his hands behind his back. He never sits down even as the others stand and pace leaving empty chairs to sit on.

Very little work is done in the office that day. Wires and Cables is hushed – the department could be under investigation, being the most lucrative in ExtelComms. Jemimah doesn't even pretend to work after she notices PK Maina pointing her out to the men. The fat guy in the brown jacket fingers the folds of fat on his scalp, rubs the top of his head hard, all the time smiling through the glass partition.

Later, she sees the fat man stand and feel PK Maina's mauve silk shirt between his fingers. The other men laugh silently behind the glass. Bessie is full of information, 'Msichana, they are coming for you! It is for you. I know that bald guy. I recognise him from when I was with Emenkua... he works at CID.'

Jemimah glares at her: 'This is China we are talking about, not Nigeria. Nothing will happen. I tell you. How can you compare a world pawa with a foo-foo drug culture?'

Lunchtime comes and goes, and the men are still in PK Maina's office. Chapati Madondo today. It's that time of the month. No one can afford nyama and this makes the atmosphere at the office more oppressive. Finally, the men leave at around 4 p.m. carrying a phone handset.

'Nothing. Nothing is wrong,' PK Maina tells her when she rushes in and asks what is going on.

'Where is your Chinese jamaa?'

'Han So is in China. His mother is sick. Can I leave early?' she asks. PK Maina waves her away. She picks up the heavy bag of GUKKI designer clothes and PANSONIC electronic samples she brought for some people at the office on the way out.

The next day the three men come back. This time they carry a large paper bag and walk straight into PK Maina's office.

After a few minutes, PK Maina comes and calls her at her desk and leads her to his office. 'These men are from the State Research Bureau.' He introduces them. 'Nyakundi, Kaboga and Rutto.' They sound like a multi-ethnic Kenyan law firm in a small town like Eldoret.

The men look at her without a word and spill cans, bottles and packets on PK Maina's desk; Royco, Vaseline Petroleum Jelly, Cooking oil, Omo, Tea, Kiwi, Homecup Chai, Lady Gay.

'We are aware that you introduced the man you call Han So to your boss, Mr Maina. We have been trying to find him for months, but he fled when he became aware. We were lucky when we learned that he is supplying a government office with fake telephone handsets. These things are costing the Kenya Revenue Authority 1 pillion a year,' the fattish man says. He is Nyakundi. Today, he is in a green metallic suit faded at the shoulders.

They hand her a *Nation* newspaper, opening it up in the middle: 'FAKE OR REAL: THE CHOICE IS YOURS,' it reads. There are photos of all the items on the desk. 'Don't worry, Madam. This can go away, as we told your boss and our friend here, Mr Maina. The Trade Descriptions Act just needs you to prove that you did not know these are fake. That you thought Han So was a legitimate businessman. And I'm sure you did not know this was a crime. That is the law for you. Ignorance is your defence.' PK Maina shakes his head in agreement. Droplets of sweat fly.

Nyakundi beckons to her to come to the corner. He whispers into her ear: 'Nyakundi and Co understand. But the magistrate might not... Even your Chinese boyfriend, Mr Han-Chu. Good friend of everyone... We need to find him. Don't worry. He is our friend.'

Jemimah tells them everything.

The verdict: Café TwendiOne. Kenyatta Avenue. 4 p.m. Alafu tumalizane. Bring 40,000.

A week later, early in the evening, there is a knock at the door. It is Mwangi, the kiosk owner. Jemimah has never seen him like that. Dishevelled and unkempt. It's time she brought up moving out of Kayole with Miano wa Miano. They can afford it – even after she paid off the three-man gang that sounded like a multi-ethnic law firm. She notices that everybody in Kayole nowadays either looks drunk or criminal.

'I've already paid for this month's milk,' she starts to say.

'Ngoja... you know the police put me inside for one week for selling curry powder mixed with flour as Royco,' he shouts. 'Your Chinese Royco. Your Chinese Omo. Asking me why it doesn't wash. Kiwi Chinese yako hardens my customers' shoes. I've closed shop. Njuguna and Kimemia also bought from your boyfriend and are still inside Buru Buru police. Wait till they get out and you'll see.'

'Fake or real, the choice is yours,' Jemimah shouts at his back, as he thuds downstairs. She can see the city's tiny lights in the distance from her balcony. She feels like she could reach out and touch them – the city lights are so near.

'That's why they were half price!' she shouts into the night. 'Shenzi!'

Miano wa Miano comes to the door and drags her in when she continues shouting and reaching out into the night as if to grab the city lights. He closes the door and explains it's just a matter of time till the police pick her up even if they have already given Nyakundi and Co. Ksh 40,000. Miano wa Miano knows these things from Kirinyaga Road.

That night, they pack with haste. Jemimah puts away all her possessions piece by piece as if she is counting the years in Nairobi. They also pack all of Han So's remaining boxes and bags full of clothes and electronics. When they leave at daybreak all that is left in the small apartment are the Kianshi brochures.

As the matatu swerves past Globe Cinema, Jemimah pictures Miano wa Miano and Kim, who have no idea the other exists, sitting in a shop in Karatina town with her mother. She already has a name for the shop. She will call it 'World Pawa'.

TREADMILL LOVE

Exactly six months before Maxwell Kung'u Kamande fell in love with the girl in the mirrors, he stirred from months of long sleep one late Limuru Red Hill afternoon and decided he never wanted to see his immediate relations again. It was during the failed long rains of 2005 and he had spent the past six months lying in his bed, drinking soup made of large bones, mouthing different farm animal sounds and masturbating himself to distraction.

That afternoon, he got out of bed and all he had on was a tight, ugly, blue knitted sweater that lacked ambition and stopped at his midriff. Wobbling to the curtain slit of light at the window, he almost slipped on the hundreds of newspaper pages on the floor, teeming with headlines, obituaries and other disquieting informations that he had pored over mindlessly during his big sleep. There were glass and plastic bottles of pills strewn everywhere on the floor and they rolled away from his dragging feet, seeming to hold a glimpse of his life in all its entropy. Some of these chemical universes burst open and hundreds of large green blobby pills, fat yellow capsules, bright orange saucers raced across the wooden floor; a fine grey powder rose, making him sneeze.

Kung'u reached the window with his hands still at his sides, his face parting the slips of curtain aside. He observed the obsessive hand of his mother in the neatly tended purple-blue bougainvillea hedge outside. In the drizzle, flowers from childhood in their wild natural colours, in between orange-reds, yellow-creams brought back Mother's cloying sweetish smell. For a brief moment this drowned the heavy pall of old news, drug-induced sweat and semen in the room.

His eyes travelled over the sharply cut edge of the Kikuyu-grass lawn, lush and arsenic-green with life. Their prickly blades made him shudder and a hot itch ran over him. There were several pangas lying on the lawn, left by the day workers. A dog appeared, loping with an aimless gait. It licked at one of the pangas and idly wagged its tail when it sensed Kung'u's presence. Reaching for the window with its forelegs and failing, it hovered there with its little pink penis flitting in and out of the piece of skin near its belly. The dog's mouth dripped with small droplets of blood from having nicked itself on the blade of the panga.

Kung'u sighed and crawled back into bed. Looking at the ceiling brought on an involuntary sob. Somewhere in his chest, he also felt a burst of uncontrollable laughter bubbling. After a brief struggle, he gave in and wept softly. In what seemed mere seconds, the drizzle outside turned into a sweeping downpour that lashed at the windowpanes. Kung'u stopped crying and the rain let up its mocking. The threatening laugh in his chest ebbed away. Yes, leaving here would be easier than living with the welcome everyday thought of killing Mother and destroying the things she had possessed with such greed all these years – his elder brother Morris, the banker, lawyer-sister Lois, fat Damaris whose kid, Kiki, was the only person Maxwell still loved in the family, though she had taken over his last-born privileges. Looking down at himself he was unable to recognise the body he had woken and found himself in, the skin folds over the stomach and upper thighs of a man suddenly in his late thirties.

When he stepped out of the room at one far end of the large house the corridor was cool and quiet. There was a pile of plates with old food that looked like mildewed droppings, which Mumbi the maid had forgotten to collect. Kung'u listened for noises from childhood but the boards remained uncreaking and the wind in the roof dead to his ear. Other dream sounds from the last six months came from what Mother called his second childhood, the sea of depression that had washed over him. She had laughed off many doctors' diagnoses as indulgences. His melancholia, in her eyes, was a weakness; she faulted herself for not nipping it in the bud when Kung'u had started tugging at her skirts as a child.

The house had been dying slowly. Years ago in the 60s it had been a shiny gleam in Nairobi's social magnifying glass. *The Kamande house is one of the proud vestiges of this country's new independence. Delicately balanced like our fledging democracy, its north wing looks out into the finest Limuru coffee estates in this country. Mixing leisure and commerce, the south wing gazes across lush meadow and fresh sedge. A small river runs through it. When I jokingly asked Edith Kamande whether they had ever considered opening a small golf course, hubby Augustine Kiereini Kamande looked up with interest...* These words had appeared in the *Weekend Nation* column, 'Going Places' in the 70s by John Fox.

Once Kung'u's father had shrunk to a brittle death from bone marrow cancer eighteen months ago, Mother had boarded up the north wing; only the upper south wing, leeward to the sun, was left open. It held the kitchen, dining hall and three small bedrooms that Mother, Kiki and Damaris had occupied before Kung'u's big sleep.

After Mathare Mental Hospital, Kung'u came back, sawed a large hole through the block board his mother had used to cut off the north wing and went into his old room without a word. It was there that he had been living and dying in turns, cut off from the other inhabitants of the house, Mother, Mumbi and Lois the lawyer when she came home for holidays. And Damaris and Kiki who left and returned unable to shrug their dependence on Mother.

It now took Kung'u five minutes to get to what passed for life in the old house through the blockboard, holding himself up against the dusty comforting walls. It was clear that the house had been abandoned by all other inhabitants, other than Mother. Beyond the hole he soon got to the dining hall, the most socially active room of the house, sat down heavily and looked around. There was nothing idle about the room, just four hardwood chairs and the large dining table that once sat up to fifteen people and looked out onto a lush Limuru countryside full of the testament of newness.

There were heavy glass pitchers of coloured water everywhere, on top of and inside the cabinet, on the dining table and even on the large European-style windowsills. Every morning, Mother sprinkled the black, blue and green liquid all over the house to ward away evil spirits sent by her enemies, and on muddy farm implements to defer potential harm to the crops. There were several bottles of vodka on the dirty shelves at various stages of depletion. The large clock, one of the remaining pieces of furniture not boarded up in the rooms upstairs, claimed it was 10 o'clock. Next to it was a large photo of a forbidding-looking man, his father, with a young woman with a determined chin, young Mother. It said *Augustine Obadiah and Edith Kiereini Kamande, London. 1951.* Mumbi the maid was nowhere to be seen.

Opening the back kitchen door, Kung'u squinted at the large sky, recently visible after more than thirty years. For most of its natural life the back of the south wing had suffered under the shadows of a copse of impressive blue gum trees. During one of his pre-Mathare impulses, a year ago, while Mother was away on a Women's Guild retreat, Kung'u went into a nearby slum and came back with a gang of men. It took three days for them to bring down the trees. Kung'u paid the men in firewood in an over-generous exchange for their labour. He had no idea that blue gum was to furniture making what Arabica was to coffee. The exhilarating after-party had also prompted Kung'u to slaughter one of Mother's prize-winning Angora goats for the men. One of the workers brewed *muratina* to usher in this new revolution. As the sun went down the men sang, ate and drank after sawing away at the trees all day with abandon. A few electronics went missing in the house. Half the huge pile of blue gum logs the men stacked in the driveway disappeared in a week, and the rest Kung'u sold for a pittance. More than anything else this prompted Mother to call her friends from the Muthaiga Police to 'discipline' Kung'u. He spent one week in jail, after which he 'cracked' and had to be taken off to Mathare, catatonic like the Limuru evenings of his childhood.

Even now the treeless back of the house remained dark and cold. Kung'u would never know that his one revolutionary act had not been futile. He had lined the pockets of the farm workers with blue gum cash. He stood there and understood that the back of the house would never acquire the life of the sunny front veranda that had been his father's side of the house. Mother had bolted the front door with his father's passing, impatient with the attention it drew away from the rest of the house. As he looked up into the sky, smelling the rain, Mother appeared on the driveway.

She was a big firm block of flesh. Her face had turned grey-black over the years, like the ageing bark of a Mugumo tree. She walked up the kokoto driveway crunching stones in black under black gumboots. She wore a large military sweater and long heavy skirt. A young sapling growing near the wall of the house caught her eye and she strode up to it quickly and efficiently, stripping its slender stem of additional side-shoots that hindered its main growth. Kung'u moved away from the doorway at her approach and she trooped inside without a word, dropping the pangas from the lawn and flower-cuttings at his feet. He heard her rummaging inside for a while and then she reappeared. She held a pitcher of black-coloured water in her hand.

He flinched when she grabbed him by the chin to examine his soft, light-deprived face. Her rough gnarly hands felt like a vice. Her small eyes filled with an ancient mischief. 'Eh, my boy Maxweo. I see you've woken up.' She gurgled softly, sprinkling the black water all over his face with thick muddy fingers. 'Unnnh…. so soft and white.' She peered at his stomach, still uncovered, and poked a thick fingernail in it till he doubled over. The sudden intake of stomach almost dropped his pyjama pants. 'Mzee, god bless that fool. He would be happy to see you wake up. We eat soon.'

'You can pray in English, Swahili or whatever tongues you been speaking day and night and day in that room,' Mother announced when they sat at different ends of the huge hardwood log table. Kung'u ignored her. In between them sat a huge pot. Mother muttered a brief prayer and pulled the pot to herself. She ladled a thick stream of boiled whole carrots complete with green tops, half-sized cabbage chunks and different kinds of seeds, peas, beans, maize, cowpeas, and lentils on her plate. Then she peered inside the pot and pulled something out with a huge clunk onto her plate – an unpeeled nduma. This seemed to satisfy her and she let go of the pot with a grunt. She spooned everything into her mouth without a word, spitting out, twisting and pulling with her hands at everything and a small pile of carrot leaves, outer cabbage remains and small husks grew at her side. The nduma was left sitting on the plate.

She heaved her large frame from her seat and went into the kitchen. She came back carrying an old enormous birika and two large tin cups. She poured a steaming gush of milky tea in one cup and sat down. After peeling the nduma onto the small pile by her side, she nibbled gently at it, sipping her tea between mouthfuls. Now and then she huffed with pleasure and wiped her forehead. Kung'u sat there till she had finished. When she made to get up he said: 'I want my money. I want my money and that's all I want.' She sat back and gave him a measured look, released an elemental sound from the depths of her largeness, stood up and trumped away, switching off the lights behind her.

Kung'u sat there all night. Fog drifted from outside into the house, swirling around his still figure. The next morning Mother came in dressed in an old cotton sack of a dress. Now that she knew what he wanted she moved with an exaggerated swagger. She dipped her finger in the cold pot from last night, put it in her mouth and looked at him mildly.

'Yes, ni kweli you have woken up.' She cleared the pot and the plates that were unused from the table and went into the kitchen. There she started singing a song about women clearing the forest. He heard her turn on the gas to heat the tea in the birika. She came back into the dining room with a loaf of bread, which she tore in huge impatient chunks. 'Your brother and sisters will come this weekend and we decide.'

'I want my money.'

'Just till weekend. Boy, you can't wait two years. You go mad. You have sold my blue gums. You have been a parking man in Tanzania. Ati depression. Depression for what? To your own mother you did this. Think... does she even look happy? You can wait till this weekend.'

'I want the Buru Buru house and one of the cars, even if it is the Mazda.'

'I don't know. Maybe it is this new government. It has changed things. Now anyone thinks they can have what they want. They leave the land. Nobody wants to work any more. Moree or *ka* Lois don't. Maybe Damaris because she is lazy with that barman boyfriend of hers.'

She scooped up the pile of peelings from last night and left him there.

'Back to the river these go. Manure for next year's ndumas.'

Kung'u sighed and went back to bed.

That Saturday, Morris the banker-brother arrived first. He slammed his Mercedes car doors shut, ignored the house and went down to the farm. His top-heavy figure, this less-sunny side of fifty, was dressed in a striped shirt and braces. Workers stopped what they were doing when he approached. They praised Mother to his face, talked of recent calfings, the size of the coffee berries that year and so-and-so's Mungiki son who had been shot by the police. Morris would make the right noises, remove his non-prescription spectacles and rub his eyes. He refused their offerings of sour milk mixed with ash, black plastic bags fall of half-rotten plums and bananas the size of his forearm. Halfway through his tour, he was summoned back to the house. Lois the lawyer had arrived.

The family met at the table. Mother sat at the head with Morris and Lois on her sides; Kung'u sat at the far end. Damaris, whose consequence in the family had flittered way after getting pregnant at seventeen from fucking one of the workers, had not been informed of the meeting. Morris cleared his throat as if to start the meeting but everybody ignored this. Mother started the accusations. 'Remeba that Luo garl you brought home Maxwell? Skinny, like I don't know what. Thin, thin, thin. The kind that white men like to go with in cheap Nairobi hotels and sin. Do all sorts of things. What was that? Tell me, what was that?' She breathed heavy and deeply. 'But now I wish you 'ad settled with her. Anything would have been better than this.' Lois, the kind of woman who thought that she had to look as ugly as possible for the Judiciary of Kenya to take her seriously, and for that matter was still not taken seriously, said seriously: 'It is good to see you like this. Maxie, we've missed you. At least you want things. It's been so long. It's a good sign.'

Kung'u glowered. '… You all have always refused me what is mine. I'm now well. For now one of the cars and the Buru Buru Phase 2 house will do. I leave Wednesday.'

'You have been taking your medication?' This was Morris.

Kung'u stood up and walked away from the table and away from the room. He found it difficult to raise his arms from his sides. He stood in the corridor and heard Mother say, 'You ka-Lois. You want to encourage him.' Then, Mother turned to Morris: 'Go see those Baluhyas renting the Buru Buru house. Tell them we need it back. We can offer them something else, maybe the house in that other place, Doonholm. Also, go to the bank – the boy will need some money for now. And furniture and things. I'm also giving him the old Land Rover. He looks well enough to me…'

'Maitu, er sore. I mean Mother,' Morris said. 'I am totally against that idea. Maxwell back in the world. Imagine.'

Mother swivelled slowly to him like a huge caterpillar truck and stared at his forehead, similar to hers. Looking at him, she wondered at his stupidity when it came to reading people.

'Moree, keep to your figures or whatever you do at that stupid bank. I know the boy. Let me handle him. The Buru Buru house, a car… is nothing.'

'Mum, I think the people in the Buru Buru house are Kisiis not Luhyas. If I remember their name from the paperwork they are most likely Maragolis,' Lois said. 'What I can't understand is why he wants to live in Eastlands?'

II

When Kung'u made the exodus from Kiambu to Buru Buru, he felt the air around him change and thicken in degrees. By the time he got to Buru Buru, he had re-adapted from the long smooth tree-lined drives of his childhood to the frequent gear-shifts of this new place, crowded with people, cars and activity. He found the Buru Buru house cleaned and laid out simply and comfortably. When he got into the main bedroom upstairs he ignored the bed. He found an old crumpled water-bed in the store, filled it up with cold water and dragged it into one of the empty rooms. He hurled himself onto it and slept for a week. When he woke up he was happy that the windows looked out onto the blank colourless face of another building. It was close enough to stretch out and touch.

He had fallen in love with Buru Buru when he had first visited his best friend Rick Kamau, in high school, years ago. Its informality, the girls who gave it up when they heard he was a Kamande from Red Hill, and the easy mobility within it had for the first time made him aware of the possibilities of class in Kenya. He had spent many a weekend driving around in an old pick-up with Rick, partying it up. That was exactly twenty years ago. He now saw that Buru Buru, the middle-class project, had become an industrial slum over the years – illegal structures had sprung up all over the place like bad teeth. But it was exactly what Kung'u felt he needed. He re-immersed himself in the estate's complete disregard of the past, its careless noises and absence of structure. There were no coffee bushes or so-and-so high-profile neighbours. There were no fresh smells, distracting butterflies and flowers. He oriented himself to the estate's courts after growing up with ridges and valleys. It was not Limuru or Kiambu with the baggage those places had, the haughty assumptions, country club accusations or land grievances. It was not Kibera or Mathare with all those NGO mzungus talking it up or full of mainstream newspaper judgements about crime. It was officially anonymous. All Kung'u had to do in Buru Buru was float on the waterbed all day, and listen to its strange moorings and urgings.

In the evening he went for walks between the box-like structures with orange brick rooftops, ugly and faded in the day but beautifully jaded in the falling sun. Hundreds of antennae reached for the sky. He watched lights come on and go off. Children cried and mothers laughed. Every now and then there were gunshots. Apart from one night when a security helicopter bathed him in light, nobody noticed him. Nobody acknowledged his presence in the small lanes that transversed the estate and this confused him no end. But still, at a distance, his neighbours knew he was a newcomer and watched him behind the upstairs curtains of their houses.

He learned the particular codes of living in an estate, and the look of vague interest exchanged on the pavement. He learned the language of the small shops and their small concerns. What bread did he want, Mother's Choice or Breadland? What milk did he prefer, Gold Crown or Tuzo? These were the things he had never thought of and they charmed him. One of the neighbouring families of his Red Hill childhood had owned the Gold Crown brand and he took pleasure in the anonymity of milk choices in Buru Buru that had never been afforded him by such privilege.

After about a month he discovered a bar in the nearby shopping centre, in one of the ugly, colourless, plaster buildings and he colonised a quiet corner. It was one of those 'new Kenya' places called 'Baada Ya Mateso Hakuna Chuki': *After The Suffering There is No Hate*. Everyone called it 'Mateso': *Suffering*. Life in the bar was different and yet similar to the estate. People talked, walked up and down, in and out of the bathrooms, with little contact. To Kung'u they seemed to be always reaching out to be part of something. They sought a national moment when they all turned to the seven o'clock news on one of the numerous TVs in the bar. But it was with a puzzled silence that they turned back to each other after they had watched the leaders they had elected. In the stream of crisis that seemed to be part of the new government they would laugh grimly and sip their beers. Laughter and buzz would build up till Manchester United or Arsenal came on, and then a hush would come over the place. The only sound was the clacking of pool balls from another room where young men lurked and played the game all day.

Kung'u grew to like being part of the flickering nothingness of the place, with its ephemeral national moments. He sensed that everyone everywhere in Kenya was doing the same thing: watching politics with hunger, talking Premier League and drinking away the years. He soon learned not to look directly at anyone in Mateso – after a few flat, hard, challenging stares were returned. He learned to watch people in the bar mirror. And since this had a degree of deniability he got away with it. After a while he became a familiar face at the bar and was nicknamed 'Mzee Chochote'. This was because he never ordered a specific drink but always asked the barman for 'anything you have – chochote.' For a long time he was thought of as being uncomplicated and friendly. The waitresses, always giggly at his unnatural lightness, eyes that became big with alcohol and his gentle manner, called him 'Muthungu'.

His success in Buru Buru gave him confidence to venture further. He drove into town and there he parked the Land Rover and retraced childhood footsteps on Kenyatta Avenue and Koinange Street. The famous Wimpy and Sno-Cream where Mother used to take him for ice-cream when they came to St Andrews were no longer there in the new Kenya. It was now a Forex. He drove to Adams and then Hurlingham, Westlands and even Nairobi West and in this re-discovery of the city tried to make out what business he would open when the time came.

One day he heard a knock at the door. The sun had barely come up. It was 6 a.m. When he opened the door, there was a little boy standing there. 'Sasa Uncle,' the boy said from the nasal depths of his Down's syndrome. It was the court's little town crier. Kung'u had seen this curious little boy out in the court who greeted everyone and everything with the same loud shriek, 'Sasa.'

'Hey,' Kung'u said. 'What is your name?'

The little boy shrieked and rushed past Kung'u into the house straight to the kitchen. Kung'u made him some tea and bread and let him shriek down the house. In the mornings when Kung'u had first arrived in Buru he'd stood just inside his gate and watched the morning rituals of the estate, the housegirl rushing to the shops to buy Brookside milk and either Mother's Choice or Breadland bread. When the estate went completely quiet after its Lords and Ladies went off to work there was lull for the rest of the morning before the housegirls finished their household chores and came out in the sun. In that period before the court was taken up by the chatter of the housegirls the little boy would come out and break the morning quiet of the court with his delightful shrieks. When Kung'u stopped watching the court's early rituals he started listening out for the little boy. He went out when he heard him and watched him, the two of them alone in this new Buru world. Amid the impenetrable solidity of the whitewashed houses and the orange brick roofs Kungu's ear started making sense of the little boy's sounds; of all the things that had started stirring in him when he had woken from his big sleep this sound touched him more than most.

Now the little boy finished his tea and bread and pulled at his hand and they went outside.

The estate's two idlers cut quite a pair. The tall, light, moon-faced man with a high forehead, scrappy beard and wild hair, all jangly and awkward with disuse, and a little puffed-up boy with a never-ending stream of snot. The little boy was always dressed up in the tightest of T-shirts that failed to cover his protruding tummy and large shorts that kept on slipping to his ankles. In his mother's absence during weekdays the housegirl covered him in a thick layer of Vaseline petroleum jelly. Everyone in the estate called him Bubu. His head was covered in ugly bald red patches of hair from the pair of scissors his mother took to his hair every few weeks. Kung'u took to wiping his nose, bought him a belt to keep his shorts in place and when he learned that the little boy's name was Anthony he tried to teach him to say it. He then bought a TV and Bubu spent the long idle days seated on the floor entranced in Cartoon Network. Once the boy had adopted Kung'u his mother accepted him and with that the rest of the court took him in too.

Since Kung'u started going to Mateso bar and sitting in the same tight corner, he had on occasion heard a pattern of noises coming up from the third floor of the building. Mateso was on the ground floor and when Kung'u asked the barman about the noises, he was told it was mad Mathare people jumping around. Kung'u assumed it was one of those new Jesus churches. It would be quiet when he got to the bar around 3 p.m. with only shouts in the pool room and the furious clacking of balls. Then the noise would pick up slowly by 4 p.m. By six, there would be shouts of exertion and some kind of dance music filtering down to his corner. By 8 p.m. the whole third floor would be lit up and then slowly die down, lights off by ten, when Kung'u was going home.

Looking outside one day, Kung'u stood up and walked up the rickety set of metallic stairs still fresh with ugly streaks of oxy-acetylene flame. The noise came closer as he clambered up the three floors. On the third floor he could hardly hear himself think as he went around a small corridor coming out into a large room. There was a large sign that said: GYM. Two of the room's walls were large mirrors, and the black rubber floor was full of indignant squeaks topped by a sky-blue ceiling that watched over old men with heaving man-tits from goat meat and forty years of independence. Kung'u saw individuals of all shapes and sizes, dressed in all colours, straining in one form of movement or another. There were several TV screens and on all of them a cheetah chased some kind of hog. When Kung'u walked in, he saw a side room with more mirrors and at least thirty women in some kind of separate aerobic activity, moving in unison. Their trainer seemed to be trying to bring the roof down with indecipherable shouts and cheers. Everybody was preoccupied with watching themselves in the mirrors.

On the far end were large horizontal windows with a bird's-eye view of Buru Buru's rooftops. There was a separate enclosed square space, a barbershop with two large leather seats and two young men hunched over customers. There were five other customers waiting, seated in right-angled fashion. Kung'u saw all this through a reflection in the large mirrors that covered one side of the barbershop.

That was when Kung'u saw the girl in the mirrors. She sat in the corner; she had a long thin neck and pinched haughty features that cried of boredom and an old wisdom. She laughed suddenly at something that was said by one of the customers. The flash of pinkness from inside her mouth was that of a newborn baby. Her face was ageless. Something stirred in Kung'u and he felt drawn to her in this new universe full of mirrors.

As he turned to the gym floor he noticed that everyone's eyes were glued to the TV screens. When Kung'u squinted he made out a strange sight on the screen – an elephant was trying to mount a rhino. People gaped, shaking their heads. Then there was convivial laughter all around. He turned and the girl was watching the copulating behemoths with a profound boredom. At that moment Kung'u decided to sign up. He went to the desk where a large young man, one of the trainers, sat watching the activity on the floor. Kung'u could not tear his eyes away from the young man's large muscled neck as he filled out the forms. 'Hey, even animals are getting on the programme. Becoming perverts. Now rhinos and elephants are doing it like you do it on the Discovery Channel. I remember this pig that was always doing it with the dogs in my neighbourhood...' the trainer said, with a strange earnestness. His neck rippled when he spoke.

Kung'u realised how young he was. 'Yeah, that shit is Darwinian – with only a handful of rhinos in the world, animal doesn't have a choice,' Kung'u offered. The trainer looked at him blankly for a moment, then laughed and raised his palm. Kung'u put out and the guy slapped it hard.

When Kung'u looked up into the barbershop mirror through the glass partition the girl in the corner was looking at him with a flat, insolent stare. She was washing a customer's head. He put his hand up uncertainly, as if to wave, and the girl, with the subtlest of sneers, he was not even sure that it had happened, dismissed him. Kung'u felt a sharp pain in his temples.

After that he came to the gym every day. He would get onto one of the treadmills and, after adjusting the machine to a brisk walking pace, watch the girl in the mirrors. When there was no work she slumped in a chair in half a doze with her long legs stretched out, watching the world. Then she would open her eyes in the barber shop mirror and catch him looking at her from the mirror in the gym in front of the treadmill. She would stare hard at him till he was forced to look away. One afternoon the intensity of her eyes unsettled him so badly that he adjusted the levels on the treadmill and started running briskly, as if trying to get away from her. Within minutes, her image in the mirror started blurring and with a huge pain in his chest he just managed to bang the machine's emergency *STOP* sign before his legs gave away. He stepped off and heaved away for minutes. When he looked up the girl was laughing hard in the mirrors.

On busy days, he observed her as she washed heads and massaged temples. This was mostly on Saturdays, Sundays and Wednesday evenings and she ignored him completely. He watched her pink mouth laughing with customers and he feared her. On those days he would leave the gym, go downstairs to Mateso and drink himself silly – once or twice he might have ignored the turn to his new home and driven back to Limuru. But after a few days he would catch her eyes on him and this would bring on a quick recovery. He started arranging his gym schedule around her work patterns. Once he realised she never came in on Tuesdays, he started taking the day off. Mondays and Thursdays, which were extremely slow at the barbershop, became the days he ran flat out on the treadmill under her scornful stare. These became his 250-calorie days.

When she was busy, Kung'u found himself unable to summon up any energy beyond a calm walk. He was lucky if he did 100 calories on such days. After two weeks of her scorn, his stomach stopped jiggling. His slow shuffle on the treadmill became a lope and his shoulders and neck seemed straighter. One day, he lost himself in his run, drifting in and out of the mirror trying to catch her eye, and he suddenly looked at the treadmill gauges and saw the impossible figure of 400 calories. Elated, he looked back in the mirrors and caught her eye on him. Her bored look was gone and there instead lingered a curiosity, a frank reappraisal that was gone in an instant. Her features became pinched again and the boredom and haughtiness returned with only the hint of a faint smile at the corners of her mouth.

As the weeks wore on Kung'u would lose himself in the calorie gauge of the treadmill machine. Some days he would go on for ten minutes without looking for the barbershop in the mirror. To maintain discipline he made friends with the trainers and exchanged pleasantries with several of the old men who came to the gym. Most of their stories were the same; they were suits who came to the gym for escape. After stripping off their shirts, specially adjusted at the girth and neck, they took to the treadmills, cross-trainers and exercise bikes with an enthusiasm that quickly faded into sweaty foreheads and heavy puffing. He saw them watching him, hating his slow smooth running figure, a 750-calorie runner. In the sauna, naked and sweaty, the old men talked politics through jiggling chins and stomachs and laughter that chimneyed through the holes in their faces. He declined when one or two invited him for a beer afterwards and felt vindicated when he noticed the girl looking at many of the old fat men with disgusted amusement.

One day as he left the gym, thinking himself cured of staring into the mirrors, he looked up and saw the girl in the corridor outside the men's changing room. She was much shorter away from the mirrors; parts of her face were dry and old. Her arms were covered in bangles and pockmarks. A waft of young sweat floated free from her figure. She looked at him as she passed and whispered: 'Una-ni ignore. Why? Who do you think you are?'

Shaken, he went downstairs to Mateso, and sat in his corner. Bees swarmed around his head. 'Buy me a beer,' a voice said next to him, shaking him out of his reverie. It was this old guy everyone called 'Twenty-five-years'. He was a civil servant who started every sentence saying: 'Twenty-five years ago... women were more beautiful; twenty-five years ago... Nairobi was a civilised place...' Kung'u gave Twenty-five-years 200 Kenyan shillings and left.

The next day Bubu appeared on Kungu's doorstep with his head freshly shorn, tufts of hair sticking out of bare patches. Kung'u put him in the Land Rover and drove to the barbershop. When he walked in with Bubu everyone stared at them. The two barbers sufficiently recovered and offered a greeting. The girl came over to Bubu, leaned over him and said, 'Has Daddy bought you to get a haircut?' Bubu stood up and hugged her. Everyone in the barbershop laughed. She turned to Kung'u and said, 'My name is Kaume.'

III

The next day at the gym Kaume waited till he was done on the treadmill and she came up to him with a small bottle of powder. 'Hii is for your son. It will help with the ma-shillings on his head.' Kung'u wondered what to do next but then two days later she came to him after his exercise and asked him whether he would be going to Mateso. 'Yes,' he managed. He sat there not knowing what to do and she came looking for him at the bar after her shift and allowed him to buy two beers for her.

She moved into the three-bedroom Buru house after one week. When she saw the mirrors that Kung'u had installed all over the house she remained quiet for a few days and then she blurted hapana – they had to go. She also asked him to remove the treadmill from the sitting room.

'On my off day tutaenda shopping. Furniture. Hii Tuesday.' They went to the NCCK furniture kiwanja near Buru Phase Five. There they found a carpenter who had a shop called 'Building The Nation?' and Kaume gave him measurements for two three-seaters and two two-seaters.

They placed the treadmill that had been in the sitting room outside in the back yard where Kung'u could continue his 1000-calorie runs when she was at work. Kaume did not say anything about the other treadmill that was in the spare bedroom upstairs that was also fitted with mirrors from bottom to top. But she never ever went in there. Or in any of the other rooms downstairs that Kungu had fitted with mirrors from ceiling to floor.

But when she noticed the families that had lived in the court for a long time staring at them she cried and shouted at the walls. So, on Sundays Kaume started tracing the neighbours' movements to see what churches they went to, sniggering over how slathered the children were in Vaseline. She decided to look into three of the churches. Assemblies of God. New Christ Redeemer Church. Life After Death Ministries. And because of the silence of her days in the house she chose the last one which was the loudest and word went around the neighbourhood that she was a Christian and now some of the women even greeted her when they saw her in the court. With the Word from Life After Death Ministries she told Kung'u that they should thank the Lord for bringing them together and so she took him to an exhibition in town to buy a suit.

The next Sunday she took him instead to the quieter Assemblies of God. Kung'u had been brought up in the hushed ways of St Andrew's and he was happy to listen to the tongues and wails of others over the next few weeks. Kaume then joined the Christian inter-church cell held by the women of the court and her acceptance was complete. Because she knew that after a few weeks she would soon have to invite the other women to the house they went off to pimisha more furniture. By now she could tell Kung'u had spent a long time away from people because of his silences when they went out of the house, how his face froze when anyone looked at him and she decided that bringing the women of the court to the house would take awhile. The house smelled like a hospital from the medicine in the sweat from his sessions on the treadmill when she came back from work. When they spent time together, walking around the estate and going to the shops in the Shopping Centre she noticed that he made his way in the world like a man discovering it anew. At first she thought he had been in Kamiti Prison because he always seemed to have money yet did not work, but after a week with him she could see he was too Babylon to have been a hardcore criminal. She decided not to think too much and enjoy moving out of Kayole into Buru Buru, one of her big life ambitions. There was also her six-year-old daughter who she had left with her mother in Nyahururu and who, at some point, she planned to bring back to live with her in Nairobi. She saw that Kung'u would make a good father because she saw how he took care of Bubu. Kung'u did not say much about where he had come from and so Kaume was happy to talk about where she wanted to go with her life.

She was tired of washing mostly old men's heads and massaging their rooster-skin necks. One Tuesday, when she was off from the salon and they had been together for two months, she said, 'We are now pamoja. And because we have become one, why are we still using mirrors to look at each other? I see enough kioos at work.'

When she came back from work the next day the mirrors had gone from the master bedroom that they slept in. They spent her next free Tuesday buying another bed, a desk and some small tables for the second bedroom. Then, Kaume took his hand and they walked around the house to take stock of all they had done. When they flopped back on the long sofa in the sitting room, registering the new furniture permutations in the house, Kaume could still feel its old noises and smells, his heaving and his sweat. She looked at Kung'u to see whether he felt the empty silence and the need for something else when Bubu was not running around the house but his moon face was as settled as she'd ever seen it.

She took his hand and said: 'I have always loved clothes.' But when she tried to say more the rest of it got stuck in her throat. He looked at her and thought he understood. When she came back home in the evening he led her to the spare room downstairs and there was a new Singer machine.

She laughed. 'And what is this?'

'For you. For you to make clothes.' She looked at her hands and became angry and ran out of the room and there was nowhere to go so she sat on the staircase. He did not know what to do so he stood behind her. Where the stairs stopped and turned there was a small window that looked out into a small field full of wild growth and underbrush.

'Argh. Angalia, how ugly it is near our house.' Her voice was full of anger. What is that kichaka doing there?'

'Have I done wrong?' he asked.

'Asante for the Cherehani Singer. Lakini, my hands are useless,' she said, spitting the words at the window and the bush outside. 'I am useless.'

'I do not know anything about clothes. Can you tell me?'

She now looked back at him and her face cleared. And they went back into the bedroom.

Later they lay in bed listening to a plane flying over the estate.

She said. 'I want to sell clothes. Ready-made. Kwa exhibition.'

Immediately she said this she wished the mirrors were back in the house so that they could only see each other's reflections. She became angry again and did not speak to him for two days. She came back from work and he was sitting there and he told her how he had changed his life over the last few weeks. And so, she told him more about the exhibition.

A friend of hers owned a stall at the exhibition and she had said that she could give her shares. Kung'u asked her how much it would cost. The figure got stuck on her tongue. The next morning she wrote it down on a piece of paper and left it on the stool next to his side of the bed while he was still asleep and went to work.

The next Saturday when Kaume went off to work, Kung'u got into the Land Rover and drove out of Buru Buru into Outer Ring Road, then Thika Road and then into Kiambu Road. Past Kiambu town he felt the air becoming thinner and he could feel the humidity on his face. He stopped on the side of the road and looked at the rolling hills and then at the side view mirror and, remembering the past, almost turned back – but when he imagined Kaume's face in there, and what she wanted, he drove on.

When he got to the old house he was surprised to realise that its memory had almost disappeared from his head. He could see it was finally dying from a lack of fresh life. The old dogs seemed to recognise him but they remained immobile and only their eyes flickered. He knocked on the oak door and Mother stood there, still an old immovable ikongo. She took time to make him out and then stepped close to him as if measuring him up.

'Maxweo, son of the devil, you have come,' she said. 'The Mzungu who sold your mzee this farm, God bless that old fool, used to like to say water finds its own level,' she said. 'Me I say blood is thick. And I see you have lost metric kilogrammes.' He let her come closer and then he put his hand firmly on her shoulder and said, 'I need money.'

'It is true. You have found a woman. Come in.' She sat down at the giant dining table and when she saw he would not sit she said, 'You will be bringing some toto grandchildren here.' And this time he could hear the wishing in her voice.

He remained quiet and she looked at him for a long time and stood up slowly and heaved away into the innards of the house. She came back with a small sackcloth and handed it over to him. He looked at her and said, 'Nitarudi December. For the rest.' He left her there laughing with a strange joy.

When Kaume came back from work that evening Kung'u gave her 150,000 Kenyan shillings. Throwing the money on the floor, her mouth trembled, her eyes widening slowly and Kung'u thought she would cry but it was just her face trying to rework itself into a rare smile.

Now with the reality of what she had dreamed of for so long her tongue loosened with new plans. She bought a quarter share in her friend's shop. She then negotiated to work for only three days at the barbershop till her share had picked up enough for her to open her own stall. On the days she went to the exhibition she came back new and improved like Omo. She talked about all the Southern Sudanese people in Nairobi who were so rich that they could spend Kshs 30,000 on one shopping trip. About new stall spaces that became available and then snapped up. How happy her mother was with the new Singer that Kung'u had originally bought for her by mistake. When her friend went shopping in Turkey for a week Kaume watched over the shop alone. Kung'u saw that she was happy and could not bear the thought of her going back to massaging the heads of old men. That evening they made Bubu and his mother supper. Kung'u had paid for Bubu to go to the Jacaranda School for Special Children. They left with Bubu's mum in tears at Kungu's kindness and Kaume looked at him and said to herself, nindathire uria ndendaga. I am where I want to be and I cannot imagine anything else.

In early December, Kung'u drove back to Red Hill. He found several cars in the compound with policemen all over, beating the coffee bushes with sticks. The workers told him that Mother had disappeared. There was a search going on all over the farm because it was suspected that she had fallen on one of her regular inspection tours, or as she was working by the river where she grew her ndumas and ngwacis.

For two days the Limuru Police searched for Mother. They interrogated the workers who at first did not tell of the shaking that had recently taken hold of Mother because they knew the police and did not want to be branded suspects in her disappearance. Finally, they told how Mother who had been indestructible for so long had started breaking into shaking fits as if there were a series of earthquakes somewhere inside her body. Old Mumbi said it was like something was trying to get out of her body and she was resisting it with all her strength. The foreman added that she had even given up on milking the cows. And then one by one the workers confirmed that she no longer ventured out every day as she once had. Then, when the police were almost giving up the search a strange hippo-like form was observed floating in the small dam. The police took a small boat into the dam and when they turned the form over, Mother was bloated to three times her size. Even if it was clear that she had slipped into the water as she cultivated her ndumas, the Limuru police arrested twelve of the workers and kept them inside for a week just to see what they would get from them. The mortuary at Nairobi Hospital soon confirmed that a series of small seismic tremor strokes had finally defeated Mother.

Kung'u went back to Buru Buru and told Kaume that he had to go away for a long time. That there was something that he had been waiting for for a long time, and now it had happened. She looked at him and laughed, wondering whether he was asking permission, looking for the past slyness of all the men who had left her in his face. Her share in the clothes shop was already picking up and she now sent most of the money home to her mother for her daughter. She wondered whether Kung'u had somehow found out about her daughter through her increased financial activity and decided not to confront her.

Kung'u left the house and she shouted: 'See if you'll find me here when you come back.' She heard the door open again. That is when he told her about Mother. And for the first time since he had moved to Buru he felt the old headache come on from the mention of Mother.

Kaume searched his face and he said: 'Now we will be okay.' That night she slept on the sofa and had nightmares of moving back to Kayole.

Kung'u joined Lois and Morris who had already moved back into the Red Hill house for a few weeks to bury Mother and to sort out the largesse of their long-dead father Augustine Kierieni Kamande. A few days later Damaris and her daughter Kiki reappeared. After Mother was buried, Morris summoned all to the dining table on a Sunday morning.

'I know that you are all challenged financially so I will offer to manage your estates for you for a year. This is the least I can offer as first-born of this family.' There was a long silence but Kung'u could see in his smile the old slyness of Mother. He stood up and held the table in his hands and started shaking it and screaming. The whole house seemed to shake. When he ran out of strength and came to, Morris had fled. Lois, Damaris and Kiki sat quietly, their faces full of memories. Old Mumbi came into the room and stood there as if waiting for instructions. Kung'u apologised and sat down. They assured her everything would be okay and she left.

With Mumbi's presence they seemed to wake up to it all. They agreed that they would buy old Mumbi a small house in a place of her choice. When they called her she begged not to leave the farm and they gave her one of the two old cottages by the small lake where Mother had come to an end. The happy look on Mumbi's face freed them of the weight of their father's sixty-year-old legacy and property and they agreed to summon Morris back to Red Hill the next weekend and get on with it as Lois said.

Kung'u went back to Buru Buru that Sunday evening and was surprised to find Kaume still there. She looked at him and said nothing and went into the kitchen and boiled some eggs. Kung'u went into the shower and stayed there for almost an hour and when he came out his skin was like a frog's, reminding Kaume of when she had first met him. They ate the boiled eggs with chips and went to bed and now she knew she would not be going back to Kayole.

The next weekend Morris addressed all of them in his banker's voice inter-mixed with the first-born attitude that had yoked the other three all their lives. Kung'u shut his eyes and remained quiet as he had promised his sisters. Then Lois said: '... that is the last time you tell any of us, at least me, what to do.' They were all seated around the giant dining table and Kung'u realised that, two decades after their father passed on, the next few years were going to be a series of endless conversations, heated accusations, confusions brought upon them by what he had owned. Kung'u stood up quietly and went outside and stood there listening to Morris and Lois arguing inside. The old dogs no longer lay on the kokoto driveway and Kung'u recognised Morris's obsessive hand – he had already started his kaburu machinations learned over the years from Mother. Just then, Mumbi, who had been cooking for them in the kitchen, now came up to him. She rarely talked to anyone these days and he was surprised.

'Your maitu loved you very much,' Mumbi said. Maybe it was the way she said it or the voices inside the house or the fact that the driveway seemed devoid of all former domestic animal life that Kung'u felt something inside him from the days of his big sleep and suddenly he started laughing and could not stop. He started up and down the driveway laughing and could not even stop when Mumbi put the small Karatasi exercise book in his hand. Still laughing, he opened the book and when he saw Mother's small neat handwriting he laughed even louder. Morris, Lois and Damaris came to the window and stared at him. He left them there and drove back to Buru Buru.

The Karatasi exercise book held the last wishes of Augustine Kierieni recorded by Mother. They could not sell the Red Hill farm. It was to be left intact in four shares belonging to all of them or donated to the Presbyterian Church as grounds for a college for PCEA pastors. They agreed to keep the farm. Now that there was nothing they could do, each of them kept their old rooms and came and went, as they liked. Morris, defeated, refused to stay longer than was necessary to finalise matters and his old room went to Kiki. They sold all the livestock and the crops, planted Kikuyu grass over the whole twenty acres and opened up the larger premises for commercial public and social events managed by Damaris.

There were also the four townhouses in Kitisuru that stood side by side. Mother had decided that she would do as much as possible to see that they never parted easily and it was clear that her plan was they would live as close as possible to each other. Only Lois moved into one of the townhouses and the rest were rented out. But as written in the small Karatasi book all else was disposable, the properties on Kirinyaga Road, the two Rift Valley farms and a beach property in Kilifi. There was no mention of the Buru Buru house. And no one asked.

A year later Kung'u opened a hardware shop that specialised in mirrors and glass on Kirinyaga Road – and in months it had grown to be the biggest shop of its kind in East and Central Africa. There he stocked every kind of mirror there was in the world. Mirrors as big as a bus, ornamental mirrors as small as one's hand. Kaume, who still marvelled at how they had met in the mirrors, refused to go into the shop. She opened her own stall and travelled to Turkey to buy clothes for the Southern Sudanese. When the wife of a South Sudanese General visited her stall she became the personal clothing consultant of all the wives of military and business leaders from Southern Sudan, who spent half their lives in Nairobi. She took more trips to Turkey to buy clothes and accessories on their behalf and started thinking of opening a shop in Juba.

When Kung'u could not find a treadmill that could make him forget the past he started running marathons.

He started with the Ndakaini Half Marathon and then the Standard Chartered Marathon. In all these places where he ran marathons he treated these trips as reconnaissances for business and more often than not he bought property. When Kaume brought her daughter, Wangui, to Nairobi they moved back to Red Hill and Kung'u started running up and down the hills of his childhood to train for the 80 km Comrades Marathon in South Africa.

One morning Kung'u woke up at 5 a.m. in the Red Hill house. The Comrades was in a few months and he was unsatisfied with his training. He watched Kaume sleeping next to him and then he suddenly knew where he would run that morning. He was soon on Kiambu Road – a slight figure heading east. He could see the road ahead of him, past Kiambu town, past Runda and then onto Thika Highway, where he would turn into Outer Ring Road. He would run the breadth of that and turn into Jogoo Road and he would soon see the orange rooftops of Buru Buru. Then he would run to Buru Buru Phase 2 and he could see the girl in the mirrors who had saved his life.

SHIKO

When I drive into the Junction Mall in my old Toyota I can't find parking for an hour. Range Rover Sports, Audis and Benzes are ushered into fake reserved spaces by the watchmen. Ngoja. Wait, they say. I come here with one of Ivy's chariots, the Prado especially, and I get parking in quick dakikas. But Ivy and I have had an epic fight about chums, what's next after two years of us, and so I have to use my own ride. I double-park, sit in the car and the ngoma from Mercury upstairs sounds like it's coming from my own music tenje. I can see all the summer bunny mamas up there in the neon. I could just go there and try to hook up and forget about seeing my old classmates from Mappen. After our fight Ivy was too mad to come over tonight. I'm home alone – a rare opportunity. I weigh that against going back fifteen years at the Whisky Bar especially given what happened with Desmond 'Dessie' Wambugu and Stephen 'Kwara' Mbatia – Dessie and Kwara, my best friends at Mappen.

A Chrysler as big as a battleship cruises in. Shit. The first I've ever seen outside of the movies. It floats past me to the parking spot that I've been chilling for. This midget in a white Kaunda suit and deep purple cravat emerges. It's fucking Eliud Wamae. The Junction did not exist fifteen years ago when we were at Mappen, which is actually not too far away. This could even have been one of those grand ideas he was always fantasising about. That's why we started calling him the Fantasist. He's now as real as it gets. A player of maana. A tenderpreneur. Now, I'm the one who can't get parking. I try and slip the watchie a fifty bob and he looks at me with bile. I give him 200 and he lets me slide into Disabled.

I enter the mall and move against all these Chaguo La Teeniez chicks, high from being out so late. When I catch their eye they sneer at me with madharau. I turn and almost get caught in their slipstream to Mercury Bar.

Victor 'Colonel' Otieno – star rugby winger, Mappen First XV '91 – is already at the Whisky Bar. We do an awkward handshake man-hug thing. 'Alan, man. Many years.' His loud laugh, I swear, is exactly the same.

'How many years, man?' His voice is uji slow. 'How many years?' Yeah, he used to repeat everything twice. But out on the wing of a rugby pitch, damn he was a bat. I used to see him at Impala and Quins when he was still playing after I was discontinued from Civil Engineering, UON. He has not put on a kg in these fifteen years; his face is still stuck in a perpetual beam. Mercury is calling. I am furious with myself. I need a Glenfiddich.

I told Morris 'The Amerucan' Munyao that I would come if he would get the whiskies. The Amerucan's the only one who's kept in touch with all of us. Ever since I can remember, the Meru bastard always wanted to go to America. We used to laugh and call him the Amerucan till he went Wall Street after community college in bum-fuck South Carolina.

For this reunion the Colonel and the Fantasist have chosen one of the long tables with the thick couches with tall backs like thrones. I sit down like King Herod and make sure I can check out the Mall thoroughfare. The Fantasist says: 'You. You. You.' I want to punch him. 'You,' he says again. I am forced to grin. In school this midget was the greatest con artist ever. How many pennies did he leave school owing us? Something's changed with his jaw since then – it juts out, makes his face the mugshot that's always in the papers. He is always in and out of High Court. Huge land and city-council deals. Tenderpreneur Number One.

I have shown this face to Ivy: 'See. I went to school with this man.'

'Fucking hell, babe. Even my father knows Wamae,' she says.

The Fantasist disappeared after Mappen. Those of us who stayed in Kenya, waliowachwa, went to UON Nairobi campus mostly. Waliotuacha, those who left, went to the States and the UK. Because we all remained babies we are here to try and make our first major investment. I feel like a rabble in front of the Fantasist. By the end of Moi times the Fantasist was a millionaire. Lately, the Government wants him for a 1000-acre parcel in Lamu that's too close to the airport. The Gupta Shah murder case that he is linked to is still in court. Fucking robber baron.

I sip the 12-year-old Glen he has ordered for me and the nectar brings tears to my eyes. It floods into the sides of my stomach. The edges of my vision turn golden. Fuck, it's been a while since I've been on the good shit.

When Ivy and I come here we always sit at the bar and fight. A month ago we brought Catherine and her friends here for Ivy's birthday. Ivy can't hold her Shiraz. Shit got messy. Ivy hates whisky. Ivy loathes whisky in me. And sure, she brought up how I become an asshole on the nectar. I started holding forth about how whisky makes me want to be the man for her.

'This negro. Gets whisky dick every time we are out,' she said to the whole place. 'How is that for being the man for me when you can't get it up?'

I got cocky. 'Whisky forever. Whisky Bar for life. Ivy, my eternity,' I proclaimed.

'You know what?' she said quietly. 'Pay for your own fucking Glen.'

I had to back-pedal. I conceded that the place was actually called Wine Bar. All of Catherine's friends cracked up. Later, Ivy paid the attendant and we made up in the toilet. Catherine says that Ivy was not mental like this before the accident. Ivy was fourteen when she got the limp. Catherine was sixteen.

As the Fantasist, the Colonel and I wait for the wazees, the Chaguo La Teeniez girls prance away in the mall. 'Wiggle it. Just a little bit. I wanna see you wiggle it. Just a little bit.' I sip at the nectar. I look at the Colonel and remember how badly he wanted to join the Air Force but then IT took off in Kenya and he went into that. I was the maths guy. Top 5 Kenya. Number 2 KCSE '91 Maths Paper 1. Then the drama of my life became small.

The wazees start to show up. They come around the corner, one by one, with that halting step of the soon-to-be-forty male. Every foot is placed with some emphasis, the insecure marker of a new prosperity. We came here because of the emails from the Amerucan and Stephen Mbatia. Paul Kiprotich, Joel Mudavadi, Michael Kieni and James Mbithi roll up.

Some of us have seen each other in passing – others have kept up serious friendships over the years. The Amerucan never let anyone drift away – he always kept in touch even when he went to the States. Even with Dessie.

When everyone settles we wait for Bertiez. That's what everyone calls Stephen Mbatia nowadays. We used to call him Kwara. That's schoolboy shit for you. In our warped minds he looked like a girl when we were rabbles. He's the one who's thrown in the Ruwa land deal by email. And of course, Desmond 'Fisi' Wambugu. I think of him and I feel like a triple whisky. That shit he pulled on me during our final Mappen year. The Amerucan told me he's fifty-fifty about this meeting. I swear I'll order a bottle if he shows up. Maybe go medieval. Fuck that. I hear he became a cop. That animal would kill me.

We mull. Now that we are all here it is clear one and a half decades have done a serious number on us – especially those who stayed. We are all '72–'73 borns but at this table some could have at least a decade on others.

I work with numbers at Heidelmann. Polls. Statistics. Market research. I take apart these soon-to-be-forty men by recreating the last fifteen years. Ivy goes at me all the time about how nyama choma and beers bring about bad life calls, bad marriages, car accidents, death of parents and ageing. I can see the twenty-year hustle etched in the faces of those who were left behind. Waliowachwa. We should all be wearing T-shirts that say 'I am a Moi-era survivor'. I can make out the dents – we look ten years older. But we are the ones who know how to get around the Ministry of Lands, the Kenya Police and City Council.

The Amerucan, Michael and Alex Nderitu are little leaguers. Mere culprits and victims of sub-prime loans, credit-card defaults and the Internet bubble, and now they want to get into the game. They have foreign savings. Waliotuwacha. We natives are here to offer local investment advice. Native intelligence. In Vino. Veritas. In Whisky. I Trust. I look at them and I can see they are smirking at the dents on our faces.

Michael says to the Colonel we should start. Bertiez has sent a text to the Amerucan that he has been held up. Ten minutes. Michael doesn't like this. He is still a bully. Obese, light-skinned, he was the Mappen First XV's Number 8. He has shrunk. No; all of us have grown to his girth. His head has ballooned like he's on Toivo and split his hair into two, right down the middle, so it clings to the sides and the back of his Mt Kenya dome. Michael was a real asshole back then — we had our problems but they were not as bad as what happened between Desmond 'Fisi' Wambugu and me.

Ten minutes. Ah, we get into the sorry state of Mappen. That's what we still call it even if it had already been renamed fifteen years before we got there. The golf course we prized so much is gone, now a maize plantation. Someone reports that Meadows, the rugby pitch of all schoolboy rugby pitches, is overgrown and is used as a cattle paddock. There is a thick joviality; some abrupt silent phases, the Fantasist looks up every now and then and the drinks rounds keep coming.

Those of us drinking whisky swirl, sniff and sip, let the golden liquid settle into our mouths, suffuse our faces and frown across the table at those who are drinking beer and wine and even Jameson. I am surprised that the Whisky Bar actually serves Jameson. Our faces loosen and age with every sip per minute. We sigh without realising.

JM Mbithi used to be the class clown with his stutter. He reminds us of a string of our schoolboy idiocies in the stutter that used to kill us back then. We laugh from the liver at gang-fucking the Mappen teachers' maids. Stealing whole trays of food from the dining hall. Sneaking out to Riruta to drink Toivo. Somebody asks whether Dessie is still coming. He was always in the middle of all the shit. The golden edges in my vision disappear. We all remember Dessie in different ways.

I look at the bar and I imagine Ivy sitting there. Ivy is mad supu with her crazy beautiful eyes and the whisky is making me miss her. I wish she were here so these clowns could see her. How I have a woman ten years younger than me. That's how I roll. Maybe Ivy and I should get engaged. I muse at this till the Colonel speaks up. The man is smiling. Unbelievable, this permanent beam he carries with all the shit there is around.

'It's a bit late and some of us are going mbali,' he says, in his calm way. Michael is seated next to him and nods. 'Can we agree on the basics? All of you have seen the emails. We all know why we are here.'

The Colonel looks at Michael and he takes over. The asshole stares hard at everyone. 'Guys, it's simple. As Bertiez said in his email, we need 10 million.' He looks up and down the table. 'If we are all in, it's about one metre each. The idea, as you know, is to buy these available plots in Ruwa. Develop high-rises. Of course, if anyone has any other business ideas we should also be still open to that.'

The Amerucan is now looking at me and he says, 'The other thing is some of us have access to important info. Some of us are proper insiders. That can translate into hard cash. That can be important.'

Michael has noticed the look the Amerucan and I exchanged. 'Amerucan,' he says, 'No free rides here. We're talking shares: ten shares for ten of us. An equal number of shares for those who front up cash.' This asshole. Sisi tuliowachwa sit up at this.

The Amerucan steps in. 'Of course, equal shares for everyone. And we leave this open to this original group. Like the email said, 50k to start with. To show commitment. Then we can sell shares at agreed-upon rates. But the info some of these gentlemen have over here is as good as cash.' He looks at JM too when he says this. I wonder whether he has the same deal as I have. Info for shares in the venture.

The Fantasist speaks up for the first time. We know we will never see him again after this first meeting. 'Let me tell you something for free,' he says. 'You might want to check out Siokimau. Kajiado. South Coast. I can send you contacts, details.' With this he puts up his hand and the waiter brings another round. 'Tafadhali, bring the bill,' he says. He stands up like a proper mheshimwa and we all fawn like rabbles. 'Gentlemen, you will have to excuse me.'

The Amerucan also stands up and walks him out. We mull. I wonder why I'm still here. The Amerucan told me that I could get into this deal if I give up the corporate investment files I have access to at Heidelmann. I should be in Mercury upstairs.

When the Amerucan comes back he is sweating slightly. He reports that the Fantasist has made a pledge of one million – he will buy a full share of whatever idea we agree on. With that small bone that we've been thrown, the gauntlet is laid.

I quickly do the math. If I can get a loan to get into the venture I will be paying 70k per year till I am almost retired. And after the loan repayments on the Toyota, that would be like two thirds of my salary a month till I'm old.

It is midnight. Fuck what they say about it being worst before dawn. Michael suggests one month for each of us to deposit 50k to show commitment. The one and a half million shillings can be done in instalments. Yippee. Fucking yay.

I'm dying for Mercury. The Chaguo La Teeniez girls have become tipsy and they chase each other around the place. The returnees leave one by one. Michael. Paul Kiprotich. The natives mill around. Then it is just the Amerucan and me. I don't think he's done more than three beers. Now that business is finished his eyes are poppin' at the Chaguo La Teeniez.

'Do the thafus of this whole thing make sense?' he asks.

I nod.

'Does that mean you are in?' The whisky is clawing at my back. I hear contempt in his voice. This is a guy I tutored in maths at O-levels. He got a B-minus because of me, for fuck's sake.

Fuck that. Fuck symbiosis.

'In how? I'm in how? You know how crazy my chums shit is.' I can't help the boo-hoo in my voice. I hold up my empty whisky glass and the Amerucan laughs but he signals the waiter. 'I'll talk to Michael kando,' he says.

There is a bowl in the middle of the long table. Everybody has left several business cards on the table apart from the Fantasist. I play around with the cards and I realise that almost everyone at the table was in Mappen's First XV '91. Paul Kiprotich second row. Joel Mudavadi fly-half. Fuck. And of course a few were part of that fourth-form secret council that held Mappen in thrall seeking out what they branded tabia mbaya. Ati Homos. Ushoga.

The Amerucan and I finish up and we get up to go to Mercury. Then he pauses, smiling at a very tall individual who has just come in. I look closely. Lo. It's Kwara but he is Kwara no more. He is now over six feet, his voice has ballast sprinkled with kokoto.

'Hey, people,' he says.

'Mr Stephen Mbatia,' I say.

He looms over me. 'Bertiez. It's just Bertiez now.' All cool. He's changed the most out of all of us. The girlish, gawky Kwara is gone.

We are in Mercury by the large windows looking out into Nairobi neon. Bertiez, the Amerucan and I are all legless. There is a very high moon that tells of the coming of the early dawn. I keep on looking for signs of the indescribable, back at Mappen, in Bertiez's face. I wonder whether he and Dessie kept in touch.

But Bertiez's face is as empty as the parking lot below us. I can see my lone Toyota. We mumble at the three tall girls we've picked. They dance silently, their blank faces try to smile and make us horny.

I pick the tallest girl and she follows me outside. In the car park my Toyota refuses to start. I look at her properly for the first time as I release the Toyota's choke. The girl is a silhouette against the window, the moon. The car remains silent. She bends out of sight and when she appears she is heading back to the mall. She holds her heels in one hand and runs like a gazelle. She is a fucking model. She is not ukimwi skinny. I wish I had borrowed Ivy's Benz, Audi or Prado. I sit in the music falling from Mercury and I think about the Ksh 1 million. A Range

Rover Sports and a Benz squat in the car park opposite me in the distance. I will need a ride from the Amerucan or Bertiez.

I sleep most of Sunday. I wake up at 11 a.m., put half my head into the guest-room toilet bowl and let it all come out till only the yellow stuff that is bitter is coming out in small stringy spurts. I sleep again to sweat out all the sour.

I find myself in a large field. A rugby field. I am on Meadows and it is a big game. I am on the blind wing. The other team is these half-gazelle half-model chicks. I recognise the girl with heels in her hand from the reunion night. She has the ball and she comes my way and tries to go around me and I chase and she giggles and throws come-hithers. She makes sure she does not quite get away from me and lets me tackle her. The cheering crowd in the stands start singing Onyango Shika Dame. Kamataa. Aah. Whisky dreams.

I head to the office on Monday ngware. I work on the Sexualities Bill file all morning. When I open my office email at 2 p.m. there is a flurry of messages from Morris titled '1M'. He says that he spoke to Michael and if I get them the right info they can waive 0.5M.

Since the Amerucan came back from the States three years ago I have been feeding him information from the files of our select investment clients. We do research for at least the top five NSE companies. This stuff gives a shark like him clues as to where the money is leaning. Where the next huge investments will happen. Where the next mall will be built. Which highways will be improved. Where the Chinese will come in. It's good shit and he knows it. He does me in kind. Whisky. A few tens of Gs here and there. I am on 140 net a month over at Heidelmann. I can't keep Ivy and the nectar on that.

Lately, we've started getting a lot of work from the big Ford Foundation grantees, the Alternative Sexualities people. Haki Elimu. Urgent Action Fund. I get back on that.

On Tuesday evening Ivy calls me after I've just popped a Xanax. Her voice trips along the line, buoyant. 'Fucking hell, babe. I haven't seen you since… We still together?'

'Your phone has been off,' I say.

'How was your Baba meeting?' she asks. Last Friday's fight is now in the ether. I think of that little gazelle at Mercury that got away. My balls ache.

'We need to talk,' I say.

'Fucking hell, babe' – Ivy's phone signature if ever there was one. 'Sure, babe.'

I do not push. I'll probably see her over the weekend. The Xanax is tipping me over. It is not the best time to bring up the 1M. We say ciao. The Xanax drops me. I dream again of gazelles playing rugby at Meadows. Onyango shika dame. Kamataa. Ah.

I leave work at lunchtime on Friday and drive into town, go past Globe Cinema to Kariokor. I stop there and get some nyama and greasy chipos. I eat while I drive. I go through Eastleigh, Majengo, Shauri Moyo, Kamkunji. I look at the sprawl, the dust, the joyous hint of violence everywhere, the cocky pedestrian refusal to move for cars on the road. I am going home. I get on Route 23. I went up this road all my life in mathrees and my dad's Vokie. I am tempted to stop at the Baha Shopping Centre. Maybe my dad is already there in the local Mateso Bar. Mateso Bila Chuki. Suffering without bitterness. These Matesos are everywhere in Nai nowadays. It's already 2 p.m. but I can't see Dad's Vokie. The place is already teeming with the 4x4s of local overlords who always come back home to show they made good. I look at these behemoths and feel the Toyota squeezing the shit out of me.

I go past Salem and I'm in Kimathi. I grew up here in these white-washed bungalows that are now the colour of brown sugar. The windows of each house are opaque with dust. The juala kiosks have spread like Kikuyu grass. Plastic bags are the new flowers of these Kimathi times. The roads are pitted and the Toyota almost breaks into two. I can't be mad – this is home. Every one of our neighbours has built a fifteen-foot wall and a black gate of reinforced steel. When I played here as a child with my late brother, the hedge fences were barely taller than us. That la vida shit ended with the eighties.

When I was in first-year campus, Mum started complaining about headaches one night. She went to bed and did not wake up the next day. My brother went approved and started hanging out in Salem. He was gunned down not too far from here in Majengo. Flying squad.

The streetlights we played under as kids, my late brother and I, lean and threaten to fall on the Toyota as I make my way to our old house and Dad. I can still hear my mum's voice when the lights still used to work, coming on in the night, us refusing to go in and playing on and on, even till 10 pm during the school holidays. Shit was safe.

I make my way down to the first row of houses overlooking Mathare Valley proper. To think this estate was named after freedom fighter Dedan Kimathi. I have yet to bring Ivy to this zoo. I keep on telling her she will be eaten alive. Driving her big cars here. Please. She begs me to bring her every month or so and I tell her we have to go in my Toyota. 'Please,' she says. Ivy has yet to believe that being jacked in Nairobi is real.

My father's old white Vokie is parked outside our house. The sound of its engine is so much part of my internal make-up that I can hear the song of Volkswagen. German engineering. I knock on the twenty-foot black gate and I hear a shout. I knock again and I hear a door open. I peep through the thin space in the middle of the gate and I see Dad coming. He has become hairier at an age when most men go bald. He still has a head full of hair. He stopped buttoning the top half of his dirty white shirt a decade ago. I can smell last week's beer even this far off. He is sprinkled with dandruff. He carries his thick open squared notebook full of esoteric equations in one hand.

He shouts 'ni nani' again before he opens the gate. His voice always surprises me – the faint English accent from his time in Cambridge. This man used to be Professor Muigai, Maths Department, Chiromo Campus, University of Nairobi. National genius.

'Ni mimi,' I say. 'Kariuki.' He opens the gate and does not move aside to let me enter but looks me over.

'Kariuki.' he says. 'Kariuki. How is the Applied Mathematician? The Statistician.' We both laugh. He looks out into the street quickly, with the old fear in his eyes and then he steps aside and lets me in. He has a scar on his forehead from the last time some vijanas broke in and came for him. This happens every other month.

He still lives with Wamaitha, our old housemaid, who is like my second mother. The best thing about the house is the perfect lawn and the bougainvillea fence that she tends every day. I look at the green carpet and know my father is not all gone. We go around the house. I want to lie there on the back lawn and go to sleep, to become a kijana again. Start all over. Bring back Mum. Bring back Ndungu, my brother. Go to Alliance. Avoid Dessie and all the other bad shit. But I hoist myself up the high-back wall on some crates and look out. Mathare Valley in all its glory. The hundreds and hundreds of paper-shack lives. The Nairobi River spine that feeds them. This is where we used to go hunting. Then I went to campus and came back to Animal Planet.

Shit, Ivy needs to see this. I climb down and look at my father and wonder how he sleeps with all this wildlife and just a wall in between.

'I am not moving,' he says. As we walk into the house he says, 'Tell me about Heidelmann.'

'Pure servitude and horror,' I say. 'Maisha at Heidelmann.'

'How is Were?' He is talking about his old professor friend who hooked me up after I was discontinued from Civil Engineering.

'I don't see the Prof that much any more. He is always in SA. They have this big deal coming up. He might be selling to some South Africans. Synovate, I think they are called. Steadmann might be going that way too.'

'Ah.' My father says. 'Were was always greedy. The millions KANU paid him for 2002, God knows.' My father thinks everyone is greedy. I don't get him. This is Kenya Inc. Kuna wananchi. Na wenyenchi. Kuna viatu, Kuna watu.

'What do they call you over there nowadays?' he asks.

'Monitoring and Evaluation Officer.'

He winces. 'You need to finish your MBA. Get into siasa poll numbers. Do the MBA and I'll talk to Were.'

We head into the house, the sitting room of my childhood, now a shrunken universe of all that was once possible in the Kenyan world but is now unlikely. Once large in the imagination of my childhood are the measly cheap leather sofas with vitambaas we were not allowed to sit on, my brother and I, till we were sixteen. As kids we watched TV from the floor. And strictly on Saturdays between 6 and 8 p.m.

Old photos of Professor Muigai adorn the walls. Makerere. Helsinki '68. Boston '72. Cairo '77. And of course Cambridge '64. All the places that my father went through. My father knew Obama Senior. He knew President Kibaki. Ati Professor Saitoti. He boasts how he taught Professor Saitoti. How he set up the current systems at Treasury, Ministry of Finance. There is Mum in all her haloed beauty – she gave up med school for this man. After his work for Treasury we were finally going to be rich. All Mum asked for was to move away from Kimathi before it became Mathare. Then the headaches came that night a long time ago and she passed on. She is the only one I told about what happened with Dessie at Mappen.

I listen to my Father's complaints against the University even if it's now at least five years since they forced him out. I wonder whether the police took away his gun after he threatened matatu people in traffic for what he saw as disrespect. That's why the vijanas are always breaking into the house.

I just come out and say it. 'Dad. I need a loan.'

He goes quiet and looks at me. 'I hope you are not thinking Treasury Bills.'

'I need one million.' He sighs, realising I am serious.

'Let me get my coat. Let's go talk about this at Mateso.'

As I wait for him, I stand up and go to a corner where there is a small shrine placed on a cow-drum table that is testament to my mathematical achievements. There are all these framed maths prizes. I do not recognise a small, framed A4 page. Old maths exercise-book page. I unhook the frame from the wall. I can tell my childish handwriting:

$a\,x^2 + b\,x + c = 0$

We head to Mateso. Suffering. Mateso Bila Chuki. Suffering Without Bitterness. We order White Caps and I tell him about the reunion, the new investment chama we want to start. As he listens he starts drawing a complex quadratic equation in his large squared notebook. When I finish he looks at me – then he turns the notebook for me to look at. He points at all these equations and figures he has drawn up. 'From what you tell me there are several variables at hand. The first is the money you, actually I, put in. The second variable is the money you say you will make.'

I soar. There might be some hope. My dad raised my brother and me up by rewarding us any time we solved a maths problem he put in front of us. I suspect I know where he's going with this. I might just get something from him. Maybe 500k. Mateso is now filling up. Kenya Inc is alive and well.

'I've been thinking about that thing you used to teach Kungu and I all the time. By some Greek. Tortoise and Hare in some race,' I say.

Kalulu Hare gives Bwana Tortoise a head start of one hundred metres in a race. They both have a constant speed. After Hare runs a hundred he will get to where Tortoise started. By then, Tortoise will have run at least ten metres. Hare then runs the ten. Tortoise runs one metre. Hare reaches where Tortoise has been but he still has further to go. Because Hare must reach where Tortoise has already been, he can never overtake the Tortoise.

That's how he used to tell it.

'Yes, the philosopher Zeno. At least you remember something I taught you. Forget him for now.' He points at the notebook. 'Look at this carefully. Let's consider the constants. You are the one and only constant.' He picks up his White Cap, looks into my eyes. He writes down a list of figures. 'This is all the money you owe me to date.'

Fuck. Fuck. Fuck.

'This is what I can do,' he says. 'I will write you a cheque made out directly to the University of Nairobi. Finish your MBA then we can talk.'

I leave him there to his notebook. I am tired Hare. I am in a series of endless infinities that never catch up. He is Tortoise.

Sato is here. Ivy has a trip to Dubai on Monday. She is not sure whether we will get together tonight or kesho, Sunday. She says she has all this shit to do. Spruce herself up. Nails. Hair salon. Her OG father is driving her nuts again.

We are on the phone. I tell her we need to talk.

'Fucking hell, babe,' she says. 'Dubs is calling.' I repeat that we need to talk. 'Now?' she shouts.

'Just tell me now, babe,' she says. 'Alan, what's wrong?' There is a pause – some activity in the background – on her end. 'You are not fucking breaking up with me. Are you?'

I laugh and she's cool.

'Babe, I love you.' She sounds relieved. 'Just chill. I'll call you. The peeps in Dubs are on my ass.'

I get off the phone. I cannot go to Barclays for 1M. I am already paying a car-loan deni for the Toyota from two years ago. The Amerucan hooked me up with some guy who I bought the Toyota from in '04. I got played on the mileage. I owe 800k. I pay 80k every month. The thafus of my life are oppressive.

Ivy finally pitches up Sunday night – when I open the door, no hug. She just pushes me aside and immediately starts going on about how she needs 320k before she takes off to Dubai to buy tyres for the Merc. Her dad won't give her the money. Ivy rarely ever uses her own money.

'Erm babe, can you help me with my suitcase from downstairs?' She throws me the Audi keys. I go outside, open the boot of the car and haul her suitcase all the way.

'In here,' she says. I take it to the guestroom.

She looks over her dresses and panties to see what she needs for Dubai. I ask her whether we can talk for ten minutes. She looks at me, placing some of her clothes aside, and ignores me while she packs for Dubai. After a while she says she feels like some Shiraz.

'Are you sure? Your flight is at 6 a.m.' I want her sober for the 1M convo.

'What are you talking about? Are you being funny? So what if I'm leaving at 6 a.m?' She sidles up to me and makes a playful grab at my crotch. I slap her hand away.

She sits on the bed. 'I can see you don't want to get me drunk. I know you won't miss me. You are so boring. Now I feel like a burger.'

I look at her bare shoulders and wonder where it all goes. She's as skinny as fuck.

'Can we order in?' I remain quiet. 'Do you have any cash?' I head back to the sitting room without saying anything.

She wanders in. 'What is it?' she asks.

I tell her about it all. The Amerucan. The Mappen reunion. Her silence gets me going.

I build into it. I take it to the bridge. I soar. I am an eagle. I am R. Kelly. How I believe I can fly. I take it to PCEA church. This is my best presentation ever. My life depends on it. I finish. Fall back to the sofa.

'Is that it?' Her face is inscrutable.

'Yes. Will you lend me the cash?'

Ivy looks at me like I am a giraffe. Then she starts to laugh. The thing about Ivy's laugh is that it's the most infectious thing there is. Fuck. Fuck. Fuck.

'Who are these idiots?' she asks.

'Morris, you've met,' I say. 'We call him the Amerucan.'

'That baba friend of yours who is going on sixty-two? Babe, seriously. Where did you meet these fuckwits?'

'School,' I say. 'Mappen.'

I start to sing: 'Clowns to the right of me. Jokers to the left. Here I am stuck in the middle with you.' She does not crack a smile. I would like to just fuck right there and forget about the whole 1M thing. My two constants, my father and long-term girlfriend, have become unreliable variables.

She shakes her head and goes off to finish packing. We watch some TV, order dial-a-delivery and fall asleep on the sofa. At some point we wander off to bed staggering under the weight of sleep.

Ivy wakes me up at 5 a.m. I have whisky dick and she is not impressed that it takes me thirty minutes to get it up.

We mercy-fuck. It's horrible. We lie there and she sighs and goes off to shower. As she gets all dressed I struggle to stay awake.

Then I wake up and she is astride of me, screaming. 'Negro, you can't keep awake for like half an hour to keep me company before I leave. You won't see me for two weeks, remember.' Then, God, it's time for her to get into the taxi. She looks spectacular. This apparition is unbelievably mine. She looks at me and laughs with some shyness when she catches me watching her.

'Look, about what you asked for – I'll think about it. I'll try to find 300k tops. If this thing in Dubai goes through. Definitely. But if it does we should also talk about what's next between us.'

She says this looking into the mirror. She purses her lips, adds some gloss. Then she turns to me. 'Fucking hell, babe. Give me a kiss.' I do that and she rubs a finger hard against my lips to rub off the gloss. I follow her to the door. She blocks me. She wrinkles her face. At times like this, she tears easily. 'You don't have to come out. It's cold.' I take her downstairs anyway.

She takes off and the world goes quiet. There is a police siren somewhere. Some cats yowl in early-morning ecstasy. At least she left the keys to the Audi. I am to email her, though, if I want to use it.

A few hours later when I wake up again, the Toyota refuses to start. The Audi just sits there. Fuck it. I cruise out in it. Inside its grand universe Monday morning Nairobi actually looks half-sane. Full of possibilities. Maybe I could sell the Toyota for 500k and get in on the game. Maybe Ivy will lend me one of her cars, any one of them, for three months till I recoup my investment.

I get to the office and go through emails. The Mappen Hall Company has been on email all weekend. Paul Kiprotich says that he's moving back to the States – Kenya is not working out for him. JM Mbithi says his father has cancer and he has to spend all the loose cash he has on his treatment. And just like that we are six men still standing in the Ruwa venture. The Amerucan says that we will all need to put in 1.5 million now.

Solar Gardens is famous for its twenty-four-hour sexual professionals and the bjs they give in the garden after midnight. During the day it's an informal office for all of Nairobi's aspiring tenderpreneurs. They play pool all day and drink between 9 and 5 p.m. and then go home like the rest of us. And they hope against hope for all the deals in the Kenyan world. It is fitting that Solar Gardens used to be a Nairobi City Council town clerk's house until he went bankrupt. The new owner is said to be negotiating with developers. A block of apartments will soon be coming up here.

I am at Solar Gardens to meet the Amerucan. I have the kind of information in the brown envelope I am holding that the broke town clerk, for the lean and mean tenderpreneurs I see skulking around, would kill for. I have what the Amerucan wants.

I walk around looking for the Amerucan but I can't see anyone sitting alone. I go to the bar and hang out there and wait for him.

Just then he calls.

'Alan, uko wapi?'

'I am here,' I say.

'The fuck where?' The Amerucan sounds drunk. Wow. 'We saw you pita us just now. We are outside.'

I head out and I make out three figures in a far corner waving at me.

I head there and I recognise the Amerucan and Bertiez, who are seated facing me. The other man has his back to me and turns. It's Desmond Wambugu. Fucking hell. I give the Amerucan a look. What the fuck? I should just give him the envelope and leave.

They all stand. We slap and dash. Dessie and I measure each other up.

'Alan Kariuki Muigai,' he growls. 'I can't believe you are still alive.'

'You look well, man,' I say. The Amerucan and Bertiez laugh at this. Wah, the man has dents. He looks like he's just come back from ten tours with GSU in North Frontier District. There is a whole bottle of Johnnie Walker Black on the table.

I place the envelope in front of the Amerucan. He takes in air, grabs the envelope and shakes it.

'You are the fucking man,' the Amerucan says. All these years and I have never seen him this drunk. He grabs at the Johnnie Walker and pours me a hefty shot.

The Amerucan says: 'Michael and I will go through this and give you a shout. Also, because Kiprotich and JM have fallen out we need more jamaas. Otherwise everybody now needs to put in 2M. Dessie says he's in. That means we only need to do 1.6M if everybody else stays.' He lists, mostly for Dessie's benefit, all the ideas that have come through the Mappen Hall Company so far.

The Amerucan continues. 'Also, Dessie knows a lot of shit that will come in handy. He knows the ins and outs of places that we might need. He has people in CID.'

The last I'd heard was that Dessie went to Moi University out in Eldoret. He says he was posted as a teacher somewhere in Kajiado. I lap this shit up. This news is excellent. A fucking mwalimu. Then fuck that, he says, he managed to get into CID training. He did a few years as a corporal and then went into private security. Entertainment mostly. But he also does a lot of private bodyguard stuff. He looks at me and asks whether I need a bodyguard. He's heard I am rolling in an Audi. His eyes have a speculative look when he says this. I need a bodyguard, yes, from this motherfucker.

Apart from the dents, Dessie's face is held together in lumps, like he also became a boxer at some point. His eyes are set deep and small in the big lump that is his forehead and the bottom half that is one huge mess. I can tell he's still super-fit though. I notice that his knuckles are all broken. If I met him at night I would be, like: 'this man is a killer'.

Malizeni. Malizeni. The Amerucan is threatening to get another bottle. I take it easy on the Johnnie Black. All three have a head start on me and things could get crazy. I am worried that the Amerucan will lose the envelope that is now my ticket.

Then someone's phone rings. Dessie picks up. He listens and laughs long and loud. Then he says to the person he's talking to, 'Are you here? Uka. Come.'

'Guys,' he says, smiling his fisi smile. 'I have some friends who have done very well for themselves who want to join us. I hope you don't mind.'

He turns on his stool and we see two women standing a bit far away, looking around. Dessie waves at them. The two women approach gingerly in their heels and very tight mini-dresses. Dessie looks at them and whistles. 'Stop the press.'

The women look like they've just woken up and rolled around in make-up to hide their dents. Shit is ridiculous. At least they are not professionals, though. The Amerucan shouts: 'This is the Dessie we know.' One of the women is tall and dark. The other is short, fat and very light. They greet us with some Kiuk contempt and introduce themselves. The tall one is Wambui Grace and her friend is Wangui Caro. Wambui says to Dessie in Kikuyu, looking at Wangui, 'Haiya, look at this one. Kwani, he started drinking in the morning.' Dessie looks at her with a baleful glance.

'You smell like you woke up with changaa,' Wambui says. Dessie reaches and grabs her neck in one fluid movement and brings her face close to his as if he's going to headbutt her. She almost topples on her heels but Dessie holds tight. He brings her forehead against his and slowly applies pressure.

'Pole,' she says like she's about to cry. 'Sorreee. Sorreeee.' He lets her go and she moves back as if she will take a swing at him. Her face is contorted in pain but there is a hot and bothered look too. He smiles slowly at her and she sits down.

'Wait till we are nyumbani,' she says.

Wangui sits next to me. The four of us look like those ugly couples on TV that fight about how much they love each other. Bertiez and the Amerucan disassociate themselves from our side of the table — they go deep into how much money there is in wheat farming nowadays.

Dessie orders a bottle of Spice Gold for Wambui and Wangui. The women also ask for one kilo of wet fry. Wambui and Dessie turn to each other. Wangui tells me that she and Wambui import mitumba. They have exhibitions all over the City Centre. They travel to Turkey every month, buy wholesale and sell retail all over East Africa. The wet fry comes and Wangui and Wambui go at it like wow. Even the Amerucan and Bertiez forget wheat and watch. The shit is national geographic efficient. Fuck. I've got to go.

But after some whisky shots I am beyond leaving. I am in the bottle and the bottle is inside of me. When I look up, the Amerucan has fallen asleep on his stool. I stand up and go to him. Dessie puts up his hand and looks at me. 'What are you doing?'

The Amerucan drools in his sleep. 'Look at him. We need to get him home. I'll get him a taxi.' Dessie laughs and looks around the table. 'Haiya. Who went and made you prefect? Si you found us here. Let him sleep for half an hour. He'll wake up feeling better.'

Dessie's eyes have gone warthog mean from the Black. I feel my balls try and go back home. I remember those eyes from back when. There goes my escape plan. Bertiez floats away to somewhere safe. He has switched to White Cap Light. Smart man.

Wangui and Wambui stand with their hands to their sides after destroying the fry. They have a slight sheen to their faces as they head off to the bathroom. Dessie watches them as they waddle away and looks at me. 'Sasa Chief. Unataka one?' You want one?

'I'm good,' I say.

'Niambie. You want Wangui? I can organise. Wambui is mine.'

I look at Bertiez. He is smiling at some very distant spot in the night that only he can see. He is somewhere in between what happened to him at Mappen fifteen years ago and the present.

'Kwara?' Dessie turns and says. 'Kwara was just telling me he's married,' he says to me with a smirk. 'That makes Wangui yours.'

'Hey man,' I say. 'I am engaged.'

'I've heard.' Dessie laughs. 'You are going out with the daughter of some millionaire. So, just that you know: Wangui also has a lot of cash.'

He laughs again and looks as if he will say something but then sips at the Black.

'Why are you here? Where is this intended of yours?'

'Majuu. Out of the country.'

'You trust her?'

I look at him and say jack. He throws back the whisky but his small warthog eyes are still on me. He pours and flashes some more Johnnie Black. Turns to me. I brace myself.

'Ama, it's something else.'

'What?'

He laughs. 'Well, I've heard she's not a hundred per cent. A kaguru. Pole man. That's why I thought you might want to test something that works one ten per cent.'

He nods as the women appear in the distance. 'Wangui is always good to go.' He grabs at his crotch. 'A night-runner in bed. I should know. She also just bought a house in Garden Estate. I'm giving it to you on a platter.' He laughs again.

'Lakini, fifteen years ago you were very different. Look at you.'

'We all were.'

Dessie holds out his hand, broken knuckles and all, spreads his fingers. And then shakes it like a wriggling snake. He laughs out loud and pours more whisky.

'What's wrong with me? Forgive me. Tuji — enjoy. I believe you. You are engaged. We should celebrate. I was just trying to be nice about Wangui.'

Wangui and Wambui come back and they have splattered more war paint on their faces. Dessie's batteries are recharged – he grabs Wambui's naked thigh and squeezes hard, grinning at me. Wangui parks herself right beside me.

Dessie points at me. 'You women should know that these two guys used to be my best friends in High School. We are going into business together. Men only.' He turns to both women. 'What is mine also belongs to these gentlemen. We shared everything in school, especially with Bertiez over here.' Bertiez makes a sound like a child's balloon losing air very quickly.

'Alan and I had some problems. I put that down to being young, not knowing how the world works.' Wangui and Wambui laugh in appreciation at this circus. The Amerucan suddenly stirs and mutters in his sleep. He froths at the mouth and sleep-talks. The fool stays asleep.

Wambui is now drunk. 'Haiya. Tha is mashetani. Evil spirits running in his dreams,' she says, looking at the Amerucan's sleeping figure. Wangui laughs and puts her arm on my shoulder.

'Let sleeping dogs lie,' Dessie says to me. 'If you wake them up they will bite you.'

Dessie stands up and comes around to where I am sitting. He looks down at me and hauls me to my feet. 'Come, let's talk.' He leads me a few metres away. The table behind us has gone quiet.

'Hey, I hope there are no hard feelings,' he says. 'Because if there are, I would have to do something about it.'

The sky is a smothering blanket. Solar Gardens is a tipping boat and I am tottering in it.

'I need a favour. Kuja with us to Simmers. Wambui and I need to fuck. But she will bring drama if Wangui does not get one of you.' He turns and looks over at the table.

'We both know Bertiez can't manage. He's just not man enough. No dume.'

Bertiez behind us makes small talking with the women. From where we are he seems to have deflated in his suit. We go back to the table. Dessie seems relaxed. I try and will myself just to get up and walk away. I stand up and head off. I find myself in the toilet. When I get back I flash what's left in my glass without sitting down. I pull out my wallet. I am not sure what I have in it.

Dessie says, 'Don't worry, we'll get it.' He looks at the two women: both of them are now drunk and they laugh. Wangui reaches into her bag and throws a wad of thousands next to the bill. Dessie pours himself another whisky and breathes in deeply. He turns to me. 'I just want to know one thing before you go back to your kaguru chick. Are you still a homo?'

The whisky portal shuts. I go as sober as a judge. There's a point where whisky gets where the immediate world and the senses lose touch. In that vacuum, lost and deep memories stream, whole portals in the brain are reopened. I look around Solar Gardens and I suddenly feel every part of me linked with all the hopeless peeps in here, their miseries and their dire knowledge. The last fifteen years and what happened at Mappen seem like yesterday. That word. Homo. I haven't heard it for a while.

We all fall quiet. Dessie stares at me hard and long. I see all the craziness in the world in there. I am the coward of the county. I did not do anything back then when I saw him with Bertiez. Flagrante. And I will not do anything now.

'Don't worry,' Dessie says. 'I love you, man. But you know what. You are still a fucking shoga.'

He stands up and pulls back his coat and stretches. We all see the gun. It is small and is holstered underneath his armpit. He does not say kwaheri. I look at Bertiez and I suddenly see Kwara – tall, gawky and girlish. After Dessie and his women leave, we sit there in some kind of mutual relief and finish the bottle. We wait for the Amerucan to wake up. Bertiez asks me whether I have managed to put together the 1.5M. I feel like a rabble again. I look at Bertiez and his eyes are dry and empty.

A few years ago Mappen was in the papers. This was after it was renamed when a new headmaster took over. A rabble had been raped by some third formers. I remember what Dessie did to Bertiez and I want to cry.

Mappen used to be King of Nairobi's National Schools. It did not have the dry swottiness of Bush. It was not as Catholic as Strath. It did not have the jock culture of Changes. It did not have the thuggery of Jamu. It did not have the ujinga of Patch. Highway and Eastleigh are not worth bringing up – they were oboho schools. And Mappen did not have the snobbery of Saints. It did not have the ugly uniforms of Starehe. With these advantages it set out to become a school between Strath and Changes.

My father wanted me to go to Alliance but I missed that by five points. I ended up at Mappen. Dessie, Kwara and I drifted together in third form because Dessie and I were Eastlands. Kwara wanted to toughen up and believed we were his best allies in this quest. By fourth form we were studying together, doing everything together. Then, Dessie made Mappen First XV flanker. He was not big but ferocious. He had to keep super-fit. That's when he convinced Kwara and I to get up at 5 a.m. to train together. Mappen had eight houses – four were far away. The other four were in an arc around the main school block.

The three of us were all in neighbouring houses on the road that wrapped itself around the main block. Every morning, Dessie would wake me first at my house. And then we would run off to the house that Kwara was in.

One morning at the beginning of the second term, Dessie came to my house-dorm and rapped at my window. I jumped out of bed and into my games kit and we set off to pick up Kwara. We reached his house-dorm and Dessie went to wake him up. As I waited, I decided to do a quick lap around the house. This was not more than 200 metres. I went off in the morning mist and when I came back to the entrance of the house dorm, Kwara and Dessie were not outside yet. I decided to go check on them through the yard of the fourth form dorm.

I reached the row of windows and I peered in. I could see that Kwara was still in bed under this white blanket he used to have. Dessie was nowhere to be seen. I was about to take off but something caught the corner of my eye. Just beneath the window I made out a form sitting against the wall. I could see that Kwara was still asleep. And then the white blanket started wriggling. I could see a hand under the white blanket. It rose and fell and rose and fell. I saw Kwara's form dancing with the movement of the hand. And then the white blanket shifted. I saw Kwara. There was a hand around his neck, clenched. As Kwara squirmed his mouth open, heaving, trying to free himself, Dessie came from under the window into view. His other hand moved up and down. My hands pushed against the glass. There they both were, locked in a silent dance. I stepped back and Dessie's head turned. In the dark, his eyes gleamed.

I ran off into the early morning dark. I ran around the block and all the way to the main school gate. It was locked and I turned back. I ran around the main school block again and again and again. Those last few months at Mappen before our finals were a haze.

There was this thing we used to call 'shiko' at Mappen. Shiko was a concept, a kind of measurement of success, a philosophy of survival in boarding-school life. But we also used it to mean a slyness, a deceptive streak and a cunning. A good cunning. The Hare versus Tortoise kind. If you dawdled, partied with others but ended up doing well in class at the end of term you were a shikoist. If you misled everyone as to what you were about you were a shikoist. Its practice was essential for success in schoolboy Kenya. It was the best apprenticeship for life thereafter. I used to be quite good at shiko. I used to be a shikoist. Then I started running. I started being taken shiko.

Dessie told the whole school I was a homo and that I had hit on him and Kwara. That's why we were no longer friends. Kwara could have turned it all around – he had all the cards. But Dessie had already turned him into the flopping fish that I'd seen that one crazy morning jerking to his tune. We both went before the secret council that fourth formers had put together to call out shoga behaviour. But what counter did I have? What could I say I had seen? I did not have words for it. Much much later and for years the phrases came and went. Forced hand-job? Strangulation with involuntary jerk-off?

Over the years I marvelled at the failure of language to describe the worst. At Mappen I had at least the language of maths that I had always understood. I took refuge in maths and blew Maths Papers 1 and 2 to forget what I had seen that early morning.

Ivy sends me emails that say that she's still chasing the same deal in Dubai. I am no longer getting emails from the Mappen House Company – the rejection from years ago when Dessie turned all against me has come full circle. I am sure he is now in the Ruwa deal.

Catherine, Ivy's sister, has been trying to call me for weeks. A few days ago, after I'd ignored her calls, she sent me a text asking when she could come and pick up the Audi.

I go through my wallet one evening after another weekend with the Audi and I find a crumpled note inside. I open it and make out a number. The name, Shiku. I call the number and I recognise the voice. It's the gazelle. 'Sasa,' she says in a voice that is weightless and unmoored.

'Shiku,' I say. 'We met at Mercury. The Junction.'

I pick her up on Friday in Kileleshwa where she shares a bed-sitter with a friend. When she sees the Audi she laughs and all is right in her world.

'Whose other car was thaaat?' she asks. We go to the other Mercury. ABC – the original Mercury. An hour into drinks, Shiku asks where I live. I say Parklands and she crinkles her nose. 'It's okaaay,' she says. Try time.

Mercury is happening. We bop at the Bar. The place is bega kwa bega full. Someone taps me on the shoulder. I turn and Catherine is standing there.

'Hey, player,' she says. The music is loud but I hear her clearly. She looks Shiku up and down and holds out her palm. I put the keys of the Audi in her hand. She looks at me and shakes her head and walks away. Shiku asks what's wrong. I can see the Audi out in the parking lot. In its beauty in the ugly night full of harsh light it is the only constant.

MOTHERLESS

Joseph 'Maish Boi' Maina Mungai, fourth-year psych student at Rhodes University, stood on the long balcony of the flat that had come to be known as the Kenyan Embassy in Grahamstown, grilling lamb and pork chops. Kim Langat, his roommate and landlord, had bought the chops from Jozi township for the party that was being held in honour of the new lecturer, Professor Macharia Mundia. The Professor had joined Maish Boi's Department at the beginning of the year and when he remembered his last meeting with the new Professor he pressed the cuts against the grill to hear the ch-ch-ch-ch-ch. He watched the trail of smoke from the sizzle as it moved out into Grahamstown CBD below, past the Town Square a few metres away, past Standard Bank to the left, to the large boulevard where Grahamstown turned African. Grahamstown was a bowl and Maish Boi could see Jozi township in the distance, hear the sirens, imagine the screams of drunken violence and angry dissatisfaction of the natives with the new South Africa.

Out on Somerset Street below, locals appeared with their KFC dinners walking up and down past Standard Bank. On quiet Sunday afternoons Maish Boi wandered in from his room, which offered the only access to the balcony, to watch the petty robberies that occurred when churchgoers withdrew Sunday lunchtime money for their families from the ATM. For now the KFC eaters went undisturbed, even if it would get interesting later. Every few minutes one of the drunker KFC eaters took in the smoke, registered its source and shouted at Maish Boi to throw over some meat boetie. Mfetu throw some meat mos. Maish Boi ignored these calls and the drunks shouted, 'Mkundu wako,' and staggered off with threats in Xhosa or Afrikaans.

Maish Boi was in Grahamstown in hiding after his father, Minister Jeremiah Mungai, had left public office in disgrace with the rest of the President Moi regime in Kenya four years ago in 2002. His father had been mentioned in several of the commissions that had been set up to investigate corruption and public misconduct after Moi but was never formally charged. The Kenyan media, however, collectively decided he was an integral part of the gross public mismanagement of those times and Maish Boi came to Rhodes in first year when the Kenyan good times had ended, dropped his surname Mungai, even though it was a common name, and cultivated a new persona. He was a carbon copy of his father and he knew the older students, the postgrads, would look at his bulging eyes, big forehead, hear the name Mungai and remember Moi's right-hand Kikuyu minister.

Once considered one of the most powerful men in Kenya, Jeremiah Mungai had lost everything after the 2002 elections. So, at the beginning of the year Dad had paid his fees, accommodation in Res, plus a pittance in pocket money and told him unfortunately he was now on his own. Maish Boi had moved into the Kenyan Embassy in January. For three years he had stayed in Jan Smuts House, an official Rhodes residency, and did not tell his parents when he left. While they still thought he was in Res, he was now paying half the cost at the Kenyan Embassy. In these new hard times for the Mungais Maish Boi needed the extra cash for pocket money.

The Kenyan Embassy flat was one of those ancient colonial constructions that are found in large cities in former British colonies, usually occupied by Asians till they prosper and move to the suburbs. His father had owned a version of several of these kind of dwellings in Nairobi when they had still been rich. One in Grogan Road. One on Muindi Bingu Street.

The Kenyan Embassy was huge. Two of the rooms were the size of halls; the balcony stretched through the length of the flat. Only the kitchen, bathroom and toilet were student size. When Maish Boi and the other occupant, a Kenyan Asian student, Shabir Gupta, had moved into the apartment they had an inkling that it also served as the unofficial social hall for the postgrads, Kim Langat their landlord's perpetual guests. But Maish Boi and Shabir did not know that they would also have to feed the whole Kenyan postgrad community in Grahamstown at least four nights a week. They did not know that Kim Langat's niece, Betty Wangui, and her friends were also already unofficial tenants. The undergraduate girls were always in the apartment, especially over the weekends watching *Generations* and *Isidingo*. Because Wangui was such a good cook both Maish Boi and Shabir did not mind too much if it was only weekends. She, however, it now seemed, was planning to move in after the July holidays to save money.

Shabir was officially in his second year but had been at Rhodes for five years, a perpetual foreign student. He'd first enrolled for a Pharmacy degree for two years, left that for a BComm degree, and now after another two years was doing a BA in Economics with Kim Langat as his private and paid tutor on top of paying the rent. Shabir's family, the Guptas, had become rich from developing a small Nakuru mattress shop into one of the biggest supermarket chains in East Africa.

Kim Langat's real name was Paulson Kimani. He had come to Rhodes years ago as an Economics PhD student. He was a Rift Valley Kikuyu born and raised in Eldoret and many of the postgrads said that he did not have the tribal hubris of his Central Province or Nairobi counterparts. He got on very well with the other non-Kikuyu postgrads. Kalenjin postgraduate students started calling him Langat when they learned that he spoke fluent Kale. Everybody else called him Kim. And that's how he became Kim Langat. When Kim Langat had come to Rhodes, Kenyan students were few and so he started an East African Society by also finding Ugandan and Rwandese undergrads. His area of study was neo-liberal economic practice in East Africa in the 1980s. Through access to the small East African population and an understanding of who came from a stable enough background to pay a full year's rent, he had recruited Maish Boi and Shabir to live with him. He was the only one who really knew that Maish Boi was an ex-minister's son but not that the Mungai no longer had any Moi-era money.

The largest room was Kim Langat's. The smaller one in the middle belonged to Shabir, who never hang out with Kenyans. Maish Boi could hear the few voices that had already come in for the party through Shabir's open windows and the main door of his empty room. The quiet on the balcony would not last long. Maish Boi could hear the early arrivals going on about the changing of the Kenyan Constitution inside the flat. In the middle of Shabir's room stood the large bong that he smoked shishah from every day.

These parties at the Embassy were nostalgic and carefree; meat-fests of Kenyan ngenge where tears were eventually shed over how South Africa could not quite match Kenya in partying, education standards, general human decency and life possibilities. But nobody doubted that SA, with its wider racial spectrum, had hotter girls.

As the party filled up Maish Boi looked up to see that some postgrads had wandered out. Beers in hand, they stood there as if they were going to fly off the balcony towards the township where they went to pick up women because they were starving at the undergraduate universe that was Rhodes. None of them was sure how they had found themselves in what was clearly a glorified private High School that was mostly white. Maish Boi smiled and placed a large vat container over the meat to increase the heat, then went past them nodding at their guttural and rural Kiswahili greetings, Deputy Balozi Habari, through his room, into the sitting room, the large hall.

Sulky undergraduate girls watched repeats of *Generations* on TV sprawled over the long couch, ignored everyone and made fun of Xhosa and Afrikaans accents from the actors, calling at each other 'mfetu' and 'wena'. Maish Boi winked at Beatu, the prettiest one of them all and she giggled to the others. Some Nairobi boys stood beside the large CD player in a mist of faux-coolness bopping to E-Sir and pretending they were back in Westie. One of them shouted at Maish: 'Boi niaje niaje,' and he acknowledged them with a small salute.

Further along the long couch the two senior Kenyan lecturers, Doctor Sebastian Wafula, Law and Professor Jonathan Ouma, Politics, held forth to a group of postgrads on the future of South Africa. Maish Boi paid homage to the lecturers and ignored the postgrads, who sneered at him from their deep loneliness.

Kim Langat threw some Swa at him, happy that the party was picking up and moved between the groups in the sitting room, the small kitchen and the balcony ensuring that the girls had vodka, the boys had Black Label 750 ml beer, the postgrads had their Fish Eagle brandy and that nobody touched the Teacher's whisky set aside for the lecturers.

'Mkubwa hajafika?' Maish Boi asked, and Kim Langat shrugged. 'Professor Mundia?' Kim Langat shook his head. Maish Boi said, 'Meat is almost.'

One of the postgrads heard this and shouted at him. 'If the nyama is ready si you bring it. You can't keep your elders and your betters waiting.' The other postgrads laughed hard.

Kim Langat smiled and said, 'We are waiting for the guest of honour.' The postgrads laughed even harder holding their bellies. The postgrads loved these parties. Outside of stiff postgrad departmental cheese and wines or the rough ways of the township these were the only real Kenyan social occasions open to them.

Maish Boi went back to the balcony and looked down on Kim Langat's Nissan. Kim Langat had bought it second-hand and cheap from Professor Mundia – after Shabir and him had paid six months' rent upfront at the beginning of the year. Kim was junior lecturer this year after years of being a broke PhD student. Neither Maish Boi or Shabir had ever asked what the rent for the whole place was because it was so cheap compared to Res. But after a few months watching Kim, Maish Boi suspected that Shabir and he were actually paying the full rent for the Embassy. And he knew for sure that they were paying for postgrad meals, and Wangui's weekend upkeep. Maish Boi also recognised Professor Ouma's and Dr Wafula's cars, a green

VW Jetta and an old Mercedes. Shabir's blue Beemer was not there. He never hung out with Kenyans.

The Professor was still yet to show. The first batch of meat was ready. Maish Boi stacked it up and took it into the kitchen. Wangui was stirring the Cameroonian peanut butter chicken in a large pot. This recipe had been inherited by Kim from the original landlord, a Cameroonian civil servant doing a Fisheries PhD, when he had moved in years ago. Behind Wangui's shoulder stood Grace Kanessa, the new Professor's sister-in-law, an extremely skinny, long girl with a lopsided face, big, sexy eyes and a knowing smile, who had just started at Rhodes. Maish Boi offloaded the braai'd meat onto the kitchen table and started stacking the raw for the next round.

'Is Prof still coming?' he asked Kanessa, keeping it clean.

'Why you axing me?' she shot him a look filled with vodka. Her laugh teetered over the lip of her glass half-full and partly in her mouth. 'Like I roll with him.' Kim Langat's niece, Wangui, now Kanessa's sidekick, laughed, recently gutsy from all the possibilities of her friendship with Kanessa.

'So what, he's married to my sister. Niko my own cross to bear...' Kanessa said, as she sidled up to him and whispered in his ear. 'Lakini, is it true that you don't roll with Kenyan chicks?'

Maish Boi kept his eyes on the meat. A few days ago he had come home early from his fourth year seminars and gone straight to the kitchen to grab a drink. Standing at the fridge, he stood aside when the door from Kim Langat's room opened. Kanessa emerged. He was not too surprised because Wangui always came to study at the Kenyan Embassy when Kim was not around. Maish Boi said Hi as he grabbed a drink and when he looked up Kanessa looked sleepy and crumpled. A rank unmistakable smell caught in his nostrils and when he turned to her she shot him an insolent look as he went off to his room. Before he shut the door she smiled at him with a wistfulness that made him twist and turn in his bed before he fell asleep with the smell of sex in his nostrils. When he came out later into the sitting room he caught her leaving with Kim Langat. Kula na kulala si kitu. Eat. Sleep. Fuck. G-town.

Maish Boi now took the last of the meat inside the flat and Kim Langat made signals to serve. Even the two older lecturers present had given up on waiting for Professor Mundia. They soon left and the party loosened up. 'Twende fully blown,' someone shouted. The rest of the night was full of half-fights, strong come-ons and drunken exchanges. In the early hours of the morning Kim Langat made a speech about Kenyan unity and everybody shouted: 'Balozi. Ambassador. Kenyan Embassy.' The undergraduates left soon after that to catch Pop Art before it closed. Then, the die-hard postgrads remaining started a post-mortem on why the new Professor had dissed the East African community. The night ended on a soundtrack of wounded patriotism, failed nationalism and reinforced ethnicity. Some felt it was because Professor Mundia was from Nyeri and those who had met him complained that he thought he was American. And then Maish Boi and Kim Langat were left alone in the large hall of the sitting room looking at all the detritus of the Kenyan evening. Maish Boi felt a pang when he thought of Kanessa in Kim Langat's bedroom vodka-sprawled.

Maish Boi slept all weekend and when he ventured out that Monday evening there were the last of that fall's brown leaves everywhere on Main Street. The late June sky was grey. Late fall into winter. Over his three years here, Mum's illusions from her student days in York, England a long time ago filled his mind. Mum had insisted on Rhodes when she saw the brochures that boasted Grahamstown experienced four English seasons in a day. She had studied in York and had become Anglophile and because his father could no longer afford to send him to the UK, here he was in Grahamstown's whistle-stop English weather.

York, she always said, had been the highlight of her life. She had received a scholarship to the UK after becoming the first Miss Kenya. His father was also a First — he had been the first Kenyan PhD in Economics at Fort Hare, not too far away from here. All this had been a long time ago. When his father had been dismissed a few months before the election in which Moi would leave, his mother had been committed to Mathare

Mental Hospital with depression. After Dr Frank Njenga and other high-profile doctors could do nothing for her, she turned all her attention to him and his younger sister, Baby. Now in all the cards Mum said, 'You are now my only hope. You are now my main man.'

Whenever he called home she likened his time in Grahamstown with its four seasons a day to her time in England years ago. Her voice trailed in his head as he made his way to campus. Every few months she sent him a huge card with a cheesy message in her girlish handwriting. Spring was eternal hope: next month in August. Summer was drunk and free innocence: Christmas in SA. Winter was discontent: cold-ass July. Autumn was fall from grace: exams.

Oaks, elms and poplars lined Main Street. As Maish Boi walked along, past the tall steeple of the main cathedral, he heard a sibilant whisper. Evening had fallen and the street lights had come on to cast a foglike glow that closed on him like a glove.

'Stiudint, Stiudint, Stiudint....' A bizarre figure emerged from behind one of the trees. Maish Boi had over the years developed a healthy fear of all non-white locals when he was outside the English campus walls. But fear now became ala. The man was of an indeterminate age and wore a crabby, determined look on his face, absurd in a brownish ill-fitting suit. Maish Boi fished in his pocket, and with a set look on his face, carefully dropped some coins in the man's hands. Maish Boi realised that they could have been his own hands – they were exact in size and hue.

'Stiudint, Stiudint, Stiudint. Mai naim iss Matteeuw Leviticass... This is Matteeuw's Strite. Stiudint, Matteeuw's Strite. Stiudint, Matteeuw's Strite. Matteuw Leviticass.'

Maish Boi turned and walked back to campus, trying hard not to run. He was relieved when he saw the Rhodes Entrance Arch with two guards on each side. There were shouts of 'mkundu wako' behind him.

When he got to the fountain at the main square, thirty metres past the Arch, he looked up at the statue. The animal's haunches were bunched in a rearing motion, and the man on the horse wore an intense faraway look that seemed to span horizons and landscapes. Both were burnished to a deep brown wood-like timelessness. Maish Boi tried to stretch out and rap his knuckles on the horse's leg and feel the cold metal but the pedestal the statue was placed on was too high. This man with the large handlebar moustache, sword hanging from scabbard, sitting on an imperious horse had been a constant in the history books of his childhood: Cecil Rhodes.

Maish Boi remembered small statues and photos of the man from the farmhouse in Limuru where he had grown up — inherited from its previous British owners. The farm had been given to his father by the former President for his loyalty. In the British colonial school he had gone to, formerly known as the Prince of Wales School — complete with rugby fields and Sunday school dress — Cecil Rhodes was also a constant. But with his father's misfortunes it had all faded into memory till he had come to Rhodes. Here, Maish Boi felt he could renew his faith in those great childhood times. This English evening. This English statue. From this statue, the English fact of the University flowed. Its blazers. Its country-club feel. It was like going back to the wonderful past of the Limuru he had grown up in. Limuru Country Club. Rolling Limuru hills. Balmy Limuru evenings.

He looked behind him before going into the main part of the University, safe from the new South Africa's dangers outside. Inside all was familiar. The further you went outside it became wilder and wilder and then of course, the township. When he went there with Kim Langat to buy cheap meat and beer the township reminded him of a wildness he associated with those terrible years after Dad had left office. The constant threat of auctioneers, the white Peugeots that followed them to school and parked outside the gate of the Limuru farm all night, white Peugeots full of police extortionists who sensed his father's weakness and thought he had stashed away millions.

A furious wind now picked up — it had been hot all day, strange for the end of autumn but completely G-town weather. Maish Boi thought about Mum, Dad and Baby in the old farmhouse they could no longer afford to heat and took off towards the Psych Department – he had exams coming up, a Masters scholarship to strive for as there was no way he was going back to what had once been home and now that there was no more money coming. No way was he going back to an apartment that Mum, Dad and his sister might have to move to soon. Possibly Parklands.

A year ago, when he was still in third year, Maish Boi had received an email from the party no-show, Professor Mundia Macharia. The email said that the Professor would be joining the Psych Department from a teaching post in the Mid-West of America. He was coming briefly to finalise matters and wanted to meet Kenyans and East Africans in Grahamstown. Maish Boi, the Professor had been told, was just the man to meet if he wanted a proper intro to G-town and the Department. Professor Mundia said in the email that his area of expertise was the role of psychology in human resources and corporate communications. Then, things had become so elephant at home that Maish Boi forgot to respond. He was still at Jan Smuts house then and there were delays in his pocket money all the time so he was working at Campus Security, sleeping late, hitting the books for his third year end-of-year exams. He only heard later that the new Professor had hung out with Kim Langat and a few other postgrads. He forgot about Professor Macharia Mundia.

So, when the Professor emailed again at the beginning of the year and reported that he was in town ahead of Rhodes fully opening in January, Maish Boi had little option. They agreed to meet at Peppers at 6 p.m. before the student crowd came in. It was Orientation week but some of the older students had already arrived.

There were only two black students in third year Psych and Maish Boi was not sure what having another Kenyan there would mean for the territory he had carefully cultivated in the Department. In the absence of black South African students he had carefully ingratiated himself as the friendly and non-threatening African to the all-white faculty. By his second year he had become an early favourite for one of the three affirmative Masters scholarships available for final years.

All that was holding him back was finding a willing supervisor who worked in his proposed area of study. Maish Boi hoped to write a Masters dissertation on the largest mental institution in Kenya – Mathare Mental Hospital, where his mother had spent time. The hiring of a Kenyan lecturer who might be willing to supervise him on his thesis could mean that the scholarship was in the bag. His proposed title was something along the lines of 'Mathare as Symbol of a National Mental Illness'. He was still looking for the right words.

Maish Boi arrived at Peppers on time and found Professor Mundia brooding over a Windhoek Lager. Up close Maish Boi saw that the man had a brown oblong face and small eyes behind large spectacles. He wore an amazing deep-brown long suede jacket and a checked shirt with bright-red thick stripes and thin green ones. Maish Boi immediately felt a deep tamaa for the suede jacket. He could immediately tell it would fit him perfectly.

'Prof Mundia, it is such a pleasure to meet you,' Maish Boi said, and they shook hands. When he sat down the Professor leaned forward. 'My young friend,' he laughed with his hands in front of him, 'I know I am in a small town when everyone I meet always comes an hour late. Now I have been waiting for you since five. Is that what they've taught you here – that time is ...' The Professor spoke in strange faux Mid-Western drawl with Nyeri-ness clinging to the Rs and Ls.

'Pole, sir. Pole, sana. I'm very sorry but I thought we were to meet at six.' Maish Boi looked at his phone. 'I am sure that your email said we meet at six.'

The Professor regarded him and for a few seconds Maish Boi felt like a lying schoolboy. The man's small eyes grew bigger behind the spectacles and then he looked away. Maish Boi looked at the man's hands. If it was not for the nails on his two little fingers that were inches long they looked surprisingly like his own. He avoided the man's face watching the thick long talons growing from the little fingers. Maish Boi remembered this little affectation from home. Ngaruiya, their houseboy who taught him how to roast meat, had one long little nail on his left hand. Maish Boi felt the little talon scratching in his ear and other small secret places and shuddered. He had to suppress a laugh. Then the man sat up as if he were interviewing him and put up a hand signalling the barman. 'What are you drinking, my young friend?'

Terry the barman brought a Windhoek Lager for Professor Mundia and a Carling Black Label for Maish Boi. Professor Mundia said, 'So, here we are. Nimeskia you are the Kenyan to meet in Grahamstown. I have been told you should have been the first person I talked to. Nobody, the Kenyans, the people in the Department have been very good at telling me what I should expect of Grahamstown or Rhodes.' He raised his glass as if it was the first day of New Year's with all in the past left behind. 'Twee hamwe.' We are together.

Maish Boi was used to this kind of weird familiarity from the older Kenyans he had met since he had come to South Africa. 'Being Pamela', as they called it back home. He put on his best primary-school face, eager and respectful, and said: 'Twee hamwe'. But inside he remembered all the 'Mkundu wakos' he had received in South Africa and sipped at his Black Label. He could not stop looking at the beautiful long, suede leather jacket that was too small for the Professor.

'Paulson Kimani,' Maish Boi said. 'That's the person to talk to. He has been here the longest.' The Professor regarded this. Simjui, he said.

'Kenyans call him Kim Langat,' Maish Boi said.

'Oh. Why?'

'He speaks fluent Kalenjin – he was born in Eldoret.'

The Professor waved this bit of information away. 'Now that you are here I like to know who my students are. When I was told that I should have looked for you I looked at your department records. I saw that your father's name is Jeremiah Mungai.'

Something in Maish Boi's pants started trying to go back into his stomach. The Professor looked at him. 'Any relation to the politician?'

Maish Boi nodded. The Professor waited. Maish Boi wished he was facing the window doors of Peppers where he could watch life streamed in all its daily normality.

'I can see the resemblance. When I met the other Kenyans they did not seem to know who you really are. Who your father is. Or was. Kenya, I can imagine, can't be too easy for your family right now.'

Maish Boi's beer was finished and thankfully Terry the barman was right at hand with the next Black Label.

'I haven't seen you here recently,' Terry now said to Maish Boi. 'Your fellow Kenyans have been here closing the bar every week…'

'The reason I also wanted to meet,' Professor Mundia continued, as if Terry were not there, 'is that because in meetings that I've had so far with the Department, I've been told that you've already formally expressed interest in staying on for a Masters at the Department next year. I found that interesting. I would imagine that you would want to do a postgrad in the UK or the US. A bigger school. A bigger place.'

'I've become used to it here.'

The Professor looked at him with no small degree of disbelief. 'Well, we all have different motivations for what we do. If you want I can supervise you. And we can start working together immediately on a suitable area of research for your Masters.'

'I am thinking of doing something about Mathare. About psychosis in Mathare,' Maish Boi offered. 'I want to look at Mathare as a microcosm of a larger national mental problem.'

The Professor laughed and the sound made him likeable for the briefest of moments. 'You have to be practical. How old are you now?'

Maish Boi muttered and the Professor shook his head.

'The trick with successfully completing a Masters degree is being practical. Choosing what gets you there, not what you think you want,' Professor Mundia said. 'When you get to your post-doc you can do what you like. If you are lucky.'

Maish Boi could smell the Old Spice on the man and it reminded him of Dad. Old Spice was officially the Kenyan fifty-something male scent. Limuru, the good times, meat and all came flooding through with the Old Spice and flittered away. Wait a minute, Maish Boi thought when he turned to look outside. Was that an old white Peugeot he had seen flashing by on the street?

'Think about it – you have a few months. Now, tell me, how does an old man like me entertain himself in an undergraduate town like this one?'

'There are two Kenyan lecturers ... Doctor Wafula at the Law Department and Professor Ouma in Politics. They might be able to answer that question better ...'

'Yes, I've been told about them. I hear they've been in Grahamstown since apartheid, when Mandela was still in jail. I am not interested in playing golf,' Professor Mundia said. 'How do you live here for more than ten years?'

Maish Boi was very good friends with Professor Ouma's son, John Ken. Professor Ouma had been like a father to him when he had come into Grahamstown and all he said was, 'Yes, the Oumas came to South Africa in 1990.'

The Professor smiled. 'My young friend. Look around you. That is a white barman. Does South Africa look free to you? What would you say the difference between 2003 and 1990 here is?'

Maish Boi drank long and hard. There were students starting to come out and the Professor grimaced at the noise now coming through from the streets.

'I have been looking at the records of some of the people who are going to be my colleagues. They expired long ago. That old man Archibald who heads the Department cannot even walk. They say they brought me here to shake things up a bit in the graduate programme. We'll see. Now I am looking for black students and colleagues. That's why I wanted to meet.'

Some students that Maish Boi knew came in and he waved at them. The Professor looked over at them and turned to Maish Boi. 'I see you've become fully integrated with mzungus. That you are still stupid nice in a Kenyan way. My time in Houston taught me well. There, they don't play nice. The mzungus in my Department were nothing. I am only here because South Africa is really going to open up. With the locals the way they are, this is the real land of opportunity for Africans if you know what you are doing. Actually, Joburg is the real land of opportunity. I am thinking of starting a communications company providing HR skills with an emphasis on workplace psychology in a few years. I'll need a research assistant. If you can tweak your Masters research for corporate communications I can get you on board as my research assistant and that would kill three birds with two stones. Of course, I will need Kenyans who I can work with. We can work on a specific topic when I start officially in a few weeks.'

The man then sprang to his feet with surprising agility after this speech, removed his jacket and went off to the bathroom. Maish Boi reached out and felt the sleeve of the suede across the table. It reminded him of those old good Limuru times when shit had been affordable. When Dad went off on overseas State trips and came back with the right clothes. When Maish Boi sat back he saw that Professor Mundia had been standing behind him watching him all along. Now he went off to the bathroom.

When he returned the man paused before sitting down, glasses in hand. 'I see you like my jacket. I've had that jacket since I did my PhD fifteen years ago,' the Professor said, and sat down. 'It helps me remember where I have come from. Now, about my plans – I hope what I've told you is something you'd be interested in. In a few years these mzungus won't be here. Who do you think will be running this place – black South Africans? C'mon.'

'Can I please have an answer for you in a few weeks when we get into term proper?' Maish Boi said.

'Why do you need that long? I can't imagine you are in a position to negotiate. But, fine if you have to wait that long. Corporate communications. Human Resources. Staff psychology. That kind of thing has a future – we could both be in Joburg in a few years,' Professor Mundia said, putting down his glass and straightening up as if this had been an interview and it had come to an end. 'Then, one last thing,' he said, and reached for the jacket. 'I am also moving my family here. My wife wants her sister to come and study here. My sister-in-law. She is young and jinga-type. I need to make sure that the Kenyan boys over here don't jump on her. Not that she has a shida with that, mind you. Plus all the other African boys here.' He looked hard at Maish Boi when he said this and stood up. He stood there looking at the bar as if he was seeing it for the first time nodding to himself — it was as if he'd forgotten that Maish Boi was even there. Then he said, 'I need you to watch out for her.' He walked away and Maish Boi went to the bar, ordered three Black Labels at the same time and drank them all in succession. He sat there and thought how in the past external threats like this had been nullified with one call to his father.

Terry, sitting behind the bar, said: 'Another Kenyan?'

'Too many of us here now,' Maish Boi said. 'Reason I left home where they are bred.'

'A mature student?'

Maish Boi laughed and shook his head. 'Nope. A nutty Professor. Just made me an offer that I can't refuse. Chaperone. Research assistant. Joburg possibilities.'

After meeting Professor Mundia, Maish Boi asked a few postgrads who had met him what they thought of the man and some shrugged that he was just another arrogant Nyeri asshole. Others said he was smart but still assholish. With this unsatisfying assessment, Maish Boi did not think too much of Professor Mundia till Kim Langat decided to hold a party in his honour. By then, his landlord and his potential benefactor were fast friends and Maish Boi was wondering whether moving into the Kenyan Embassy with all its entanglements had been such a good idea.

Before the party Maish Boi bumped into Professor Mundia on the corridors of the Psych Department several times. The man kept on telling him that he was still waiting for him to come and see him, but whenever Maish Boi went to his office the door was always shut. When somebody pointed out the sister-in-law on campus, Maish Boi laughed out loud that the Professor would have imagined that this girl with the long, odd face needed any looking after in a varsity population that had three girls, one and a half cute, for every two boys. In a varsity that was in *Guinness World Records* for partying. In a varsity where one in three girls was hot and willing. He saw that the chaperone task had clearly fallen to Kim Langat and Maish Boi thought no more of it. After all Kim Langat was thirty-seven and Grace Kanessa was twenty-three. Kim Langat would make a better handler. Till Maish Boi saw what he saw. Kula na kulala si kitu. Eat. Sleep. Fuck. G-town.

It had taken Maish Boi a long three years to find his campus life sweet spot. Over the first two years he steered clear of Kenyans, especially the postgrads because they were old enough to remember his father as Minister Mungai. Once the President's right-hand man. Ati part of the economic dream team the President had put together to pacify Kenyans on all that was going wrong at the end of the millennium. The drunken over-familiar and wealthy postgrad Kales probably knew but did not care too much. The strange intimacy that the Kiuks tried to infer on him in those early years betrayed their vague suspicions. They did not seem to understand that he could do nothing for them one way or the other.

When he first came to Grahamstown he had found the lack of expectation, the lack of obligation that he had grown up in, exhilarating. No longer under his father's hand and his demands, away from the needs of those who had lain at their feet. The Limuru family house had always been full of political hangers-on who needed something, who orbited his father's star.

The Psych Department was not too different from Hillcrest or any of the private schools that he had gone to when things were good. Most of the students were middle or upper class. He made sure that he made them aware of his childhood access to Enid Blyton and they came to see him as one of them. He'd done two years at USIU before he had come out here while his father put together the money so he knew the ways of the private university.

Outside of Smuts and the Psych Department, Maish Boi, adrift from Kenya, discovered early that South Africa had even more issues. In those first months he decided to place himself mid-way between the extremes in the student population – straddling the equator. Issues. The word peppered the phone conversations he had with his parents and Baby. Back home his dreamy attempts at flight had always ended up with treading water – a runner's cartoon nightmare – when he tried to achieve enough life speed to take off in deciding what he wanted in life without the help of his father. His father's power and wealth, at least a decade ago, had created a utopia that made it difficult to take life too seriously.

So, he was relieved when he arrived in G-town, South Africa, anonymous – ending up in-between: with Coloureds at times, with Blacks sometimes, and Whites other times. All these people were cooked a certain way, and would not bend to his attempts to fit them into his spectrum. He watched Premier League football with the smooth-accented Zimbabweans at Smuts; met up at the Union with the history-free private school Black students who called themselves DeKaff in his other classes. He also hung out with South Africans of English origin in the Psych Department and exaggerated his knowledge of rugby; they still kept him at arm's length.

Maish Boi also fell in lust with a fellow first-year student called Catherine De Kock. He met her at the Freshman's Dinner – he had already seen her in classes trying to play favourites with the lecturers in the Psych Department. And because she was in Atherstone House next to Smuts he had seen at the dining hall their houses shared.

Students turned up for the Freshman's Dinner in casual clothes in spite of the dress code and the hushed physicality of the large dining hall. There were no grand entrances, formal speeches, prayers or felicitations. The only ceremony was in the old framed pictures and large wooden board etched with English names from the past. Maish Boi plonked himself on the first empty table he came to. From the vantage point of the high table he could see the eddy and flux in the large room. The male students gravitated to certain pre-selected tables and sections of the dining hall. Colour seemed the determinant aspect in these choices. He would learn later that other variables like looks and interests were factored in. After some weeks he was able to mouth the boxes everyone put themselves in: crude in any other country, necessary here. Tanned jocks and their bubbly Britney Spears-looking 'I'm not that innocent' chicks. Foreigners with mostly Shona–English accents. Arty Farties carrying either books or guitars. ANC Comrades hissing: 'You Muusst Empathissse!' Indians cheeky, and accentless ('Did you know', said a young Indian woman to him, 'that Chatsworth is the largest English-speaking suburb in South Africa?') So-called Coloureds, ultra cool, sitting with and next to the foreigners.

Then he looked around and he realised he was on a staff table. That's when he caught her looking at him. She was seated with three other friends and they were already drunk. When she waved at him her friends pushed her and they all giggled. Maish Boi had noticed in the few weeks he had been there that the girls were more integrated and kept to groups of twos and threes. Over the months he saw that some of the girls did not keep habitual territory in the Dining Hall. They were fluid across colour and geography – one of the great things about the 'New SA'. At first, he did not recognise her but he waved back.

She shouted at him: 'Why are you sitting there?' Then, he remembered. Psych 101. She was in his class. Caroline. No. Catherine. De Kock. She patted the seat next to her and her friends burst out in laughter. Maish Boi went to the table with the three girls.

They all spoke in chorus. 'Why were you sitting there?'

'*In vino ... veritas,*' he said.

'What's your name?' they all chorused.

'Joseph,' he said. 'He of the techni-coloured dreamcoat.'

'You are not from here?'

'Grahamstown. South Africa?'

That was the moment. The beginning of his strange ongoing on-and-off thing with Catherine De Kock. She tilted her head, as if listening to his accent and said, 'Yes, you are not from here.' Her two friends quickly became bored and giggled their way to other tables once they had eaten and the place was starting to empty out. All the while solitary individuals drifted to the table. Sitting at the table, then upping and leaving when neither Catherine nor he made overtures to communicate. At some point, when the wine was almost done, Catherine stood up and he looked around wondering what next.

'You want some more vino?'

They went out of the dining hall and turned into the path that led to Atherstone House, her res. He waited outside and she came back with a bottle of wine. They drank from one coffee mug as they watched the orange sky fall beyond the horizon with the dark in hot pursuit. The large blood-red moon. They hung out together for those first few weeks of first year. When they both got to know their way around she abruptly stopped talking to him in public and he knew well enough the ways of the place than to pursue what she had started. She held the power and so she, for a while, only spoke to him in psych class. He saw her all over the place: in a Joburg groove of rugby jocks, fast cars and life at the Rat and Parrot. Then, one day early in third term he went to the Union late at night. A girl staggered past him and then stopped and shouted his name and laughed. They slept together for the first time that night. But she still did not speak to him in the dining hall where heads would turn. She became his clandestine.

By then Maish Boi found that few local students had any idea where exactly Kenya was – and so he explained that it straddled the Equator. Some laughed at the earnestness in his tone and he held back his retort. Some laughed at his faint British accent (they said) intermixed with misplaced emphasis on the wrong syllable – at least that's the way the English South Africans saw it. In his mind South Africa was down here – anti Mediterranean, straddling the Tropic of Capricorn.

Maish Boi also had countless sessions with black South Africans on the meaning of names. When asked what Maina and Mungai meant he invented tall myths, keeping a straight face as long as he could and playing games with those who asked. At times he told them that his father's name meant 'from God' and they nodded with some kind of new regard even when he told them that the man was anything other than that. He found himself negotiating the boxes of South African colour. Later he realised that his black South African interrogators saw names as clues to character – or background. When he told them the truth: that his own name meant nothing, or that he had no idea what it meant, that's why everybody started calling him Maish Boi; they lost interest in him.

One day in exasperation, he made the observation to yet another Sasco interrogator that, 'At least I know where my tribe came from!' This was received with curt nods of approval. So as the approval bubbled and frothed, he continued, 'My tribe, the Gikuyu's are Bantus, like the Zulu and the Xhosa. We all come from Cameroon.'

'Ayibo! Upi Cameroon?' he was asked.

'West Africa,' he said.

They were waiting to go into the dining hall and someone in the audience retorted that South Africa did not come from Najeriaa. There were angry voices among his listeners. Who was he to tell them where they came from?

He spread his arms and smiled, 'But ... we are all Bantu?'

He listed the words in common, 'ku-Kufa, haiko, mkundu wako.'

They all laughed at the last phrase: Your arsehole.

Against his better judgement this encouraged him to go to a Sasco party that was being held in the weeks before his second-year exams before he knuckled down to start swotting. He planned to drink himself motherless, a South African word he had picked up.

The party was on Anglo-African Street. When he got there it was full of an uneasy mixture of locals, both black and coloured and African students who could not afford to live on campus. Though he did not remember all of it – he was told later by a 'friend' that he'd first removed his shoes and tried to burn them in the middle of the small dance floor because they were not suede. Everyone had found this funny and ignored him until he threatened to remove all his clothes. The narrator of this particular night of his life left soon after that and didn't really know what happened to Maish Boi next.

Removing clothes when drunk was considered white-boy behaviour by black South Africans. He could picture the scene.

'Coconut. Brown on the outside – white on the inside.' Motherless, that's what he had become. Not only completely drunk but unable to understand himself in front of all these Africans.

Maish Boi did remember wandering off outside to the braai stand. There were some middle-aged black Xhosa men and they offered him Fish Eagle brandy.

'Make you fly like fish eagle, Mos.'

He had three or four shots – and then he blurted out at the men by the braai stand:

'What do you really think of Mandela? Let me tell you what Mandela did. You think he negotiated everything he could for you behind the closed doors of Codesa? He sold you to the whites. Political freedom for Africans. Economic status quo for whites.' This was from a History 101 class. Convention for a Democratic South Africa. He remembered their faces later, flickering in the firelight – pulling shapes in the shadows.

'It also happened to us. Kenyatta did that to us at Lancaster ... Fuck! Mandela and Kenyatta betrayed us.' At this stage someone took him into one of the rooms. On the bed he fell on a supine figure. He did not care.

Then much later, something yanked him awake. He could not tell how many hours later it was. His hands were held close to his chest – the callused hand-wedge held him against the bed and with a harsh calmness chopped away at his face. Then a scream from his side. The squeak of bed springs being relieved of a body. A figure running away. The girl by his side. In his drunkenness it had all seemed to be happening very far away from him, the brownish haze of stupor turned crimson. Almost supplicant, hands in some form of worship, Maish Boi fell back as his attacker's breath slowed and his heaving stilled. That's what he got for dissing Mandela, comparing him to Kenyatta. Mkundu wako.

When Maish Boi woke up he could smell ripe blood in the air. Two of his front teeth were loose and his face was swollen. The sun's rays sliced into the bare room. His vomit was laced with dining-hall beetroot, an English root vegetable. From afar, he remembered old VOK documentaries – black-and-white images of white men with dogs and hoses chasing black men. And he lay back and bled.

After the Anglo-African beating he never drank himself motherless again, and stuck to East African parties where you could get away with murder. He forgot all the Shona words he'd learned by hanging out with Zimbos – and he was not displeased by the cash desperation that he started noticing with them now that Bob Mugabe had gone mad. He also retreated to the Psych Department where he joined camp with the English students of his third year class.

His thing with Catherine De Kock remained clandestine and unpredictable – over the second year they drunkenly fell into bed at least three times. After that first time at the Union when they were in first year, then after some cheese and wine in the Department in second year. Then, once after class when they had left together. And then, weeks later, after he had run into her in the library and they had been unable to concentrate. He had hardly seen her during their third year – she had a serious boyfriend who beat the shit out of her when he got drunk. In between these encounters she continued to ignore him in public, taunt him in class and flirt with him one on one.

He started hitting the books and came second in his final-year exams. The Department took his photo like it always did the top students and placed them on frames along the corridor of the Psych Department. When he went in one day, his photo had been defaced with the scribble underneath: Affirmative Action Prize. He stood there smiling and when he turned he found Catherine standing next to him. He crossed out the Affirmative Action Prize and instead wrote below – Motherless. She peered closely and laughed and linked her arm to his and pinched his cheek. She shrugged at the photo. And just like all the times before when they slept together she studiously ignored him thereafter for weeks, months even. It was part of the Rhodes code. But they both knew the incident had brought them even closer.

It was at one of the East African parties shortly after this that Kim Langat convinced him to move into the Kenyan Embassy. He felt his still loose teeth, his torn lips and thought about being motherless and agreed to become Deputy Ambassador.

Maish Boi now reached the Psych Department. All Honours and Masters students were given keys for access to the Department and when he removed his he looked at his hands, remembered the homeless man he'd just seen and shuddered. The Department was quiet. He paused at the main corridor, checking out the picture frames of all those final-year graduates from over the years. The Masters students. The few PhDs. At the end were the photos of prizewinners. There he was.

'97 – THIRD PRIZE WINNER 1ST YEAR
'99 – JOINT THIRD PRIZE WINNER 3RD YEAR

Of the five serious contenders for the three Psych Masters scholarships, Catherine De Kock was Maish Boi's biggest competitor. They had jostled for number three all these years at Rhodes. The third year prize had been shared between them. He had missed out in his second year after being beaten by her by one mark.

The top student, Megan Grogan, a quiet red-haired girl, who everyone agreed to be a certified genius, was a given and her photo was the biggest. Kathy Du Preez, super-fit and kindly was more or less in there next to her. Sasha Bretton would have been a shoo-in but she was Zimbabwean and with all that was going on with the economy she had decided to be practical and go for TV journalism. Anita Naidoo, another genius of sorts, had a breakdown at the end of third year and had taken a year off to recover. This last spot Masters scholarship was now just between him and Catherine De Kock. He looked at himself in the picture and then went up to the toilet on the third floor. Before he entered a voice called out down the corridor.

'Hello. Grace. Is that you?'

Maish Boi realised that the open door at the end of the corridor was Professor Mundia's office. He went into the toilet and when he came back the man was standing at the door waiting. Professor Mundia wore the same brown suede jacket from Peppers and it was even smaller than when they met a year ago.

'Young man, how are you?' the man said. 'I thought you were my sister-in-law, Grace. I am waiting for her so we can go home. Would you know where she is?'

Maish Boi remained quiet.

'Of course you don't. Why don't you come into my office? We might as well also talk about your Masters plans now that we are both here. God knows I've been trying to get you to meet for a while.'

Maish Boi followed him into his office where the professor asked him to sit down and give him a couple of minutes. He continued working at the desktop. The desk was full of books and papers. There were shelves all around. Professor Mundia, Maish Boi saw, had clearly settled in.

Then, he turned to Maish Boi. 'You have not bothered to come and see me? Have you changed your mind about your Masters?' He pushed aside the papers on his desk as if he were trying to swim against a very strong current.

'Professor Archibald told me that you've already been to his office to talk to him. I am not sure why you have not come to see me. I thought we agreed that we needed to keep on talking? In fact, if I remember correctly, we tentatively agreed that you would think up a tentative topic in psychology in corporate communications.'

The Professor reached out behind him and pulled out a file.

'I have been looking at your records properly.' He opened the file and Maish Boi could see copies of his transcripts.

'Very impressive. You have always been among the top five in all your units. Also, the muthungu lecturers really like you. Archibald especially.' The Professor laughed.

Maish Boi remained silent. The last time he had seen Professor Mundia was at the Rat and Parrot with Professor

Archibald. Other than himself Prof Mundia was the only other black person in there. The Professor had intently watched Maish Boi as he chugged them back with his fellow psych students. When Maish Boi had waved Professor Mundia had ignored him. Now the man leaned back.

'It does not look good when you go around me and see the Head Of Department when I am here now. We are both Kenyans. People talk if they do not think we are close. We had a meeting amongst the senior staff and the Department agreed that it would be best for all involved if I was your supervisor. But I am yet to formally agree. Before we work together I just want to make sure that we are clear on some of the things.'

Maish Boi looked past Professor Mundia, at the Grahamstown evening, a wind picking up fast. 'I am yet to work out whether this impressive record of yours in front of me is not an act of affirmative action. Maybe you have managed to fool the muthungus here very well.'

Maish Boi looked at Professor Mundia. 'Please Mwalimu. What is all this about?'

'Young man, do not try that mwalimu crap on me. I am Professor to you. I have been waiting for you to come to see me but yet you have gone to the Head of Department. The time when us Kenyans should have stuck together is long gone.'

'We are still in the middle of the year – I did not know I needed to think about this yet.'

'This is your future we are talking about. It is never too early. What have you been doing? Don't tell me you've been working – I hardly ever see you in the Department.'

There were voices outside in the corridor and Maish Boi waited in faint hope for them to come this way to save him but they drifted further away.

Professor Mundia continued. 'The other day someone told me that you live in what is known as the Kenyan Embassy and then I understood why I never see you here. I know what goes on there. I thought when we met last year you and I understood each other. I mistakenly thought you a serious young man who wants to further his career.'

Maish Boi saw the tree outside the window behind

the Professor lean towards the building in the wind. Grahamstown's famed four seasons in a day – it had been hot all day and Maish Boi now remembered reports of hailstones coming from the East.

'It has also come to my attention that you are in collusion with a member of staff who is breaking one of the most serious laws in the teaching profession. Sleeping with a student. Not to mention that the same member of staff has a wife back home. A young daughter.'

The Professor's voice continued at a distance: 'The conduct of a psychologist is one that requires a lot of moral rectitude ... we are like members of the medical profession. There are standards to uphold. I cannot support your application until you prove to me that you are worthy to study a postgraduate degree in this Department.'

The Professor sat back and looked at him. 'So I want you to think about this and then we talk.'

Maish Boi remained silent and decided to try. 'Sir, the reason I want to study Mathare is because of my mother. It is actually because of my mother that I am doing psych. I always wanted to do journalism. But I want to look at Mathare because of the time she spent there.'

The Professor leaned back, his glasses now steaming, removed them and wiped them on the sleeve of the suede jacket.

'My mother ...' Maish Boi said. 'She had problems when my father was dropped from government. I wanted to understand what happened to her. When I went on visits to Mathare I saw all these people there ... all these people who had been dumped by their families. All those people who showed a certain side to life in Kenya ... '

The Professor sat up and looked at him. 'Why didn't you tell me this the first time we talked?'

'Sir, I was not sure you would like my choice ... what you said when we first met. I don't know. I was stupid. I am sorry.'

Professor Mundia regarded him. 'But that's not really it. Is it?'

'What do you mean, sir?

'This is about your father – you really do not want anyone

here to know that you are one of the sons of the men behind the Moi regime. Biwott. Saitoti. Your father. Their children scattered all over the world in hiding. Ashamed.'

Maish Boi smiled at the ceiling. 'Yes, maybe that too. You've seen the papers. What happened to my dad. That would not be a good thing for everybody to know ...'

The Professor leaned back and Maish Boi could see lightning flashes. 'I do not know whether to really believe you. But you know, it does not matter. Life has a way of balancing the ledger. The benefits of the past are always held against the price of the present. Young man, do you know why I left Kenya?'

'No, sir.'

'Because of what Moi did to the country. Moi destroyed the possibilities that were open to my generation. That's why I am sitting here with you now. Because of men like your father there was nothing for me in Kenya. I am sure you did not have the same problems when you were growing up ...'

'Yes, and that is partly the reason I do not broadcast who my father is.'

'I admire your cause – I really do. And yes, it could be true you are here because you want to understand what happened to your mother. Look, I can and will recommend you strongly for a scholarship. I can also make sure that you get a long-distance supervisor that we can both work with because I will have to tell the Department that it is not an area of strength for me. How about that? Forget Joburg. But I can only help if you show me you are serious. You know a member of staff having inappropriate relations with a student. Kim Langat, as you call him. I need you to go see the Chairman of the Faculty and report this member of staff. You do that and we'll understand each other. That is all.'

Maish Boi stood up and the man said, 'Last thing before you leave. Whose idea was it to invite me to the party in this place you call the Kenyan Embassy to laugh at me? Was it Paulson Kimani? To have me as a figure of fun for the whole Kenyan Grahamstown population. And this after I sold him a car at buying rate ...'

The Professor had turned away and was now facing his desktop computer speaking into it and Maish Boi knew he had been dismissed.

'I need to get on with my work. I am sure my sister-in-law will not be coming home tonight. We both know where she is. The ball is in your court.'

Maish Boi left the Department and walked to Smuts, his home for those three years when things had been so simple. He always called home from the reliable public phone in the Smuts common room. He needed to hear the sound of the Limuru hearth. His Mum picked up with a little scream at hearing him: 'How are the green rolling fields out there ... Is it balmy?' He could hear the meds in her words. She always put on a little voice when he called.

'The mists are rolling in, Mum. Autumn is refusing to die.' His mum's tears came easily these days and he'd learned to be light-hearted. Before she could vent how much she missed England, his dad got on the phone extension willing some authority down the connection.

'Joseph, I've been trying to call you at your Res for the last few days. All the students that picked up could not seem to find you. They even seem unable to find you on the room list. Why is that?'

'Dad, the exams are a few weeks away — I do not spend that much time in my room. I study in the Department. In the Psych Honours room.'

His father made a strange noise on the phone. 'Have you managed to deposit the fees draft for the second half of the year? Don't want to see you at the doorstep tomorrow saying you've lost the draft.'

'I paid it in immediately, Dad. I'll fax the receipt tomorrow morning.'

'You know the fax here is not working, Joseph. Always waiting for tomorrow to do what can be done today. I hope you've started reading the book I sent you.' This was a tattered copy of *The Young Man in Search of a Better World* by British philosopher C.E.M. Joad. The slim volume had been given to his father as an eager bare-footed young man by an English missionary called Melchiot Andrews who had been his mentor at Fort Hare. Maish Boi shuddered, expecting another version of this story. When the finances had run out any gifts his father gave him came with little tests, second-hand books instead of pocket money. This last draft his father was asking about was possibly the last wire that he would ever receive.

'Read that book,' his father now said. 'If you don't get that scholarship for your Masters it might help.' His voice was still public, honest and earnest. Maish Boi could hear Oprah in the background and pictured his father munching roast corn off the cob, his meaty slump of shoulders and wrinkled Kenyan map of a face. Rolling fingers and mouth working like a man breathing into a mouth organ.

His father, in their new genteel poverty reincarnation, believed that a family that watched Oprah together was a family together. That was his father – the only honest man in a regime full of billionaires. All the kids Maish Boy had grown up with were still filthy rich and could not believe that the Mungais did not have any money. Maish Boi waited and the regular soundtrack to these conversations played out. How the man had started off by supporting his now dead mother, Maish Boi's grandmother, by fixing wheelbarrows in the village. When he left government his father had even tried to start a wheelbarrow factory for a while but that, like all else, had failed. All doors, even the banks, were closed to him. Maish Boi wondered what new social plan his father was trying to put together to uplift the andu-a-moko who had worked for him all these years.

Thankfully Baby now came on the other extension and asked him whether he was being faithful to the diary he had promised to keep for her.

'I can't wait to read it when you get home at the end of the year – even if Dad says you are not coming. I know you will come. I have been praying. How's your Joburg girl?' Maish Boi had mentioned Catherine De Kock lightly to keep her entertained, lied that she was his regular girlfriend.

'A journal. I am keeping a journal. I am here on a journey remember,' Maish Boi now said to Baby. 'You guys watching Oprah? Is Dad still feeding you guys on seeds?' he asked. He felt weary thinking about maize. Beans. Peas. Cowpeas. The sausages and the Mombasa holidays of childhood now a thing of the past. Baby did not seem to mind – even if she was fourteen she seemed innocent of all that had passed. He thought about the possible move to Parklands and her walking through its mean streets and winced.

Mum came back on the other extension. 'I am sure you are excited about your plans for next year. You know you can't come back here. The country is just not what it used to be. Your father has aged ten years in the last two months. We need you more than ever to succeed. I don't know what will happen if we go to Parklands.' Her voice wavered and Maish Boi thought she would cry. This was a woman who had once graced all the covers of the East Africa social magazines. A former Miss Kenya, even said to have the ear of the President. And of course, the whispers about an affair.

Maish Boi remembered the years when they thought that Dad would become Vice President and all she had thought about was becoming Second Lady. Then, his father had been snubbed and how the Kenyan media had crowed. Maybe that's when Mum's journey towards Mathare had started. There had been more whispers that all this had happened when Mum had refused the big man's overtures. After that snub his father had been sidelined and eventually the announcement had come just months to the 2002 elections. Maish Boi would never forget seeing her being taken away. Maish Boy knew the only reason his father still paid for the landline phone was so that his mother could talk to him regularly, afraid that she would relapse again.

'Mum, things might now work out here. I'm now thinking UCT. Cape Town.' He thought about Professor Mundia.

'Your father cannot afford Cape Town. You will have to remain there.' Maish Boi suspected that his mother had managed to stash away what she called a few shillings here and there without Dad's knowledge. He remembered when she had visited at the end of his first year, going among other parents, stalking and beaming at the Freshers' afternoon welcome event. 'Just Call Me Cecilia. I studied in England.'

'Mum, I'm sure you can kick in the extra 100k for me for UCT. I have been here for four years. Think about how you could come to see me in Cape Town,' Maish Boi said. He could now hear her thinking about that.

'Okay, we'll see. I have to think of your sister too.' Maish Boi could hear her weighing Baby's future against a visit to UCT. Cape Town against Parklands.

Then, Mum said, 'You know who we saw the other day? The Wahomes. They told us that there is a new Kenyan lecturer they know who has come to Rhodes. Have you met him? The Wahomes say he's in your Department. I am sure that it will now be easier to get the Masters scholarship.' The Wahomes were their only remaining friends in Limuru – the only ones who took their calls after his father had gone down.

'Do you want me to get in touch with this man through the Wahomes?'

'Mum, please please do not do that.'

'Why? The man is Kikuyu. He can help.'

'Mum. Grahamstown is a small place. The Uni is too white. In Cape Town I could even start working while I did my Masters.'

Somebody came into the Smuts Common Room and when Maish Boi turned he recognised a fat bespectacled round-headed boy with a silly cap on his head; he was walking around the room, hands behind his back like a school prefect. Richard Wilkins Junior, who had been his next-door neighbour when he had still been at Smuts. Wilkins Junior stood in front of the large mirror in the room jawing his face side to side.

'White means that the standards are high then,' Mum was saying. 'But it doesn't hurt to have another Kenyan there. I'll ask the Wahomes to talk to him. You were to send us some photos.'

'I'll do that, Mum. Send the photos. Please do not ask the Wahomes to speak to Professor Mundia.' Maish Boi heard a voice, his father's voice calling, 'Cecilia, Cecilia.' His father, after a few beers, liked to sing, 'Cecilia, you're breaking my heart.' Maish Boi imagined his mother getting all tremulous and shy, becoming her old girlish self. She said 'hold on' and went off. The former Fort Hare Economics Professor and the former Miss Kenya. Maish Boi tried to picture them in England. They had run their course and he had to make his move. He was decided. They still had each other.

As he waited for his mum to come back to the phone, he watched Wilkins Junior wondering whether the boy remembered him after they had stayed in rooms next to each other for two years.

Maish Boi rolled his eyes and murmured to himself, 'Wine glass number five. Red. In Vino …' Mum drifted back. 'Okay, I will not ask the Wahomes to talk to the new mwalimu yet. So, that's it. Just be happy, son. Don't think too much. Enjoy yourself − it's nice to be young and starting your life somewhere else…'

Maish Boi interrupted, knowing what was coming next. 'Okay, Mum, I have to dash. We'll talk soon. I've got to hit the books.'

'I don't know…. when we'll speak to you next… You know now that you are my only hope − your father is not who he used to be. I could never imagine my life would become this − oh, the idea of living in Parklands.' Her voice started breaking. He said bye. He could hear his father's voice. Cecilia, you're breaking my heart. He had to get out.

Over the next few weeks the Kenyan Community held small caucuses in different corners of campus to discuss why Professor Mundia had not attended the party held in his honour. The undergrads spread the word that the Professor was a kaburu because he never let Kanessa leave the house after 8 p.m. That he dropped his sister-in-law off at campus and then she had to go to his office so that they could go home together as if she was in primary school. The postgrads felt that the snub warranted sending a PhD delegation to make a peace offering. When they went to Professor Ouma and Dr Wafula for advice the two confessed that they were yet to meet the new Professor.

The postgrad traffic at the Kenyan Embassy increased in the evenings to discuss the matter. Some put this all down to Nyeri Kiuk arrogance. All sorts of things about the Professor were reported. Somebody even managed to retrieve an old colleague of Professor Mundia's in Denver and sent him an email to get a sense of what kind of man they were dealing with. The former colleague reported and confirmed the strange ways of Professor Mundia even when he had been in America.

Grahamstown emptied out for the mid-year holidays but most of the East Africans, as always, remained. The Grahamstown festival came and went. One evening when some postgrads had just left the Kenyan Embassy, Maish Boi, Shabir and Wangui were watching a movie on the E channel when they heard a knock on the door. It was 11 p.m. and they did not expect any visitors. Maish Boi opened the door and Kanessa was standing there with a suitcase. Wangui helped her take her things through the small door at the end of the hall into Kim Langat's room. Shabir turned to Maish Boi and said, 'Ai. I feel like I'm living in a dorm. Back in High School. I have to get away. I'm driving to Cape Town first thing in the morning. Wanna come?'

Maish Boi looked at him. 'I am working campus security this holiday. Night shift – pole.' They continued to watch the Arnold Schwarzenegger movie and Maish Boi wondered whether Shabir knew how poor he was.

When Rhodes reopened for third term the Kenyan community turned its attention to the new development of the extra tenant at the Kenyan Embassy. The postgrad women felt that Kim Langat should step down as the patron of the East African Society. EASOC had become the most vibrant African society and provided access for students from smaller African populations such as the Ghanaians, Namibians and Zambians. All the non-Kenyans in EASOC thought that the Kenyans had dominated things for so long and were happy at all these cracks between Kim Langat and the new Professor Mundia. They wondered aloud whether they were better off going to join ZimSoc or WestSoc because Zimbos and Nigerians had suddenly become easier to deal with than Kenyans with all their drama.

The rent-paying occupants of the Kenyan Embassy stayed away from it all. Kim Langat was hardly ever seen anymore. Shabir spent most of the time driving in his Beemer up and down the streets of Grahamstown. He played pool at the Union all day and at Pop Art all night. Maish Boi spent all his time in the Psych Honours room.

A few weeks later, one October evening, Maish Boi walked into the Swot Room and it was completely full, student heads stooped under the looming end-of-year exams. The BComm Accounts Zimbos, the Africans in BA. Econ, the few Sascos who were still not on Foundation Courses. One of the unspoken rules of the Swot Room was that nobody acknowledged each other. It was so uncool to be there. Maish Boi found a desk against the wall and placed his Pharmacology notes to the left of the desk. He also removed a brown envelope and a large brochure. The colourful brochure said 'Student Work and Travel Programme (SWTP) USA'. It asked whether he wanted to go to the USA and have a working and travelling experience in the most amazing country in the world. He could hear his father singing in his head: *Cecilia. You're breaking my heart.*

He began with the letter to the Student Work and Travel people. When he finished that, Maish Boi started a second letter to the University, asking for all the money against fees for the second term, fourth year be transferred to his name. He carefully replicated his father's signature and he looked up and breathed in deeply at what he had done. None of the students in various panic modes, end-of-year hell were looking at him. Then, he made out Catherine De Kock at a desk right at the front of the room. Very few white students came to the Swot Room and Maish Boi could see that everyone was now watching her. He had hardly seen her since second term. Yes, a few times in class where she'd been distant and polite. Now she had her eyes fixed on the books in front of her but kept on untying her ponytail, removing the band and then pulling back her hair and tying it again.

Maish Boi stood up and thought about going up to her but instead went outside. There were a few students smoking and blowing out into the summer sky. When he went back into the Swot Room he found Catherine De Kock sitting on his desk waiting for him. She was reading the US Work and Travel brochure.

She looked up at him. 'Were you ever going to tell me?'

Maish Boi laughed at this.

'Does anybody know at the Department that they won't have their favourite Kenyan boy around anymore? I thought that now you have a Kenyan supervisor in your corner the scholarship is a given ... why? Why are you leaving?'

Maish Boi laughed, thinking of Professor Mundia in his corner.

'You know when you think you want something really badly ... and then one day you just wake up and ...'

She stood up and pushed him. 'What are you talking about?'

'Well, one day you wake up and feel ...' Maish Boi paused, 'motherless. You feel motherless.' He laughed at the word.

'Kenyans,' he added. 'That's why. It's less straightforward than you would think.'

'Can I buy you a drink?' she said. 'I'd like to hear about this African thing between you and the new guy.' She laughed out loud as she said this and Maish Boi remembered why he had always liked her. Everyone glared at them as they left.

They drove to the Monkey Puzzle instead of the Rat and Parrot because she was scared one of her ex-boyfriend's jock friends might see them. She said she had finally dumped him after he had slapped her at the Union recently. Maish Boi knew this had happened countless times and was sure they would be back together by the end of the week. They could not go to Pop Art because all the East Africans would be there. He showed what it meant to get motherless when they drank till the Monkey Puzzle closed at 3 a.m.

The next morning they lay in her bed going through the Pharmacology notes.

She sighed trying to get into it. 'You are so lucky, going to the States – I am not even sure why you still need to go through this Pharmacology stuff?'

'I am not going to the States. I am thinking about going ...'

'I can feel it, You are not here anymore. You are done ... you've always been intense; don't you know that's why I like you – but that intensity does not live here any more.' She poked his naked chest and flopped back. 'Very sexy. Have you thought what will you do there ... in the States?'

'Wait on tables. Pick fruit in an orchard. Hey, it's still a vague plan. I am waiting to hear from my cousin who lives there. He went to Cape Cod end of last year from UCT. His name is John Biko Kamau.'

She laughed. 'You have a cousin called Biko? That is sooo struggle.'

'Maybe come back when I've made enough cash and do not need a scholarship or any of the BS that has happened to me over the last few weeks with this Kenyan guy. I'll do a year and come back. I might try and do a Masters there.'

Catherine laughed. 'Stop trying to make out like you are disadvantaged. It's not like you are township ...' she crinkled her nose. 'We will miss you around here.'

'I am not disadvantaged. I have told you I am just motherless.' Maish Boi said this and tried to laugh but something else leapt from his throat.

'What does that even mean?'

'Adrift.' And the thing crawled from his throat.

Catherine turned to him. 'That laugh scares me. There is this very hard thing in you. I knew it when I first met you ...'

He looked at her and said, 'I believe I am your first subject, Miss De Kock.'

'Fuck you,' she said, and went into the bathroom.

Maish Boi let himself out.

The week before the exams Maish Boi went to see Kim Langat in his office in the Economics Department. The small office smelled of sleep and bananas. Maish Boi found Kim looking out of the window onto the lawns. Students were spread out chasing each other, lying spread-eagled on the grass. Kim Langat turned to him and they both looked at each other and just laughed.

'Things are elephant,' Kim said. 'Aren't they?'

They remained silent for a while. Kim said: 'You know I've been offered a job in Maputo. An Economics consultancy. Maybe I've been here too long. What is happening is just a way of telling me that I've been here too long ...'

'Professor Maina wants me to go to the Dean,' Maish Boi said, 'and say that you've been sleeping with a student.'

Kim Langat shook his head. 'Ati to say what. What can he prove?'

'Kim, actually I am not here for that. I don't give a shit. I am here about the rent. I know I'd asked you to give me some time till my next draft came from home.'

Kim laughed. 'Maish, always the practical one. Kenyan kabisa. You really don't care about this thing with Kanessa ...'

'What can I say? Kula na kulala si kitu.'

'Okay.'

'I wanted us to talk about the way the rent works. I can't pay the whole rent if Wangui and Kanessa have been living with us. I can't afford to. You know how it is with me ...' Maish Boi said.

Kim looked at him. 'If you leave right now things will become more elephant. Everyone will think the Deputy Balozi ... is against me.' They both laughed.

'We are now five people staying together ... pole, but that is not what I signed up for.'

Kim Langat waved this away. 'Sawa about the rent — we can do the math. Split it into five since the two girls moved in. Are you staying for Masters like you said? Why not let all this die down — you don't have to pay anything for now — wait till towards the end of the year and then we agree on what's what ... for this year. And start next year. Clean slate.'

Maish Boi looked at him. 'That's the other thing. I am also done with G-town. I think I'll do the US Work and Travel thing. Go make some cash for next year. That's why I need the extra rent cash to pay the Work and Travel guys. I can only pay some of the rent now and then the rest of what I owe in March next year when I am back.'

Kim Langat sat back. 'Hey, pole — is it because of this thing with Kanessa and Mundia?'

'Uh uh. Stuff nyumbani. Things are not great at home.'

'Well … maybe I should come with you.'

'Well, this thing with you and Kanessa has fucked up things for me at Psych. I doubt whether Mundia will recommend me for the scholarship … he thinks I am in cahoots with you. The man is a lunatic.'

'Mathare certified,' Kim Langat nodded. 'When do you leave?'

'I am not sure yet – trying to head out after my last paper. Is Kanessa okay?'

Everyone knew that she had been admitted to the Sanatorium for a nervous breakdown.

'So-so,' Kim Langat said. 'These young girls … a man cannot deny them …'

They looked at each other and laughed again at this.

'Last thing. Someone told Mundia who my father is …'

Kim Langat looked out at the students on the lawn without a care in the world and he shook his head. 'Ndio yes, Maish. Pole sana … who knew what the guy was like …'

'Kenyan unity, right. What to do?'

Maish Boi spent the week after his last paper at Student Registration. He took the 319 authorisation letter that he had forged to receive the money from the last draft the old man had sent made out to Rhodes. Because he was no longer in Res he was given a refund, which he sent to Cape Town for the US Work and Travel fee. Part of him had hoped that the Registration people would try and call his father but at this time of the year they were too busy and he went to the cashier and received the most rands he had ever held in his hand since he came to Rhodes. He felt alive again. He knew Rhodes would hold his final year results till he cleared the fees; the fees that were now taking him to America. He would write to Archibald and ask him to defer his Masters Acceptance for a year. By then he would have enough US dollars. Already his cousin, John Biko in Cape Cod, was emailing him furiously, asking him whether he was serious about coming.

When he returned to the Kenyan Embassy with all his business done he found a middle-aged woman having tea with Kim Langat and Kanessa. He had already heard that Kanessa's mother had flown into Grahamstown to take her daughter back home. Over the last few weeks Kanessa's eyes had become bigger and she had lost even more weight. Her mother was an older version of her but with an upright posture like a steel rod. Kim Langat asked Maish Boi to join them and he could not refuse. They made small talk about the summer pollen in the air and how bad it was for Kenyans. Then, the three retreated to Kim's room for high-level talks.

The day Maish Boi received the letter from US Work and Travel he went to the Psych Department to pick up his books in the Honours Room. Once he was packed he went upstairs to the toilet. On his way in he saw that the door of Professor Mundia's office was open. When he knocked on the door there was no answer and he went in. The room was empty. He stood there for five minutes but Professor Mundia did not show up. He could see from the desk that the man was around – there was an open book, *Mathare Mental Institution: A Case Study*, with a pen and glasses lying next to it. The window was open and Maish Boi could feel the summer heat. Then, he saw the suede jacket folded neatly to the side on the other small desk in the room. There was no one on the long corridor he could see. Maish Boi went to the window and looked outside. The window looked out onto the back of the block. There was a deserted path, a floor bed and a small hedge. Maish Boi picked up the jacket and threw it outside the window. When he reached downstairs he went out back, picked up the jacket, put it on and said goodbye to the Psych Department. The jacket fitted him perfectly.

THE CAPE COD
BICYCLE WAR

The Bicycles

We came to Orleans, Cape Cod that winter after 9/11 to work at the local Wendy's. Students from Eastern Europe, Latin America and Africa, new to America and dorming at the Wendy's house. Juanita Gomez and Carmela Dos Santos from Bogotá moved into the house and because they were there first took over the TV. Then Juanita made the green Schwinn with the large tyres and low-slung seat hers; Carmela chose the red Chopper with the tall front handlebars and front small wheel. Kudzai Farai, a Shona boy who had already been around the year before in some sort of self-exile from Zimbabwe, kept the large mountain Schwinn. João Da Silva from São Paulo chose a large traditional bicycle, heavy as a farm horse, that Georgo Moldovanu from Moldavia called a Soviet worker's bicycle. Georgo rode a large black Trojan, the newest bike in the house. John Biko Kamau from Kenya and Brazilian Roberto Perez were left without bicycles because they had come to Orleans last. At first João shared his bike with Roberto. Kudzai and Carmela let John Biko use their bikes whenever he wanted. The bikes were not a problem before it became cold. In the final weeks of autumn the girls preferred to walk anyway so there was always a free bike. But we were eight and there were only six working bicycles and winter was coming in. Four bikes needed minor repairs. At least another five were in some slow form of decay.

Mostly it was a difference of days that each of us got in, even hours, spread over two weeks. One by one on the night bus over two weeks in late October and early November. Tumi and John Biko came through JFK – we thought it was because it had the best security. Georgo came directly through Logan, Boston. Juanita, Carmela, João and Roberto landed in Miami and then flew to Boston. When we compared notes later we realised everyone had taken the Bonanza bus from Boston to Orleans. Through all the small toy-towns in Cape Cod in the dark, sleeping under the first snow flurries of that winter. Brewster, Barnstable and all the others only Georgo could not remember.

We were all picked up by our new benefactor, Mr Malcolm Pudephatt, at the Orleans bus station. We had all received a Hello letter from him when we were in our countries. We expected a tall old man with a white beard like Noah or Moses, some Old Testament figure. But there he was in the snowy night, a short man in large spectacles with dark thick hair and dark eyebrows.

'Malcolm Pudephatt,' he said. 'You must be Work and Travel Employee number … ' He knew all our work numbers. Later, Georgo said that's all we were to him – Numbers. So, to revenge, we'd started calling him Mr P to pretend all that he was to us was just a letter. Or maybe Juanita and Carmela had started calling him Mr P because they could not say his name. In arrival, in all the things that we found in America we were equal. But not with the bicycles.

Mr P had three Wendy's shops – the other two were in Brewster and Barnstable. We all wanted to work in the bigger shops but we were stuck at the Orleans Wendy's. At the end of every winter, Mr P offered a one-year visa sponsorship to one student worker to stay on and become permanent. We talked a lot about who Mr P would choose at the end of that winter. We wondered whether 9/11 meant that Mr P would not be allowed to choose one of us. After a week we already felt like suspects. We talked about how crazy it was that Mr P had sponsored Kudzai the previous year. That's before we learned that he had lied to Mr Pudephatt that he was an orphan.

We learned that saying you were an orphan from Africa could just about get you anything in America.

Mr P picked us up and drove us to the large house in a wide clearing surrounded by trees moving in and out of a blanket of fog by the river. This would be our home for the winter. This mansion. Mr P led us into the large sitting room which was like the lobby of a hotel. 'Here you are,' he said, showing us to our rooms. 'Good luck. One of the managers will see you tomorrow.' He did not say anything about the bicycles.

Mr P disappeared from our lives but remained everywhere in the house. All the bills that were brought to the house by the postman were addressed to him. The cheques we received every two weeks had his signature. There was a photo of him and his family in the restaurant – his wife and daughter, a teenage girl with braces that all the boys came to want to marry so that they could get one of the shops.

We woke up after our first night in Orleans to find a note beside the bed. *Welcome to Orleans. My name is Ahmed Abu Samed, Manager here at Wendy's. Please come to the Wendy's shop as soon as you can.* There was a small hand-drawn map and directions. Wendy's was built like a very big cottage – Georgo said it looked like Red Riding Hood's cottage. He always said weird things like that. We walked to that first Wendy's meeting still half-asleep. The first thing we heard in the shop as we waited to meet Ahmed Abu Samed was a loud-speaker voice coming from the drive-through window:

'Hi.'

'How are you? Welcome to Wendy's. What can I get you today, Ma'am?'

'I'd like the Wendy's No. 5.'

'Will that be all, Ma'am?'

'What was that?'

'Would you like anything else?'

'No. Thank you.'

'How are you, Sir?'

Over and over it went and it would become the soundtrack of our lives. Later we tried talking like that. When we went back to our countries in the Spring (the Africans no longer talked of long rains and short rains but of summer, autumn, spring and winter) the soundtrack would play in our heads for years. Our families would ask why we talked funny even if we had been in America just for a few months. It was to remember till we were old, that winter, the War with the bicycles.

Before Ahmed Abu Samed put us to work he gave us his little 'welcome' speech in the office he shared with Midge Bush the other Wendy's manager, an owl-spectacled woman of forty with a pretty, blinking face, a round body and a loud laugh.

Their desks and every open space were strewn with Wendy's merchandise: Wendy's letterheads; Wendy's uniforms; Wendy's toys for children and Wendy's menus. The soundtrack continued from the overhead speaker from the drive-through window and Ahmed spoke to us over it. Ahmed handed over a contract. It said: *You will earn USD 6.25 an hour and will work for 4 months.* All of us immediately started doing the math in our different currencies. All our contracts ended at the end of April, and then we would all be back in Cape Town, Moldova, Bogotá and São Paulo. We expected to have 5000 US dollars. The contract was ten pages – nobody read it all. We pretended to because it made us feel important. We told each other contracts for what – we just wanted to get paid. That was a mistake. Among other things we should have looked at the contracts to read what they said about equipment, especially the bicycles.

The small short-circuit TV in the top corner facing Ahmed and Midge's desks swept across the shop again and again – it showed the drive-through window, then the front restaurant, the cash register area, the grill and fryer area, the kitchen, the back of the shop and even the office in quick succession. Every five seconds the small TV gave a short snapshot of strange black and white human figures with static on their edges. Seeing each other on that small screen for the first time, those images never quite left our heads. Strange black and white figures with sudden, jerky movements. Shadows.

Ahmed's eyes jerked between us as we pretended to read the contract and monitor the small TV. As we told him about ourselves, he put a hand up, looked even more closely into the small TV, stood up and peered into it. Then, satisfied, he sat down. For some of us, Midge was also on duty during our first meeting and he turned to her: 'Look at this. Look at this. Can you believe?' Midge Bush gave out her loud laugh.

Once the contract was done, Ahmed gave us some hard yellow envelopes to keep the contract and the other documents safe. House Rules. Safety Regulations. First Aid. The many forms that we had to fill. Social Security, Insurance, Wendy's Confidentiality Clause and Work Injury Form Disclaimer. The envelopes were great – each of us kept them so that we could carry them back to our countries and use them to keep our school certificates, school transcripts, birth certificates and other important papers of our lives. We also found it difficult to throw away anything we were given for free that winter in America. We had become used to the endless stream of paperwork that came with coming to America. We had become good at signing things but poor at reading.

Ahmed advised us to take away the contract and other papers and look at them after the shift. But, no: we pretended to be speed-readers, and after a few minutes handed him back the forms with our signatures. He did not react to our disregard for fine print. We learned later what taxes really meant when we did our recalculations and our projections plummeted. From projections of USD 5000, we learned that we would only make USD 3000 that winter.

So nothing was said about the bicycles that came with the house. Later, when things had escalated and we had searched in the nice envelopes we came across a sheet of paper that said 'House Rules' and there was the mention of the bicycles under 'Equipment'. None of us had looked at it. It was the finest of fine print:

Every member of staff will be granted equipment required for him to carry out his tasks to the best of his abilities.

The bicycles, we would of course learn, were crucial to our survival that winter, not just to carry out our tasks. We were put to work on the shift after our first meeting with Ahmed Abu Samed and remained half asleep all winter. Tumi and

Carmela became part of the front shop. Georgo Moldovanu was taken to the grill. Roberto and João were placed in the kitchen. John Kamau Biko at the frying station. Juanita was told to go to the drive-through window.

We discussed the rationale of these choices. Juanita and Carmela, both students from Bogotá University, spoke terrible English with an innocent earnestness for America that charmed everyone they met outside the house but irritated all of us. Juanita was chubby with a pretty and somewhat insolent face full of contempt for the rest of us. She saved her brilliant smile for Americans, mostly customers at Wendy's. She had a plump fidgety form that she was constantly 'working' into a restless vague sexiness. Maybe that's why she was sent to the drive-through window. Beautiful Carmela with her long, thin face, blonde, almost white hair, was as fragile as a vase, as if recovering from a long illness. We all loved her. Juanita and Carmela woke up to Zumba videos in the morning – Carmela was trying to put on some weight, Juanita was trying to lose some. We could see why Carmela was at the front shop.

Kudzai had opted to stay on after the last batch of student workers from Africa, Latin America and Eastern Europe had left. He constantly reeked of Wendy's frying oil. He was two credits short of a Bachelor of Commerce degree at the University of Cape Town and was in Orleans saving up for a big push to get his degree, move to Jozi and get a BComm accounts job and from there, to move on up in the world. The sheer effort of his BComm degree and spending a year in Orleans at Wendy's had made him sly and scornful. He was always trying to get into Juanita's pants. When he teased her she lost her insolence and winked at him and repeated 'mira mira' after him, and she said she was looking for an American with a green card. Kudzai worked all over the shop and we could see Ahmed's thinking with him because he'd already had a year's experience.

Tumi Dottie Leboshile, from Lesotho but studying in South Africa, never spent any time with us – she'd become friends with some local teenagers and was on fast track to Americanisation. She was careful to tell us that she'd gone to High School in South Africa and never went to Lesotho unless it was to visit her grandmother. Tumi only really spoke to John Biko. Tumi was driven around everywhere by her American teenage friends, Stephanie and Melanie, who worked at Wendy's part-time just for fun. The girls drove past us on the bicycles and laughed at us. Tumi was perfect for the front office.

John Biko Kamau was light, round-headed and before long we decided he was a liar. He shared the attic-room with Roberto Perez, a silent, finicky, awkward born-again Christian from Brazil. Roberto was always with João Da Silva, also Brazilian, a bulky, pleasant individual with a broad face and small, intelligent eyes. Despite being overweight, João gave the impression of great physical strength. He was always cooking, nibbling things or sleeping. Roberto spoke in a stutter, mostly only to João in Portuguese. His eyes seemed strangely focused on a spot directly above and in front of him. He scared us with his silences and that look. He dressed in formal clothes that were too big for him. He had the thickest wrists that we had ever seen. John Biko and Roberto were sent into the kitchen, manual labour. Georgo Moldovanu from Moldavia had a lot to say about the world because he was clever and when he said that Roberto looked like something straight out of *National Geographic*, *Grimm's Fairy Tales*, the Old Testament or Middle-earth, we agreed with him but also called him a racist behind his back. Kudzai, however, said that Georgo was a racialist. Kudzai said to see real racists you had to go to Cape Town. When somebody asked what a racialist was Kudzai twisted his crooked mouth even more and asked what? You don't know what a racialist is? We could see why Georgo was placed at the drive-through window. He had amazing confidence.

Roberto was never still; he always seemed to be doing something – shining his old São Paulo shoes, chewing on a stick he had broken off the Douglas Firs that were planted around the Wendy's shop, washing and ironing his Wendy's uniform. He wore his Wendy's uniforms even when he was off shift. He was the neatest in the house – his bed was always well made with the iron placed at the foot of the bed next to a small tin cup. Yes, he was born for the kitchen sink.

Georgo Moldavanu resembled the good-hearted last-born son in a Grimm Brothers' fairy tale, a broad and thick-bodied kind soul. We hardly ever saw him in the house – he was usually shacked up with some local girlfriend till he got together with Carmela. Georgo liked to test his English on us and say things like: 'Entering Cape Cod seemed like a plunge into the great nowhere.' We shouted at the fucker but he went on. 'Cape Cod', he said, 'is shaped like the tail of a sea-horse carving into the Atlantic.' This was from the tourist pamphlets he'd picked up from the library. George could name all ten towns on what he now called 'the stretch'. After a few weeks we thought that Georgo could be Wendy's Assistant Manager.

The small business district of Orleans was a long semi-circle of sorts bordered by the main road. The banks, the main shops, the supermarket were located within an elongated oblong – and then the small suburbs just outside of it. The Wendy's house sat on a lane on the southern border of the oblong. When off shift we took to that road outside the house on bikes and rode left for about three kilometres in a long arc that turned right along a main fare that whistled with SUVs and trucks. This eventually turned sharply right into Main Street, the radius that topped the long arc. We rode across it and turned left again and after about forty-five minutes we found ourselves back at the Wendy's house after riding in a long arc that turned to the right. When we rode on Main Street again, and down a road that split it into half, we found ourselves back at Wendy's. It was in that stretch that the bicycles set us free.

As winter came on we hardly saw any pedestrians on the street. Other than Georgo all of us had grown up in highly populated cities. We started riding up and down Orleans imagining ourselves alone in the whole town. On the bikes we even competed to see who could see the most strangers walking in the street over a week. We tried to figure out how all the people we saw indoors kept from being outside. In the shops there were always people. Customers came into Wendy's all the time. There was even a mid-week, mini lunchtime rush between Wednesday and Sunday. But as the temperatures dropped and the days became shorter, Orleans became our moonscape, strange and alien – at least from the other side of the counter at Wendy's. When we left the shop, either by bike or on foot we were the only ones on the other side of a split Orleans, between foreigners and citizens, between funny and American accents. We even saw ourselves as Wendy's citizens outside of the Orleans world – when we spoke to Americans they could barely understand our accents. For the first time in our lives we became those other people. But at least we were on bikes.

In mid-November, after three weeks in the shop, when we started to become tired, the bikes became even more important. Our backs, our legs and shoulders went numb from standing and tipping fries into boiling Wendy's oil. Standing by the flat grill flipping burgers and washing endless vats, fryers and utensils, our nostrils became lined with Wendy's smells. The buzzers and timers that we constantly pressed after every cycle continued ringing in our ears when we went to bed and in our dreams. Our faces and mouths and even our eyes crinkled in pain because of smiling and saying: 'Hi-How-waya-Welcome-to-Wendy's-What-can-I-get-fo-ya-today-Ma'am? You'd like the Wendy's No. 5?-Will-that-be-all-Ma'am?-What-was-that?-Would-you-like-anything-else?-No?-Thank-you.Have-a-nice-day-Ma'am-Here-How-are-you-Sir?...'

The bikes became our only source of pleasure. We gagged at the free staff meals, Wendy's Chicken, Wendy's Fries. We could not stop eating Wendy's even as we tired of it. We noticed that the manager Midge brought in her own lunch and never touched Wendy's food. Our faces became rounder and sleeker, our breath slowed down. We started panting when we walked for short distances. And the bikes became even more important. In the mornings and at times at night when we stood at the kitchen window of the house and looked out to the river we saw a sleek and rounded animal shape that could barely walk sliding in and out of the water. The water dripped from the fat slow-moving creature like Wendy's oil and we felt its sluggishness come over us as we entered the winter.

Other than biking around, we became tired of everything. The second-hand Old Navy clothes that we still kept on buying; the sofas, the beds, the old fridge in the Wendy's house. Each of us became tired of the stale breaths and sounds of the person we shared rooms with. João and Tumi tired of sleeping in their own tiny rooms. João and Roberto argued in Portuguese, frustrated from working in the Wendy's kitchen together all the time. Carmela and Tumi tired of watching each other clack away at the keys of the cash registers. Standing by the drive-through window, Georgo and Kudzai start calling each other African and gypsy. John Biko lied that the heat from the grill and the fryer were making him dizzy.

Then, the first real snow came. We became excited at the change in the world. When we walked to the shops white flakes fell around us and we put our faces against it and it felt cool. We watched it from our bedroom windows and used words we had heard from the Americans in the shop: wind chill factor, slush and black ice. We became like small furry animals. We stopped talking much with our mouths. Only hot air came out when they opened. Kudzai and John Biko seemed to be affected most. Kudzai's dreadlocks dried up and stuck fast to his scalp. John Biko's short hair shrank and his head and his face became rounder. The other Africans' noses and mouths shrank back into their faces away from the cold air and became flat, grey. The rest of us, when we were not biking, started walking hunched forward, arms close to our sides, moving backwards and forwards as if we were in water swimming river-style with the smallest of movements. Our necks disappeared into our shoulders. We started to sleep more. We fell asleep standing even if our eyes were open. Georgo, who was used to this kind of weather in Moldavia, asked us why we were so somnolent. We did not answer him because we had agreed that he was a racialist and we were not sure what somnolent was.

In these sleepy states we pined for Johannesburg, Nairobi, Maseru and Harare, Bogotá and São Paulo. It was too cold to shed tears but we shuddered ourselves into a warm sleep without even noticing. We sleep-cried and sleep-screamed at the unfairness of it all in the dead winter tomb of the night. All efforts were spent moving from one inside space to another. The shop, the house, CVS, Stop and Shop and, of course, the Old Navy Store.

During our free evenings at the house when we tired of talking about Mr P we talked about Ahmed. We had all seen the framed photo on Ahmed's desk of a woman with a narrow face holding a very young baby. There were also numerous Wendy's certificates with Ahmed's name. Now we all wanted to become like him and live in a small town by the river, drive a Honda Acura and go home to a white wife and a baby. Some of us disagreed that Ahmed's wife was white.

When we talked about 9/11 we fought about whether Ahmed was an Arab or an African. Kudzai said that Ahmed had been a water engineer in Egypt before he moved to America a few years ago. Juanita laughed and said that was bullshit because she'd read about Egypt in the Old Testament and it was a desert. When Kudzai asked her whether the Latin version of the Old Testament mentioned the River Nile, she turned back to watching the telenovellas. Kudzai told us that Ahmed's wife was from Iran and we all said damn. Some of us felt she would be kicked out of America soon after 9/11 and we were happy that Ahmed would no longer be our boss. We agreed that the FBI were now everywhere but if we shared any information about Ahmed we might even get green cards.

We worried whether we could come back next winter because of 9/11. Someone said the US government would stop giving visas to our countries. Ahmed, we thought, would know about this. We started planning how to bring this up with him when we were on shift. We wondered how we would find out whether his wife had been called in by the FBI.

Juanita listened to these conversations as she watched telenovellas but remained silent. When the commercials came she laughed at us and shouted that Ahmed did not care about being Arab or African or 9/11. All he cared about was being

American. We all knew each other well by now and agreed that Juanita was a slut anyway. John Biko was a liar. Roberto was an angel. Georgo was a racialist. Kudzai was not an orphan. João was psycho at night when he was tired. Carmela was a child because she cried easily. Tumi was a snob of the worst kind. Mr P was a capitalist. Ahmed was harbouring a 9/11 suspect. Midge Bush was an undercover FBI agent. There was no way a real American could be working with us at Wendy's in the winter in a small town in Cape Cod.

The snow fell harder and the cold moved into our bones. Our skins, however, became oilier as we ate more Wendy's. The trees and the grass went grey and we thought we would die. We were the only ones on the street — our African and Latin American shoes folded into strange shapes, cracked in the cold. We became angry at the cars, the SUVs that slid past us. We went into the supermarket and everyone was still kind and smiling and we wanted to kill them. Then, ourselves. The whole of Orleans turned white under the snow. This new beauty meant nothing to us. Wendy's Red Riding Hood's cottage became just Red Riding Hood's cold, white cottage. Cape Cod became like a Sony TV screen that we were not part of, that we could not feel. It became like those pictures in a children's Bible. We became tired again and to forget we tried to breathe in, eat, wear, fuck and abuse everything when we could. There were no more second-hand summer clothes at the Old Navy Store. We now bought strange roll-necks. Colourful polo-shirts. Soccer-mom jeans. We stared at every young American man or woman who came into the shop. As it became colder even those older than us seemed desirable in their warmth and their smiles. We called home just to hear a voice in Africa and Latin America and before we knew it the phone card would beep and there would be a click and then the voice from Verizon (fuck) said goodbye. We said goodbye to Verizon in the anger of all our languages: Kwaheri. Tsamaya hantle. Sarai zvakanaka. Adios. Tchau. La Revedere.

Tumi and Carmela did not become as tired as the rest of us. Maybe it was because they only stayed at the front of the shop and took money and smiled and said: 'Hi-How-waya-Welcome-to-Wendy's-What-can-I-get-fo-ya-today-ma'am?-I'd-like-the-Wendy's-No. 5-Will-that-be-all-Ma'am?-What-was-that?-Would-you-like-anything-else?-No?-Have-a-nice-day.Thank you-How-are-you-Sir?' Maybe it was because the Wendy's Fries oil did not enter their skin and nostrils. They did not use their arms and backs to stand all day and throw burgers on the fssshing flat grill or fries into the fryer. We watched them to see whether they were smiling for real at the customers.

Then, one day, we stopped being tired. It was like we had been exercising for a long time and we had become fit and strong. We were still quiet with each other even on Mondays and Tuesday evenings when most of us were off and at the house. Carmela and Juanita now watched the telenovellas with the volume off because of exhaustion. The rest of us sat in the kitchen and watched the river slowly go by the house. We no longer saw that animal shape we'd seen before going in and out of the river.

After one and a half months, none of us had ever truly unpacked. We slumped half-dead onto our beds, at times still in our uniforms, whenever we could and woke up in half-shock, scurrying into our bags and running out into working America. When we were not in bed the things around our beds became our little private universes. We started sneaking out Wendy's garbage bags. We built little piles of belongings next to our beds that grew every day. When we bought new American things we threw the things that we had come with from Africa, Latin America and Eastern Europe into the garbage bags. But we were still learning. When we were indoors we were too hot and sweaty, outside our skins froze immediately even as we sweated under the three T-shirts and two pairs of pants we wore because we did not have winter clothes. At times we found ourselves in front of the cash machine at the Stop and Shop without knowing how we got there. We printed out slips of our bank balances without taking out any money. We stored the slips in our purses and wallets and removed and looked at them when we were tired, just for reassurance. In our new fitness the managers stopped ordering us around as much as they had when we were new.

So, finally one day Georgo asked Ahmed about 9/11. Ahmed looked at him and said that it had taken him two years to get a visa to come to the US from Egypt. We pretended that we were working away at our stations but we listened carefully. Ahmed did not say anything else but just looked at Georgo. Some of us thought that the question had made him angry. Juanita looked at us as if we were mad and said that Ahmed was more American than the Americans because he had worked hard to come here. We were happy because our visas had not taken more than a week and Ahmed's had taken two years.

As Christmas approached there were few customers after 8 p.m. – the locals went into hibernation. Business at Wendy's slowed down to the point where our shifts were reduced. There were now only two rush hours – lunch and dinner. Ahmed reduced the number of people required during the morning shift. With the reduced Christmas hours we started calculating again how much we would need to go to Cape Town, Moldova and Bogotá while thinking about the USD 6.25 hours we were losing. Because of the reduced hours it became even more crucial to use the bikes to avoid being exposed to the cold weather for long periods of time. We walked in a stupor around town or flew on the bikes past the beautiful streets. We pedalled harder thinking about the US dollar, mad men and women pursuing the wind. Christmas came and went.

In the New Year, the snow was like a blanket. We were now always wet. The bicycles saved time and energy. Riding meant an extra twenty minutes of sleep before a Wendy's shift. It meant less exposure to the cold even though when we rode the wind-chill factor cut up our cheeks. At times we slipped on black ice and almost broke every bone in our bodies. We soon learned to tell the difference between hard snow, soft snow, mush, snow and mud. We rode faster and became colder even as we tried to minimise our exposure to the weather. Now the bicycles became all important.

The War

One Sunday morning in late February we saw John Biko Kamau's figure emerge from the kitchen window. We saw him scratching like a big chicken amongst the slew of broken bicycle parts, metallic weeds in the sparse winter grass. We could tell it was very cold from the small clouds coming from his mouth. We could see the cold metal burning his un-gloved hands. On Sunday mornings the shop only opened after 10 a.m. so there was no rush. He had not seen us and we were enjoying his suffering. Before we went off for our shift we rapped on the window and when he looked up and shouted at us we all burst into laughter.

All week we zoomed past John Biko Kamau on the sidewalk. He looked like a toddler in a blizzard rocking this way and that way, learning to walk. He had been unable to salvage anything from all the ruined bicycles. We would have liked to stop and watch him struggling against the snow but it was too cold. We rushed indoors and as we got warm we all looked at each other and someone pretended to stumble and struggle in the snow like John Biko and we all laughed hard. Whenever we saw anybody walking on Orleans streets, it would be John Biko.

But on the morning the War started, we woke up and while some of us were waiting to head out for the morning shift we heard Georgo shouting outside. When we rushed outside he stood there in his cassock holding his bike. His twenty-one-gear black Trojan did not have its nice black leather seat.

'Somebody is playing,' Georgo kept on repeating. He glared at all of us and jumped on the bicycle and rode away standing. Wendy's was not too far. Georgo was strong enough to ride standing all the way to Brewster if he needed to.

Then, a few days later João's bicycle was missing a pedal. We ignored him and got on our own bicycles and rode to Wendy's. On the way, when we looked behind us to laugh at John Biko, we also saw João moving along slowly with John Biko behind us in the snow. We reached the shop and laughed twice as hard at the sight of the two idiots struggling along.

When Carmela's front tyre went flat after a few days we stopped laughing and became pensive. We no longer cared about Carmela but did not want to be out there like John Biko and João. Then, the weekend came and the gears of Juanita's Schwinn got stuck.

Our main thoughts were protecting our own bicycles as we would protect our own children but once we went into shift we forgot because we became tired again. We now understood those parents we saw at Stop and Shop who let their children run wild in the aisles. We had our suspicions about all these events with the bicycles. When Roberto realised that João would not share his bicycle, he spent a few nights tinkering around the heap of remaining bicycles and managed to get the small child's BMX working. So, in the New Year, only John Biko was left without a bicycle of his own.

Once upon a long time ago Juanita and Carmela had walked everywhere. Juanita had also ridden in cars with her weekly American boyfriends. Carmela walked because she had been scared of falling off her bicycle when she was alone. She had even let John Biko use her bike whenever he wanted. But after Juanita got dumped by another man she met at the Wendy's drive-through window she told Carmela: 'Mira, ride with me what you fearing?' Then, when they got together Georgo helped Carmela get used to her bicycle and she could not get enough of it. Carmela was like a child that way. And so she no longer let John Biko take her bicycle. But Juanita and Carmela were constantly falling out with each other because of Carmela's thing with Georgo.

Every evening they turned on each other in Spanish. We sat on the sidelines and watched this live version of telenovellas. So, now we were not sure it was John Biko or Juanita meddling with Carmela's bicycle or Georgo's. Or whether it was Carmela messing about with Juanita's.

João and Roberto were no longer that close because João's drinking had become epic as winter set in. Roberto said that because João was always hungover he did less in the kitchen and ordered him around like he was Ahmed-boss. We laughed when he said it like that. Roberto said he did not like bosses. So, we assumed Roberto had messed up João's bike.

We agreed that Georgo's bicycle had been messed up by Juanita. Roberto had definitely messed with João's bicycle. We could not really agree on who would fuck up Carmela's bicycle – maybe Juanita again. And when the gears of Juanita's bike got stuck we suspected Kudzai. We were still waiting for something to happen to Kudzai's bike.

Juanita talked Carmela into walking with her while her bicycle was being fixed. Those two. From make-ups to break-ups. Telenovellas, just the two of them. We were surprised to see John Biko on Carmela's bike. Carmela said that John Biko had fixed her flat tyre for her at the gas station and so she felt she could share with him.

When we rode past the two girls, Juanita shouted and waved at us: 'You fat bitches, walking is good for you. I need to lose my ass. Caliente is what I am going to be at the end of winter.' Then, the next day we saw the two Brazilian boys walking together. Someone had snapped the chain on João's bike. Then, we saw John Biko on the small BMX because Roberto had lent it to him. We could not keep up.

After Georgo lost the seat to the Trojan he had managed to unscrew a plastic seat from one of the decaying bicycles and fix it on his bicycle. So, when he now found the gears stuck fast we watched to see what he would do. We were not sure that someone had tampered with his bike. It had one of those back-pedal brakes that were known to develop complications with the cycling mechanism.

The War with the bicycles was now four weeks old. And because of it we became tired again. One slow Monday, we were riding home from the day shift when we saw Georgo and Carmela. They were both on her bicycle coming into the shop for the night shift. Georgo's broad back was arched, his feet hooked onto the back wheel and he held Carmela's waist as she cycled and held the handlebars. Their faces glowed. They looked like a couple in an Italian love film. If Georgo was not part of it we would have asked him the name of the film and he would have remembered. We felt more tired than we ever had as they went past us. To outdo Carmela, Juanita convinced John Biko to ride with her on her bicycle. We watched them practise outside the house. Juanita was too heavy for John Biko, who was not as strong as Georgo. We watched them wobble all over the road. John Biko gave up and got off and Juanita rode off in anger. Not long after she came back storming. She rushed to the kitchen and switched on the hot plates on the electric cooker to warm her hands.

We noticed that Tumi had started going into John Kamau Biko's room every evening. We knew there was nothing going on between them because Roberto, who shared a room with John Biko, was also in there fast asleep. We wondered what John Biko and Tumi were talking about. Our bodies had started making decisions for us and we could see that with Tumi. That is why she was doing this new thing because there was something she needed. This made those of us who were alone angry and needy.

To make it worse Georgo and Carmela kept up their Italian love film bike thing. In the evenings they lay on the large sofa intertwined watching telenovellas. They made a good-looking couple. Georgo, the good-hearted last-born clever son in a Grimm Brothers' fairy tale, broad and thick-bodied with an easy smile. Carmela, with her thin face, beautiful blonde almost-white hair.

Georgo enjoyed riding like the wind, going out on the H-1 and racing with trucks. One day he picked up speed while he was carrying Carmela near the CVS and they fell. The Italian love film went Hollywood. Carmela, with her stick-bones only suffered few bruises. Georgo broke his nose and did something funny to his elbow. When he came back from the hospital in Brewster, Carmela said that his elbow was distendedated. In the shop, Midge Bush laughed hard when she heard this. She had been a nurse before she became a Wendy's Manager. She had been very many things, that's why we suspected her of being FBI.

'Distendedated?' she asked. 'You mean "distended".' Carmela repeated 'disendedated', and looked as if she would cry because she had come to America to learn English.

We all wanted Georgo's shifts as he recuperated. John Biko asked Midge whether he could have them but she stalked off to her office. We laughed at Carmela's English and John Biko's greed for US dollars. Even if we were tired and did not have that much time because we were somnolent, Georgo's fall had made us start thinking. What if we got hurt and did not make our projections? So, we wrote down what was happening with the bicycles to try and figure it out.

- When Georgo's bike lost its seat and got the gears messed up he rode with Carmela
- When Carmela's bike tyre went flat she rode with Georgo
- When João's bike lost a pedal, Roberto stopped riding and followed João on foot
- When Juanita's bicycle was disabled, Carmela gave Juanita her bicycle and rode with Georgo

We stopped there. It was too much. We could not agree on who was benefiting the most from what was happening. We however discovered that these four bicycles had the most effect on the status quo. Kudzai's bicycle was never touched. Nothing happened to Roberto's small bike so we started thinking they were the ones who were fucking things up. We all knew Kudzai's contempt for us. Because he had been around for a year he had decided he was a permanent and we were all temps beneath him. We all knew how strange Roberto was. We even tried to have a meeting to go through all this information but we could never find a time because we were spread out over the shifts.

If it hadn't been for what was going on with the bicycles and the cold, life would have been great. Everyone now had some money in the bank. We had all become even sleeker, rounder and better fed – like our river creature. In the common bathrooms there were a lot of new shampoos and products. The old smells of the house started to disappear.

The old fridge heaved and sighed because it was so stocked. João and Juanita took over half the space and became plump like the partridges that ate all the stuff from Wendy's that was put outside in the large bins. There was always a large

Ziploc bag of flour tortillas labelled 'Juanita' in the old fridge. João stocked his cupboard with nachos and beers.

While we now only wore American clothes, Roberto still dressed like a factory or farm worker. He still wore shoes that carried the dirt of São Paulo. He dressed like he was resigned to a life of toil. Like those peasants you saw on *National Geographic* in the Amazon. We looked at Roberto with his old clothes and the child's bicycle and pictured him walking along the Amazon over epic distances. We wondered why he even needed a bicycle. We agreed that if he gave John Biko his bicycle that our problems would come to an end. When João came to the kitchen he was hungover and heard us and he shouted that São Paulo was nowhere near the Amazon. We stopped talking to João for a few days. We thought maybe the War would not have started if Roberto had not acquired a bicycle.

The thing with the bicycles spread inside the house. Juanita started complaining that the quesadillas she cooked were disappearing. They were the best thing anyone had ever tasted – better than anything at Wendy's. They were so good that Kudzai had started calling Juanita 'Tortilla', licking his lips and twisting his mouth even more.

João's beers started disappearing too. When he discovered a six-pack gone after a Friday shift we heard him stomping all over the house and talking to himself in Portuguese. We all stayed in our rooms till the house went quiet. Then, a pair of Kudzai's Nikes went missing. We expected him to go completely crazy but he said nothing – which was worse. Now, none of us wanted to be in the house for any period of time. When Kudzai found his Nikes inside one of the washing machines he started calling all of us monkey temps. Things kept on going missing and then turning up in strange places. Georgo found his cassock under the large sofa facing the TV. Someone hid Roberto's Bible in one of the old shelves in the kitchen. Somebody tore off John Biko's contract that he had put up on the wall of his bedroom as an incentive and left the pieces on his bed.

Then one day we were told at the shop that Ahmed wanted to come and see us at the house. We rarely had official meetings at the shop, let alone in the house, only impromptu sessions that started with 'Hey, can you all listen up?' by Ahmed. These impromptu sessions tended to be for introducing new things to the menu, a new starter usually. Wastage was a big theme too. We knew this was serious but we were also excited because Ahmed never came to the house. Somebody said that maybe he was coming to tell us what a great job we were doing. We sat on the couches waiting. Some of us fell asleep. And then there was Ahmed at the door. He did not move inside and come and sit with us. He looked around for a few seconds as if trying to make sense of what he saw and then said: 'Listen up. I know what is happening. It is my business to know all that is happening. This nonsense with the bicycles is affecting your performances.' His eyes swept over us right and left.

'Look at me. I came to America just like you. I was stupid. I did not understand how America worked. Unity.' He went silent and looked at us. There was a question on his face.

'Yes,' he said. We were puzzled. Then, he said, 'Three straikes'. This is what he liked to say when Roberto burned the fries or John Biko blackened a burger pattie.

Then Ahmed said: 'Okay. Who does not have a bicycle?' We kept quiet. Nobody wanted to go official that they did not have a bike in fear that would become status quo.

Then, John Biko put up his hand as if he was in a classroom.

'Why do you not have a bicycle?'

'Because I came last to Orleans.' His voice was trembling and we wanted to laugh. 'Because of status quo.'

'How many bicycles are there in the house?' Ahmed asked.

We all remained silent. He opened the door and the fog rushed in.

'Come with me,' he said.

We followed him into the back garden. We refused to look at him or each other. We could see the river moving slowly, somnolent. We looked for the oily river-animal shape but all was still. Every night we'd been hearing something heavy in the ceiling and we knew that the animal shape had moved in with us. Warming itself along the hot water pipes and making ugly furry babies. When the animal's movement woke us up at night and we thought about everyone else in the house and what was happening with the bicycles we became angry and could not go back to sleep. We became even more somnolent during the shifts.

Ahmed now counted all the decaying bicycles.

'Is this stupid or what? Fourteen bicycles. You are only eight.' He only wore a sweater and a wind-breaker but we could see he was not cold. This Egyptian who had adapted to America with his green card and now did not feel cold. We hated him even more. 'Fourteen bicycles and you are fighting. Wait here.'

He marched off. We stood there in the cold and he came back with one of those hard yellow American envelopes that we liked so much. He removed some forms and handed them to us. The first two were some kind of equipment forms titled 'Part 2 House Rules'. All along there had been a Bicycles Section after all. But it was in the finest of the fine print. It was so cold that we pretended to speed-read the forms. There were two questions under all the rules.

- Why do you need a bicycle?
- What does the bicycle you have need?

'I want those forms back after forty-eight hours. Read the fine print,' Ahmed said. We watched him go through the wet grass to his Honda Acura and drive off to his Iranian wife and little baby born American. It was all very unfair she had not been arrested so that they could be deported together. All of us went to the electric cooker and switched on the hot plates and put our hands over them.

Over the next few days we talked about status quo. We complained about having to read the fine print. We agreed that in America you shaped up or shipped out. Tumi said we were all stupid and bicycles were for farm workers in Lesotho.

After Ahmed's intervention there was a kind of lull in the War. Carmela continued to ride with Juanita and Georgo on different days. She also gave her bicycle to John Biko on other days. Roberto and João continued to ride together. Some days when they fought in the Wendy's kitchen, we saw John Biko on the small BMX.

Then, it was the last week of February. Some of us were in the house when the phone rang – there was a Mr Alan Pabast looking for John Biko. We never ever received phone calls and we were surprised. The calls continued.

At the end of the week John Biko came into the house and said he had landed a second job. We had laughed at him during those weeks of riding and walking around Orleans looking for work. He had become the most well-known face in every Orleans establishment that was open that winter. The CVS Pharmacy, the Stop and Shop Supermarket and the Old Navy Shop where he spent most of his money. The gift shop.

The following week he started work at the Mobil and disappeared from the house. After a week when he was off-shift we found him with a bottle of Jack Daniel's in the kitchen celebrating. He forced us to his room and there on the wall was a new note:

> *You will now earn an additional USD 9 an hour. In addition to the USD 6.25 an hour you are earning at Wendy's this will now be USD 15.25 an hour. By the end of April, back in South Africa, you will have 10,500 USD. At the current exchange rate, that works out to nearly seventy-five thousand rand. The fees for your MA tuition are only R 5,000. Your rent is only R 700 a month. You will have R 55,000 to spend in 2002 at the dollar-rand rate. That is some serious partying money in South Africa. You will suffer as Work and Travel Employee Number 23 but you will enjoy the rest of the year.*

We wanted to kill ourselves. Even Juanita was impressed. John Biko would take home USD 5000. He had conquered American taxes – we knew he was not lying.

All our Wendy's shifts were generally split into morning and evening. We worked six days a week. Three days in the morning from 8 a.m to 4 p.m. Or 6 a.m. to 2 p.m. And three days from 4 p.m. to 10 p.m. or later. John Biko arranged things so that he either went to Wendy's in the morning, slept till 10 p.m. then went to Mobil for the graveyard shift, or slept in the morning, reported to Wendy's at 4 p.m. and went to Mobil at midnight.

Even if the bicycles were still being messed with we had become used to it and we started watching John Biko. We were happy when we noticed that he was losing weight because he was riding so much that the wind was reshaping his features. He was now always more than a few minutes late for his Wendy's shift, which meant losing a full hour. He was always in a rush, always shouting: 'Time. Time.' Screaming 'Masaa', which we learned was time in his language. When Midge Bush was on the evening shift at Wendy's she took forever to close the shop and he got to the Mobil late. His face started becoming longer.

When Carmela was working the same shift and John Biko did not have a bicycle he offered to pay for the use of our bicycles. We did not use our bikes at night or at 6 a.m. When he got back from his graveyard shift he paid us. Kudzai made most money from his bicycle this way.

One morning Roberto came to breakfast and called us to the room he shared with John Biko who was still in bed. John Biko made sounds like his chest was stuffed with feathers. Because of his new job he had been riding more than usual. We now hardly saw him in the house at all. We shook our heads and asked him whether he wanted us to tell Ahmed or Midge that he was sick. He looked at the note on the wall, the contract beside his bed and shook his head. We wondered who would get his shifts. When we went outside the air had been let out from Georgo's bike. The seat had also been removed from Juanita's Schwinn.

When we came back at the end of our shift in the afternoon there was an ambulance outside the house. John Biko was admitted to hospital for three days. When he came out he looked like a real African orphan and we wondered whether he would get the permanent position offered by Mr P. By then the tinkering with the bikes and the long winter had disrupted our lives so much that we started forgetting the old arrangements. Now everybody picked up any bike they came across at any time that was working. But the worst of the War was still to come. We woke up the morning John Biko came from hospital and none of the bikes were working. But it did not matter – winter had set in such a way that the roads had become treacherous with black ice and it was too dangerous to ride. Energy levels were low. The bikes now remained frozen and untouched on the front lawn.

Then, we realised our time in Orleans was coming to an end soon and that's how the War stopped. We all wanted to be friends. We blamed Ahmed for not getting us enough bicycles. We blamed Mr Pudephatt for being a capitalist. We blamed Midge Bush because she was FBI and had not done her job and deported Ahmed and his wife. We blamed America for making competition a way of life. Shape up or ship out. Fine print. Status quo.

Our last week in Orleans came upon us in April. The days became warmer. We had all started walking around again. We looked at each other to see what changes had happened since we came to Orleans. In these last few weeks Juanita had grown as fat as the oily animal shape we saw going in and out of the water again. But she was still a slut. João had grown his hair and his beard but he was still a psycho when he was tired at night. Roberto now looked like a mountain man with a small furry animal on top of his upper lip. Carmela had grown less brittle and no longer looked like an underfed Colombian child. Tumi had become an American teenager from hanging out with Melanie and Stephanie and spoke like them. Georgo had fallen in love for real for the first time with Carmela but he was still a racialist. Kudzai was rich with all the money he had saved all these months and did not speak to any of us at all.

Ever since he had fallen sick John Biko Kamau had remained quiet and did not lie as much. He'd also started drinking every other day. We sensed that he had decided to do a Kudzai and stay for the year. He started carrying around his notebook again, this time calculating figures for the year. He was not good enough to be sponsored by Mr Pudephatt so we suspected he would have to disappear elsewhere somewhere in America. He was not as sly as Kudzai and could not talk Ahmed into putting in a word for him. We could already see him somewhere as an illegal in Dallas or New Jersey. There was also the small matter of finishing his degree. He still had one more year in South Africa. We knew he was telling himself that he would make enough money for a year and go back to finish – we knew that this was not going to happen. One morning we came down for breakfast and we saw that John Biko was very happy. He announced that he had convinced his cousin who was studying in South Africa to come down and be with him in Cape Cod later in the year. John Biko boasted that his cousin was doing this for fun and he came from a rich political family in Kenya. When he told us his cousin was called Maish Boi, Georgo asked him why his family had such funny names. And if his cousin was so rich why would he come to work at Wendy's? We were surprised John Biko did not get angry; instead he seemed to be thinking. But all he said was that his cousin's real name was Joseph Mungai. And that they had been supposed to meet up at the beginning of winter. Georgo said he thought Joseph Mungai was just another fiction of John Biko's. We did not know whether Kudzai was going back – he was used to being here. Maybe he would talk to John Biko and tell him not to be too sad about staying – many Africans before him had been seduced by America. We were all scared of leaving and scared of staying.

That last week in Orleans, we went to the kitchen to fix breakfast, and we found a large sketch on the wall. It had been drawn by Roberto. It was beautiful. There we were fighting each other over a heap of broken bicycles. Roberto had captured all the changes that had happened to us. We all wanted a copy of the sketch. We begged Roberto for copies and he said he would see what he could do.

Then, the day arrived and Mr P started picking us up one by one. We looked at the large house that had been our home for winter for maybe the last time as we drove away. We said the usual things to each other – we would be in touch by email, we would come back and see each other. But we knew this would not happen.

We drove away with Mr P. The bikes lay on the small lawn in various forms of decay waiting for the summer. We looked at the house for the last time and we noticed a brand new bicycle, the last one standing next to the house. It belonged to John Biko.

Acknowledgements

These stories span my writing life over fifteen years and because it has taken so long to bring them together under one cover there are many people to thank and acknowledge. If I have forgotten you, nisamehe.

First and foremost thank you to Binyavanga Wainaina who read several of the early pieces in draft form, especially all those which appeared in *Kwani?* He was an incredible champion of those stories he read and they wouldn't be here if it wasn't for him.

Many of these stories were drafted in spaces conferred through the kindness of individuals who gave me a room to write. Thanks to the Danish Union of Writers, Rhodes University, Iwalewa House, Northumbria University and to Peter and Claire Wheeler for their house in Lamu.

Some of the stories have been published before, often in a slightly different form, in *Kwani?*, *Granta*, *McSweeney's*, *Imagine Africa*, *Enkare Review*, *The Caine Prize Anthology* and *Postcolonial Text*. I thank all those spaces that housed these stories in their earlier versions.

I am grateful to those I worked with at Kwani, which gave me a literary home for so many years and also allowed me to write. I thank Angela Wachuka, Velma Kiome, Mike Mburu and Maya Muturi. My editorial colleagues Otieno Owino and Clifton Gachagua. Tom Maliti and Malla Mumo. Asante.

I have been lucky to have so many creative interlocutors whose time and imaginations have directly or obliquely fed my own. To Parselelo Kantai who has critiqued, excoriated and praised in equal measure many of my creative attempts. Asante chief. To Muthoni Garland and Yvonne Owuor who have made my life in Kenya sane through their literary friendships. Asante. Martin Kimani and Daniel Waweru thank you for your friendship and continuing intellectual fuel. To Ntone Edjabe, a creative collaborator whose kindness to my work and whose space Chimurenga has inspired so much of the thinking behind these pieces. This extends to Dr Joyce Nyairo and 'Prof' Kimani Njogu. Mukoma Wa Ngugi. Mikhail Iossel and Ed Pavlic. Ngala Chome and Usama Goldsmith. Judy Kibinge. Asante, asante.

To Ellah Allfrey who patiently worked on my final versions of these stories and improved them further. Vimbai Shire for the Augean task of making these stories presentable with her eagle eye. Otieno Owino for his useful comments and support. Thank you.

Louise Umutoni-Bower and Lucky Grace Isingizwe from Huza Press – thank you for giving these stories a home.

Thanks so much Ankush Vohra, Diganta Joshi and Margdarshan Productions for your professionalism and the work we've done together. And for pulling out all the stops for this collection.

Dad and Mum. Siblings Gakuya, Shiru, Shiku and Kinyua. You are why I have come so far.

To Kate Wallis and Ella 'E' Haines, with love.

Billy Kahora is the author of non-fiction novella *The True Story of David Munyakei* and was highly commended by the 2007 Caine Prize judges for his story *Treadmill Love*; his story *Urban Zoning* was shortlisted for the prize in 2012, *The Gorilla's Apprentice* in 2014. His short fiction and creative non-fiction has appeared in *Granta*, *Chimurenga*, *McSweeney's* and *Kwani?*. He wrote the screenplay for *Soul Boy* and co-wrote *Nairobi Half Life* which won the Kalasha awards. He worked for nearly a decade for Kenya's leading literary publisher Kwani Trust, editing seven issues of the *Kwani?* journal.